Emma Hornby lives on a tight-knit working-class estate in Bolton and has read sagas all her life. Before pursuing a career as a novelist, she had a variety of jobs, from care assistant for the elderly, to working in a Blackpool rock factory. She was inspired to write after researching her family history; like the characters in her books, many generations of her family eked out life amid the squalor and poverty of Lancashire's slums.

You can follow her on
Twitter @EmmaHornbyBooks and on
Facebook at www.facebook.com/
emmahornbyauthor

www.penguin.co.uk

Also by Emma Hornby

A SHILLING FOR A WIFE
MANCHESTER MOLL
THE ORPHANS OF ARDWICK
A MOTHER'S DILEMMA
A DAUGHTER'S PRICE

For more information on Emma Hornby and her
books, see her website at www.emmahornby.com

THE MAID'S DISGRACE

Emma Hornby

CORGI BOOKS

TRANSWORLD PUBLISHERS
Penguin Random House, One Embassy Gardens,
8 Viaduct Gardens, London SW11 7BW
www.penguin.co.uk

Transworld is part of the Penguin Random House group of companies
whose addresses can be found at global.penguinrandomhouse.com

Penguin
Random House
UK

First published in Great Britain in 2021 by Bantam Press
an imprint of Transworld Publishers
Corgi edition published 2021

A CIP catalogue record for this book
is available from the British Library.

ISBN 9780552175777

Typeset in 11/13.25pt ITC New Baskerville by Jouve (UK), Milton Keynes.
Printed and bound in Great Britain by Clays Ltd, Elcograf S.p.A.

The authorized representative in the EEA is Penguin Random House
Ireland, Morrison Chambers, 32 Nassau Street, Dublin D02 YH68.

Penguin Random House is committed to a sustainable
future for our business, our readers and our planet. This book
is made from Forest Stewardship Council® certified paper.

For Mark – *my* mountain. And my ABC, always x

Slowly comes a hungry people, as a lion,
creeping nigher . . .

Alfred, Lord Tennyson

Chapter 1

'YOU MUST PROMISE me, Phoebe.' The woman's grainy voice scraped the stuffy air between them. 'Please. Let me go to my Maker with peace in my heart. *Promise* me.'

Phoebe Parsons gulped back a pain-filled sob. 'I do, Lilian. I promise.'

The small white face relaxed a fraction, the paper-thin skin lifting at the corners of her mouth in the shadow of a smile. Moments later, Lilian Yewdale took her final earthly breath and was gone.

'I promise.' Dipping her head, Phoebe, too, closed her eyes, and wept silently.

This was it. What she'd feared for years had today become reality. She was on her own. Completely, terrifyingly alone.

When she'd awoken this teeth-chatteringly cold mid-autumn morning, she had no idea that her life was set to change for ever. Of course, she'd known her mistress was ill but she'd never imagined, never dreamed . . . Even the doctors had assured her that Lilian would rally. But they had been wrong, for she was dead. Gone in her thirty-fifth year, leaving Phoebe with no one. And if she

1

knew Warwick Yewdale, she was set to lose a whole lot more before this day was through.

Phoebe stood and crossed to the rosewood washstand to swill the grief from her face. After smoothing the creases from her dark grey bell-shaped skirt and tidying her thick brown hair in the mirror, she took several long breaths. Then she headed to the door and, for the first time in days, left the sickroom.

Her boots sounded unnaturally loud on the polished wood floor as she made her slow way to the new master's study. *The new master.* Phoebe shuddered at the thought. God help the domestic staff beneath this roof from hereon in with Warwick at the helm.

'Enter!' came the booming demand to her knock.

'Sir.' Phoebe addressed his stiff back. 'Sir, your step-mother has gone.'

He lifted his head from the papers he'd been looking at but didn't turn. 'Gone?'

'Dead, sir.'

'Hm.'

Silence descended. Phoebe shuffled on the spot. 'Is there anything I can do, sir? Anyone you'd like me to inform—?'

'That shan't be necessary.' He rose and finally swivelled his head around to look at her. His stance was emotionless, collected. 'You may leave, Miss Parsons.'

She felt her face grow hot then the blood drain away again with horrifying clarity. She swallowed hard. 'Leave . . . for good?' she murmured.

'Naturally,' he threw back. 'Your services at this house are no longer required.'

'Now, sir?'

'This instant!'

'But Lilian – Mrs Yewdale,' she corrected at the

2

audible grind of Warwick's teeth, 'she gave me her solemn vow that I could remain here until I had secured alternative employment—'

'And that vow died with her.'

Phoebe licked her lips. Tears threatened, and she'd begun to shake. 'Please, sir. It's late and I . . . I have nowhere else to go.'

'That is no concern of mine. Now' – he returned to his desk – 'you've wasted enough of my time. Gather your belongings and leave.'

'But sir—'

'At *once*, Miss Parsons. Or I shall be forced to deal with you as I would any common trespasser – which of course is exactly what you now are.'

As though by some unspoken order, the three black dogs lounging by the fire lifted their heads and emitted low, menacing growls.

Phoebe backed away. 'May I be so bold as to ask from you a character reference, sir? With Mrs Yewdale gone . . .'

To her surprise and relief, although he sighed in annoyance, Warwick snatched up a piece of paper. After scribbling out a few lines, he folded the sheet and sealed it with a wax stamp. He held it out to her.

'Thank you, sir.' Then, given he'd been forthcoming in this regard, she thought she might as well try: 'May I be permitted to see Mrs Yewdale one last time before I go, sir?'

'Certainly not.'

'I would like to say goodbye.'

Amusement gurgled in Warwick's throat. 'Whatever for? My stepmother is past the capability of receiving such trivialities.'

'Even so, sir—'

'No, I said! Now leave!'

Phoebe hadn't time to press her wish further as, at the click of their master's fingers, the hounds leapt up and bounded at her, teeth bared. With a cry, she flew from the room, slamming the door behind her just in time.

Warwick's cruel laughter filtered through to her as she stood, panting with terror, in the hall. After a last hate-filled look towards the study, she turned on her heel and ran to her bedroom to pack.

The wrench minutes later when passing Lilian's room, now clutching the small portmanteau containing her worldly possessions, was unbearable. Phoebe dragged herself on with grim resolution. Warwick Yewdale would have no qualms in setting the dogs on her again should she disobey him and sneak a visit to her mistress – would likely take the horse whip to her into the bargain. Having to be content instead with saying a final farewell in her mind to the dead woman, whom she'd miss more than she could ever express, she headed downstairs.

The servants glanced around as she entered the kitchen.

'She's gone.'

A collective breath whispered through the room. It spoke of regret and sorrow and of dread. Lifting up her bag, Phoebe sighed.

'He never has . . .' The cook shook her head. 'It wouldn't have harmed him none to let you stop on 'til you found yourself another position.'

'He refused the notion point blank, Mary. I'm to vacate the house forthwith.'

'I'll not be far behind!' cried the parlourmaid, who had been enjoying a cup of tea at the table. 'I'll not serve under that tyrant's rule. Nay, never!'

'I'm of the same mind on that, Kitty lass,' murmured the cook, whilst even the housekeeper nodded agreement.

4

But Phoebe saw in their eyes the uncertainty, the fear of the unknown, and knew they would suffer it. It wouldn't just mean giving up their jobs but their home, too. A regular income. Security. No one could afford to risk that – particularly so at present, with the country in the grip of mass unemployment. *Not if they had a choice, at any rate, unlike her.*

'Where will you go?' asked the housekeeper, and Phoebe wanted to scream at her that she didn't know, that she was ruined, done for . . . But she didn't.

'I'll be fine, Mrs Tibbs,' she assured her, forcing a smile. 'I have a friend who will put me up until I'm back on my feet.'

The staff gathered around her. 'Goodbye and God-speed, lass,' they said in turn, patting her shoulder and squeezing her hand in farewell. Choking back her emotion, she thanked them and hurried from the house.

There was no friend.

Coming to a standstill at the end of the road, Phoebe peered around through a blur of hot tears.

There was no one. *No* one . . .

The dark and dangerous streets were to be her home now.

Across town, forty-year-old Victor Hayes was realising a similar fate.

How in *hell* had it come to this? his numb mind asked again of the passing traffic. He'd had it all just one short week ago and now his future – his life – was shattered to dust. And for what? He'd done nothing wrong! Nothing that warranted losing his job, and consequently his home and wife, at any rate.

His eyes creased at the thought of Kate. Daft mare. She'd believed the rumours, same as everyone else.

Surprised him, that had. He'd thought she at least would have taken his word, but no. She'd packed a bag for him whilst he slept, had been waiting in the chair by the window for him to waken, back ramrod straight, mouth set, gaze bright with angry tears.

She'd caught wind of the whispers, knew what folk were saying. Even when he'd explained again, insisting that what he spoke was the real truth, it hadn't made a difference. He'd disgraced himself both professionally and personally, Kate was adamant – and with someone like *her*, a low woman of the night, of all people! Well, she wanted no part of it. She wanted him gone. And leave he did, for he'd rather have that than cause his wife further embarrassment. But he'd done *nothing*. Hopefully, with time, he'd make her see that, make her see sense. Make them *all* see he'd had no immoral dealings with Suzannah Frost.

Now, as his musings switched to the streetwalker in question, his bushy brows drew together in an uneasy frown. Not because of the gossip – no, no. That wouldn't have affected her. It was the trouble she'd fallen into, the low-bellied scum she'd become entangled with – and the threat they posed to her – that worried Victor.

He'd seen it a hundred times before, and rarely was the outcome a positive one. The pimps and bullies took over their lives. The vulnerable became their property and with that came their freedom and income. Suzannah didn't deserve that. None of the sex workers of this municipal borough did, but she was different. He saw something in her he didn't very often with the others. She had potential to be better. But potential without the wherewithal to change was pointless. And now, stripped of his position, his contacts lost and his reputation in tatters, he was powerless to help.

6

'I should have just kept well out of it,' he growled, a line he'd told himself countless times over the past few days. Yet he knew he couldn't have done that. It wasn't in him to turn a blind eye to anyone's suffering, whoever they were. Class certainly didn't come into it, as it had with some of his colleagues. *Every* person was deserving, and the solemn oath he had taken all those years ago when embarking upon his new career, to serve and protect the people of Manchester, he'd taken very seriously.

Sighing, he scanned the throng of passers-by without much seeing them. His thoughts were on finding a place to lay his head that night and the rest to follow, and just how long the money he had squirrelled away would support such a haphazard lifestyle. But first, he must find somewhere to get a bite to eat.

Victor rose from the edge of the public horse trough he'd been perched on for the past hour and stretched his back. His canvas-sack bag, which contained what few bits his wife had deemed essential to stuff inside – shirts and trousers, a pair of boots and his comb and razor – sat by his feet, and this he threw over his shoulder. Then he pulled the collar of his jacket up around his chin against the stinging cold and set off towards the string of eating houses along Oldham Street to fill his grumbling stomach.

He ordered liver and onions and a mug of strong tea. Whilst he waited for the serving girl to bring the meal, he sat close to the open fire, holding out his hands gratefully to the flames.

The hot food was tasty and quickly restored his flagging energy; he was sorry to swallow the last morsel. He deliberated whether to request another helping but, mindful of funds, decided against it, opting instead for a second cup of tea. He was sipping at the piping brew and planning in his mind where best to seek out cheap lodgings when another customer entered. He gave her a cursory glance then swivelled his eyes back again to see she'd been crying. She sat at a small table to his left and placed her portmanteau on the floor by her chair. Then, as though sensing she was being watched, she half turned towards him.

Victor directed his attention back to his drink. The woman was giving her order now and he heard her ask for a cup of tea. Nothing to eat; though, in his opinion, she could have done with it. She was a little on the thin side, he observed, his gaze flicking back discreetly. In fact, she looked to be wanting of more than a good feed. The pinched face peeking out from her straw bonnet was void of colour and the purple smudges beneath her brown eyes showed clear signs that she hadn't slept properly in a while.

He wondered what had brought her here, not only alone but at this hour – daylight was rapidly leaving the October sky. Night-time on the streets of this borough posed dangers enough for man; for the fairer sex, it was tantamount to suicide. Such recklessness was just asking for trouble.

By her neat and clean attire, she didn't appear to be a vagrant. A drifter, then, who had happened upon Manchester in search of work? Possibly. Though judging by her white and uncalloused hands, it was evident she wasn't used to heavy toil. His curiosity mounted. Then, with an irritated click of his tongue, he inwardly shook himself. It was of no concern to him. He must stop this. It was time now to concentrate on himself and him alone. Other folks' issues had nothing to do with him any more.

When she rose shortly afterwards and disappeared into the darkened evening, he ordered a last brew with a resolute nod, telling himself to hell with everyone else. He had problems enough of his bloody own.

Shivering uncontrollably, Phoebe drew her sealskin capelet more securely around herself. A cast-off of Lilian Yewdale's, which she'd been delighted to accept when her kindly mistress had offered it her, it was Phoebe's pride and joy. However, though attractive, it really wasn't adequate for this time of year, she admitted to herself. A thick woollen shawl would be much more suitable. She'd have to locate a pawnbroker's tomorrow and exchange her capelet for one, she decided. She'd be sad to let the garment go but she must be practical. She'd not survive the harsh weather out here otherwise.

A fresh flurry of noise from an inn facing leaked across the cobbled road. Women's shrill voices, intermingled with the shouts of men, angry in drink, rent the air – lowering her head, Phoebe quickened her pace.

When, sometime later, a sign affixed to the window of a house in the centre of a tumbledown row proclaiming 'Beds Vacant' caught her attention, she breathed deeply in blessed relief. Low and miserable the dwelling might be but, by God, it had to be better than remaining a moment longer on these mean streets. The sights she'd seen . . .

Phoebe shuddered at the memory of this, her first day of destitution – and wanted to weep herself hoarse to think there were many more to come. *Lord help her.* She'd witnessed suffering and depravity in all its forms.

Rag-clad women, some with babes in arms, almost all with a huddle of emaciated, barefoot children clinging to their skirts, teeming around the doorways of every beerhouse she'd passed, their desperate eyes as they begged the revellers for a penny tearing at her heart like

9

a blade. Streetwalkers and their customers carrying out carnal acts in shadowed corners, the sights and sounds leaving those passing by in no doubt as to what was taking place. Males and females alike, any sense of pride they possessed dulled with drink, vomiting or urinating by the roadsides. Ribald language and bawdy songs, ferocious arguments and punch-ups . . . It felt as though she'd stumbled straight into hell.

Now, after extracting some coins from her portmanteau, she hurried on for the common lodging house.

She was nearing the door when it burst open and two young men tumbled on to the front steps, feet and fists flying. There came a muttered curse from inside, undoubtedly from the lodging-house keeper, followed by the door swinging shut again with a resounding slam which rattled the panes in their rotten frames.

Phoebe had moved hastily back – now, watching the ongoing skirmish from a distance, she bit her lip, unsure what to do. Before she could decide whether to go in search of another place, the men's anger was spent, the altercation over as fast as it had begun – swearing and yelling threats, they parted ways and disappeared in opposite directions.

Silence descended once more on the moonlit street, yet she hesitated still. Could she bring herself to approach? What further horrors lay in store inside the house? But what choice had she? she reminded herself. The simple answer was none. Thank goodness she was by nature frugal and had always put a bit by from her wages, but what money she had wouldn't stretch far. She couldn't afford to squander it on a better class of establishment, for who knew how long it would take her to secure employment, even with her precious reference? No. She would just have to endure it.

The unkempt woman in her middle years who answered Phoebe's knock confirmed she had room for her but refused her entry until the threepence fee was in her palm. With a flick of her greasy head, she indicated that she should follow, and Phoebe stepped inside.

A host of indeterminate smells each as rancid as the others enveloped her in a clogging veil; it took all of her willpower not to retch. Black mould bloomed on the ceiling and walls, and the filthy bare boards underfoot felt spongy with rot. If this first impression was anything to go by then, Mother of God, she could just imagine what the sleeping quarters would be like . . .

'Up there to the top of the house, first door on your right,' the keeper said, thrusting a thumb towards the staircase. 'You're to be up and gone in t' morning by eight o'clock sharp. No fighting, or you'll be out on your arse right away. I'll have no trouble beneath my roof.'

'I understand. Thank you,' Phoebe told her retreating back – already the woman had turned and was disappearing down the hall.

'Oh aye, I nearly forgot.' The keeper looked over her shoulder. 'That there's the communal lounge.' She pointed to the door directly in front of her. 'Cook yourself some grub, brew a sup of tea, whatever you fancy. Just be sure to clean up after yourself when you've done.'

Once more, she ambled off, and Phoebe was alone. Glancing from the lounge to the stairs, she screwed her lips in deliberation. Her mind made up, she headed in the direction of bed.

The sloped-ceilinged room was lit by a candle at either end. In the dimness, she could just make out rows of long black shadows and her brow furrowed in confusion. They looked almost like beds, but surely not . . . There couldn't be so many crammed into a single room, could there? As her vision gradually grew accustomed to the gloom, her heart dropped to her boots. There could and there were. Bar a narrow gap down the centre, the entire space was filled with bed upon bed – profit was clearly more important to the keeper than were her customers.

Sniffs, coughs and snores rumbled into one continual medley which jarred the nerves, and the gut-turning stench of bodily excretions and other nauseating odours hung like a noxious fog, choking the very air. Phoebe didn't know what to do first: cry or be sick. There was one thing she *couldn't* do, however, but wanted to more than anything else, and that was turn tail and run. This was her life, now, after all. She *must* front this out.

Picking her way across the floor, she squinted at each bed she passed in search of that which she'd occupy – and her horror slowly rose to manic proportions. None were vacant. Worse still, it wasn't, as she'd naively assumed, one to a bed. There were at least two or three persons, sometimes up to four, squashed into each. These poor, destitute souls were sharing beds with complete strangers and in their pathetically desperate state were grateful to do so. The cruel reality brought a lump to her throat. What hell on earth was this?

''Ere, lass. Squeeze yourself into ours.'

Phoebe turned towards the source of the voice and could just make out the craggy face of an elderly woman. Snuggled beside her lay sleeping a teenage girl.

'It's just me and my granddaughter in here – come on, there's room aplenty.'

'Thank you,' Phoebe murmured, moving to the opposite end of the bed and pulling back the threadbare blanket.

Even in the darkness, she couldn't fail to notice the

small black critters, disturbed by her action, scuttle for cover. It was overrun with vermin. *Dear God . . .*

'Cockroaches,' her bedfellow informed her on a yawn. 'It's the rotten straw in the palliasse, you see. Don't fret none, they'll not harm thee.'

Biting down on her tongue to stop herself from crying out in utter disgust and devastation – *how* had things come to *this*? – she lowered herself gingerly on to the bed. Within seconds, it became evident that cockroaches were not the only thing it was infested with; wincing, she scratched at the itchy bites that had sprung up on her arms and legs.

'Oh aye, there's fleas, an' all.' A gravelly laugh leaked from the old woman's toothless mouth. 'Them buggers you *do* have to pray don't eat thee alive by the morn.'

Phoebe had no response. Blinking back tears, she stooped to remove her footwear.

'Nay,' the woman hissed when Phoebe made to place the boots under the bed. 'God alive, lass, don't leave them there, else you'll be leaving this pit come the morrow in your bare feet.' She waved a hand around the room, indicating the other occupants. 'We're amongst all manner of foul and thief – they'll have thee stripped bare the minute your eyes are closed. Nay, never let nowt out of your sight in t' lodging houses. Same goes for that pretty bag of yourn,' she added, nodding to the portmanteau. 'Stuff your boots inside, stockings an' all, and use the bag as a pillow. That way, you'll feel it and waken if someone does try to have it away in t' night.'

Painfully aware that she had a lot to learn, Phoebe did as she'd been instructed. Her bonnet, she left where it was. Careful not to lie on the tangle of limbs, she shuffled herself into the gap between the two, pulling the grubby blanket up around her nose against the odour from the pairs of unwashed feet either side of her head.

'Goodnight, God bless, lass. I'd add, don't let the bedbugs bite, but well . . .'

'Goodnight,' Phoebe answered thickly, past the lump in her throat.

'You must promise me, Phoebe.' The deathbed plea hours before whispered like mist in the breeze. *'Please. Let me go to my Maker with peace in my heart. Promise me.'*

And her response: *'I promise.'*

But how, Lilian, how? her mind begged of her departed friend as she fell into a fitful sleep.

Chapter 2

'BASTARD! I'LL SNAP your filthy fingers!'

Awakening, Phoebe bolted upright with a gasp. The room was still dark, but she could see two shadows struggling by her bed.

'What's it to thee, anyroad?'

'I don't much care for thieving parasites, that's what,' the one who had spoken first growled. 'Shift yourself. Move!'

'All right, all bleedin' right, leave go!'

The taller of the men slammed his scrawnier opponent against the iron headboard. 'Get out of here whilst you still have the use of your legs. *Now.*'

When he'd scuttled out, Phoebe, shaking uncontrollably, stole a look at the one who remained. He was staring straight back, his breathing heavy with fury, and she shrank further beneath the blanket.

Several people in the surrounding beds had stirred during the ruckus, one or two lifting themselves on an elbow to squint over, but no one had attempted to intervene. And by the look of this man here, it was easy to see why. Tall and thickset, with jet-coloured hair and neat beard and piercing dark eyes, he cut an imposing figure.

'Are you all right?'

His tone was completely at odds with the harsh one

15

from moments ago. She nodded. 'Who are you? What's happening?'

'That one just now, he was attempting to steal your portmanteau. I wakened and caught him in the act.'

Phoebe was shocked. 'I didn't hear or feel a thing, I . . .' She shook her head. 'Thank you, Mr . . . ?'

'Hayes. Victor. And you're welcome.'

She watched him cross to a bed on the opposite wall, but he didn't lay down his head. Instead, he sat on the edge, his arms folded.

Filled with an odd sense of security at the sight of his presence, Phoebe fell back to sleep.

When she woke again, her bedfellows were gone. In fact, besides a few remaining stragglers determined to snatch what precious extra seconds of rest they could before a new day of clawing to survive began all over again, the room was deserted. Victor, however, was still present.

'Good morning, Mr Hayes,' she said with a small smile.

'Is it?' he retorted. Then his face softened a little and he half smiled back. 'Sorry. Good morning.'

He was shrugging on his jacket and Phoebe hurried to put on her stockings. 'May I buy you a cup of tea, Mr Hayes, by way of thanking you for last night?'

He hesitated, and she thought he'd decline the offer. But he didn't. He nodded then waited by the door whilst she quickly laced up her boots. She secured her capelet and picked up her portmanteau and they left the room and descended the stairs.

Stepping outside into the sulphurous air created by thousands of industrial and domestic chimneys, Phoebe drew in a blessed deep breath. Even this was preferable to the reek of the hovel they had just vacated. Without a word, they crossed the road and headed towards the eating house she'd visited the previous night.

16

'Two teas, please,' she told the serving girl when they were settled at a table. She turned to Victor. 'Do you want something to eat as well . . . ?'

'Will you?'

Phoebe shook her head. 'I'm fine with the tea, but please, you feel free.'

'The mistress does a lovely bit of porridge, mister,' the serving girl chipped in.

Victor smiled. 'Then porridge it shall be. Twice,' he added with a lift of his eyebrows to Phoebe when she made to protest. 'Some bread and butter, too, I think.'

'Very good, mister. It shan't be long.'

'I said I was fine with just tea,' Phoebe said when the girl had left.

'Like yesterday, you mean?'

She frowned. 'I don't under—'

'I saw you in here last evening. You ate not a scrap then, either.'

'Come to think of it . . .' She nodded slowly. 'I do remember you, after all. You were seated over there.' She pointed to the table in question.

'Yes.' Then: 'Tea alone won't keep you going for long. You've got to eat, or you'll make yourself ill,' he pressed.

'I haven't much of an appetite of late,' she admitted, lowering her eyes.

'Me neither, if truth be told.'

His gaze had taken on a troubled edge and she wondered what his story was. What had brought him to where he was now, dossing down in some low lodging house, living out of a bag, same as she? He didn't seem like a vagrant. Not the ones she was accustomed to, anyway. She'd spied them on more than one occasion when she'd been down in the kitchen in the Yewdales' house. Men, normally, but sometimes women, too, would knock

17

at the back door to plead a heel of bread or sup of water, and kindly Cook had always obliged. But Victor wasn't like those poor unfortunates, wasn't dirty or dressed in ill-fitting rags. So what, then?

'Hello?' Victor's voice cut through her thoughts and she blushed pink to have been caught second-guessing his affairs. His business really had nothing at all to do with her!

'Sorry,' she told him, shaking her head. 'I was in a world all of my own. What were you saying?'

'I said you know my name, but I as yet don't know yours.'

'Oh. Yes. Phoebe. Phoebe Parsons.'

They shook hands awkwardly and laughed. Then the serving girl was back with their order and they tucked in gratefully.

'You see?' Victor announced when they had finished their breakfast and were sipping at the last of their tea. He inclined his head to her empty dish.

She smiled in admission. 'Yes, you were right. I do feel better now.'

They sat in easy silence for a while, enjoying their full stomachs and the heat from the fire, until Phoebe said, 'What time are we permitted to return to the lodging house, Mr Hayes?'

'You're really that eager to?' he asked incredulously.

'No, no. It's terrible. Only . . . Well. I haven't anywhere else to go. I can't very well sit in here all day – I'm sure the proprietor wouldn't like that – and the lodging house does stave off the worst of the elements, I suppose.'

'Sometime later tonight, I'd say.'

'Oh.' She swallowed hard. How on earth was she meant to pass the time until then?

'I'd better be going.' Victor rose and reached for his hat on the table.

'Oh,' Phoebe said again – it was all she had. Her heart had dipped with the prospect of being adrift for the remainder of the day *and* alone.

'Goodbye, Miss Parsons.'

She wanted to ask him whether he'd be staying at the lodging house again that night but decided against it, deeming it too forward. Though she did hope he would be. 'Goodbye, Mr Hayes.'

After he'd walked away, she closed her eyes. She could order another cup of tea? That would buy her a little more time in the warmth. But what then? What about the rest of the long day and evening stretching ahead?

Her mind drifted to the luxurious house she'd left behind and her friends below stairs. How were they faring with Warwick Yewdale? And what of dear Lilian? Had her stepson even informed the odd relative or two she had in the world of her passing? Probably not, knowing him. He'd likely not deem the occurrence important enough to bother. *Damn him.* Oh, how she wished things hadn't changed, that her mistress was still here. She could see her now, stretched out in the drawing room on the satin chaise longue, one of her beloved books open beside her, ash blonde ringlets bobbing about her ears and her pearl-like teeth sparkling behind her pink lips as she laughed at something Phoebe had said . . . Lord, how she missed her . . .

No, she told herself firmly, dashing away the tears that had pricked with the back of her hand. She wouldn't wallow in self-pity, wouldn't dwell on all that was lost, refused to. She must think, be practical.

Glancing down at her capelet, she remembered her plan regarding acquiring a sensible shawl. She nodded, her purpose renewed. And afterwards, she'd take a walk around the main thoroughfares and try her luck at gaining fresh employment. With another nod, she drained her cup and rose.

'But . . . the mister you were with paid afore he left, miss,' the serving girl revealed in puzzlement when Phoebe went to settle the bill before leaving.

With a wry smile, she thanked her and set off towards the centre of the borough.

As he'd suspected, Kate wasn't home.

Victor glanced left and right along the quiet street and released an irritated sigh. His wife would have gone to her sister's house to gripe about his shortcomings from there. And so it had begun: discussing their business with all and sundry, damn her. And talk she had, if the twitching of next door's curtains was anything to go by.

He gave his neighbour a sarcastically bright wave and she let the material drop back into place with her nose in the air. Gossiping hag, she was nothing else. And all the time he'd done nothing! He could shake Kate for her knee-jerk assumptions, he really could.

Dragging a hand through his hair, he stepped back into the road and turned once more to look at his house. He could kick the door in, he surmised. As the man, he was more than entitled to take full claim of his castle, after all. But Kate wouldn't stand for that, and where would it leave her? She'd refuse point blank to continue residing with him whilst her temper was still up, would no doubt stop on at her sister's indefinitely, and he couldn't let that happen, wouldn't see her evicted from her home. She was blameless in all this, too – more so. It was all such a bloody mess.

But what *was* he to do? If he had to spend another night beneath the roof of some stinking lodging house, he'd go mad. He could possibly afford to rent a couple of decent rooms until, God willing, all this foolishness blew over. But how long would his funds last, and what then? Besides, that option seemed a little too permanent, too *real*, for his liking. This was his home, here. Soon, when everyone came to their senses, all would be as it had been again. Soon . . .

A vision of his bedroom, of his wardrobe and what was hanging up in there, swam into his thoughts and a stab of something so painful that it snatched the breath from him struck.

His uniform. Blue trousers and frock coat embellished with white embroidery and silvery buttons. The diamond-and-circle-patterned collar patch, emblazoned with his number and the letter of the geographical division for which he worked – or at least had worked . . .

The three-quarter-length thick woollen cape, invaluable when out pounding one's beat in all weathers – a rain-sodden uniform would have been hazardous to the health – fastened in place with a chain-and-hook fixing at the neck. At the risk of it becoming an encumbrance should a constable find himself in a scuffle, the soft alloy chain could be snapped easily, allowing him to remove his cape quickly. Lastly, his sturdy boots, the shine on them like black glass, so bright you could see your reflection in them, standing beneath on the floor of the wardrobe alongside his smart top hat . . . He could see it all clearly in his mind's eye.

His truncheon he'd been forced to hand in to his chief constable upon his dismissal, along with his rattle for summoning assistance. The uniform would be requested back shortly, too, no doubt.

The Duty Band, a piece of white-and-blue horizontally striped cloth with a buckle, was attached to the uniform when officers were on duty. When *off* duty, it was the only item they were permitted to remove – bar to bathe or go to bed, they wore their uniforms at all times. Glancing down at what he wore now: a white flannel shirt, best broadcloth suit in gravy brown and woollen coat two shades darker, finished off with a round, narrow-brimmed hat, all somewhat stained and dreadfully crumpled – more than likely lousy now, too, he suspected with a ripple of disgust – from his night in the lodging house, Victor frowned. It was still an oddity to him, wearing civilian apparel again; he doubted he'd ever grow used to it.

The prestige his role had given him – all gone. Along with his marriage, his home and his unblemished good name. For what? His gaze swivelled westwards towards Ancoats and Suzannah Frost residing in the slum district's poverty-riddled belly. His feet jerked with the desire to seek her out, check she was well. But his common sense told him it was unwise to and, with a shake of his head, he swung around and clumped away in the opposite direction, resisting the urge to shoot his abandoned home a last look over his shoulder.

Market Street, with its high-end shops and counting houses, was as always a hubbub of noise, teeming with transport and people. Taking his time, eager to kill some hours, Victor strolled leisurely on through the throng towards Piccadilly, lined with warehouses and huge hotels, continuing on further for London Road.

Here, though the grimy working men's quarters were still mostly concealed from the eyes of the genteel patrons, the surrounding premises gradually grew less impressive. The shops and factories and works, churches and chapels and beerhouses, catering more towards the labouring populace and all mulched together in a hodgepodge

22

mass, squatted beneath a sky the colour of crushed grey pearls, whilst a hundred sounds and smells rapped at the senses.

The shouts of hawkers plying their wares and cart drivers urging on their horses or warning folk to make way, the nerve-jangling scrape of iron-rimmed wheels and merry clop of hooves interweaved with the odd burst of child laughter, greetings and general conversation, whilst wafts of tobacco, fresh fish and newly baked bread amongst other smells from the surrounding businesses mingled with the cloying stench of hot manure.

Drinking in everything, Victor was reminded how much he loved his home. His mouth curved in a fond smile. There was no place quite like Manchester in the whole of the world, he was certain. It held an unassuming specialness that he couldn't even describe – he wasn't a man of words, was no poet or philosopher – but he knew it to be so without question, and he felt it instinctively deep in his breast. That pride, warm and solid and sure, which every Mancunian emerged with from the womb.

As he approached a busy corner, he was accosted by a stunted child, his thin face wreathed in misery; the tip of his dripping nose was cherry red, his lips tinged mauve from the cold. Clutching the tools of his trade in chapped hands, he gazed up at Victor with hungry desperation:

'Polish your boots, mister?'

Peering pityingly down at him shivering in his suit of rags, his feet shoeless and encrusted with filth and sores, Victor nodded assent and placed a foot on the small wooden box positioned before him. In his current situation, it was an extravagance but, as well as wanting to help the boy to earn a crust, he did like to look his best and old habits die hard.

The urchin blacked and buffed to an agreeable standard and Victor rewarded his efforts with a generous tip. 'Are you destitute, lad?' he said quietly, knowing full well the answer but asking nonetheless. The weather was worsening with each new sunrise. These unforgiving streets would likely carry him and countless others of his ilk off before the next spring. Unfortunates young and old swarmed in depressingly high numbers; but what was the alternative? The majority would sooner perish from cold and hunger in the streets – and this they did in their droves – than knock upon the door of the much-feared poorhouse, and that was the truth.

At the question, the boy's sharp eyes narrowed and he backed away. 'Mebbe I am, mebbe I ain't,' he offered in a tone low with unease. Then he licked his lips and glanced both ways, as though expecting the workhouse van to rumble around the corner at any moment and bundle him inside.

Victor could only sigh helplessly. Despite his earlier inward praising of his borough, like so many others it wasn't without its flaws. The gap between rich and poor was painfully, shamefully acute and he hated the fact.

A recent trade crisis, leading to economic recession, was still very much affecting the populace. It had gradually increased in severity and by the time the stifling summer just passed had rolled around, industrial depression was at its lowest ebb. Unemployment figures were high, and those who managed to cling on to their jobs saw a drop in wages – a devastating blow when food prices were soaring. Suffering and sick of it, tensions inevitably spilled over and mass strikes had broken out across the country.

Districts in Lancashire and beyond had ground to a halt as almost half a million workers forced into revolt ceased productivity, causing mills, factories and more to shut down. Here in Manchester, thousands upon thousands had marched through the streets – peaceful and dignified but determined for change. 'A fair day's wage for a fair day's work' was the maxim. Was that really asking too much? they wanted to know. Surely it was the basic right of every man?

Victor certainly thought so. His profession, however, had required him to assist in 'managing the mob', and he'd hated the feeling of being on the opposing side, so to speak. Though the general consensus amongst the ruling lot was that the working class had got above themselves and had no right defying those in authority and dictating to their betters, Victor hadn't agreed. He empathised with the poor and felt deeply for their plight.

The strikers held out doggedly – to the death for some – until desperation as their families slowly starved had forced them back to work. Though some wage cuts were withdrawn, achieving the small victory had come at a heavy price – the hardship had been immense.

'Steady on, lad,' he began now to the boot polisher, but the boy was already turning about.

'Ta, mister,' he called, indicating the precious coins gripped tightly in his fist. 'I'd best be on my way . . .'

Victor watched him skitter off to become lost in the crowd. With another sigh, he moved on once more.

Sometime later, he paused to purchase hot pigs' cheeks from a street vendor and leaned against the bricks of a nearby inn to enjoy his feast. A glance heavenwards had him frowning – pewter clouds had gathered ominously, heralding a downpour in which he was reluctant to get caught. The food had warmed his insides but the stiff wind that had started up was turning his face and fingers to ice; looking behind him, he nodded. A rare sup beside the inn fire would remedy that.

He'd pushed open the scuffed door and was about to enter when, to his right across the street, a familiar figure caught his eye. His brows lifted, his interest piqued. He stopped and watched her disappear inside a pawnshop.

Victor's hand lingered on the door a moment longer. Then he dropped his arm to his side and made his way across the cobbled road.

The door creaked shut at her back, blotting out the day, and the dimness closed around her like a shroud. Phoebe peered through the musty-smelling interior and was glad there were no other customers present. She crossed to the man behind the cluttered counter.

'Yes?'

'I, erm, I'd like to . . . pledge this, please, sir,' she mumbled, loosening the clasp at her throat and removing the capelet from her shoulders, both embarrassed to be here and unsure whether she was conducting the business correctly – she'd never stepped foot inside one of these places in her life before.

'Hmm. Yes. Nice.' He spoke to himself, running the soft material through his hands then scrutinising the fur collar for moth damage. She knew he'd find no complaints there. She'd always been careful to wrap the garment in linen washed in lye and place pieces of cedar wood in her drawer, to ward off pests, when the capelet was not in use, during the warmer months. Finally, he turned his attention back to her. 'Five shillings.'

Phoebe nodded in surprise. True, the garment was fine quality and held virtually no sign of wear, but it was a good few years old – third-hand, now, she realised – and very much out of fashion. She should be able to purchase a warm shawl out of that and still have shillings to spare.

The pawnbroker had begun to count out silver coins into her hand when, suddenly, he paused. His gaze had travelled to her chest, and his eyes, two dark amber slits like those of a cat who had spotted a mouse, lit up. He smiled, and Phoebe squirmed beneath his scrutiny, acutely aware of their state of isolation. Her arms crossed instinctively to shield her small bust. *Let him try anything with me – I'll scream blue murder, scratch the flesh from his face* . . . she swore silently to herself, her heart beginning to drum.

'That there.' He pointed. 'If you're for selling it, I can give you a good price.'

Frowning, she glanced down. The brooch pinned above her left breast winked back and she felt her colour rise. She'd thought he . . . when all the time . . . A relieved laugh gurgled in her throat. 'This?' She fingered the cherry-sized ornament with its intertwining bronze leaves studded with imitation emeralds. Pretty enough, but by no means valuable; at least, not in a monetary sense. 'It's but a cheap bauble, sir.'

'Ah. Yes.' He was quick to agree, his head bobbing on his neck in a nod. 'Indeed it is, indeed it is, but my wife has a weakness for such things, and I'd be only too happy to take it off your hands—'

'Oh, I couldn't, sir! It was a gift from my mistress on my last birthday.' Sadness gripped her chest, as always, at the thought of Lilian Yewdale.

His face visibly fell. He eyed the piece again. 'As I said, my wife . . . I'll give you twelve pounds for it.'

'Twelve . . . *twelve pounds*?' Phoebe was agape. During her position as lady's maid, she would have had to have worked an entire year for such a sum. It had to be some kind of trick or mistake. Who on earth would pay that amount for this – however much it may please their spouse? It was madness. 'Sir, I don't think you understand—'

'Fifteen, then.'

She drew in a breath. For the briefest of moments, she was tempted to accept – and on his head be it! Besides, surely Lilian would understand … Then shame, like a chill wave, washed through her. She shook her head. 'Thank you, but the answer is no. I couldn't ever part with it. However, I *would* like to buy something from you,' she added, looking around. 'A shawl, please. The thickest you have.'

He motioned to the far wall, where hung an assortment of woollen clothing, and as she made her way across to peruse them she surveyed the array of goods set on wide shelves all around her. From boots and trousers and dresses to pots and pans, sheets and counterpanes and tablecloths, clocks and jugs and vases and pictures in frames, coal buckets and curtains – the list of unredeemed and purchasable items on offer was endless. All the while, the owner's eyes remained locked on her. Ignoring his stare, she concentrated her attentions on the outdoor garments.

Phoebe selected a near-new shawl in dark blue with white tassels, and after paying and thanking him turned to leave, but he stopped her:

'If ever you change your mind …' He once again glanced with longing at the brooch. 'You know where to find me.'

Hoping beyond hope that she'd never have cause to accept his offer yet realistic enough to admit that circumstances may force her hand in the future, however much it would pain her, she nodded. Bidding him good-bye, she wrapped the shawl around herself and left the shop.

'Oh. Hello.' Phoebe smiled up in surprised delight into Victor's face.

'Miss Parsons!' He appeared equally surprised to see it was she. 'I didn't recognise you for a moment – the shawl,' he explained, motioning down.

She explained about the growing cold and her pretty but unsuitable capelet. 'I'm glad I spotted you, actually. Let me buy you lunch. I insist,' she pressed when he made to decline. She lifted an eyebrow. 'You paid for breakfast, after all.'

'Ah. That.' He flashed a crooked smile.

'It was very kind of you, but please, you must allow me to return the compliment.'

'I've eaten already . . . All right, then. A cup of tea would be nice.'

When they were seated in their usual eating house, she asked, 'So how was your morning, Mr Hayes?'

'Unremarkable.'

He didn't seem to want to divulge more, and she left it at that. Whatever he'd been doing and where was nothing to do with her. 'Are you sure you won't eat something?' She nodded to the serving girl making her way across.

'No, thank you. Tea will do just fine.'

She ordered two cups and they sat sipping the piping brews in companionable silence. Phoebe wanted to ask him if he did plan to spend the night at the lodging house – the thought of staying there alone after the previous night's antics scared her – but he might think her impertinent to probe his movements. Instead, she sent up a silent prayer that he would and returned her attention to the world passing by beyond the window.

When at one point a police constable went by and Victor, having spotted him, too, ducked quickly out of sight, Phoebe frowned in confusion, and this swiftly gave way to curiosity then unease.

'Mr Hayes?' she murmured questioningly.

He didn't respond. His face was wreathed in dread coupled with acute embarrassment – she could almost feel his discomfiture across the scrubbed table.

'Mr Hayes, is something—?'

'No. Nothing.' A last quick glance through the pane and he rose back into his seat. His gaze remained firmly fixed on his tea. 'Nothing's wrong.'

Phoebe watched him discreetly over the rim of her own cup. Why had he felt the need to act so? Unless . . . She swallowed hard. People only hid from the law for one reason, surely? He was a wanted man, had to be. *God above.* And yet he seemed so . . . normal, upstanding. Could it be true? And if so, was she as safe as she'd thought herself to be in his company? What crime had he committed? What was she to *do*?

'It's not what you're thinking.'

Victor's voice had pierced her fretting and it was as though he'd read her mind. Her cheeks flushed brick red. 'I don't know what you mean, I—'

'I'm not a wanted man, Miss Parsons.'

For reasons she didn't understand, she believed him instinctively. Nor did she push him for an explanation; his business was his alone, after all. She simply nodded and they returned their attention to their tea.

A short time later, Victor, who had barely spoken again following the incident with the constable,

30

announced, 'Don't let me keep you, Miss Parsons, if you have plans for this afternoon.'

She was about to deny any such thing, was quite content to sit here in his company, but there had been an edge to his tone and a hint of, if not annoyance, then a brooding desire to be alone with his thoughts, within his deep eyes. She reached for her shawl. 'I did think to look for employment. I suppose there's no time like the present. Well, goodbye, Mr Hayes.'

Victor nodded without looking up. Phoebe lifted her portmanteau from the floor beside her chair, shot him a last quick look then left the eating house. Whatever his reasons for wanting to avoid the law were, it was weighing heavily on his mind. What *was* his story? she wondered.

After enquiring at several businesses, she eventually secured an address – taking a sharp right turn, she headed off for the servants' registry office.

Filling vacancies for affluent households was big business. Whether full or part time, from ladies in need of temporary cooks and waiters for special occasions – though even these instances could result in full-time roles if a good enough impression was made – to more permanent positions, there was always demand for domestics.

Those seeking staff relied on agencies and in turn, many out-of-work servants turned to such establishments in the hope of gaining employment. If a servant was suitable for a situation and agreed to the terms and requirements outlined, their details were forwarded to the potential employer and an interview was arranged. In the main, it proved a smooth affair. Phoebe just prayed she'd be successful and would soon be in a steady, live-in job once more.

Outside, she read the large notice in the window:

MRS FONTAINE, RESPECTABLE SERVANTS' AGENCY.
Employer registration 1s/6d (plus an annual
12-shilling fee for details of recruitable employees).
Domestics seeking employment, registration 1 shilling.

She rummaged inside her bag and extracted the correct amount. Then, clutching the coin and Warwick Yewdale's reference, she pushed at the door.

Locked.

Frowning, she scanned the window again, spotting now in the bottom corner:

Opening hours 2–6 p.m.

The time wasn't yet one; she'd have to try again later.

She wandered around for a while before turning and making her way back. Sure enough, the premises were now open, but already the reception room was packed with applicants on the same mission as herself. There were but a handful of males present; females predominated greatly. This was no surprise. There were few opportunities for women in particular besides domestic servitude. Furthermore, be it because of ill or unwanted treatment or to improve their prospects and wages, maids frequently changed jobs. Picking her way through the crush, Phoebe approached the high mahogany desk.

'Yes?'

She had to clear her throat before she was able to address the formidable-looking registry keeper with the stiff back and stern face. Her nervousness was mounting by the second; her whole future depended on this going well. 'Good afternoon. I'd like to register, please, if I may.'

One look at Phoebe's serviceable clothing and shawl and the woman was in no doubt as to her role: 'You're seeking *work* as a servant rather than looking to employ one, am I right?'

'I'm a fully qualified lady's maid and until very recently worked for a highly respectable family in Cheetham Hill. I understand perfectly the duties required: hairdressing, dressmaking and millinery, amongst other things—'

'More importantly, you're honest and strictly sober?'

Besides a celebratory sherry at Christmastide and New Year, which Lilian used to insist she join her in, not a drop of alcohol passed Phoebe's lips throughout the rest of the twelvemonth. 'Oh yes.'

'Very well.' The woman reached for a form. 'If I can just have your particulars . . .'

After providing her full name and age, nodding to confirm 'lady's maid' as the position trained for then shaking her head in answer to whether she was married or had any dependants, she gave her last place of employment and its duration.

'And your current address?'

Looking to the floor, Phoebe shook her head once more.

'You're destitute?'

'Yes,' she whispered, both embarrassed to admit how far she'd fallen and worried this would lower her chances here. However, she was pleasantly mistaken:

'Not to worry,' the woman told her. 'I also offer a female servants' home. It provides a safe place for those in need when out of work. There, see.' She inclined her head towards the window; across the road stood a row of plain grey apartments.

Phoebe could have cried. No more bedding down at the lodging house – or worse, the street! Everything was finally slipping into place. 'Wonderful. Oh, thank you!'

'The home is under my superyision and I must warn you, I run a very tight ship,' she continued. 'My rules and regulations must be wholly adhered to, you understand?'

'Oh yes.' Phoebe agreed without hesitation. Right now, she'd have promised the keeper the world if she'd asked.

'I expect all those dwelling there to practise high morality, cleanliness and order. You are also required to attend morning church service each Sunday. One last thing: you must be back at the home before 9 p.m. each night. If you do require to sleep elsewhere, at a relative's for instance, you must first come to me to obtain permission.'

'Yes, of course.'

'All conveniences such as candles, fire, bed and linen are provided. Food, however, is not. The rent is three shillings a week. My terms are satisfactory to you?'

She nodded readily. 'They are.'

'Good. Now, where were we . . . ?' The woman flicked her gaze back to the form. 'Ah yes. What was your reason for leaving your last position?'

'My mistress . . . she died.'

'I see.'

'I am in possession of a reference. It's from Mr Warwick Yewdale, my mistress's stepson, and attests to my good character.'

'I should think so,' she stated, taking the letter from her and breaking the seal. 'I deal with only the very best, and my agency boasts an impeccable reputation to prove it. No applicant can possibly be considered without a first-class reference.'

Phoebe nodded her understanding. 'That, I trust, will prove satisfactory.'

The woman scanned the lines then paused to glance up. Once more, she turned her attention to the paper and read it through again, this time thoroughly. Finally, she met Phoebe's eye. Her lips had stretched into a thin line and a frown was pulling at her brows.

'Is something wrong?'

'This is some ridiculous pastime of yours, is it, wasting people's time?'

'What? No, I . . .' Phoebe shook her head in perplexity. 'I'm sorry, I don't—'

'Really,' she cut in, flinging the reference across the desktop. 'Read that.'

Miss Phoebe Parsons is both an idler and a liar . . .
A shameless harlot with unscrupulous morals . . .
Disagreeable, dishonest, unprincipled, incompetent . . .
Would not recommend her services to neither man,
woman nor beast . . .

The unbelievable words danced a devastating jig on the white paper. She could feel her heart beating in her throat.

'I'm afraid I'll have to ask you to leave, Miss Parsons.'

'No . . .' Phoebe shook her head again, sending tears of injustice spilling down her cheeks. This couldn't be. Even he wouldn't stoop to such a callous low, such utter cruelty, surely! 'It's lies. It is, it—!'

'Good *day*, Miss Parsons.'

Her shoulders fell with terrible truth. His damning – and totally false – testimony had sealed her fate. He'd scuppered her chances of ever gaining employment in her chosen field again. Warwick Yewdale had effectively ruined her for the fun of it.

Reaching the street, she gulped in lungfuls of air.

Her devastation was absolute. She should have guessed he was hoodwinking her when he'd agreed to provide a reference, should have known him helping her was too good to be true. He never did anything for anyone even out of common obligation, never mind decency or kindness. Why? *Why?* What in God's name was she to do?

She turned and made her slow way back towards London Road. There were of course the 'Situations Vacant' columns in newspapers, but what would be the point? Without a character reference, those, too, would yield the same result. Reputable households didn't take on just anybody and everybody. The lack of a character would scream unsatisfactory candidate. No decent employer would touch her without one. She was finished. Unless . . .

The only possible option left open to her now, she realised, was the unlawful practice of falsifying one. Could she do it, despite the risk of detection and subsequent punishment? Then again, should it work . . . She bit her lip, red-faced with guilt to even be considering such a notion. *But I'm desperate,* her mind insisted. *Surely, I have no choice?*

No one, not even Warwick Yewdale, need ever find out. Former masters and mistresses were not legally obliged to provide a reference, after all – any responsible person, therefore, was permitted to write one.

The idea was still heavy in her thoughts later when she climbed the lodging-house steps. She was making her way past the communal kitchen towards the stairs when Victor's voice reached her:

'Evening, Miss Parsons.'

'Mr Hayes,' she murmured in greeting.

'Tea?' he added when she made to continue on her way. He encompassed the room with his arms. 'It's early

36

yet, there's nobody else here, so we can enjoy a cup in peace?'

After a long moment, she nodded in defeat and crossed the hall. She took the low stool next to his and accepted the chipped mug he held out to her. 'Thank you.'

'You're all right?'

He seemed easier of mood than he had been that morning, and she was glad of it. Then her own trials bore down on her once more, scattering all else from her mind. She swallowed a sigh. 'Yes.'

'Really?'

'I said *yes*, Mr Hayes. Sorry,' she continued when he glanced away; worry had made her tongue sharper than she'd intended. 'No. No, I'm not all right.'

Victor waited in silence. When she wasn't forthcoming, he encouraged her with a slight incline of his head. 'A problem shared, Miss Parsons . . .'

'There is no relieving my troubles, Mr Hayes, and most definitely not by half,' she whispered thickly, her throat filling with tears. 'You see, I'm ruined.'

'Ruined?'

She nodded. 'And there is no rectifying the fact. I'll never . . . never . . .' Putting her head in her hands, she burst into silent sobs.

'Phoebe . . .' Without realising it, it seemed, Victor addressed her by her Christian name. He laid a gentle hand on her arm. 'What in the world has happened? Don't take on so,' he soothed in his soft, deep voice. 'Tell me what's occurred. Happen I can help—'

'You cannot, Mr Hayes, no one can!'

'Try me. Please.'

'The servants' registry office. I went this afternoon and . . . and they . . . Dear God in heaven. It was so humiliating!'

'Surely no . . . Not again, it *can't* be.'

Victor's tone had her raising her tear-streaked face to him in confusion. 'What do you mean?'

'Those places – and countless other "agencies" besides. Not all are as scrupulous as they claim, are they? You're . . . all right?'

'Besides bruised pride – yes, I suppose so.'

'You're certain, Miss Parsons?'

His insistence baffled her. She shook her head. 'I'm sorry, but what exactly . . . ?'

'You've discovered to your cost this day, have you not, that fraudulent practices operate all over this city?' He shrugged his shoulders in bitter regret. 'It's clear you've led a rather more sheltered life than most. Your blinkers of innocence have been forcibly removed from you, it seems. I do hope your ordeal wasn't too great? Of course, I must insist you report this at once to the police.'

'Mr Hayes, I think you misunderstand me.' Phoebe was completely flummoxed. 'What is it that you mean?'

'I thought, when you said . . .' He cleared his throat. 'My mistake, think no more of it. Well, you see,' he continued when she urged him on with a pressing stare, 'there was one such agency plying a similar trade not so long ago. Except it wasn't.'

'I don't . . . ?'

'It claimed to be a servants' registry office, only it was something else entirely,' he explained. He looked decidedly uncomfortable. 'Their tempting pledges and syrupy assurances in the newspaper articles they put out were believable enough, I will admit – more so to those folk desperate to have it be true. Summoned by the keeper, scores unwittingly flocked to register, with some poor lasses even upping sticks from the country to skip like the proverbial lambs to the slaughter. They suspected

38

nothing untoward, and why would they? Reality was, they hadn't the slightest clue what they were really walking into.'

Phoebe's hand snaked up to her throat. She'd gone cold all over. 'What happened, Mr Hayes?'

'Upon arriving at the office, the girls were directed to the servants' home; therein they were to dwell, in cramped and wretched conditions. Days passed and, despite their questions with regards to securing domestic positions, the keeper offered up no information but instead insisted all would be finalised in due course. It was to later transpire that positions did not in fact exist. They had been lured to the agency under false pretences.'

'For what? Why ever else were they there?'

Victor stared into the meagre fire. 'The one thing that makes this sorry world of ours go round. The one thing many people value above all else.' He turned to face her and his dark eyes were hard as flint. 'Money.'

'But surely if the servants were out of work, then they had none to give,' said Phoebe with a frown.

'Where there's a will, Miss Parsons, there's a way.'

'Tell me.'

'The girls had been tricked into going there in order that they should lodge at the servants' home, thereby fetching in a profit to the registry keeper. Inevitably, however, as you yourself pointed out, with no situations forthcoming and thus no income at their disposal, they were unable to pay the rent. Now in their host's debt, they were obliged to earn the fee in an altogether more undesirable capacity.'

'You mean . . . prostitution?' Phoebe was aghast.

'That or, as they were threatened with, face prosecution. The terrifying, and very real, prospect for young naïve girls of being hauled before the courts, resulting

39

in incarceration in the debtors' prison, left them with what they believed to be no choice. They had to settle up somehow. They were at the keeper's mercy.'

'Why didn't they simply flee? Surely they could have tried . . . *some*thing?'

'It wasn't so simple. Once they had fallen into that life, of course they found it nigh-on impossible to break free. The shame and self-loathing, not to mention the ongoing fear owing to fabricated, added expenses, kept them right where the keeper wanted them.'

'Kept them from returning to the safety of their families' bosoms,' she murmured, her chest aching with remorse for every last one of the victims and her hands trembling in anger for their devilish persecutors.

'Exactly. Those new to Manchester were adrift in a strange place; impoverished, alone and helpless. Even to the local girls, escape seemed impossible. Once they realised what a terrible and wicked ruse they had been drawn into, they not only felt foolish but thoughts of returning penniless and with the truth, to scorn, fury or disappointment – those back home were depending on their wages – was a devastating notion.'

'How was the horrific business eventually exposed?'

'One of them finally found courage to seek the help of the police. It blew the whole operation out of the water. Those girls might very well be languishing there still but for her.'

'Thank God for her strength and fortitude. She must have been so scared.'

'Petrified.'

'It's terrible, just terrible.'

There followed a silence. Then, closing his eyes, Victor spoke on quietly: 'Can you fathom it, Miss Parsons? The Slavery Abolition Act was passed throughout the

British Empire almost a decade ago now and, excellent as that was – our involvement in such a heinous practice shall for ever be a blot on our escutcheon – yet it goes on still amongst our own people, in many guises, in plain sight. Here, in one of the greatest, most prosperous, forward-thinking nations in the modern world, we have enslavement on our own doorstep.

'Why? Why *any* of it? So that the land sharks may live in luxury? We're talking mortal beings, for God's sake! But, negro or white, plantation or grey cobbled street, it matters not one iota to some. If money can be made off the back of another, you can be sure it will be. The evil of man never ceases to amaze me.'

The passion of his speech touched her deeply; on impulse, she reached over and pressed his hand. Then, embarrassed at her display of overfamiliarity, she pulled it back again and lowered her gaze. 'I cannot make sense of it, Mr Hayes, no.' Of one thing, however, she was in no doubt: here was a good man and she was glad to call him her friend.

'You're certain the offices you visited today were proper and above board?'

'They were perfectly reputable,' she was quick to reassure him.

'Well, I'm glad to hear it. The risk is very much there, for it goes on still. Registry offices are not licensed, but they should be. That way, should a complaint arise, they would have said licence withdrawn by their local authority; it would soon stamp these practices out. However, until the law sees fit to act . . .' Holding up his hands in a helpless motion, Victor sighed. 'There's nothing to stop others falling into similarly depraved traps. People must simply try to avoid fraudulent agencies by relying on personal recommendations only. It's the wisest way.

So, Miss Parsons,' he added, and his voice had softened. 'What *was* it about your experience today? You were mightily upset upon your return . . .'

'The character reference given to me by my last place wasn't . . . up to muster, shall we say.'

'Oh?'

Not having energy enough right now to go through it all again, she played the matter down: 'It's fine, really. Only, as a result, the registry keeper refused my application. I'm just so disappointed. What with the servants' house and all – well, it was ideal.'

'If you were to explain the situation to your former employer, they would be willing to write you a more detailed reference, I'm sure,' he said, assuming it was that which was the issue. *If only it were that simple . . .*

'I'm sure you're right,' she lied, blinking rapidly as her eyes filled with despondent tears.

By now, the kitchen was steadily filling with drifters. As though of the same mind, Phoebe and Victor rose as one and headed for the stairs. It had been a long day, it seemed, for the pair of them.

'Mr Hayes?' she said as they reached the landing, the thought occurring. 'Those girls. How do you know all that?'

'I know, Miss Parsons, because I helped to shut that registry down last year.'

For a long moment, she stared back at him with a frown. Then, as realisation dawned, her brow cleared and she emitted a small gasp. 'You're a policeman.'

'Please, keep your voice down.' His gaze flitted about with definite unease. 'Plenty of folk beneath this roof wouldn't take too well to knowing that.'

She nodded understanding. Every manner of criminal passed through the lodging houses. A constable in their midst . . . Victor's very life could well be in danger should it get out. 'I do apologise,' she whispered, 'but please, tell me, why would someone in your position be here?' Her eyes widened in excitement. 'Are you working on some important undercover case, maybe, or—?'

'Nothing as sensational as that, I'm afraid.'

But Phoebe wasn't convinced – her imagination was working overtime. Why in the world else would a respectable lawman be suffering such a place as this unless he had to? Of course, him being who he said he was, it all made sense to her now. He'd possessed from the start a certain air; he exuded authority. One felt safe in his presence.

'I can trust you'll keep to yourself what you've just learned?'

'Oh yes. But Mr Hayes, what—?'

'I'm sorry, Miss Parsons, I really am very tired,' he cut in, continuing on for the sleeping quarters, and she had no choice but to quell her curiosity and questions.

A space beside a young mother and her baby was available; Phoebe hurried to claim it before someone beat her to it. Reassuringly, Victor had settled in the bed closest to her; she smiled at him through the dimness and he returned it with a nod.

A policeman.

She knew she'd sleep a little easier this night.

Chapter 3

'SAUSAGES?'

Raising herself on her elbow, Phoebe squinted through the morning light. The other lodgers all around her were mostly still at slumber, grabbing what sleep they could before the house keeper kicked them out for the day.

'We have half an hour or so before we must vacate the place,' Victor added. 'We may as well take advantage of the facilities.' He held up a small, paper-wrapped package. 'I'll meet you downstairs.'

When he'd gone, she rose and stretched then put on her boots. After tidying her hair and bonnet and straightening out her clothing the best she could, she picked up her portmanteau and padded out and down the stairs. A handful of others, faces locked in usual misery, squatted on broken stools around the walls. Avoiding their eyes, Phoebe headed for the fire. She stood beside Victor, who was bent over the flames, an aged frying pan in his hand.

'I called at the butcher's earlier,' he explained, rolling his wrist and sending the melting block of lard, like an oily snowball, swirling around the heated bottom of the pan. 'I picked up a screw of tea, too.'

'I'll give you some money towards my share,' she said

as she went in search of the communal teapot. 'I can't allow you to fritter your funds feeding me.'

'There's no need—'

'I insist, Mr Hayes.'

'All right, if that's how you feel, why don't you buy something to break our fast tomorrow? We could alternate it: I buy provisions one day, you the next. Deal?'

'Deal,' she agreed. However, a frown had appeared at her brow and before she could stop herself, she added, 'But surely you won't be here for very much longer. Your duties—' She clamped her mouth shut when he threw her a warning look. 'I . . . What I mean is, won't you be shortly moving on?'

Victor opened the paper package, extracted four sausages and placed them in the pan before answering. 'I've no plans to for the time being.'

Cursing her slip in front of the others, Phoebe let the matter drop; she could have chewed off her tongue at her thoughtlessness. She really must watch what she was saying – she'd never forgive herself if she got him into trouble. *I'm sorry*, she told him with her eyes; catching it, he inclined his head in acceptance, much to her relief.

A bucket, intended for swilling out tea dregs from the pot, stood by the hearth. She crossed to it and peered inside and her lips bunched in a grimace. It seemed the water hadn't been changed in days. The contents were murky black in colour and a thin layer of scum rested on top of the rotten leaves, as though someone had swished a greasy spoon in it. She really didn't know how much longer she could bear it here, she thought, as she went to rinse the teapot under the pump outside instead.

They ate their meal straight from the pan, washing it down with the tea, which they supped from the only drinking vessels going spare – empty jam jars that Victor had located in a rickety cupboard on the wall. Phoebe determined to buy a few cheap crockery items today; she'd store them in her portmanteau when not in use, save them being stolen. Preparing meals here did make sense – dishes they could cook and consume quickly then be out of the kitchen again. It would prove less costly than to keep eating out.

'May I, mister?' a gaunt youth asked, sidling up when Victor and Phoebe moved from the fire and were donning their outdoor garments. He flicked his sharp chin towards the frying pan and, at Victor's nod, flashed a black-toothed grin and hurried to dip the precious hunk of bread he was clutching into the tasty meat juices. Victor nodded again towards the pot, indicating there was a little tea left, and the youth snatched it up, cradling the ceramic to his chest like a mother with her suckling babe as though afraid someone else might swipe it away, his gratitude falling breathlessly from his lips. It made Phoebe realise, not without a little shame, that despite her terrible position, she wasn't as badly off as some of the poor souls of this town. Yet.

The lodging-house keeper shooed everyone from the premises shortly afterwards. As soon as they were out, Phoebe drew Victor aside.

'Mr Hayes, what we spoke of last night . . .'

'Yes.'

'Please, I must know: what is your business here? Should I be concerned, vigilant? *Are* you on someone's tail back there? Am I sharing a house with a dangerous criminal?' she forced herself to ask – the worrying thought had plagued her throughout the night.

'No.'

'Then *why* would a member of the police be lodging at—'

46

'I'm not a member of the police,' he murmured, his hooded eyes on the road ahead.

'But . . . You said—'

'I was dismissed from the force last week. As a result, I've lost my marriage and my home. I've lost everything. So you see, Miss Parsons, I'm dwelling at the lodging house for the same reason as you and everyone else: because I'm destitute. I'm *ruined*, don't you see?'

She gazed back mutely. Never would she have guessed this. *The constable passing the eating house that day, whom an embarrassed Victor had taken pains to avoid* . . . He'd been a former colleague, she realised.

Victor now had tears in his eyes and she winced, disliking herself intensely for having been the one to cause them with her incessant probing. She would have liked to have put her arms around him and soothed away his sorrow, but of course she couldn't. Nor would she ask why he'd been relieved of his duties. She'd meddled enough in his affairs – it really was no concern of hers, none. 'I'm sorry.'

'My wife hates the sight of me. She's banished me from the house, and nothing I say will have her see reason. I must simply hold on to the hope that one day soon she'll come to realise . . .' He broke off to swallow hard. 'It's all I can do.'

Knowing him the little she did, Phoebe couldn't believe his downfall had been wrought by something he'd done that was so very bad. Perhaps those in authority had made a mistake? He was a decent man, he was. It shone from him like a light. This added blow, being cast on to the streets . . . A wife ejecting her husband from his own home? Who ever heard the like? 'But she's a woman,' Phoebe pointed out simply. 'She has no rights whatsoever, legal or otherwise.'

47

'And moral rights? Those, I believe, she is entitled to exercise. I've hurt her deeply.'

'What will you do?'

'I'm on my way home again now. Hopefully, she'll be present and this time will listen to the truth.'

'I wish you luck, Mr Hayes,' Phoebe told him, and she meant it. It didn't prevent a ball of dread from forming in her guts, however, at the prospect of him leaving the lodging house and her never seeing him again. She'd come to rely upon – perhaps selfishly, she realised – his presence and quiet protection. 'If we don't meet again . . . thank you, for everything,' she murmured. 'My first days here would have been infinitely more difficult without your friendship.'

'What of you?' His voice was soft. 'Will you visit your last place of work for another reference? Finding a new position is likely your only ticket out of your current situation. Do it, Miss Parsons, and take *my* best wishes along with *you*.'

When Victor had gone, she shot a sideward glance in the direction of Cheetham Hill. Should she return, beg from him another? Was it worth her trying? Then again, as Victor had pointed out, what option was she left with? *But dear God, the thought of seeing his hateful face again . . .*

She *must*. Phoebe straightened her shoulders and gave a resolute nod. Warwick Yewdale couldn't damage her any more than he had already; but maybe, just maybe . . . It was worth a shot. She'd do her utmost to convince him, would appeal her very hardest to his good side. Surely even he had one, however deeply buried it may be.

Gradually, the air grew wholesome as she approached what only an exclusive few were fortunate to belong to: an existence of comfort and luxury. Positioned on remote and breezy heights, with elevated views of the surrounding countryside, the fine neat homes and sprawling villas reeked of self-importance and of freedoms. Out here, as in Pendleton and Broughton, Chorlton and Ardwick, away from the commercial districts and their businesses of work, from the poverty and grime, the smog and want and squalor, it seemed millions of miles from the world she'd just left behind rather than the mere two or three it actually was.

This was where the bourgeoisie made their homes. The wealthy merchants and manufacturers, their fortunes mostly in cotton – and booming still on the back of rapidly growing industrial Manchester. In rural idyll and leafy splendour, their lot was a whirl of balls and banquets, and of ignorance of and indifference to the struggling poor all around them in their stark brick prisons, clawing on daily for just the basic necessities of life. The gap between masters and workers had never been wider. Little wonder then that the country had been for years, and was very much still, in the grip of social and political crisis.

In the midst of all the problems, the Corn Laws – essentially a tax on bread – had brought Britain to its knees. As was usual in times of austerity, it had had a far greater impact on the poor. Bread was, after all, the fundamental staple of their diets. Not a day went by that hungry men and women didn't stalk the borough begging for food, some literally dying of starvation in the streets.

However, to the more privileged lot, who could afford meat aplenty, it was merely a mild irritation at best. Bread wasn't *their* chief article of sustenance, the situation didn't overly affect them, and so the issue didn't appear to carry too much importance. Whether they really

49

didn't understand or simply chose not to care, Phoebe couldn't say. Mind you, they didn't exactly have a reputation of showing interest in the needs of the lower classes, did they?

The working man was tired of wanting, and their 'betters' feared a national uprising in the none-too-distant future. Phoebe, too, believed it was coming. The Manchester-formed Anti-Corn Law League was at its peak, so she'd heard from her former servant friends, and battling on doggedly in its quest for reform. Class conflict had become impossible to ignore. Something would have to give, and soon.

For now, though, the Warwick Yewdales of this world still very much wielded all the power, and as Phoebe passed the bowling green and the school then the new Perpendicular Gothic church of St Luke's and its graveyard, drawing her ever nearer to the house, her earlier resolve began to crumble. Would he take his horse whip to her this time? Set the dogs on her again? Or, by some miracle, would he comply with her hardly unreasonable request? She was soon to find out.

The grey stone mansion dazzled in the high sun's rays like polished marble. To her left, beyond the wide gravelled path, stood a line of stables and, further back, on a natural slope, stretched the orchard lawn. Blossoming pear and plum, apple and apricot trees, renowned for their lustrousness in their varied, vibrant hues, were cosseted by a semicircle of cedars and Scotch firs, buffering them from the blighting northern winds. Phoebe's destination lay in the opposite direction – turning right, she made at a brisk pace for the rose trees bordering the walled gardens.

Here, the herbs and late blooms released a plethora of perfumes – rosemary, balm and sage, primroses, jessamine, lavender and blue violet, amongst others – making her senses dance and momentarily soothing her frayed nerves. She continued past an alcove seating space and sapling-shaded pond until she reached the servants' and tradesmen's entrance at the back of the property. Taking a deep breath, she plastered in place a bright smile. Then, lifting an arm, she knocked twice.

'Miss Parsons, lass!' Cook was both surprised and delighted to see her. Flinging wide the door, she invited her in with alacrity. 'Where've you been stopping? How are thee?'

'Hello, Mary. Hello, girls,' Phoebe added, giving the young kitchen maids busy rolling pastry at the oaken table a wave. 'I'm lodging with a friend.' This wasn't an altogether outright lie, was it? 'And I'm very well, thank you.'

'Ay, it's glad I am to hear that. It's fair worried about your welfare we've been, you forced to leave so sudden like, as tha were.'

'That's sweet of you all, but there was no need, really. I'm managing just fine.'

'So what can we do for thee, lass?'

'I came to speak with Mr Yewdale. Is he home?'

'Oh.' The servant's eyebrows rose to meet the edge of her frilly white cap. 'Aye, he is, but lass . . .'

'I know, I'm the last person he'll expect or want to see. However, he must, it's important. In the library, is he?'

'Aye, but—'

Phoebe thanked her and quickly made for the red baize door that led to the house proper, before the cook could persuade her otherwise. Much more talk and her already wavering resolve would trickle away to nothing. Then where would she be?

Pausing in the passageway between twin cherrywood

side tables holding alabaster vases and rose-gold candelabra, she drew in a steadying breath. Gaze fixed on the library, she bobbed her head in a far from confident nod and forced herself forward once more.

It was the gilded mirror between the room's tall windows that she noticed first. Even before she realised the door was ajar, the looking glass within had grabbed her attention. But it wasn't the mirror itself that refused to release her and had her rooted to the spot, but what was reflected in its cool surface. There were two figures by the fire.

One stood with his back to the leaping flames. His trousers were crumpled around his ankles, his fleshy pink thighs studded with dark hairs standing out starkly. At his feet knelt a woman with long red hair. He had one hand at her nape, a fist full of her fiery tendrils, and was directing her head up and down in rapid strokes.

Phoebe's gaze travelled the length of the mirror, up . . . up . . . to the face contorted in rapture showing there – and let out a shock-filled gasp of horror.

Good God above . . .

The woman turned at the interruption, poppy mouth still open, her ice-blue eyes holding a look of surprise. Now that she'd shifted position, Phoebe was assaulted by a clear view of the object of her desire. Warwick Yewdale's swollen member, its shaft glowing bright red from the woman's attentions, jerked like a living thing against his stomach. He tried to cover it with his jacket, at the same time releasing a bellow of such thunderous proportions that both women almost leapt from their skins.

Staggering into a bookcase and sending leather-bound tomes crashing to the floor, his eyes bulged fit to pop: 'Be gone!' he almost screamed.

Phoebe didn't need a second telling; skidding on the polished floor, she turned tail and pelted for the front door.

Her boots sent gravel spraying in all directions as she flew down the pathway and on, away from the house, from them and what she'd witnessed. She'd just drawn level with the church when she heard the voice:

'Wait!'

Glancing over her shoulder, Phoebe frowned in fear and confusion. It was the woman with the red hair, and she was running down the lane towards her.

'Please, wait.'

Curiosity got the better of her. She slowed, saying when the woman caught up, 'Look, I'm sorry, I didn't know . . . the door was open and—'

'It's all right.'

'It is?' Phoebe was nonplussed. 'Then what do you want?'

'We gave thee quite the shock back there. I wanted to check you were well.'

On close inspection, she saw that the young woman was breath-catchingly beautiful. It was clear, though, that she didn't possess Warwick's breeding; her hat and clothing were undeniably inexpensive and she spoke with the blunt Lancashire accent. Phoebe's intrigue mounted. Just how had she and Warwick become acquainted? More to the point, when? Phoebe hadn't once caught a glimpse of her in all the years she'd dwelled in that house under Lilian Yewdale's employ.

'So, lass? You're all right?'

Phoebe shrugged then nodded. 'I'm only here today for a reference. My mistress, Mr Yewdale's stepmother, she died, you see, and he provided one in her place.

Only it was a testimony of lies intended to besmirch my good name and I didn't deserve it. I came to ask from him another, for otherwise, I'll never work again. After the scene back there . . .' She flushed furiously. 'I realise that's a definite impossibility – he'll never agree now – so if you don't mind, I'll just take my leave and—'

'I could speak to him for thee?'

For a moment, she was too surprised to speak. 'You?'

'Aye. If you'd like me to.'

'I . . . well, I don't know—'

'Leave it with me,' she purred, her generous mouth curving in a smile. 'I'm sure I can persuade him.'

The implication was clear. Phoebe's blush deepened. 'Well . . .'

'Come back tomorrow afternoon. He'll have the character reference waiting.'

Though desperate to believe it may be possible, naturally, Phoebe was unconvinced. She shook her head.

'*Trust* me,' the woman murmured. She reached inside a small, black velvet pouch dangling from her slender wrist and extracted some coins. 'Fare for the omnibus back into town. Here, take it,' she insisted, pressing the money into Phoebe's hand. 'Don't forget. Tomorrow afternoon.' With that, she turned on a whish of her domed skirts and was gone.

Phoebe continued on her way in a daze. Reaching Cheetham Hill Road, she spotted the omnibus making its half-hourly service and hurried to catch it.

On the journey back to the centre of Manchester, her mind remained locked on the flame-haired woman. She had seemed amiable, Phoebe admitted – and totally at odds with Warwick Yewdale's beastly personality. She'd spoken kindly, her voice like the soft flap of a bird's wing compared to the jarring scrape of stone on

54

stone that was his. Just what was the appeal? What did she see in him, at all?

That she could bring herself to touch him, engage in ... *that* – with him of all men! The notion made Phoebe's flesh creep more than any vermin-ridden lodging house ever could. Were the servants aware? Of course they were, her head answered for her. Hadn't Cook tried to dissuade her from seeking him out but, impatient for that damned reference, she hadn't waited around long enough to listen. Now, the images she'd been faced with would be seared in her memory for ever. He really was an utterly unpleasant specimen, both inside and out.

And tomorrow? Would she return? Her lips bunched together in uncertainty. The woman had been so confident that she could successfully bring Warwick around. Surely it was worth her going, was worth trying just one last time? And yet ... something was niggling in the back of her brain, telling her not to, that she should stay away, though she couldn't pin down why. But what choice had she? She *needed* that reference.

Her thoughts were still in disarray when she alighted and they were still no nearer to being clearer when she reached the familiar eating house. She pushed open the door, entered and glanced about. Victor Hayes was at a far table, his head resting on one hand, and staring into space as though in a world of his own. Listlessly, she made her way across and took a seat facing him.

Though they acknowledged one another's presence with a tilt of their chins, neither said anything, simply sat, lost in their own despondency.

'You were unable to mend things with your wife?' Phoebe asked – it was evident from his mood that his day had been as unsuccessful as hers.

'She wasn't home again.'

'I'm sorry.'

He gave her a half-hearted shrug. 'You were unable to obtain a fresh reference?'

'He . . . wasn't home either,' she lied, without knowing why. Embarrassment more than anything.

'Then I'm sorry, too.'

'Thank you.'

They lapsed into quietness once more.

So far as she could see, she had but two choices open to her. She could keep the rendezvous tomorrow and just pray Warwick would indeed comply – and if he didn't, blackmail him into doing so for her silence regarding the shocking conduct she'd witnessed. But no, of course she could never do that, hadn't the courage. The second option was to abandon all hope with Yewdale and falsify a reference herself. Again, this alternative – and the repercussions should her deception be discovered – scared her witless. She would have liked to have put the idea to Victor, but obviously that wasn't possible, him being an ex-lawman. He'd never approve of such a thing.

What, *what*, was she to do? She *must* have funds and soon. 'Perhaps I should simply forget about references altogether and just sell the brooch and have done with it. But how long would the money from that last?' Sighing, she dropped her head in her hands.

'Sorry?'

Phoebe lifted her gaze, confused for a moment, until she realised that without thinking she'd spoken the last part of her rumination out loud.

'You mentioned something about a brooch . . . ?'

'Yes.' She shifted aside her shawl to show him. 'This one.'

'Pretty.'

'Yes.'

'And you're considering selling it?'

She scratched absently at a bug bite on her arm. 'I may have to. I . . . I've been offered fifteen pounds for it.'

He lifted an eyebrow. 'By who?'

'A pawnbroker not very far from here.'

'No.'

Phoebe frowned. 'Mr Hayes?'

'If a pawnbroker is willing to pay such a sum, then he knows something you don't. Its true valuation must be around the twenty mark at least. I could put you in touch with a jeweller. Mr Rakowski is a decent fellow and honest as the day is long into the bargain. Why not have him take a look at it before you make a decision?'

She smiled. 'Yes, thank you. That would be sensible.'

'May I ask how it came to be in your possession?'

His countenance held now a look of mild discomfort – Phoebe tilted her head. 'You don't believe me as trustworthy as your jeweller friend? You suspect I came by the brooch through dishonest means, that I stole it?'

'Please don't take offence, only I had to ask . . .'

'Forgive me, I was just teasing you. Of course you must ask. It wouldn't do your friend's reputation much good were he to be found dealing in pilfered goods.'

Victor flashed a lopsided smile. 'No.'

'It was a gift from my late mistress. I was a lady's maid,' she explained. 'It was the best four years of my life. But Lilian – Mrs Yewdale – passed away after a short illness and, well, I was no longer needed and her stepson dismissed me from the house. So here I am.'

'You haven't family you can lean upon?'

'No.'

'None?'

Phoebe shook her head. 'The cholera carried them from this life.'

'The great outbreak of '32?'

Now, her head moved in the opposite direction in assent. The pandemic had swept across Europe like a wildfire, consuming all in its path, killing tens of thousands in Britain alone. Its hellbent mission one of simple destruction, it had in the main sought out with its cruel touch the poorest communities. Sniffing out Manchester – where there was no shortage of slums and squalor – as its next target in late spring, it had claimed during the course of almost nine months yet hundreds more. Its appetite for flesh had been insatiable.

'It seized my mother first,' Phoebe murmured. 'Already delicate and half famished, she didn't stand a hope. The next day, my father and brother began with the stomach cramps. Vomiting and cold sweats followed, then their skin turned greyish-blue . . . By then, of course, we knew the signs. Knew what the end result would be. How they suffered so! I did my best to nurse them back to health, honest I did, but it wasn't enough and—' She broke off to swallow hard. 'Within the space of three days, my family were all dead. I was twelve years old and on my own. Only God Himself knows why He saw fit to spare me.'

Eyes creased, Victor sighed. 'It carried off a brother of mine, too, along with my grandparents.'

'I'm sorry.'

'As you say, why He chose who He did to stay and who to go, we'll never fathom.'

'The thing is, I told no one,' Phoebe admitted in a wide-eyed whisper. 'No one knew they had died. I'd seen the van in our street more than once, watched it cart off our friends, our neighbours . . . I couldn't let my loved ones go, didn't want to say goodbye, and I . . . I . . .'

'Oh, lass.'

'I'd been there, alone with their bodies, for two days before anyone found out. The sanitary police had ordered that our lane be evacuated and its dwellings disinfected with chloride of lime to halt the disease's spread, you see. They discovered us and removed me to the home of a great-aunt, who took me in. She died six years later. Alone once more, I answered an advertisement for a lady's maid and, to my great good fortune, Lilian Yewdale took me on. I had no experience, none at all, but she took a chance on me anyway. She was a wonderful woman. Now she's gone, too.'

'Where was it that you grew up, Miss Parsons?'

'By the River Irk below Ducie Bridge,' she revealed, and at once recognised in his face that he knew of its reputation. Ruinous and overcrowded, it was where some of the borough's worst housing was to be found. She nodded. 'My father and brother worked in a nearby tannery, but both liked the drink a little too much and we were always wanting. Our home was a stagnant, grime-riddled cellar. You recently remarked that I'd led a sheltered life, Mr Hayes. Well, you're quite wrong.'

He had the grace to look shamefaced, and she saw in him that a new level of respect for her was born. 'So I see. I'm sorry.'

'Don't be. Oddly, despite the wretchedness and filth and hunger, I miss it, my childhood. I do.'

'Your Mrs Yewdale's refined speech rubbed on to you, I see, as I suppose it would after a time, you two being in such close and constant company with one another.'

'I suppose it did. She taught me so much. She saved me, really. I miss her a lot.'

'I admit, I did wonder at the ease with which you've coped with the horrors of the lodging house.'

At this, her smile resurfaced. 'It's not pleasant, by any stretch of the imagination. But you're right: it's not completely overwhelming to me. I've lived in worse conditions. Mind you . . .' She scratched again at the raised lumps – a result of her bedfellow critters' midnight feasting. 'Right now, I would give anything for a good cleanse. I feel ever so mucky. Funny, isn't it: even prisoners receive a bathing when they're brought into custody. Us, our only crime that we are destitute, are not even afforded that small luxury.'

'You're right.' Victor nodded purposefully. 'Come with me.'

Frowning as he rose and strode off into the street, Phoebe hurried after him. 'Mr Hayes? Where are we going?'

'You'll see,' was all he'd tell her.

They arrived at a neat residence shortly afterwards, where he halted and inclined his head.

'Where are we?'

'Home.'

'This is where you live?'

'Where my *wife* lives, alone – for now at least.'

'But why are we here?'

'Why not?'

Phoebe was filled with puzzlement. 'But . . . you said yourself that she's banished you from here, that you wouldn't even consider forcing your way back in—'

'A man can change his mind, can't he? Besides, Kate's away visiting her sister. She'll never know.'

Biting her lip, she glanced up and down the street. 'Oh, Mr Hayes, I don't know . . .'

'A quick clean-up, maybe a bite to eat, and we can be on our way again. No one will be any the wiser,' he insisted, already making for the door.

Phoebe dithered for a few moments more. Then her need to wash won through and, against her better judgement, she scurried after him. In barely any time at all, he was in: where he'd acquired his knowledge in house-breaking, she never queried. His time as a policeman, ambushing criminals' hideouts and the like, must have helped hone the skill, she surmised.

She should have been worried at being alone with a man in a deserted house, but she wasn't, not with him. Neck-deep in steamy, sweet-smelling water, she closed her eyes and heaved a sigh of sheer bliss.

After donning from her portmanteau the one set of spare clean clothes she possessed, she got on with preparing them both a quick meal, whilst Victor dragged out and emptied the bath then refilled it with a fresh supply for himself.

'The food is ready,' she called sometime later over the splashes coming from behind the curtain, which he'd hastily pitched up to afford them privacy. 'Best get it now before it grows cold.'

'I feel like a fugitive in my own home,' he said quietly as they ate. 'But until this mess is remedied, what's to be done? I'm loath to worsen matters with Kate.'

Phoebe itched to ask him what had occurred to bring about his current circumstances but held back. When and if he wanted to reveal them to her, he would. 'We'd better be making a move soon, Mr Hayes.'

They tidied around, making sure they had left everything as it had been, and under the cover of the darkening evening slipped out.

As they made back for the centre of town, she turned to him with grateful eyes. He'd taken a risk in going there today, more so with her in tow, yet he'd done it anyway – for her sake, she knew, rather than his own. It was evident that the sorry story of her past had affected him, that he'd wanted to do something for her, bring her just a little happiness. She was deeply touched. 'Thank you, truly. I feel infinitely better.'

Glancing down at the clean shirt and trousers he now wore, Victor nodded. 'Me too.'

Sensing the morose cloud that had appeared over him, and no wonder – being home again had clearly reminded him of all he'd lost – she tactfully fell silent. Would he indeed succeed in reclaiming his life? For his sake alone, she sincerely hoped so.

In bed that night, cushioned between two old fogies who stank to high heaven of ale and snored worse than two dozen pigs, Phoebe couldn't contain a crooked smile. Even the *pop pop* of cockroaches as they fell from the ceiling and hit the bare boards couldn't dampen her spirits. For in her imagination, she was somewhere different entirely.

She was back in Victor's house. They were sat side by side before the kitchen fire; warm, comfortable, content. And they were holding hands. In this moment, she'd never known peace like it.

'Together,' she mouthed to the darkness as she drifted into sleep.

Chapter 4

WHY HAD HE come here?

Hadn't he told himself repeatedly that he shouldn't? Shaking his head at his own foolishness, Victor turned and walked away from the decrepit house. However, he couldn't stem the growing concern in his guts for the woman who had been instrumental in his downfall.

No, that wasn't fair, he reminded himself. Suzannah Frost hadn't forced his hand, had she? She hadn't begged that he stay in touch, hadn't pleaded with him to keep regular checks on her well-being. He'd done so off his own bat; it was his choice. He alone must accept responsibility – and now must pay the price.

She hadn't been back to her two rooms in days, according to a neighbour, when he'd enquired about Suzannah's whereabouts after knocking and receiving no answer.

'No one's seen hide nor hair of her. But fret not, she'll return, she allus does . . .'

But would she? Thrusting his hands in his pockets, Victor chewed on his lip. Suzannah was vulnerable – and those who looked to exploit that knew it. However, for now, his hands were tied. He'd just have to drop by again soon and hope she'd resurfaced.

Kate sprang to his mind next and he paused in consideration. Then, with a hard nod and his mouth set, he headed left in the direction of her sister's. This nonsense had gone on long enough. He'd see her today and he'd finally get answers if it killed him.

His sister-in-law's perpetually waspish face screwed up further upon discovering he was the visitor – Victor offered a disarming smile, but it had no effect: 'Kate doesn't want to see you.'

'Well, I want to see her,' he responded, planting a boot in the hall and halting her attempt to slam the door in his face.

She sighed theatrically. 'Just go away, Victor.'

'I will not. Now, listen to me, I'm not budging from this step until I see my wife, do you hear me—?'

'What do you want?' It was Kate. Her uninterested voice floated to him from behind the human shield that was her sister. Then her face appeared, strained and unmoving. She folded her arms. 'Well?'

'We need to sort this ridiculous mess out, Kate.'

'And what mess would that be? The one of your own creation? The one I could never forgive, never mind forget, even if I lived to be a hundred? The *mess*, as you call it, that is utterly repulsive to me – to any right-minded woman with an ounce of self-respect?' She threw the words at him like knives, her eyes spitting steel, two angry circles of colour sitting high on her cheeks. 'Well?'

'Miss Frost and I, we—'

'Don't speak that whore's name to me, Victor Hayes. Don't you dare!'

'There was nothing between us. For Christ's sake, Kate, it's the truth—!'

'Ha! Your depraved brain doesn't understand the meaning of the word! Our marriage is *over*, Victor,' she slung at him, much to her smirking sister's obvious delight. 'Nothing you or anyone else can say will change

64

my mind. Much better to be shunned by society for walking out on my home and my husband than spend the rest of my days with a beast like you!' With that, she swung the door shut with a resounding slam.

Victor stared at it for an age, dazed. Stupid *bloody* woman! What the hell did this mean?

Of course, separations between man and wife occurred, but not very often, and it wasn't something that would ever happen to him – or so he'd thought. He cared naught for what people would say; most of their circle had already turned their backs on him anyway. And well, if it didn't much bother Kate either . . . ?

He shrugged. To hell with her then. Let her do as she liked – she would anyway, always had. They would never endure without trust. That was no sound foundation for a union, was it? But by God, why wouldn't she at least hear his side – the *truth*? Or was it more convenient for her not to? he wondered suddenly.

Maybe this was the excuse Kate had been looking for to escape the bonds?

He just didn't know any more. She *had* seemed to fall out of feeling with him rather swiftly after the consummation. Never really appealed to her, had that aspect of their marriage. As for that sister of hers, well, she'd never taken to him, had she? Moreover, she was recently widowed so would be glad to have Kate there to keep her loneliness at bay. She'd no doubt fed the flames of his wife's hurt and rage and influenced her decision, spiteful cow that she was.

Yet what surprised Victor more than anything was that he wasn't nearly as shattered as he perhaps should be. He'd taken his wedding vows seriously and, he suspected now, had seen it as his duty to get the marriage back on track, make it work. But he couldn't force the woman, could he? If she was unwilling to put in the effort to try to fix things, too, then what could he do?

His heart lifted slightly when he caught sight of the eating house in which he now spent much of his time, but then he remembered that Phoebe Parsons wouldn't be there and his face fell. He could have done with her calming influence just now.

How long would it take her to trek to Cheetham Hill and back? Not very, if her visit there yesterday was anything to go by.

His mind made up, he found a table and ordered a cup of tea. Forcing all thoughts of Kate from his head, he fixed his stare on the window to await Phoebe's return.

Why had she come here?

Drawing her shawl more securely around herself, Phoebe scanned the surrounding land, barren of life bar grazing cattle. She'd convinced herself she wouldn't return, yet here she was. And it seemed her journey had been in vain, just as she'd known it would. *Stupid, stupid.*

Throughout the morning, she'd barely given the red-haired woman's words a second thought. However, as noon approached, she'd found herself thinking more and more about her promise and the prospect of the precious reference, and on impulse had hurried out here again to see if she could be proven wrong.

She wasn't.

Neither Warwick nor his lover had been at the house, and Phoebe felt a first-rate idiot.

Now, as she made her way back through the rural surroundings to the bustle of Manchester, she was more angry than upset. Why had that woman tricked her into returning like this? What in the world had she thought to gain from sending her on this wild goose chase? Vindictive, that's what it was. And to think that Phoebe had judged her to be nice. Well, she'd certainly had her fooled.

On top of everything else, the weather was foul. The broody sky had darkened ominously and plump storm clouds squatted on the silver hilltops like well-fed woodpigeons at roost. She gasped as a hare darted for cover nearby. Then the air seemed to hold its breath. Moments later, the first fat raindrops fell from the heavens.

Lifting her skirts, she hurried past a strip of shaded woodland – where a noise from beyond the trees shattered the heavy silence.

Phoebe stopped dead in her tracks. A bird, perhaps, seeking shelter from the elements? A fallen branch? Her racing mind weighed up the possibilities whilst, inside her breast, her heart hammered a painful beat. When no further sound followed, she set off again, quicker this time, her sodden boots muffled in the thick grasses.

It was the flash of dappled grey against the green expanse that caught her gaze. Blinking raindrops from her eyes, she peered across the vast swathes of open field and watched as a horse appeared over the crest of a hill. Its rider, tall and lean, had the animal at a harsh gallop, and as they crossed through Halliwell Lane and jumped a drystone wall, she realised they were headed in her direction.

The trees concealed the horse and its rider for a few seconds, then they emerged suddenly from behind a high thicket just yards away. They were so close now that she could see the whites of the horse's eyes and the fog of hot breath from its wide nostrils – shrinking back, she cried out in fear.

'Good afternoon, Miss Parsons.'

Wha—? Who?

Forcing her stare upwards, she found herself looking into the grim face of Warwick Yewdale.

Immaculate as ever, he wore a moss-coloured jacket and doeskin breeches of the same shade, and shiny riding boots. There wasn't even a dark hair out of place, in spite of his speedy pursuit. Seeing him again made her feel queasy but, God help her, she was desperate for the reference.

'S—sir,' she stuttered. 'Your . . . friend, she said I was to return this afternoon. I called, called at the house, but—'

'Most *dread*fully sorry to have missed you,' he drawled with definite sarcasm. 'Please accept my most humble apologies, m'lady.'

The tension between them was thick as stew. Phoebe's cheeks burned with embarrassment and, to her horror, she felt humiliated tears close by. She wetted her lips. 'Forgive me if I misinterpreted your friend's meaning, Mr Yewdale, sir,' she said, though she knew she hadn't, 'only I was led to believe—'

'Silence.'

He'd delivered the word through gritted teeth. She closed her mouth abruptly.

'Whatever you believe you witnessed in my library yesterday, you are quite wrong. If I should hear even a whisper that you've told anyone, anyone at all, I—'

'Sir, I wouldn't do that. Your business is yours alone; I wouldn't dream of concerning myself in your affairs. It isn't my place.'

'Damn right it isn't.' His eyes were mere slits in his pale face. 'After all, you know what happens to tell-tales who bleat lies about their betters, don't you, Miss Parsons?'

Phoebe shook her head. 'No, sir,' she whispered.

'Then allow me to enlighten you.' With a brush of his

68

heel against the horse's belly, he moved the animal forward, directing it to encircle her in a jerky prance. The dull thump of its iron shoes filled her ears and her brain. She froze. 'They live to regret their folly,' he continued in a hiss. 'Oh yes, they do.'

Phoebe's wary gaze shifted from Warwick's hateful face to the large hooves, which were edging frighteningly closer towards her. 'Sir . . .'

'I warn you, don't cross me.'

'Sir, please—'

'I could make life *very* difficult for you!'

Phoebe screamed as, with a sharp kick and a brutal yank of the reins, he sent the distressed beast rearing into the air above her.

For a second, the ear-splitting whinny and petrifying vision of looming thoroughbred muscle robbed her of her senses. Her arms moved up to shield her head – too late. As the horse's front legs returned to earth, she felt pain shoot through her as a hoof clipped her face, the force knocking her backwards on to the wet grass.

'I am newly betrothed to a highly respected merchant's daughter,' he snapped down at her, 'and if any rumour were to circulate from your lips, the entire arrangement would be finished. Now you listen to me, and listen well—'

'No, you listen to *me*.' Scrambling to her knees, Phoebe glared up in bone-shuddering fury. Her fear had dissipated completely in the face of such unjustified barbarism; she could have clawed the flesh from his face for him, so much was her blood up. 'I gave you my word that I wouldn't speak of what I saw you and your *friend* engaged in, and still you felt the need to terrify that poor animal into launching an attack upon me, threaten me into submission. Just who do you think you are?' She

69

stood facing him now, chin thrust forward, her body shaking with barely containable temper.

Warwick's mouth hung loose, his astonishment absolute. 'How *dare* you speak to me in that manner—!'

'I'll speak to you as I see fit that you deserve,' she retorted grimly, cutting short his bluster. 'You've always been a bad apple, Warwick Yewdale. Your father, God rest his soul, was a good man, a man of honour. As for dear Lilian . . .' Phoebe's eyes were dry – there was no upset in her levelled speech, no hysterics, only unadulterated rage. 'Lilian loved you as a son. She did, you know. In return, you treated her like muck beneath your boot the moment she joined your family. You did, I saw it, and why? Not because you deemed her too young for her husband. Nor because you resented her taking your late mother's place; no, no, nothing as sentimental as that. You hated her because you were terrified she'd inherit your father's wealth.

'That was it, wasn't it? Money. That's all that keeps your pulse beating. No doubt the poor woman who's soon to become your wife is fetching with her a handsome dowry – she'd hold no attraction for you otherwise, would she? You don't care for her for *her*, I'll bet – I'd stake the clothes off my back on it, in fact. Well, do you know what, sir? I pity you.' Phoebe nodded to emphasise her statement. 'Rich in wealth you may be, but poor in love you're set to always remain. Lord above, I wouldn't swap places with you for a gold clock, and that's the truth.'

She'd been unable to stem the torrent once it had begun to trickle, then gush, and by God she felt the better for it. She'd tolerated his contempt, disrespect and degradation for years with the meek and accepting servitude that befitted her station, but no more. Today, the invisible bonds of class that had held her prisoner, made

70

her bow and scrape to him – to *all* of his lot – had been severed, and to hell with the consequences.

For a full minute, Warwick stared back wordlessly. Phoebe held his gaze with quiet dignity. Then: 'Take it, you wretched peasant,' he murmured, reaching into the inside pocket of his jacket and producing a folded sheet, which he flung at her feet.

The reference. She picked it up and scanned its contents. This one was perfectly adequate. Not exactly glowing or singing her praises to the heavens, but nowhere near the document of lies he'd first provided. And he'd had it all along. All this, the horrible scene just now, had been completely avoidable. She really couldn't fathom him at all.

'Now be gone from here. I never want to see your face again, not *ever*. Do you understand me?'

'Perfectly,' she said, slipping the priceless piece of paper inside her portmanteau. Then she turned and walked away.

As she joined the stretch of Cheetham Hill Road which would take her back to Manchester, she thought she spotted someone hunkered down behind a hawthorn hedge up ahead. And had that been a flash of red hair . . . ? *Warwick's lover*. Phoebe's mouth tightened.

Had she watched that entire encounter from afar? Lured her here with more in mind than to help her? Had she known she would be threatened, hurt?

True, she'd got her reference in the end but, by God, things had grown more than a little heated back there. She'd been injured, for one thing, and had even thought at several points that Warwick would leap from his horse and kill her with his bare hands, so incensed had he been. And the woman had stood idly by and done nothing? Just what was her game?

71

However, upon reaching the site where she thought she'd spied her, Phoebe saw it was deserted; neither the woman nor anyone else was there. Frowning, she continued on her way.

Settling in the omnibus shortly afterwards, Phoebe caught a few queer looks being directed at her from the other travellers – she lifted a hand to her injury. Blood came away at her touch and she searched inside her portmanteau for a handkerchief to stem the trickle. After dabbing it clear the best she could, she returned the now soiled cloth and placed the bag at her feet.

She had a reference at last!

Despite her still-shaken state, she couldn't contain a relieved smile. Finally, it was now in her power to get her life back on track. She'd visit the servants' registry office again this evening, she determined. Hopefully, once she'd spun some explanation of there having been a mix-up with the characters, the keeper would accept her on to her books. Who knew, this time next week she could be settled in a fresh household with a new mistress. Until then, there was always the servants' home. Fingers crossed, she'd spent her last night at the lodging house. *Please Lord.*

'Mr Hayes!' Stepping inside the eating house, her mood lifted immediately upon seeing him. She hurried to join him at his table. 'I wasn't expecting to see you here. I thought you had planned to visit your wife again?'

'I had. I did. I went to see her at her sister's house.'

'You were finally able to discuss . . . matters?'

'We were.'

Phoebe waited, but nothing else was forthcoming. She leaned towards him, pressing gently. 'Mr Hayes?'

'Yes?'

'Would you like to talk about it?'

'Not really,' he began, then he paused and shrugged. 'Oh, you may as well know. My marriage is over with. Kate wants nothing more to do with me.'

'Oh, Mr Hayes.' She lowered her gaze, at a loss for what to say. 'There is no chance . . . ?'

'I don't believe so.' Then, with more conviction: 'No. She shan't be swayed. She's strong-willed, and stubborn with it. But more than that . . .' He frowned softly. 'It was the look in her eyes. I won't ever forget it. I repulse her, Miss Parsons.'

The look in *his* eyes now was tearing at *her*. 'Please don't give up hope.'

Victor tried a half-smile, nodded – more for her sake, she suspected, than from any prospect of possible reconciliation he harboured. Then he stretched his mouth again, this time with better results. 'And how was your day? More successful than mine, pray?'

'Oh yes.' Though her heart ached for him still, she couldn't keep the brightness from her tone. 'I got the reference, glory be to God. This time it's perfectly satisfactory. Here, take a look,' she added, reaching down beside her. However, her hand stroked thin air. Glancing to the ground then back to him, she blinked, stunned.

'Miss Parsons? What's wrong?'

'My portmanteau . . . It's gone.'

'Gone?'

'Gone, Mr Hayes! Where—Oh *no*,' she croaked, queasiness gripping her insides as realisation slammed home. 'The omnibus . . . I think I left it on the omnibus!'

'Oh, lass.'

'Everything I possess in the whole world was in that bag.'

73

'The reference also?'

Screwing her eyes closed, she nodded. 'What am I going to *do*?'

'You understand that the chances of you locating it are slim to none, I'm afraid . . .'

'I know.' Of course she wouldn't get it back. She'd seen the last of it beyond any reasonable doubt. Someone would have come across it and swiped it away in less than a heartbeat of her alighting in Manchester. 'Everything . . . it's all . . . My clothing and bits and pieces, what little money I had, the reference, and with it the chance of my ever working as a lady's maid again . . . gone. I have only what I stand up in.'

Victor frowned suddenly. 'The brooch?'

The brooch!

Hastily dragging back her shawl, Phoebe fumbled at her chest – and let out a loud sigh. Blessed be the Lord! 'I have it.'

Thank God she'd attached it to her clean dress after her bath! If she'd left it on the other, which had been in her portmanteau . . . The prospect didn't bear thinking about. She truly would have been done for.

'So what will you do now, Miss Parsons?'

There was no way she'd get another reference from Warwick, that was for sure. Not now. Even were she to go to him on bended knees – not that she'd ever lower herself to do that, to beg; she would sooner starve in the gutter first – he'd never oblige her again. She bit her lip to stem the hopeless tears now threatening to consume her. 'There's only one thing I *can* do. I must sell the brooch. Please, does your offer of introducing me to your jeweller friend still stand?'

His eyes had creased in pity. 'Yes, of course.'

'Tomorrow?'

'Tomorrow,' he agreed.

And until then? Her chin wobbled in realisation. 'I cannot pay for a bed at the lodging house tonight, Mr Hayes, and I was wondering . . . Could you possibly . . . possibly loan me . . . ?'

'Miss Parsons—'

'I do so hate to ask, I do, only . . . only there's no one else I . . .' Choking on a sob, she pressed her fingers to her quivering lips. 'I'm sorry.'

'Phoebe.'

She glanced at the large warm hand he'd placed on hers on the tabletop. His thumb moved in smooth strokes across her wrist; at his touch, fire bolted through her veins. Breathless, she lifted her eyes to his.

'I won't loan you a penny.'

The popping inferno fizzed and went out. Hurt and confusion tugging at her brows, she drew her hand away. 'Oh.'

'I *won't* because you shan't be spending the night at the lodging house,' he hastened to reassure, though he didn't attempt to take her hand again.

'Then where . . . ?'

'Well, I have a big empty house standing doing nothing. Think about it, it makes sense, really. Kate won't be returning and we're desperately in need of somewhere to stay. So why not?'

'But, Mr Hayes, you and I . . . alone?' A quick wash and something to eat was one thing. To spend the night there together, however innocent, was another. 'What would people say?'

'What people?'

'Your neighbours, for one. Someone's bound to see us coming and going.'

'Oh, I'll think of something to prevent the tongues

75

from wagging,' he responded mildly. He seemed unconcerned and this lent Phoebe confidence in the idea.

'I won't deny, Mr Hayes, that the prospect of not having to suffer the lodging house for one night is appealing,' she admitted with a glimmer of excitement. 'And so, if you're certain . . . ?'

'I am, Miss Parsons.'

'Then I accept and gratefully so.'

Victor nodded, smiled. Then he rose and without another word left the eating house, Phoebe following behind at a trot to keep up with his long stride.

Having purchased some provisions on the way – boiled ham, a tiny brown loaf, tea and half a dozen eggs – they let themselves into the house and Victor immediately saw to laying the fire whilst Phoebe prepared the meal.

Soon, the chilly dark kitchen was warm and cosy-looking and, as she waited for water to boil, she went to hang up her shawl and headwear. Victor had been laying the table but stopped as she re-entered the kitchen. Scrutinising her face, he frowned deeply.

'Mr Hayes?'

'You're cut. Your cheek, there . . . how did that happen?'

She'd forgotten all about that; her wide-brimmed bonnet, which she'd pulled further forward on the omnibus owing to the stares, had concealed it until now. Her fingers fluttered to her injury, made more apparent by the pink blush highlighting it. 'I slipped,' she lied. 'On the way back from Mr Yewdale's house. A patch of mud had iced over . . . I spotted it too late.'

'It looks nasty.'

'No, not really,' she responded easily, turning her attention back to the pan, and was glad when he let the

76

matter drop. She didn't want to speak of it, of Warwick and the red-haired woman and the set-to she'd suffered. Besides, she'd made a promise. She'd told him she wouldn't tell anyone about what she'd witnessed in his library, and she'd meant it. Whatever had occurred afterwards with his horse, she still intended to keep her word – and this she'd struggle to do if she opened up to Victor, for he'd surely want to hear the whole story.

She just wanted to forget about the entire thing. The reference was lost and that's all there was to it. So far as she was concerned, she'd never see Yewdale again; the matter was over with.

After they had eaten, Phoebe made a fresh pot of tea and they settled themselves in the chairs either side of the hearth. Outside, the temperature had plummeted – she'd glanced through the window shortly before when drawing the curtains, and the street and houses were blanketed beneath a frost sheen, twinkling like powdered diamonds in the low moon's glow. She'd shut out the world and, hugging herself, returned to the fireside with a contented sigh.

'I'll take the chair, here, tonight,' said Victor, knuckling his tired eyes, as would a small child. 'You have the bed.'

'Thank you,' she murmured. And seeing that he wasn't fit to stay awake much longer: 'I'll go on up now then, if I may, Mr Hayes.'

'Of course.'

He led the way upstairs and showed her to the bed-chamber. *His and Kate's bedchamber*, Phoebe couldn't help thinking, her eyes flitting to the four-poster bed with its dark green damask curtains. They were happy once, had to have been; why wed else? *Their marital cocoon, where they had shared their love for one another nightly* . . . Flushing at her own thoughts, she dragged her eyes away. Victor, on the other hand, barely gave it a second glance. Having paused in the doorway, he pointed towards a pair of matching wardrobes dominating the far wall.

'You'll find a nightdress in there, Miss Parsons, I'm sure.'

'Your wife's?'

'Yes.'

She nodded, though the idea of poking through someone else's possessions didn't sit easy with her. Yet what choice had she? She had no belongings of her own now, had she?

'I'll bid you goodnight, then.'

'Goodnight, Mr Hayes.'

He stared at her a moment longer, inclined his head and left her.

Phoebe crossed to the wardrobes and opened one tentatively, feeling like a thief in the night. Though a few empty spaces indicated that Kate had taken some items with her, her clothing appeared virtually intact. She reached out and stroked a pretty dress in light blue with white lace edging. Then she moved to the narrow shelves set to the right and plucked out a cream nightgown.

She undressed quickly. Naked, she stood for a moment, revelling in the feel of the cool air on her bare skin. Having to sleep fully clothed in the lodging house, she hadn't been afforded the pleasure of stripping from soiled garments, besides when she'd bathed, in what seemed for ever. It would be lovelier still to sleep in something fresh for a change.

When Phoebe slipped beneath the soft sheets, she almost cried out at the sublimity. With a languid stretch of her arms and legs, she released a drawn-out sigh.

Aromas of hair oil and cigars reached her nostrils – Victor's smell still lingered on the sheets. She shuffled to what was clearly his side of the bed and snuggled down, tucking the blankets all around her. Safely embraced in comfort and warmth, she was slumbering in seconds.

Chapter 5

PHOEBE AWOKE WITH a smile on her lips – she doubted she'd ever slept so well. She had a spring in her step as she rose and padded across the room to fetch her clothes.

As she dressed, she resolved to head downstairs quietly and have breakfast ready for when Victor roused. It would be nice for him to waken to a hot meal, she thought, slipping on her boots and returning to the bed. Here, she lifted the discarded nightgown from the pillow and shook it out before folding it neatly. Then she crossed to the wardrobes.

Pulling at a door, a frown appeared as she stared at the unfamiliar contents inside; then she understood: she'd opened the wrong one.

This was Victor's wardrobe. The uniform made that clear.

She couldn't help herself – reaching up, she lifted out the smart police frock coat and peered at it in closer detail. An image of Victor striding around the streets in it, bravely apprehending all manner of dangerous criminals without a thought for his own safety, came to mind and she smiled with a feeling of pride for her friend. Then she remembered that was in the past, he *wasn't* a lawman any more, and her old curiosity resurfaced, stronger now. What had transpired? Why *had* he been dismissed from his duties?

'Good morning, Miss Parsons.'

'Oh!' Phoebe spun around with a guilty gasp to see Victor's large frame filling the doorway. She saw him glance from her to the uniform still clutched in her hand and back again. 'Mr Hayes . . .'

'There's tea in the pot.'

His face was expressionless; she could read nothing from it but sensed his displeasure instinctively. She stepped towards him. 'Mr Hayes, forgive me. I wasn't snooping, really. I was returning your wife's nightgown and opened the wrong wardrobe, and I, I saw the uniform and . . .'

'You wanted a better look at it.'

'Yes.'

'I understand. I'm not offended, Miss Parsons. Far from it. Actually, I'm rather flattered at your interest.'

She smiled, relieved. 'I am interested, yes.'

'Kate never was.'

'No?'

He shook his head. 'I learned early on to keep that aspect of my life to myself.'

Phoebe replaced the coat and closed the wardrobe door. Then she turned back to face him. 'What happened, Mr Hayes?' she finally asked him. She'd told herself she wouldn't pry but, right now, the time seemed right. She had to know.

He closed his eyes for the briefest moment. Then he nodded. 'You trusted me enough to be open about your past, and so . . . Come,' he murmured, and she followed him down to the kitchen.

They spoke not a word whilst he poured them tea and she set a pan of water on the heat to boil eggs for breakfast. Only when she'd sat after cutting slices from the loaf, and he'd tapped with the back of his spoon then removed the top of his egg, did they break the silence. Both spoke at once then paused to smile.

'Sorry. You go first,' Phoebe told him.

'No, you. Please, I insist.'

'Well . . .' She cleared her throat, awkward now. 'I just wanted to say that whatever the reason you were removed from the force . . . I shan't judge you, Mr Hayes. You're my friend and I, well, I will do my best to understand.'

He blinked with a mixture of relief and surprise. 'And I value that friendship, Miss Parsons.'

'As do I.' And she meant it, more than he could know.

'They found me to have committed the offence of "behaving in a manner unbecoming a police officer by associating with an undesirable person",' he said in a rush.

'An undesirable—?'

'A prostitute, Miss Parsons. I visited a prostitute.'

'Oh,' was all she could whisper.

'I had, in their words, neglected to work my beat for fifteen minutes and stopped by a dwelling house for an improper purpose. Initially, I was disciplined with a two-shilling fine. The next time it occurred, they felt they had no choice but to come down on my conduct severely. I was urged to resign forthwith. When I angrily refused – in my eyes, I was blameless of wrongdoing – the accusation of using insolent language and disobedience of orders was added to my list of misdemeanours. My punishment was instant dismissal.'

'You said, "the next time it occurred".' Though she knew she had no right to the feelings of slight hurt and disappointment that had come over her, she couldn't help them. She'd wanted to believe him decent, that his

82

superiors had been mistaken, but how so, now knowing what he'd done – and not once but twice? The revelation had thrown her. 'It wasn't a lapse in common sense and character, wasn't a one-off case?' she asked, almost begging that he'd correct her, that she'd heard wrong.

'No, Miss Parsons, it wasn't.'

'But you're a good man,' she blurted. 'I don't understand why . . . ? Were you prompted into acting so by your failing marriage? Were you . . . seeking comfort? Is that it?'

'I was never unfaithful to my wife! Not that Kate believes a word of it. I wouldn't . . . couldn't do that.'

'With all due respect, Mr Hayes, you can't blame your wife for suspecting it. You paid addresses to a prostitute. For what other reason could it have been but to—'

'I'm not guilty of what they accuse me. I'm not, Miss Parsons.' Now, it was he who sounded pleading. 'Not in the sense they mean, at any rate. You have my word on it. Please.'

'Oh, Mr Hayes. Don't take on so,' she soothed. 'I believe you.'

His voice was thick. 'You do?'

'If you say you're innocent of . . . that, then yes of course.'

'Miss Parsons. Phoebe.' He leaned forward across the table, his brown stare intense with gratitude. 'Thank you.'

'For what?' Her heartbeat had quickened at his closeness; she could feel his breath on her face so near was he.

'For your faith in my word and in me. You're the first person . . . It means a hell of a lot.'

'What really happened?'

The food grew cold; Victor prodded at his absently with his spoon as he spoke. 'The servants' registry office and its keeper who tricked girls into a life of debauchery – you remember me telling you?'

'Yes, of course. One brave girl found the courage to alert the authorities.'

Victor nodded. 'That's right. Suzannah Frost. It's she who I'm accused of having a liaison with.'

'I see.' It was all making a little more sense, now.

'A fortnight after the case was over and the girls were freed, I spotted Miss Frost sleeping rough in a doorway. She said she couldn't return home, that her family assumed she'd forged a decent life and would be disappointed if they knew the truth. She wouldn't be persuaded and I . . . well, I felt a duty of care towards her somehow. She'd helped all those other girls escape a terrible fate but was herself living still a miserable existence. So, I resolved to do what I could for her.

'I found her lodgings and promised to help her secure work. Days later, however, when I called on her to see how she was faring, she stated she'd found a position in a cotton mill, which I was pleased about. She thanked me for my help, she seemed settled, happy, and we parted ways. I said I'd visit her when I could to check on her progress, which over the following months I did, and she appeared to be doing well. Only one day, I was seen leaving, and the matter was brought to the attention of my superior. It was he who informed me that Miss Frost wasn't working in a mill at all but selling herself on the streets.'

'And he wouldn't believe that your visits to her were of a purely innocent nature?'

Victor shook his head. 'It didn't help matters that I went to see her again shortly afterwards. I had to. I needed to know why she'd lied, to try to talk sense into her to change her ways, but my attempt fell on deaf ears. She wouldn't listen.'

'That's when you were spotted there again and they had no choice but to dismiss you?'

'Yes.'

'And there is no hope, none at all, that—?'

'None,' he cut in miserably. 'I'd never be accepted back into the force. It's finished.'

Sighing, Phoebe reached for the pot. 'And Miss Frost?' she asked as she poured the tea, flicking her eyes up to look at him.

'I don't know how she is. I called on her yesterday, but she wasn't home. Her neighbours haven't seen her in days.'

'You're worried about her?'

'A little, yes.'

'Perhaps . . . well, perhaps it's time to let Miss Frost stand on her own two feet. You said yourself she wouldn't accept your advice. You've sacrificed your career and marriage already; what else? You owe her nothing, she isn't your responsibility – and I mean that in the kindest way possible. You can't rescue everyone, Mr Hayes. Besides, not everyone wants to be saved. You're a good man, but if you don't mind my saying so, I think it's time to let her go.'

He nodded. 'You're right, of course. I just wish . . .' He paused and shook his head. 'It doesn't matter.'

'Tell me,' she said softly.

'I wish the world was a better place, Miss Parsons. I wish everybody had a decent roof over their heads and full bellies. I wish everybody was safe and comfortable. I wish everybody mattered, you know? *Every*body, whatever their class. But . . .' He spread his arms wide. 'As you say, you can't rescue everyone.'

His generous soul touched her. She nodded. 'I wish all that, too. Do you think we'll see it come true in our lifetime, Mr Hayes?'

85

'One day, perhaps, things *will* lean in the poor man's favour, but it shall be a long time in the coming. Right now, the wants and needs of the rich hold precedence and to hell with the rest, caught in the middle of this wealth war that rages on.'

'But it's terrible.'

'And set to get a whole lot worse before it gets better. The only solid hope for improvement lies with the Chartist Movement winning the common man a voice in government, but . . . We'll just have to see.'

Phoebe gazed at him. His face was flushed with passion, and the anger of injustice sparked from his eyes. This was like his speech about slaves; again, his empathy for the working-class plight was plain.

'This is why you became a policeman, isn't it?' she said suddenly. It made perfect sense. 'Your desire to help people.'

Victor considered this before nodding slowly. 'I suppose it was, yes. I was one of the first to be accepted when the Manchester Borough Police was established three years ago,' he added proudly. 'When adverts appeared in newspapers inviting applications for the post of constable, I was drawn to it right away. I don't mind admitting I breezed through the necessary drilling.' He puffed out his chest as he spoke. 'The day I was sworn in was one of the most defining of my life.'

Her stare softened in pity. 'You miss it a lot, don't you?'

'That I do. We were a fine body of men. Not that we were popular with everyone, mind you, and still today there is much public contention towards the police. Our Prime Minister's hope when he founded the first force, London's Metropolitan Service, was to avoid lawmen being likened to soldiers. After all, when brought in to restore order during riots and even peaceful demonstrations, they are well known for their brutal treatment of the people. Sir Robert Peel insisted, therefore, on his police wearing plain clothing rather than the ostentatious uniform of the militia, to have them appear more approachable.

'The same is true of an officer's tools – his handcuffs and truncheon are concealed in hidden pockets in the tail of his coat rather than on show like those of the armed hussar. Alas, *still* suspicion surrounds the police. However, things are still in their infancy. We can but hope that the public will eventually grow accustomed to their presence and see that their main aim is to uphold safe and good living on our streets.'

'I like your uniform,' Phoebe told him, smiling. 'It's a lovely shade, very smart.'

'Yes, I agree. I'm glad that Manchester has its own independent force rather than being clubbed with the county force of the Lancashire Constabulary. Their uniform is of a dull dark green, you know.' He pulled a face and chuckled when she laughed. 'Blue is much nicer. When it's not covered in spittle, that is.'

'Spittle?' she echoed, grimacing.

He shrugged. 'As I said, the public are a suspicious lot. It was a nightmare in the early days. To say we were unpopular is putting it mildly . . .' Here he paused, and his cheeks took on a reddish hue. 'Forgive me for prattling on,' he told her. 'I must be boring you to tears—'

'No, no.' It interested him and so she wanted to hear it. 'Please, go on.'

'Well,' he continued, with evident delectation at her attentiveness, 'both ends of society strongly resented us: the poor because they believed us oppressive, the rich because they saw us as an unnecessary expense. The latter I can sympathise with – it's ratepayers who fund the force, after all, and must continue to unless the government step in to shoulder the cost.

'Mind you, I can even understand the ill feeling of the lower class, too. Well, some of them, at any rate. The orderly poor would be inclined to view us more favourably, but for our sorry reputation. As in all things, bad apples will burrow amongst the good, and the police force is no exception. Lawmen haven't become known as blue butchers for nothing, I'm afraid. There are some who go mad with the power and for whom brutality is the order of the day.'

But not you, thought Phoebe, knowing instinctively he'd been a fair and just officer. Never you.

'The lawless poor, of course, are another breed entirely,' he went on. 'There's no love lost between them and the force and never will be. Both verbal and physical attacks on the police by that lot are commonplace, expected even. There's no low to which man will not sink to evade arrest. I've been assaulted in the street, kicked and bitten, pelted with stones – and yes, spat on . . . You name it, I've had it. But well, it goes with the territory. And do you know something, Miss Parsons?' A wistful smile touched his lips. 'I don't regret a single moment, would do it all again in a heartbeat if I could.'

'I'm sorry.'

'Don't be. What's gone is gone. I suppose I miss being part of something worthwhile, making a difference, you know? Like my father before me, it felt almost like I was playing a part in our history somehow.'

'Your father? He was a lawman, too?'

'Yes, he was a watchman. And his brother also; my uncle was a lock-up keeper. I can still see them now.' Victor smiled again in remembrance. 'My uncle, in his brown uniform with "LK" emblazoned on red collar patches, kept order on Manchester's streets during the day, along with the beadles and runners. Then, when darkness fell, the watchmen took over the patrol.

'Though it must be said that watchmen had a reputation of dozing away the night in their boxes whilst the criminals ran amok, my father wasn't one of them. He was diligent and dependable. He kept his truncheon, rattle and lantern well cared for, and his low-crowned hat with its yellow band impeccable. I'd watch him paint his number on to his greatcoat in ochre each evening before he left for work, saw the pride in his face . . . He took his role of protector to persons and property seriously. He was a credit to the police.'

'It seems you were destined then to follow in their footsteps,' she said, biting her tongue too late when self-reproach clouded his features. 'I'm sorry, Mr Hayes, I didn't mean—'

'Please don't keep apologising. It's my doing, I who went and threw it all away. I'm just glad that neither of them is alive to see it.'

In the ensuing silence, the small cuckoo clock in the hall chirruped the ninth hour. Remembering today's plan, Phoebe fingered her brooch and plucked her lip.

'You don't have to let it go if it means that much to you,' Victor told her quietly.

'Yes, Mr Hayes, I do.'

'What I mean is, I'll see you all right until you're back on your feet. I have some savings, and you're welcome to stay on here—'

'Thank you, but I can't let you do that. It would feel I was taking advantage. I must have money, must pay my way. Can you understand that?'

'I can, of course. Well, if you're sure . . . ?'

'I am,' she said, rising from the table and crossing the room to collect her shawl. 'Let's go and see what Mr Rakowski has to say.'

The jeweller's stood on the edge of Rochdale Road and at no great distance from Victor's home – he and Phoebe set forth at a brisk pace against the coldness.

They were midway through their journey when she turned to him, asking, 'So, Mr Hayes. We have discussed the past and thrashed out our hopes for the future – what about the present? Tell me, what, were it in your power, would you choose to do with yourself? It's true that our first choices of lawman and lady's maid are lost to us, but what else? What would make *you* happy?'

'Why, what would be your dream?'

'Ah, no. I asked you.'

'Ladies first,' he insisted, smiling, making her feel warm inside – no one had ever referred to her as a lady before.

'All right, we'll go at the same time. Deal?' she offered, feeling a little silly now and half wishing she hadn't brought the subject up – he'd surely deem her long-held wish absurd.

'Deal.'

With lopsided grins, they took a simultaneous deep breath. Then: 'Tavernkeeper!' they blurted in unison.

Halting mid-step, they gazed at one another in stunned silence before laughing out loud.

'What? I don't believe it!' spluttered Victor. 'What are the odds of that?'

'Indeed!' Phoebe was as amazed as he. 'I never anticipated that, Mr Hayes!'

'Well, I know my reason for it: my grandfather had his

own tavern when I was a boy. I always fancied the business myself, I've just never had the funds to pursue it.'

Her mouth dropped open. 'Mine too!'

'*Your* grandfather ran a tavern?'

'Yes! The Abbie, which he named after my grandmother Abigail, on Withy Grove. I used to stay over as a child and was fascinated by the place. Like you, I've always fancied trying my hand at it. I can't believe this! What was your grandfather's name?' She laughed, joking, 'Here, it wasn't Giles, was it, like mine?'

'What in the world . . . ? It *was* Giles, yes.'

'No . . . No, it can't have been, it can't—!'

'You're right, it wasn't,' Victor cut in with a wicked chuckle. 'Mine was called George.'

'Oh, you! Mr Hayes, you had me there!' Laughing, Phoebe swatted his arm. 'I was beginning to wonder what on earth was going on!'

'I'm sorry, I couldn't resist,' he said, wiping tears of mirth from his eyes. 'Now that really would have been one coincidence too many!'

They were still grinning as they entered the small shop. When the slim and wiry man behind the counter spotted Victor, his bearded face spread in a beaming smile.

'Why, Mr Hayes! My friend, come in!'

'Good morning, Mr Rakowski. You're keeping well, I trust?'

Shaking Victor's hand, the jeweller nodded. 'Cannot complain, cannot complain. And you? Hey, and what is this, no uniform?' he proclaimed, taking in the length of Victor with a sweep of his arm. 'Not at work, my friend?'

'Er, no. Anyway,' he added, swiftly changing the subject, 'we wanted to ask your advice on something.'

91

'Oh?'

'This is Miss Parsons, a friend of mine. She has in her possession a rather fine brooch which she wishes to have valued.'

'Pleased to meet you, Miss Parsons.'

'And you, sir,' she said, though her attempt at a smile fell short. Now she was here, being separated from Lilian's gift had become horribly real and her eyes felt gritty with approaching tears.

'A brooch, you say?' Mr Rakowski asked in his soft Polish twang, stroking the greying hair at his chin. 'May I see it, my dear?'

Phoebe unpinned it from her bodice. She stared at it for a moment, gave the bronze leaves a last caress and handed it across.

Turning the piece between his thumb and forefinger, the jeweller lifted his brows in surprise. Light from the narrow window behind him had caught the stones, sparking thin cream-gold prisms. 'Very nice. Very nice indeed. Early Georgian period, I believe.'

'As old as that?' Phoebe was shocked.

'Most definitely.'

'How much is it worth?'

His lively eyes flicked up to look at her. 'You are willing to sell?'

'I'm afraid I must.'

Nodding understandingly, he stroked his beard once more. 'I am very interested in buying it, Miss Parsons. I would be willing to pay . . . hmm, let me see . . .' Again, he studied it, then turned back to her. 'One hundred pounds?'

Phoebe gasped. Victor grinned. Mr Rakowski smiled from one to the other.

'I don't believe . . . A hundred pounds?' she whispered.

'A pawnbroker offered but fifteen for it. Are you certain it's worth as much as all that, Mr Rakowski?'

'My dear girl!' The jeweller laughed. 'You are honest, I will say that. Not many would question an amount such as the one I have just suggested to you, nor ask if I wanted to reconsider! But I stand by my offer and will say that whoever this pawnbroker may be, he is driven by both dishonesty and greed. He saw the piece for what it is and thought only of himself. You would do wisely to avoid future dealings with him, yes?'

'I will, I . . . I still cannot believe . . . Though it pains me more than I can put into words to let it go, I must, and so . . .' She nodded bravely. 'I am willing to sell it to you, sir.'

'Excellent, excellent.' His delight with his purchase clear, he turned to shake Victor's hand. 'My thanks to you for thinking of me and bringing Miss Parsons here. Be sure to bear me in mind again with more of your friends!'

'I doubt a second opportunity will arise, Mr Rakowski,' responded Victor, and his gaze deepened as it locked with Phoebe's own. 'Miss Parsons here is a rare find.'

Her heartbeat quickened at what she'd sensed to be an added meaning behind his words. It wasn't only her being in possession of the brooch that made her stand out as unique to him, was what he'd meant. Surely that *had* to be what he'd meant . . .

'As you're without a portmanteau now, would you like me to carry it for you for safekeeping?' Victor was saying to her now – she blinked back to the present, confused.

'Pardon?'

'The money.' He nodded to Mr Rakowski, who had counted out and was holding aloft the fortune. 'Have I to . . . ?'

'Oh yes. Yes, thank you, Mr Hayes.'

Outside, she dragged in several deep breaths. A hundred pounds! Lord, she'd never even begun to imagine such wealth in her wildest dreams.

'Are you all right?' There was a hint of laughter in Victor's tone. 'You've had quite the shock.'

'Yes. I think so.'

'What is it?' he asked when she frowned.

'Do you . . . ?' Phoebe felt suddenly choked as a thought occurred. 'Do you think Mrs Yewdale knew its true value when she gifted it to me?'

'Without doubt. You said it was part of her personal collection; those of her breeding don't possess cheap jewellery, Miss Parsons. She knew its worth, there can be no question.'

'I didn't think of that, I didn't. I honestly assumed it to be worthless. But why didn't she tell me?'

'Would you have felt it proper to accept it if she had?'

'Probably not, no.'

Victor smiled. 'Then you have your answer. Either way, she wanted you to have it. You clearly meant a great deal to her.'

As had she to her. Oh, that dear, sweet lady . . .

'My promise. Of course!' Phoebe gasped as realisation dawned. Then seeing Victor's puzzlement, explained, 'She had me vow something to her on her deathbed, wouldn't rest until I did. She made me swear to her that I'd be happy. That I would do everything in my power to make it so, to never give up. Realise my dreams, whatever they were and however hard it might be to achieve them. She needed me to promise, and I did.' She turned eyes shining with a feverish excitement on to him. 'The tavern, Mr Hayes. Let's do it, you and I. Let us *both* make

94

true our wishes. For us. For Lilian. It's within our power now, don't you see?'

His voice, shaky with disbelief, was little above a whisper. 'Miss Parsons . . . You really mean it?'

'More than anything else in my life,' she shot back on a squeak.

'Yes.'

'Yes?'

Taking her by the arms, he nodded, grinning. 'Yes!'

Adding her laughter to his, she allowed herself to return his hold. She wanted nothing else at this moment but to be alone with him in the quiet warmth and discuss their plans; on impulse, she grasped his large hand and drew him in a run towards his home.

Phoebe spotted her first. It was the dress she wore that she recognised, the same light blue with white-lace edging that Phoebe had seen hanging in the wardrobe the night before – Kate. Juddering to a stop outside the house, Phoebe's recent joy melted like wax to a flame. She flicked her eyes up to Victor, standing stock still beside her. His face now wore a stone mask.

'Well, this is cosy.' Kate descended the few steps by the front door and came to stand in front of them. Her eyes spewed venom as they settled on Phoebe and Victor's still-clasped hands. 'Very cosy indeed.'

Mortified, Phoebe broke her hold from his and dropped her gaze, her cheeks ablaze. What must she think? Just as everything had been going so well, too. Lord, this was the last thing they needed.

'What are you doing here?' Victor asked his wife, slicing through the iced atmosphere.

'I came to collect my things.' She jerked her chin towards a dark-wood trunk by the front door. 'I could see from the inside of the place that you'd been back – and that you hadn't been alone,' she added, swivelling her glare to Phoebe. 'So. This is who you threw our marriage away for? *This* is the filthy little slut, is it? You didn't waste much time—'

'You're wrong, Kate.' Victor spoke quietly, though a muscle at his jaw had tightened at her abusive remark. 'This isn't who you believe her to be.'

'Like hell it isn't!'

'I'm not Suzannah Frost, Mrs Hayes.' Phoebe spoke gently, desperate to defuse the situation; passers-by were beginning to crane their necks in their direction. 'My name is Phoebe Parsons and I . . . I'm a friend of your husband's, just a friend, and—'

'I'll bet,' she snapped, marching forward to close the space between them. 'You really are disgusting, do you know that?' she told her husband, thrusting her face into his.

'Kate, will you *listen* to what Miss Parsons is saying? It's the truth—'

'Truth?' she cried, advancing on Phoebe with murderous eyes. Phoebe backed off with a cry. 'You shameless whore, I'll—!'

'Stop!' Victor grabbed his wife's wrists as she made to claw at Phoebe's face. 'Christ's sake, woman!'

Phoebe had heard and seen enough. She had to get away, had no business here anyway, none at all between this husband and wife. Her presence was only adding further fuel to the woman's fire of fury – for all their sakes, she must leave. She should never have *come* here in the first place. Head down, she turned and walked away.

'Phoebe, wait.'

Ignoring Victor's plea and Kate's jeers, she crossed

the street. When tears threatened to choke her, she picked up her skirts and set off at a run, away from the house, from him – from their future, which had seemed so certain just minutes before, now shattered to dust.

Chapter 6

THE PEARL MOON had long since chased the sun to bed when Phoebe finally stopped walking. She'd roamed aimlessly for hours, going over the day's fluctuating events, and still her head and heart were no more at ease now than they had been when she'd fled the unpleasant scene.

For all that she understood Kate Hayes's hurt, to be branded a slut and a whore in the middle of the street – unjustifiably so – had been both painful and mortifying. She hadn't deserved it and she was determined not to put herself in such a position again. Her and Victor's friendship was finished, had to be. For her own peace of mind and reputation, not to mention her safety – hadn't Kate gone for her, after all, intent on causing her an injury? – she couldn't maintain the connection, however much she valued it. Better for everyone that she steered clear and he forgot all about her.

She'd pushed open the eating-house door and found herself an empty table before she even realised where she was – she'd wandered here automatically. Sighing, she was about to leave, couldn't risk Victor seeking her out here, when the serving girl appeared at her elbow.

'What can I get you, miss?'

'Actually, I . . .' Phoebe began, then glancing through

the window at the rain that had started up, she hesitated. Already she was frozen to the marrow, her fingers, toes and the tip of her nose numb with cold. Furthermore, she was bone tired; the mere prospect of tramping the streets again brought a groan to her lips. A few minutes to rest up and warm herself through wouldn't do any harm, surely? 'A cup of tea, please,' she relented.

The girl skittered off to fetch the beverage. Alone once more with her thoughts, Phoebe swallowed a sigh. *Their own tavern.* Oh, but what a wonderful, if short-lived, dream it had been. She was heartsore at the loss of what would now never be. They would have made a great team. She, impeccably trained in serving others. He, practised in dealing with all manner of people and in defusing difficult situations. And both of them besides knowing their way around a tavern since childhood. It would have been perfect. It really would. And now . . .

'Here you go, miss.'

Glad of the interruption, Phoebe forced her mind elsewhere and murmured a thank you to the girl. A few sips of her tea later, she was feeling a little better. However, in no time, the cup was empty; biting her lip, she contemplated ordering a refill. The rain was showing no sign of abating and she was just beginning to thaw out. But in the end, she shook her head. She couldn't risk it, couldn't see Victor again today, hadn't the strength for it. Best that she left before all the lodging houses filled up. She really would be in trouble if she allowed that to happen with only herself to look out for her welfare now.

Reluctantly, she rose and made her way towards the counter to pay – and stopped dead in her tracks. *Oh no . . .*

Her money. Victor had offered to carry it for her and had it still. She hadn't a single copper coin on her. How would she settle her bill? *Good God, this was all she needed.* 'I . . . I . . .' she stuttered to the serving girl, lost for an explanation. A blush was creeping up on her and a lump of hopelessness had lodged in her throat. 'I'm afraid, I . . . I don't have any—'

'I'll get that,' said a smooth voice behind her.

Turning in surprise, Phoebe watched as a broad-shouldered man with thick dark hair leaned over and dropped coins into the serving girl's hand.

'And two more teas, please,' he said to her with a smile, before motioning for Phoebe to follow him to his table. And, too perplexed to refuse, Phoebe did.

'Thank you very much for that,' she mumbled when they were seated facing one another, both embarrassed by and overwhelmed with thankfulness for this stranger's generosity.

'Don't mention it.' He held out a hand. 'Dick Lavender.'

Her gaze locking on his, she shook the proffered hand without seeing it. He was without doubt the most beautiful man she'd ever laid eyes on. 'Phoebe. Phoebe Parsons.'

'Well, Phoebe, I'm very pleased to meet thee.' His cut-glass blue stare creased in playfulness almost and his generous mouth followed suit, bunching slightly in a whisper of a smile. He leaned back in his chair in the manner of someone completely at ease with himself and his surroundings. He exuded confidence in fact, and she suddenly felt shy without knowing why.

'I have money – or at least I did, only . . . a friend's looking after it for me,' she explained. 'Once I'm in a better position, I'll pay you back, Mr Lavender.'

Draping an arm across the top of the empty chair beside his, he shrugged. 'No need. Making your acquaintance is payment enough.'

Not knowing how to respond to the compliment, she lowered her eyes with a smile. 'Well, if you're sure . . . ?'

'I am. Now,' he added, lifting an eyebrow curiously, 'what's a decent lass like thee doing out, all on her lonesome, in this part of town and at this time of night?'

'Oh, I wasn't intending staying out much longer. I was just on my way to the lodging house across the way, you see, and— Oh!' She slapped a hand to her mouth, her gaze above it widening in sheer horror. If she hadn't the means to pay for her tea, she certainly wasn't in a position to secure a bed for the night. Dear Lord, she was done for!

She'd just have to return to Victor's after all, collect her funds. But what if he was angry with her for dashing off as she had? She couldn't face that. Worse still, what if Kate was still there? What if she and Victor had settled their differences and she'd returned home? It was possible – who knew what had taken place once she'd left? Her turning up again would likely cause merry hell between the pair; she couldn't have that on her conscience. And yet, what options were left open to her? What else was she to do? Simply forget about the money altogether? But she needed it, had nothing more, no other way of supporting herself. *Oh, what a quandary! Think, think . . .*

Realising her predicament, Dick clicked his tongue sympathetically. 'You haven't the brass forra roof above your head the night, have you?'

She bit down on her bottom lip, now dangerously aquiver. 'No. No, I haven't.'

'Then it's a good thing our paths have crossed, ain't

it, Phoebe? For I just happen to know someone who runs her own lodging house but an arrow's flight from here – and she's an amiable sort into the bargain. She'll put thee up once I've explained the situation, I'm sure.'

A determined tear made its escape to splash to her cheek. She swallowed several times to dislodge the lump of gratitude. 'You'd do that for me?'

'What are friends for?' he answered simply with a wink.

'Thank you, Mr Lavender.' Her relief was indescribable. 'Thank you, truly.'

'You're welcome. And please, lass, call me Dick.' He rose and sauntered to the counter to pay his bill. Then, returning to Phoebe, he crooked his arm towards her. 'Shall we?'

Linking her hand through, she smiled up into his face. Then, nodding, she followed him out into the cold black night.

They came to a halt just minutes away on Garrick Street. Peering into the pockets of dancing shadows, Phoebe chewed the tip of her thumb. She wasn't accustomed to this part of Manchester, as nearby to what she *did* know as it may be, and her uneasiness began to peak. Yells and curses, aggressive in drink, carried on the wind in seemingly every direction and the very air felt steeped in desperation and danger. She hid a shaky breath. Then Dick was rapping at a paint-chipped door and she hadn't time to question her surroundings when a tall and strikingly handsome woman appeared, her cautious gaze relaxing to see her visitor. She stepped aside, swinging the door wide, and Dick entered. Not knowing what else to do, Phoebe followed.

'Evening, Mr Lavender.'

'Betsy.' He touched the tip of his cap briefly in acknowledgement – not exactly what you might call cordial, Phoebe thought, as he'd recently made out their acquaintance to be.

'And who's this, then?'

Dick ran an approving gaze over Phoebe. 'Miss Parsons. She finds herself . . . somewhat indisposed and I said my good friend Betsy would be only too happy to help a lass in distress.'

'Did you now?' Betsy retorted, arching a perfectly shaped brow, though it was clear by the spark in her heavily made-up eyes that she was teasing. 'The lass is in need, then?'

'Aye. She—'

'I need a bed for the night. Just one night, that's all,' Phoebe cut in, disliking that they were talking about her as though she wasn't even present. 'I'd be most grateful, Mrs . . . ?'

'Just plain owd Betsy'll do me, lass,' the woman responded easily, and her mouth twitched as though something had amused her, though Phoebe couldn't figure out what. 'Come on, come this way.'

Dick motioned that she should follow and they passed along a narrow passageway, which opened out into a good-sized kitchen.

'You've no possessions, then?' asked Betsy, lowering herself into a chair at a table littered with used dishes.

'No, I . . . I lost my bag, you see.'

'Aye. Well, no bother. I'll see you right with a nightgown and suchlike.'

She blinked in surprise, was touched by the gesture. 'Really? Well, I appreciate that, Betsy. Thank you very much.'

'That's all right, lass. 'Ere,' the woman added quietly

to Dick, her eyes, still on Phoebe, creasing, 'is tha sure about this one, only she seems a delicate little thing, with impeccable manners, to boot. I mean to say, she ain't what you normally fetch round here—'

'She's perfect,' Dick interrupted, a clipped edge to his tone now. Then, noticing Phoebe's puzzled expression, he laughed and a breath-snatching smile appeared at his mouth, transforming his face into one of even more beauty. 'I've helped one or two lasses afore you what were down on their luck,' he explained. Then: 'Come,' he murmured, cupping her elbow and guiding her from the room. 'You're fagged, I'm sure, will be glad of a lie down in a comfortable bed. Betsy, here, shall show you the way. Won't you?' he added to the woman, who had risen and moved with them to the staircase.

Betsy folded her arms. Then her eyes met Phoebe's and she nodded. 'Aye. 'Course I will.'

'Good girl.' Dick planted a swift kiss on her cheek. Then, to Phoebe's amazement, he leaned towards her and repeated the action, his smooth lips lingering a little longer on hers. He took her hand and squeezed. 'Well, goodbye, Phoebe. Pleasant dreams.'

'Goodbye, Mr Lavender . . . Dick . . . and . . . Thank you!' she called as he disappeared, the front door rattling shut at his back. She turned to Betsy. 'Are you sure you don't mind . . . ? I haven't the money to pay,' she admitted, realising now that Dick hadn't filled the lodging-house keeper in on her circumstances. 'Mr Lavender, you see, he assured me—'

'Fret not, lass.'

'You're sure?'

'Fret not,' Betsy repeated. She motioned for Phoebe to follow. 'Come with me.'

The house was tastefully decorated in cream and dark green – it was clear that the place had only recently been painted; and the stair carpet, though not of the best quality, was fresh and had been diligently swept. Several prints of ladies in varying poses, hung in overtly ornate frames, lined the walls leading up to the landing. Here stood six doors – three to the left, three to the right – and Betsy paused midway. Turning to Phoebe, her expression was unreadable in the dim light of the candles suspended in holders dotted along the walls. She leaned towards her, looked as though she might impart something, before straightening again. Then she motioned for her to follow once more.

The bedchamber into which Phoebe was led resembled nothing she'd been expecting. Pretty floral-printed paper hung at the walls, and silky counterpanes in rich deep red adorned the beds. Most of all, everywhere was clean and, shock upon shock, bug-free – she was dumbstruck at its attractiveness.

'Choose a bed, lass,' Betsy told her, sweeping her arm to encompass the four present. 'T' other girls shan't be back forra bit yet; you make yourself comfortable wherever you like in t' meantime.'

'Other girls?' she asked, still gawping around at what seemed plush splendour after the other lodging house to which she'd grown accustomed.

'Aye. They're away watching some show or other at the music hall, so you've your pick of the beds. Now,' Betsy continued, crossing to a wooden stand holding a broad washbowl and tall pitcher. 'You get yourself settled and I'll fetch some nice hot water for you to freshen up, like. I'll bring thee up a cup of tea, an' all, whilst I'm about it, shall I? Or would you prefer summat a bit stronger?'

'Oh no, thank you. Tea would be perfect.' Phoebe could hardly contain her pleasure at all this. 'Are you certain you don't mind, Betsy? Only this isn't what I've become used to. The last lodging house I stayed in . . . Well!' she said, chuckling. 'It's . . . a lot different to this, shall we say.'

The woman had paused by the door, pitcher in hand. Despite Phoebe's laughter, *her* face held not a trace of mirth. Finally, she flashed a weak smile, saying, 'I'll not be long,' before disappearing.

Alone, Phoebe frowned slightly at the closed door. Then the room stole her attention again, and Betsy's reaction just now was forgotten. She gazed about and nodded in approval. Then she made her way down the centre of the room and selected the bed to her left, between two others. Perfect, she thought when she sat on the edge and felt herself sink into its feathery softness. What a boon that she'd happened to cross paths tonight with someone as wonderfully kind as Dick Lavender. She shuddered to imagine what she would have done, where she'd be at this moment, otherwise.

Thoughts of him conjured up his perfect features and she felt herself blushing despite herself. She was, admittedly, curious how he and Betsy knew each other, but decided it wasn't her business to wonder. And yet, she couldn't stop herself from feeling a slight pique of envy that the other woman clearly had some sort of connection with him. Nor could she help hoping that their paths would cross a second time. She'd like to see him again. Yes, she would, very much so.

Minutes later, Betsy brought up the clean water and a drink and left again soon afterwards, and Phoebe was on her own once more. By the warmth of the crackling fire, she stripped to her shift and washed herself all over. Then she re-dressed, climbed beneath the bedclothes with her tea and sighed in contentment.

The fraught day coupled with the quiet and relaxing surroundings took their toll; placing her empty cup on the floor, she snuggled down in the bed. Within seconds, she was snoring softly.

''Ere, look at this!'

The voice, high in surprise, pulled Phoebe from her doze. Blinking, she peered in confusion at the sea of faces staring down at her.

'You new, then?' asked a short plump girl with a beaming smile.

'I . . . Yes, I suppose I am,' Phoebe stammered, still groggy with sleep and not a little alarmed now to see that, as well as other females, several men had entered and were smiling across at her. She sat up, pulling the covers around her chin.

'What's your name, then?'

'Phoebe,' she answered the girl, breaking eye contact with a light-haired man close by whose gaze she'd caught.

'That's nice. Aye, I like that. I'm Anne.'

'Nice to meet you, Anne,' she murmured, her stare still on the man. To her unease, he was making his way towards them, his face creased in a slack-mouthed grin. Swinging her legs out of bed, she reached for her shawl which was lying at the bottom of the bed and draped it around her shoulders, eyes downcast.

The occupants had now made themselves comfortable and were sitting or sprawling across the other beds, laughing and talking in pairs. That all had enjoyed a drink or two too many was evident; Phoebe could see their glassy looks and smell the alcohol fog on them

107

from where she sat. She turned to where the girl who had spoken to her had been standing but found her gone; scanning the space, Phoebe saw her now engaged in playful conversation with a young man on the bed facing. He leaned across to stroke her cheek and she smiled and draped an arm around his neck. When their lips found each other, Phoebe glanced away quickly, her colour rising.

For all the other lodging house's faults, she hadn't witnessed this sort of behaviour beneath its roof, that was for sure. She was at a loss what to make of it, less so what to do.

'All right, love?'

It was the blond man. He made to sit beside Phoebe and she rose swiftly to her feet. 'I'm sorry, but if you don't mind, I'm rather tired and—'

'Why leave the bed, then?' he asked on an ale-slur, patting the counterpane. 'Lie thee down, lass, and rest with me.'

'No, thank you.' By now, her heart was beginning to beat faster – his eyes had taken on a wolfish glint, deep with intent; she needed to get away from here before things got out of hand. He wasn't in his right mind in his inebriated state, couldn't be to be suggesting what he was to her – in full public view, no less. Not that anyone else seemed even mildly bothered. In fact, they were much too preoccupied with their own affairs, Phoebe saw, her mouth falling open in disbelief and horror as she glanced around. Some couples were locked in each other's arms, others kissing passionately.

The plump girl she'd spoken with now lay beneath the bedcovers with her male friend, her milky-white breasts exposed. In the next moment, he climbed on top of her, and Phoebe looked away sharply with a gasp.

Just what on earth was this place? her mind screamed. Dick had insisted it was but a common lodging house, and Betsy had said nothing to the contrary – had they been deceiving her all along? But why? Why had she been brought here in the first place? It was clearly some mode of bawdy house . . . well, she was getting out of here right now!

''Ere, where you going, come back!' called the blond man as Phoebe hurried without a backward glance from the room and skittered down the stairs. She met Betsy in the passageway.

'Phoebe, lass?'

'Had I known what this establishment really was, I would never have come here,' she told the woman, cheeks blazing with mortification and indignation. 'I'm leaving.'

Betsy moved towards her. 'But Dick, he said—'

'I don't care what Mr Lavender said! Why did he bring me to this house, exactly?' she added, wanting to know despite herself. 'Tell me.'

'Well, ain't it obvious? Girls what have fallen on hard times . . . He was helping thee, is all—'

'Helping me?' she cut in again, shaking her head. 'I don't need *that* kind of help, thank you.'

'But where will you go?'

'Anywhere, I don't care.' Her body had begun to shake with building anger and disappointment, and tears stung her eyes. 'Anything is preferable to this!'

'But Dick, lass . . . He'll not be best pleased when he discovers—'

'I care naught for that. Naught at all!' With that, Phoebe stalked to the front door and wrenched it open. Then she was running again, out of the house and

109

along the pitch cobbled lane as fast as her legs would carry her.

He'd been so bloody *stupid*.

Cursing his actions and the whole of this horrible day in general, Victor trudged on grimly down the next street.

So that was that. His wife was gone from his life for good. He'd insisted she take all of her possessions, had hoicked her back inside after Phoebe had fled and had personally helped Kate to stuff all of her things into another trunk. He'd then ordered a hansom cab to take them and her back to her sister's, had waited with her at the roadside until it arrived and had even paid the fare. An extortionate cost, however worth it to have her gone.

He'd hung around at home for an hour or two afterwards in the hope that Phoebe would return, but she hadn't, and he'd been forced to wrap up warm against the elements and go in search of her. He'd been hunting for her ever since.

Fully expecting to find her at the eating house, he'd been surprised when he'd entered and found her absent. Then he'd nodded and, making his way back the way he'd come, he'd headed for their usual lodging house. But again, despite a thorough search of the place, she wasn't to be found, and worry had begun to coil his insides.

She had no money, so far as he knew. Nor did she have anyone she could have turned to. She'd relayed this knowledge to him already, had she not? So where had she gone? How would she cope?

'I'm sorry, lass,' he murmured to the biting night as he walked. He should never have let her dash off as he had. Because of him, she was on her own and, very

110

potentially, in God alone knew what danger. 'Where *are* you?'

Passing down yet another grimy stretch filled with warren-like dwellings, he almost missed his footing on an uneven flagstone; muttering an expletive, he righted himself – and a small gasp left him as, up ahead, a flash of blue disappeared around the bend.

Phoebe.

It had been her shawl, he just knew it. Thank God! Calling her name, he set off after the vision at a run.

The narrow entryway he found himself in when he hurried around the corner was deserted. Slowing, he frowned and scratched his head. He was debating what to do next when a hand on his shoulder had him almost leaping from his skin – he whirled around, fists raised in readiness.

'My, my, Victor. You are jumpy these days!'

'Miss Frost.' He blinked down at the young woman in astonishment. 'What are you doing here?'

'I were passing and thought I recognised thee. What you doing skulking about this part of town at this time, then? You on someone's tail?'

'No, I . . .' *She didn't know he'd been dismissed from his position, dismissed in the main because of his connection with her.* He hadn't the strength for all that right now. 'I thought I saw someone I knew.'

'Pardon me if I startled thee – I thought tha were about to land a left hook on my nose for a minute there!'

He smiled sheepishly. 'Sorry. As you say, this part of town . . .'

'Who knows who might be lurking in the shadows,' she finished for him, and he nodded.

'Well.'

'Well.'

111

'Hello.'

'Hello,' she responded with a slow grin, her teeth glistening white in her heart-shaped face. She reached out and tapped his arm playfully. 'How's tha been keeping? All right?'

Victor nodded. 'You?'

'Aye, can't complain.'

'I came to see you.'

'Oh?'

'Your neighbour said you were away and didn't know when you'd be back.' He flicked his gaze over her and was relieved to see she did indeed appear well. 'You're eating enough, have somewhere safe to stay?'

Suzannah nodded. Then her eyes softened and she closed the space between them. She nudged him with her elbow gently, saying, 'How's about we get a sup of tea, eh? Have a chat and catch up, like?'

Victor was about to accept when Phoebe's face slammed into his mind; he shook his head. 'No, I'm sorry. I can't, not tonight.'

'Oh?'

'I have business to attend to. Important business, and—'

'Oh, but Victor . . .' She lowered her gaze then glanced back up at him from beneath her long, coal-black lashes. Her full mouth had bunched in a pout. 'I've not seen thee for ever such a long while and . . . Please?' she asked, brushing his hand with her cold fingers. 'You can spare just a little of your time for an owd friend, can't you? For me?'

He wanted to. He was glad to see her. He'd worried about her and now here she was, happy and healthy, and he was pleased of the fact. She was asking for some company, his company, for she trusted him – was she lonely? he wondered, and his heart softened in pity. She had no one else, did she, after all, not really. And yet . . . Phoebe . . . He bit his lip.

'Just one cup of tea won't do no harm, will it?' she pressed in a small, childlike voice, her eyes creased in hope.

'No. I don't suppose it will . . .' he heard himself say.

One cup. Then he'd resume his search for the other woman who needed him, he resolved. Nor would he stop until he found her. Phoebe couldn't spend the night on these streets, penniless and alone. She couldn't.

Suzannah laughed quietly in delight. She hooked her arm through his and turned him around, and the two of them headed off towards the centre of town.

Her tears grew icy on her cheeks, but she made no attempt to wipe them away.

Hunkering down further behind the high wall, Phoebe buried her head in her arms. Victor had come. He'd come looking for her; proof that he cared. Then that woman had apprehended him and he'd forgotten all about her. He'd chosen the other one, walked away with her, Phoebe's welfare now seemingly unimportant in his priorities and his mind.

She'd heard him call her name and had juddered to a halt, overwhelming relief rushing through her. She hadn't a clue where she was headed, had simply needed to get away from Betsy's and what it stood for – what she'd clearly represented to Dick Lavender. That was how he'd seen her? A common whore who would willingly spread her thighs for a few pence?

Had he hoodwinked her, or had she read something into their chance meeting that wasn't there? She'd believed them to have developed instantly some rare form of connection. She thought him a new friend whom she could confide in and trust, and had. He'd seen her as nothing more than another poor unfortunate who would do anything to earn a crust. Well. She wasn't that down on her luck, not yet. She had some way to go before she sank to those levels of depravity.

Then Victor – strong, reliable, her saviour since the start – had said her name and she'd retraced her steps in search of him. Then she'd seen *her*. The woman had approached Victor with obvious pleasure, and he'd greeted her with the same. Miss Frost, he'd addressed her as. Suzannah Frost, whom he'd spoken of only that morning.

Sticking to the shadows out of sight, Phoebe had looked on in a haze of confusion, struggled to make sense of it still. For she'd recognised the woman, too. Only she knew her as the flame-haired piece who kept rather less civilised company with one Mr Warwick Yewdale.

She'd held her breath when Suzannah had put the invitation of going for tea to Victor. Crossing her fingers, she'd waited for him to turn her down and resume his searching, prayed he'd choose her. But no. He'd agreed, and the two had left together arm in arm.

The pain of betrayal had seared through her breast like a blade. Had he been aware she was there, watching, would it have altered his decision? She didn't know. Should she have made herself known? Possibly. But something had made her hold back, hadn't it? What? Perhaps she needed to see with her own eyes where his loyalties lay, was that it? Whom he'd pick whilst under no duress? And he had. He had.

Had everyone been justified in their suspicions about the pair after all? Was there more to the couple's relationship than she'd been led to believe? Was Victor hopelessly under the beautiful vixen's spell?

The long and lonely night ahead stretched in front of her like a bad dream on a loop.

Pulling her shawl tightly around herself, Phoebe drew her knees up to her chest and closed her eyes.

Chapter 7

VICTOR CHEWED THE hunk of bread without tasting it. Leaning against the wall by the window, his eyes flicked continually to the clock and back outside to the street.

He'd failed to locate her.

He'd scoured every inch of the town's centre throughout the night, had reluctantly returned home only an hour before, parched and fit to drop. A few more minutes of rest and he'd set back out once more.

Slipping his hand into his trouser pocket and fingering her money, he shook his head and sighed. Where was she? What kind of hellish night had she endured out there without a penny to her name? Had she slept; if so, where? No lodging-house keeper would have taken her in without the means to pay, no matter her desperation; this he knew without doubt. Profit was king, and charity came a very firm second. Was she safe? *Please let her be safe.* Damn and blast it, this was all his fault.

He swung away from the wall to pace the rug in front of the fire. *Should harm have come to her* . . . The prospect made his breath quicken, whilst a hundred and one horrors that could have befallen her swam dizzyingly through his mind. He felt a definite sense of duty towards her. He cared, probably more than she knew, certainly more than he'd as yet let on. If something had happened . . . He'd never forgive himself.

Heading for the hall, he shrugged on his jacket and reached for his hat. Then he nodded determinedly and opened the front door – and drew in a sharp breath of surprise and utter relief to find Phoebe standing on the step, arm raised, preparing to knock. 'Miss Parsons . . .'

'Mr Hayes.'

'Oh, lass, you look terrible. Come, come.' He ushered her inside. 'The fire, there. Take a seat whilst I brew some tea.'

Phoebe perched on the edge of a chair and he hurried to put the kettle on the heat. She looked frozen to the marrow, with dark circles beneath her eyes, and her clothing was dishevelled. Sitting on his heels in front of her, he smoothed back tendrils of hair which had escaped their pins and were falling across her face. 'I looked everywhere . . . Where have you been?'

'Around.' She shrugged. 'There is no need to concern yourself over me. I'm perfectly all right.'

'Well, of course there is, I—'

'May I please have my money, Mr Hayes?'

Her demeanour and tone were new to him; it was like a stranger sitting before him. Rising slowly, his brow knotting in a frown, he nodded. 'Yes, of course.'

The moment the hundred pounds was in her bunched fist, Phoebe stood abruptly. Not quite meeting his eye, she murmured a thank you. Then she inclined her head and skirted past him to the door.

'Wait!'

Though she paused, she didn't turn. Victor crossed the room and halted behind her.

'Miss Parsons. Phoebe . . .'

'Goodbye, Mr Hayes.'

117

'But why?' he asked. 'Kate's gone. For good, this time. Yesterday . . . I shouldn't have let you leave as I did, I . . . I'm sorry. Stay. I want you to. Please.'

'It would never work,' she rasped.

'Phoebe. Look at me.'

'I must go.'

Victor turned her around by her shoulders. Tears glistened on her lashes; the sight constricted his heart. He would have liked to have taken her in his arms and reassured her she didn't have to leave, that she had a home here if she wanted it. But he didn't. He couldn't, for he had no right to do that and knew not how she'd react to him crossing that boundary. Instead, he sighed. Then he stepped back and nodded. She had to make the choice for herself. He couldn't decide for her.

He waited, realising he was holding his breath, noting with growing surprise what this meant to him, how much he wanted her to remain here. When her shoulders sagged and she lowered her head, her face crumpling, he released air slowly. *Thank God.*

'You'll stay?'

'I'll stay.'

He smiled.

'Thank you.'

'Sit down, warm yourself,' he told her. 'I'll see to that tea.'

A little later, lying back in the bath behind the curtain, the steam from the hot water performing a swirling dance around her grateful body, Phoebe heaved a long breath. She'd had no other alternative but to seek Victor out, had needed her money. The terrible night she'd spent huddled in a refuse-littered backyard had been one of the worst experiences of her life; the prospect of

118

suffering another night like that had been enough to silence her vow that she wouldn't return. Yet she'd gone further than that – she'd stayed. Why?

She sighed again. Was she making a mistake? Would it really be better to put the past days – and the people she'd inadvertently come into contact with during that time – behind her? Victor, his wife. Suzannah Frost. Though Kate was gone, what of the other woman? Phoebe wanted no dealings with her, wanted part in nothing associated with Warwick Yewdale. Besides, there was something about the red-haired female she just didn't trust, however much Victor seemed to hold her in high regard. What, she couldn't put her finger on, but it was there all the same and Phoebe was unable to shake the instinct.

Would remaining in Victor's life mean seeing more of Suzannah? She feared so. She'd debated telling him about their previous encounters but hadn't. The first was too shocking to relate, and the second . . . Well. She couldn't be sure that Suzannah had been watching Warwick's assault on her and had done nothing to intervene, could she? Not with absolute certainty. Nor could she prove that Suzannah had somehow orchestrated how the meeting had gone, as she now even more strongly suspected.

Her encountering Warwick as she had on the barren hillside instead of him awaiting her return visit in the relative safety of his home was beginning to seem somehow planned, the more she mulled it over. It was almost as if Suzannah had wanted Phoebe hurt; but why? None of it made sense. And if she couldn't understand it, how could she expect Victor to? No. Best she kept this to herself.

There was one thing, however, that she didn't hold

back on, and that was her ordeal at Betsy's lodging house. Victor was horrified.

'You're certain that nothing . . . that no one made you do . . . anything?' he insisted on knowing, the meal Phoebe had cooked for them after her bath now forgotten.

'No, no. I was away from there before anything could occur. I'm fine, really. It just came as a bit of a shock.'

'I should never have let you leave here yesterday.'

'I couldn't very well have remained, Mr Hayes, could I? Your wife was, naturally, upset seeing us two walking towards her hand in hand—' Flushing at the memory of her impulsiveness, she paused to glance away. 'My staying would only have worsened the situation.'

'I'm glad you came back,' he told her. 'I was worried. I looked for you throughout the night – and oh,' he added, reaching for his fork, 'I had a chance meeting with Miss Frost at one point.'

Phoebe turned her own attention back to her food. 'Oh?' she asked quietly.

'Quite out of the blue.'

'She's well?'

'Yes. Though lonely, I suspect. I took a few minutes out from my search to have a cup of tea with her and to thaw myself out.'

Swallowing a piece of potato without tasting it, Phoebe said nothing to this, though self-reproach had begun to set in – Victor must be exhausted from tramping the streets, and temperatures last night had been cruel . . . The fact he'd bothered enough to want to find her at all said a lot about him; so what if he'd taken a break to have a hot drink, whether that was with Suzannah or not? What he did and with whom was none of her business. She'd been being churlish, not to mention self-ish, in the extreme. Realisation brought another blush. *I'm sorry.*

'Miss Frost shared my concerns when I told her what I was doing. She insisted on helping me look for you.'

Phoebe flicked up her gaze with a surprised frown. 'She did?'

'After the best part of an hour, she was blue with cold; I insisted I'd continue on alone, despite her protests. She'll be both pleased and relieved to hear you're safely back.'

'Did you mention my name to her?'

'Erm . . .' Victor thought for a moment then shook his head. 'I don't believe I did, no. I just said I was looking for a friend. Is that a problem?'

'No, no problem.'

There was no ulterior motive. Suzannah hadn't known she was searching for her. She'd willingly given up her time for what was in effect a complete stranger. That wasn't the action of someone capable of having ill intent in their heart, surely? She could only have done such a thing through sheer goodness. Had she got the woman all wrong after all? Phoebe bit her lip. It certainly sounded so, now, in light of this. What was wrong with her judgement of late? Why was she seeing the worst in others, finding badness in people that was neither there nor fair? Her shame intensified.

'Are you all right?'

'Hm?' Pulled from the guilty thoughts, she nodded. 'Yes, sorry, I was just thinking . . . Thank you,' she murmured earnestly. 'I'm grateful to you. And to Miss Frost also. Really I am.'

'What say we put it behind us and instead start looking to the future?' There was a definite twinkle in his eye. 'You see, I might not have had luck locating you last night, however I *did* find something.'

In spite of herself, her curiosity was piqued. She tilted her head inquisitively. 'You did?'

'Oh yes.'

'What was it, Mr Hayes?'

Victor smiled. He left the table and disappeared into the hall. Returning moments later, he'd donned his jacket and hat. He held out her shawl to her.

'We're going out?' she asked, puzzled.

'We are.'

Her mouth stretched to match his as she wrapped the garment around herself. 'But where are we going?'

'You'll see.'

See, she did. Phoebe gazed around in wonderment.

'Well?'

'It's perfect. Just *perfect*.'

'So then you haven't changed your mind about our venture? I thought, perhaps, after you left . . .'

'No, oh no. Oh, Mr Hayes!'

The tavern boasted an ornate tiled frontage, double bow windows and a corner-positioned entranceway reached by two narrow steps. Yet it was its location – nestled in the heart of the district's knot of streets above the bridge, in mere spitting distance of where Phoebe had been born and raised – that called out to her. Memories of her long-departed family swarmed her mind and heart like a warm mist, bringing tears of loss but also comfort. She nodded. She'd be happy here, she knew, for the place was in her very blood. She belonged.

'It's like I've come home.'

He smiled. 'I hoped you'd say that. The thing is, when a constable joins the force, the division he is allocated to

122

work must be different to the one in which he resides. That way, he has no connections with the locals and can act totally impartially. I was on the Ardwick division and, though I'm no longer with the police, people around that end will recognise my face, should I stray too near. Nor would the lawless amongst their number be pleased about the fact. I knew, therefore, that the opposite direction would be a wiser choice in which to set up business. That you have ties with this area fits in all the more. I want you to feel comfortable; here, I believe, you will. It's ideal.'

'Oh, it is.' She could have hugged him, so touched was she at his thoughtfulness.

Victor motioned to the left-hand window, in which was affixed an official-looking sale notice. 'You see, they're advertising for a new owner,' he said in excitement, and Phoebe shared his enthusiasm. 'Tavern – to be sold,' he read out, 'with immediate possession. For many years held by Mr Fredrick Fennel. Premises boasts an extensive business in the beer and spirit trade.'

'That I can believe; it's a very populous neighbourhood, after all,' Phoebe pointed out.

Nodding, he went on: 'Consists of licences, fixtures, stock and household furniture. Brewhouse attached, replete with every utensil requisite for brewing.'

'Can you brew?'

He nodded. 'I used to assist my grandfather.'

'Me too, at working the malt,' she said. 'Between us, we'll have it covered.'

'For inspection of an inventory,' Victor went on, turning back to the notice, 'and for further particulars, apply on the premises or to Messrs A. and S. Brownlow, solicitors, 38 York Street, Manchester.'

'Will it go to auction?'

'Most probably.'

'Shall we take a look inside?' she asked with definite impatience and a grin that refused to be contained.

'I don't see why not.'

Phoebe pushed at the door – it didn't budge. She turned to Victor questioningly. 'Locked?'

'Hm.' He seemed equally miffed. Victuallers never shut shop if they could help it. 'We could try the Misters Brownlow first, instead?' he suggested, scanning the notice one more time for the address. 'We'll call back to the tavern on our return; perhaps the place will be open then.'

Minds made up, they set off through the grey streets for the solicitors' offices.

They were discussing their plans for the business when, suddenly, Victor stopped dead in his tracks.

'Mr Hayes?' asked Phoebe, frowning, then gasped as he pushed past her and launched himself into the road's busy traffic. 'Mr Hayes!'

She could only watch, frozen in horror, as he made a grab for what appeared to be a dog heading beneath a laden cart's wheels. He snatched it up in his two arms, turned and dived back towards the pavement and safety, drivers' angry shouts following him on his way. The duo hit the flagstones, rolled several times and landed at Phoebe's feet in a panting ball. With a cry, she dropped to her knees.

'My God, are you all right? Just what were you— Oh!' she exclaimed as Victor released his hold on the rescued party and she saw it wasn't an animal at all but a dark-haired toddler.

'I spotted the little mite skittering out into the road,' said Victor breathlessly. 'God only knows what would have befallen him if I hadn't – a trampled head, no doubt. Where the hell is his mother?'

Whilst gathering bystanders, alerted by the hullaba-loo, clapped and cheered, Phoebe and Victor checked the whimpering child over. Mercifully, he appeared to have escaped his ordeal unscathed.

Phoebe picked him up and rocked him soothingly. Glancing around, she caught sight of a young woman hurrying in their direction, tears streaming down a face wreathed in terror. 'I believe this may be her, Mr Hayes,' she told him, nodding ahead, and he rose from the ground to stand beside her.

'My baby! Oh, my good God! Is he injured? Pass him to me, please!' the woman howled, grasping the lad from Phoebe and crushing him to her bosom, which heaved with sobs. 'Oh, you naughty, naughty boy! I'm sorry, my love, so sorry,' she immediately followed the chastisement up, raining kisses on her son's hair and dis-solving into tears. 'It's all my fault; I should never have taken my eyes off you! I'd never have forgiven myself if you'd got yourself killed, I wouldn't, truly!'

'But he didn't, so no harm done,' Victor broke through her lamentation with an understanding smile. 'Don't torment yourself so. These things happen.'

The woman hiccupped and sniffed. 'I was browsing the material hanging outside the draper's across the way. I turned my back for just a second and . . . You saved his life. How can I ever repay you?'

'If a man can't extend the hand of help to a fellow crea-ture in need, without expecting something in return, then the world's gone mad. You owe me nothing, Mrs . . . ?'

'Fennel,' she offered with a watery smile. 'Thank you. *Thank* you.'

'Let us walk you home, Mrs Fennel,' Phoebe said, tak-ing her elbow. 'You've had quite a shock.'

Nodding, the woman motioned ahead and led the way.

When minutes later she drew to a halt, saying, 'Here we are,' Phoebe and Victor looked to each other in surprise.

'This is where you live?' he asked, indicating with his chin the tavern they had recently left.

'Yes; though not for very much longer, with any luck.'

Before he or Phoebe could question this statement, she banged on the door. Almost immediately the scrape of the bolt being drawn back sounded – she pushed past the man who had answered her summons and stormed inside. He followed, and after a few moments Phoebe and Victor did likewise.

'See that good gentleman there?' the woman announced to the man, who was clearly her husband, throwing a thumb towards Victor. 'Mr . . . Mr . . .'

'Hayes,' Victor offered, looking decidedly uncomfortable.

'Mr *Hayes* has just rescued our son from certain destruction!'

The tall, thin man, some years older than his wife, opened his eyes wide. 'What?'

'You heard me. Now I'm putting my foot down here and now, Tim, and I'm telling you I want out of this town immediately! I hated the place the moment we stepped in it. I said it was a grimy, dangerous hole; didn't I say? Well, I won't remain here to see our one and only child ravaged by death's jaws. I'll not; no, no! Find a buyer for this place – today! – or I'm returning to Bolton town without you. And I'll be taking our son with me. Do you hear? Well, do you?'

The henpecked Tim paled at the threat. Eyes contrite, he opened his mouth to placate his fuming wife but didn't get the chance:

'We were here just a short while ago for that very purpose!' Phoebe, unable to stop herself, blurted out.

'You were here?' jumped in Mrs Fennel. 'You want to take this place off our hands?'

'That's right.' Victor nodded his agreement. 'We do.'

'Well, then!' The woman's demeanour changed instantly. She rushed forward to grasp her husband's hand. 'Did you hear that, Tim? We have a buyer. That settles it – oh, we can *finally* go home!'

'But my dear . . . we can't just accept the first offer to walk in off the street. You see, it doesn't work like that.'

'Tim—'

'The tavern is going to auction, remember? There's more chance of making a higher profit on it that way.'

'*Tim*—'

'Not long now,' he went on, seemingly oblivious to the flaring of her nostrils and the narrowing of her gaze. 'Just a few more weeks – perhaps a month – and the tavern and Manchester will all be behind us—'

'Tim!' she finally exploded.

'Yes, dear?'

'We. Are. Selling. We're *selling*! Today!'

The silence hung between them, thick as soup. Then, in a calming tone:

'I can assure you, Mr Fennel – *Fennel*, of course!' Victor exclaimed as an aside, nodding to the woman still clutching her child. 'I should have recognised the name when you introduced yourself earlier as being the same as that on the sale notice.'

'Fredrick Fennel was my uncle-in-law,' she explained. 'He opened this place in the early twenties; it's never passed through anyone else's hands. Sadly, he's newly deceased and the inheritor – his nephew, my husband here – has no desire for it, and nor do I. And so we're selling. I couldn't dwell here, oh no,' she continued, shaking her head in sheer horror at the prospect. 'We reside in a pretty spot called Breightmet in nearby Bolton town, surrounded by fields and meadows as far as the eye can see. Nothing but peace and beauty and fine, wholesome air. Give up all that? For this smelly, dull and colourless place? Be trapped in a nightmare of fog and filth and never-ending brick? Oh no. No, thank you.'

Though Victor's mouth had tightened somewhat – like Phoebe, he was affronted by the slur on his home; though Mrs Fennel either failed to notice or didn't care – he nodded amicably. It wouldn't do at this point to lose favour and scupper their chances with the one wielding all the power. Whatever silent *Mr* Fennel's opinion was on the whole matter was anyone's guess.

'Anyway . . .' Victor said, shaking his head as though to bring his mind back to the present. 'As I was saying. I can assure you that if you agree to go ahead with a private deal, with us, then quick sale or no, we're more than willing to offer you a decent sum.'

Tim glanced from Victor to his wife, who pursed her lips warningly, then back again quickly. 'How decent?' he asked.

'Name your price.'

'Well . . . It *is* an old-established tavern. It's also in a prime location here between Manchester and neighbouring Salford. Besides, businesses such as this will always do well within the labouring quarters. The lower classes certainly like their tipple. Yes, a very eligible situation for carrying on the wine, spirit and beer trade. Definitely a valuable investment. You'd make a small fortune in a short time—'

'How much?' Victor pressed.

'According to the books, the place is currently doing considerable trade. Add to that the vault and the house's contents and fixtures . . .' Looking around the attractive

space, he scratched his balding pate. 'Capital spirit foun-
tain with nine taps, stop taps and piping, puncheons
and troughs . . . plain and cut decanters, tumblers, tankards, dram and wine glasses . . . the mahogany card,
Pembroke and snap tables, drinking tables and all of the
seating . . .

'Then there's the stock,' he went on. 'A quantity of
foreign and British spirits: gin, rum, brandy, whisky . . .
ale and porter, wines and cordials . . . And not forgetting the spacious stone-arched cellaring with brewhouse
below, complete with copper pan and pump, numerous
thirty-six- and eighteen-gallon barrels, cooler, mash tub
and mash staff, hop sieve and malt hopper, stillages,
thermometer . . . As for the living quarters above—'

'So then?' Victor interjected, and Phoebe worried he
was close to losing his patience with the man's incessant,
nasal chatter, as had his wife. She stepped forward.

'I believe what Mr Hayes is trying to say, Mr Fennel, is
that we may as well know how much you want for the
place before details are gone over in case we're unable
to reach the price. It will save us all much time and
embarrassment, I'm sure you'll agree.'

Victor uttered agreement, followed by an exasper-
ated Mrs Fennel.

Finally, Tim nodded. 'Two hundred and fifty pounds.'

Phoebe almost choked on a gasp. She looked to Victor, her eyes creased in disappointment – they could
never afford that – but his gaze remained locked on the
other man. Then, to her astonishment:

'Two twenty,' Victor murmured.

'Two hundred.'

They all turned to Mrs Fennel in surprise.

'Two hundred,' she repeated to her husband, her
tone brooking no argument. 'Yes, worth more than that

this place might be, but he saved our son's life, Tim. On *that*, we cannot put a price. You were wrong, Mr Hayes – we do owe you,' she added, turning to Victor with a gentle smile. 'We owe you a great deal. Call this compensation. Please?'

'So, Mr Hayes.' Tim's expression now matched his wife's. He held out a hand. 'Two hundred. Do we have a deal?'

Victor looked to Phoebe, who gazed back expectantly. He gave her the softest of winks, which spoke of trust and reassurance and of dreams being made, before turning back to the couple. He clasped Tim's hand between both of his. 'Yes. Yes, we have a deal.'

'It's been nice doing business with you, Mr Hayes. I'll inform my solicitor of the development and have him draw up the necessary papers and go through the deeds. I'll meet you at his office, say . . . Friday morning at nine?'

'Friday morning it is.'

'Did that really just happen?' Phoebe asked dazedly moments later, drawing Victor aside. 'It's . . . ours, Mr Hayes?'

'It's ours.'

'We really have the funds between us?'

His grin seemed rooted to his face. 'I have just over a hundred pounds in savings. The excess, once we've gone half and half on the sale, shall go towards extra stock – that which Mr Fennel listed won't last long – and should keep us going until the money starts coming in.'

She smiled through her tears. 'Half and half.'

'Split straight down the middle.'

'Equal partners,' she murmured, sighing happily when he reached for her hand and squeezed. 'Oh, Mr Hayes . . .'

'Here's to us, Phoebe, and a brand-new start.'

'So then, you two,' Tim called to them, cutting through their private talk. 'You've seen the main drinking area; how about a tour of the rest of the place?'

'Oh yes, please, we'd love to.'

'Well, like I was saying earlier,' he began, getting back into his stride, 'the living quarters above boast capital four-post mahogany beds in feather and flock, washstands and dressing tables, painted wardrobes . . .'

Casting each other a smile, Phoebe and Victor followed him across the tavern towards the narrow stairway.

That evening, they were relaxing by the fire discussing their plans for the premises – Victor resting his feet on the hearthstone, Phoebe with her legs tucked beneath herself and a blanket around her shoulders – when he brought up the subject of the rooms above the tavern.

'I've been thinking, the living quarters that come with it . . .'

'Me, too,' she said, nodding. He'd already expressed his desire for her to stop on at his home here; disliking the prospect of dwelling alone she'd readily agreed, and to hell with possible gossip. 'There is a perfectly adequate sitting room and kitchen, plus two good-sized bedrooms up there. We could rent them out, don't you think? It would add nicely to our profits.'

'Exactly. And I have just the person in mind.'

'Oh? Who?'

'Miss Frost.'

Phoebe's smile slipped. Despite the more recent favourable conclusion she'd come to regarding Suzannah, thoughts of her being so closely entwined with them and the business brought a roll of displeasure to her insides. 'She's in *need* of fresh lodgings?' she asked, hoping he'd say no.

'Yes. She told me so over tea last night. Her current rooms are in a terrible state, damp and verminous, and she's desperate to be out. It pains me to know she's suffering such conditions. It's no way to live, is it? In any case, it's better that someone sleeps on the premises; folk will be less likely to think of breaking into the place than if it were lying empty of a night. You don't have any objections, do you?'

What choice had she? She had no plausible excuse to offer. She shook her head.

'That's settled then.' Victor nodded, smiled. 'I'll call on her soon and put to her our offer. I'm sure she'll be only too pleased to accept.'

Your offer, Phoebe corrected him silently, knowing that Suzannah was sure to jump at the chance all right. And the extraordinary day lost a little of its sparkle.

Chapter 8

'WOULD YOU CARE to do the honours, Miss Parsons?'

'Really?'

'Go on, I insist.'

Phoebe took the key that Victor held out to her. The November morning carried a snappy wind but she barely noticed, the excited fervour coursing through her veins warming her more than any summer sun could.

This marked their first day in their new venture; neither had slept a wink the previous night. They had gone over every possible detail and, now, they were more impatient than anxious to get started and about what today would hold.

She paused to flash her partner a bright grin. Then she took a deep breath and unlocked the tavern door.

'Ready?' asked Victor later, eyes shining, when everything was set.

'Ready!'

Hearts banging, they fixed their gazes on the door and waited. And waited. And waited some more.

Phoebe grew increasingly worried. She was just about to question Victor on their lack of custom when the door swung wide and a man's head appeared. She almost cried out in delight. It was really happening!

'Youse open, then?'

'Good morning, sir,' Victor called across in greeting. 'We are indeed.'

Smiling, the punter entered. 'I weren't sure it would be, thought I'd call in on the off-chance. Place has been bolted up since owd Fredrick passed.'

'His nephew, who inherited it, wasn't much interested in the trade.'

'So youse have bought the place, then?'

'That's right.' Victor held out a hand. 'Mr Hayes – Victor. And this is Miss Phoebe Parsons.'

'Big Red,' the man responded in his booming, jocular voice, pumping Victor's hand and flashing Phoebe a wink. 'Pleased to meet youse.'

'What can we get you, Mr . . . Big Red?' she asked.

'Porter, lass, ta.'

As Victor went to fulfil the request at the barrel nearby, Phoebe could have burst with happiness. Their first customer! And what a friendly sort the carrot-haired, bushy-bearded giant seemed. They couldn't have wished for a more agreeable welcome.

'Eeh, that hits the spot,' Big Red announced, taking a deep draught of the dark drink. He released a loud burp and wiped his wet whiskers with the back of his hand. 'A finer quality by far than that on offer at Col Baines's across the way. Don't know how he gets away with selling the ditchwater he reckons passes as ale.'

'Col Baines?'

'Aye.' Big Red flicked his chin in the general direction of the street. 'Runs that little beerhouse on t' corner over t' road.'

Victor nodded. 'I've noticed that premises.'

'Aye, and you'd do *well* to only look, an' all, let me tell thee. *I* made the mistake of doing more than that and actually sampled the place. That inferior sup of his had me chained to the privy for nigh on three days – rotted my insides summat chronic, it did!'

'It's a widespread problem, all right. I don't know why this government won't just scrap that daft Act it dreamed up and have done with it. It's clear to everyone that it has failed its main objective.'

Big Red nodded agreement. 'You're right there, lad. It'll be a gradely day when we see the back of swindling buggers like that one across yonder. Mind, I can't imagine it occurring any time soon, can you?'

'No, sadly.'

'Mr Hayes and I were adamant when deciding on this new venture of ours that it would be a fully licensed place or nothing,' Phoebe joined in. 'People are inclined to take a premises seriously – and treat it with that bit more respect – when they know it's traditionally approved by the local justices.'

'You've got that right, lass; I'm one of them there folk you speak of. Mind, there's plenty more don't care a fig for that, are content to fill their bellies with *any* class of ale so long as they don't have to dig too deep in their pockets. Drink owt, some will, and worry about the gut-rot the morrow!'

She and Victor shared a look, knowing he was right. They just had to pray that others held the same level of standards as Big Red; otherwise, they had made a disastrous mistake going into this trade with everything they had.

Passed some twelve years previously, the Beerhouse Act had been an attempt at reducing what those in power believed to be a serious problem with drunkenness amongst the lower classes. They felt that cheap strong spirits were leading to the public's ruination and so, in a somewhat blinkered approach, the government had decided on a bold new aim: to flood the working people's districts with weaker beer and cider instead.

It was widely accepted that beer was harmless – healthy even, brewed and purified as it was of deadly disease, given the state of the unsafe drinking water. Even children regularly partook of small beer, a lower-alcohol-content version. Surely then, the government reasoned, this course of action would prove successful?

And so, a justices' licence was no longer needed. With a one-off two-guinea payment to the local excise officer, any rate-paying householder in the land could now apply to brew and sell beer. Coupled with the scrapping of the beer tax, such widespread availability would lead to a lowering in ale prices, which in turn would attract the poorer masses to this cheaper alcoholic option, thus flushing out spirit consumption. Better they turned their backs on the gin palaces in favour of the beer-houses' offering, right? Or so the logic went.

Rather, with much easier accessibility to alcohol, drunkenness was as bad as ever. So simple was it to gain permission, so few were the restrictions and so lucrative was the trade, that beerhouse numbers exploded astronomically – and were rising still. To have previously managed some mode of public house wasn't even a requirement. Retailers of every description, from cobblers to bakers to clockmakers, began doubling as beer sellers, plying ale alongside their usual wares to boost income.

A great many others – Col Baines amongst them it would appear, by the outward look of his place – simply turned their dwellings into drinking dens, which were barely distinguishable from customers' own homes. Conditions and consequences meant little. Behind those doors, revellers could and did do as they pleased. So long as the money continued to flow, so too did the drink – and this it certainly did, with opening times now extended from fifteen to eighteen hours a day.

Those who had blasted the old problem of a spirit-glugging populace were once again voicing their displeasure, now over the excessive consumption of ale. The dilemma was a scourge of the town. Drunkenness led to crime, and the common beerhouses attracted every type of undesirable. Finding it increasingly difficult to keep a rein on the people, the police and clergy, aided by the Temperance Society, pressed on at the authorities for stricter magisterial and licensing controls, to no avail. Premises continued to choke the slums in ever increasing numbers. The current situation, so it seemed, was here to stay.

'We've decided, Miss Parsons and I, not to take full advantage of the foolishly excessive trading hours,' Victor told Big Red now. 'Noon 'til 10 p.m. will be our maxim.'

'A controlled and respectable house – that's what I like to hear,' the man agreed. Then his mouth stretched in a grin and he shook his head. 'Mind you, you'll have a fair row on your hands from some of the blokes hereabouts. Swear by their sup of porter or two afore work, they do. Sets them up for the day, they reckons.'

'Then they shall just have to suffer Col Baines's offerings, won't they?' responded Victor, quietly but firmly. 'A common practice it may be, but I won't promote nor actively encourage drunkenness, not on my premises.'

A rumble of laughter rolled through the large man's stomach and escaped on a bellow to echo around the room. 'Aye, well, you're the boss. Ah!' he cried in the next breath as the door was tentatively pushed open

137

and the weary faces of several men appeared. 'It's my pals. Come in, lads, come in.'

It was evident from their appearance that they were employed at one of the many nearby cotton mills that dotted the riverside. White spores clung to their hair and rough clothing, as though they had been caught in a violent snowstorm. Phoebe and Victor smiled a welcome.

'What can we get you fellows?'

Served and seated with Big Red at the rectangular table minutes later, their friend proceeded to introduce them. He pointed first to Phoebe and Victor, informing the men, 'These here are the new proprietors, Victor Hayes and Phoebe Parsons. Victor, Phoebe, these are brothers Seth and Elias Dodd,' he said, indicating the two tall, dark-haired young males to his left. 'Joe Stone,' he continued, referring to the next man along. 'And last but not least' – he flicked his hairy chin to the final one: a squat, downtrodden-looking individual in his middle years – 'King Henry.'

Phoebe and Victor shared a grin, the latter asking, 'Why King Henry, then? Have you a penchant for having many wives?'

'Have I bloody hell – the one wench I'm lumbered with is more than enough! Nay, they calls me King Henry 'cause my name's Henry King,' the man answered, rolling his eyes at his chuckling friends. 'Think themselves clever, they do. Daft buggers they are, these lot.'

During the next few hours, a steady stream of customers, thirsty after a day's toil, chanced upon the tavern. Further millhands, hawkers and market traders, and foundrymen who could sup the Irk dry owing to the heat of their work, ensured that the barrels were hardly left still for a moment and kept Victor and Phoebe rushed off their feet.

Here, surrounded by a multitude of works employing hundreds of regular labourers, they had been confident that the business could be a success. However, as the night wore on, proceedings surpassed even their expectations – they had done a roaring trade. Finally, shattered but happy, Phoebe alerted Victor's attention to the clock; nodding, he called time.

'Right then, gentlemen, let's be having you!'

Downing their drinks, and amongst many friendly slaps on the back for Victor and touching of their caps to Phoebe, the customers expressed their gladness at them taking over the place and their best wishes for the pair's future here, and drifted off home. When the last few stragglers had gone, a smiling Phoebe flopped into a seat and heaved a long sigh.

Victor eased himself down beside her. 'What a day!'

'What a welcome!' she added.

'Thank you.'

Phoebe turned her head to face him. 'What for?'

'This. Everything.'

Her tone was just as soft. 'And the same to you.'

They stared at one another through the rose-gold light of the open fire. When she saw his hand move to hers resting on the table, she reached across to meet his touch. Their fingers entwined for the briefest moment, then he stood suddenly, breaking the contact.

'Well, we'd best be heading for home.'

'Yes. Yes, I suppose we must,' she said, rising reluctantly. Glancing around, she pulled a face. 'What about the mess?'

'Leave it, we'll sort everything out tomorrow.'

Nodding gratefully, she went to collect her shawl from out back whilst Victor gathered the day's takings. She was wrapping it around her shoulders when his voice reached her:

'Oh, in fact, would you mind clearing up in here in the morning by yourself?'

'Of course not, but why?'

'I said I'd help Miss Frost across with her belongings first thing.'

Phoebe's hands stilled on the garment, heart sinking. Glad of her back to him, she closed her eyes.

'You haven't forgotten she's moving in tomorrow?' he pressed, on her lack of response.

As if *that* could have slipped her memory. The thought had dominated her mind for most of the day. 'No, Mr Hayes. I haven't forgotten.'

The tavern locked and secured, they set off for home through the deserted dark. And again, Phoebe was bitterly aware that another happy day was marred for her thanks to Miss Suzannah Frost.

The fire she'd built upon her arrival was chasing the cold away nicely. Hands on hips, Phoebe turned her attention to the stained tables and floor and the dirty glasses. Then, avoiding the clock, and Victor and Suzannah's impending arrival, she nodded determinedly and got started with the cleaning.

Sometime later, the place was tidied and swept and, having made herself a pot of tea, she was on her second cup, but still there was no sign of them. Frowning, she crossed to the window.

Besides the odd beshawled woman passing by, out making purchases, the narrow street was empty. Like the men, children were away at work. Infants too young for toil would wisely be by their meagre fires; it was far too cold for outdoor play, inadequately clad against the elements as the poor slum dwellers were. Then a movement across the way caught her eye and she glanced in the direction of the beerhouse. A thickset man with curly brown hair was staring straight back from the doorway, arms folded.

Col Baines? she wondered. It must be. She inclined her head at him in a nod of greeting, but he didn't return it. Nor did his stony face alter when instead she tried a smile. Seconds later, he turned and went back inside his premises.

Unsure what to make of the incident, she was pondering on his behaviour when a noise beyond the tavern door sounded. Instantly, all thought scattered – *they're here*.

Victor, a canvas bag in his hand, entered first. Then there was Suzannah. Phoebe clasped her hands together in front of her to prevent any fidgeting; she felt oddly nervous seeing her.

'Miss Frost, this is Miss Parsons. Miss Parsons, Miss Frost.'

They exchanged pleasantries. However, though Phoebe had to drag hers to her mouth, Suzannah's didn't appear forced at all. Phoebe had wondered what the woman's reaction would be when they met again: surprise, horror even. This total indifference, she hadn't anticipated. If Suzannah did recognise her, then she was a fine actress – her face gave away no indication. But no, she couldn't fail to, she *had* to know. And yet . . .

'I really am pleased to meet thee, lass,' Suzannah gushed, her face breaking into a devastatingly beautiful smile. 'A friend of sweet Victor here is a friend of mine.'

Watching the way he looked down at Suzannah, seeing the pleasure that shone from his gaze, was too much for Phoebe; groaning, she held a hand to her brow.

'Miss Parsons? Are you all right?'

'Headache, I think,' she lied to him, adding, 'I might go home and have a short lie down before this afternoon's opening, if that's all right?'

'Yes, of course. Let me take Miss Frost's things upstairs and I'll walk you—'

'There's no need,' she interrupted quickly, anxious to be alone and collect her thoughts. 'Really, I'll be fine.'

'Hope the rest does thee good, lass,' Suzannah called out as she reached the door.

Mumbling a thank you over her shoulder, Phoebe escaped into the dull and breezy morning – but not before catching the unmistakeable glint of malice in Suzannah's cat-like stare.

Arriving at home, she made straight upstairs, where she threw herself on to the bed and pulled the coverings over her head. Her eyes felt gritty with tears, but she blinked them away furiously, wouldn't cry, refused to give that woman the satisfaction of seeing her puffy and red-faced later. For Phoebe was certain now. Suzannah remembered her, all right. How would that bode for her, for all of them?

Victor could see no wrong in her, it was plain. Would he scoff at anything Phoebe could tell him, anything that set Suzannah in an unfavourable light? Possibly – and this, she wouldn't bear. What she'd witnessed in Warwick Yewdale's library between the pair, her strongly renewed conviction that Suzannah planned her lover's assault upon her, the unshakeable sense that the woman just wasn't what she seemed, was calculating, perhaps even dangerous . . . would Victor consider a word of it? Did she really want to take the risk to find out?

The foundations for a fresh new beginning were in

place. Her painful past, the loss and struggle. The uncertainty, destitution, fear . . . all that had mercifully left her, was over with. She had a home, a business. Happiness, security . . . and she had Victor back. Their friendship had almost been ruined once through Suzannah's presence – she was adamant it wouldn't happen again.

Already, within mere minutes of that woman's arrival, here was she, running away. Well, that stopped right now. Never again would she do that. The first opportunity she had to get Suzannah alone, she'd have it out with her, would demand to know what she intended to do. If Suzannah planned on making trouble for her, she'd have no option but to tell all to Victor. Should that spell an end to their friendship, to everything she had and held dear, then so be it. If, however, the woman desired only to put what had passed behind them and never have it mentioned again, then she would agree. All Phoebe could do now was pray Suzannah made the right decision.

Suzannah's expression when Phoebe returned to the tavern soon afterwards showed clearly her surprise. She must have believed she'd got shot of her for the rest of the day, surmised Phoebe, painting on to her face a wide smile, determined to hold the upper hand from hereon in.

'Ah ha!' Victor came across to greet her. 'You're well now, Miss Parsons?'

'Much better, thank you,' she assured him before addressing Suzannah, saying with what she hoped was confidence, 'I'll take over now I'm back, Miss Frost.' She held out her hand for the bucket and cloth. 'I'm sure you have more important things to be getting along with.'

The woman opened and closed her mouth. 'I don't mind, honest—'

'I insist,' pressed Phoebe brightly, plucking the items from her hands and giving her attention to the window that Suzannah had been engaged in cleaning.

'Well, I'll go up and unpack my things,' she announced. 'Unless there's summat else I can be of use with . . . ?'

'No, thank you,' chirped Phoebe, without turning.

'You're sure you're all right, Miss Parsons?' asked Victor when Suzannah's footsteps had died away on the stairs.

'Never better,' she murmured, secretly marking off her first small victory in her mind.

Chapter 9

SUZANNAH REMAINED IN her rooms for the rest of the day. When evening was drawing around and there came a lull in the work, Phoebe took the opportunity to slip upstairs.

'Can I speak with you?'

Sitting up in the bed, Suzannah nodded. 'What about?'

'I'd have thought that was patently obvious, wouldn't you?'

The atmosphere immediately grew thick with tension. In the ensuing silence, Phoebe kept her nerve and gaze steady.

Eventually, a slow smile spread over Suzannah's face. 'You recognise me, then?'

'Well, of course I do!'

'And Victor? Does he know we've . . . met before?'

She shook her head.

Releasing a theatrical sigh, the woman folded her arms. 'So. You've landed on your feet, ain't yer?'

Phoebe ignored the jibe. 'Why are you here, Miss Frost? The real reason, I mean.'

'Victor asked me to come.'

'Ah yes, your inadequate rooms.' She raised an eyebrow. 'You might be able to fool him, but not me. Just what is it you're after?'

'What's it to you, like?'

'Mr Hayes is my friend—'

'Aye, and he were mine long afore you showed up, so just you keep your nose out of it.' Suzannah's normally beautiful face had twisted in ugly hostility. 'Victor wants to help me, allus has done. I ain't about to turn owt he can offer me down, am I?'

Suzannah was merely using him, taking advantage of his golden nature for what she could get. She *knew* it. Anger had her curling her lip and shaking her head. 'He sacrificed his career for you, you shameless—!'

'I meant not for that to happen! Victor's told me what went on, but . . . it weren't no fault of mine, none!'

'If you say so. Anyway, what about your other male friend?' she shot at her before she could stop herself. 'You know, the one you witnessed hurting me on the hillside and did nothing to help – encouraged him into it even, I suspect?' Suzannah's lack of a denial at this spoke volumes – Phoebe's anger mounted. 'Well, where is he, then? I don't see the high and mighty Warwick Yewdale doing much for you. What's wrong, Miss Frost? Got what he wanted and grown bored, has he?'

The woman looked as if she might strike her but regained her composure and smiled. 'Me and Warwick have summat special. The moment we clapped eyes on each other in the town one night, we clicked. Sparks flew.'

'Oh, for heavens' sake . . .'

'You'd never understand. Bet you've never even known a man's touch, have yer? Nay, thought not,' she added, smirking, when Phoebe reddened. 'And who can blame them, plain runt like you?'

'Rather that than a whore!' she fired back, immediately regretting being drawn into an argument; she refused to lower herself to the other woman's level. She closed her eyes and breathed deeply. 'Look. This isn't getting us anywhere. I'm an equal partner in this business, am going nowhere. Victor, God help him, wants you here so, for now, it seems you aren't leaving either. Therefore, we must try our hardest to rub along the best we can, for all our sakes.'

Suzannah was regarding her with guarded interest. 'Aye? How?'

'We forget what has passed. Victor needn't know our paths ever crossed before this day. It's the only way for a peaceful life.'

'More like you're frickened he'd not stand for you bad-mouthing me. That's it, in't it?' she crowed. 'He'd choose me over thee any day of the week, and you know it. Do owt for me, would Victor.' Her eyes creased slowly as curiosity replaced smugness. 'D'you love him?'

'He's my friend. I won't see him hurt.'

'I am fond of him in my own way,' Suzannah acknowledged. 'He's a kind man. Reliable, you know? Loyal, an' all, once he's taken to someone.'

'Like you, you mean?'

'And you.' Suzannah nodded. 'He were fair daft with worry when you did your disappearing act. I felt sorry for him, even helped him look.'

'So I heard. Will you answer me one question?'

'Go on.'

'Would you have bothered had you known it was me he was searching for?'

'Probably not, nay,' the woman admitted with a quiet laugh, and Phoebe couldn't help but smile.

'A last thing, Miss Frost.' All trace of amusement had left her now. '*Were* you in any way involved in Warwick Yewdale's actions that day he decided to take his horse to me?'

147

'One question, you said—'

'Tell me. I must know.'

Suzannah was silent for a long moment. Then she shook her head. 'Nay. Nay, I weren't.'

'Really?'

'Aye, really. I knew nowt about any of it until afterwards.' She shrugged. 'I wanted only to help.'

Phoebe wanted to believe her . . . Besides, what did all that matter now? It was finished, over with. She nodded. 'All right, I'll take your word for it. So,' she added, 'are we in agreement that we put all this behind us? For Mr Hayes's sake?' And at Suzannah's nod: 'Good. Now, I'd better return downstairs. He'll be wondering where I've got to.'

'Before you go . . .'

Midway to the door, Phoebe paused and turned. 'Yes?'

'Will you answer *me* one question?'

'If I can.'

'How did you do it?' Suzannah spread her arms wide. 'This place, finding the money for it. You were fair desperate for that reference, for fresh employment, were on the brink of ruin. How did you manage it?'

'Through the means of a brooch gifted to me by Warwick Yewdale's stepmother. I'd thought it to be worthless, but no. Mr Rakowski, a jeweller friend of Mr Hayes's, bought it.'

'Well, fancy that.' Suzannah gave her a smile. 'That were a turn of good fortune, eh, lass?'

'Yes. Now, I really must get back to the tavern.'

'Bye for now.'

Phoebe nodded and left the room. Outside, she paused for a minute and took some steadying breaths.

That had turned out better than she'd thought it

148

would. They had concluded their talk on almost friendly terms. More surprisingly still, she was glad. That the issue had been put to bed would, she was certain, make life easier for them all.

When she reached downstairs, she saw that the place had filled in her absence; flashing Victor an apologetic smile, she hurried to help him. Busy as she was with the thirsty punters, she didn't see Suzannah weaving her way through the throng until the last moment.

The woman drew her shawl over her head and slipped out of the tavern, but before Phoebe could wonder over her late-night departure, another customer claimed her attention and her curiosity was forgotten.

'I've been thinking,' said Victor later as they snatched a short break. 'What would you say to us serving food in here?'

'I'd say it's a good idea, Mr Hayes. But how would we manage with the extra workload? We're rushed off our feet as it is. If I'm to be busy in the kitchen—'

'It wasn't actually you I had in mind for the role.'

'Miss Frost?' she asked as realisation dawned. 'Employ her here at the tavern?'

'You're averse to the idea?'

'I . . . don't really know,' she answered honestly. 'Can she cook well? Will she even want the position?'

'Customers won't be expecting anything elaborate. I'm sure she's capable of producing simple fare. Bread with fish or ham, potato pies, that sort of thing. I'd very much like for you to give the matter thought, Miss Parsons,' he continued earnestly. 'This could be the making of Miss Frost. It would offer her security.' He lowered his tone. 'Respectability also. With our help, she'd have the chance to improve her life, to turn her back on how she currently earns a living for good.'

Remembering now that she'd seen Suzannah leaving earlier, Phoebe sighed. There was no doubt where the woman had sloped off to: to ply her trade on the mean streets out there. Better that Victor wasn't informed. He'd only worry himself over her welfare – more so now Suzannah was residing beneath this roof. 'You're right, of course,' she said. 'All right, Mr Hayes. Let's give Miss Frost a trial run, see how she gets on.'

His face spread in a smile. 'Excellent. Oh, back to the grindstone,' he added, motioning to the door as a group of males entered. He greeted them cordially. 'Yes, lads, what can I get you?'

A pock-faced youth pushed his way to the front. Chin tilted at a cocksure angle, he flicked his eyes to a barrel. 'And don't take all night about it.'

Phoebe was shocked at the blatant rudeness. A quick glance at Victor showed her he was more annoyed than surprised; his mouth had hardened and a muscle at his jaw twitched ominously. Nevertheless, he kept his tongue and fulfilled the request.

The lad drained half of the glass in one gulp. 'Ugh!' he exclaimed loudly with a grimace of disgust, bringing heads around in his direction. 'Tastes like sheep shit! I want my sodding brass back.'

'Now look here—'

'I *said* I want my brass back!' the customer repeated menacingly, thrusting his face into Victor's. 'Right, lads?'

The half dozen others behind him loomed in, snarling their agreement.

Afraid the situation was set to worsen, Phoebe touched Victor's arm, saying through the side of her mouth, 'Perhaps just do as they say, Mr Hayes . . .'

'No.' Victor stood his ground. 'No one is getting a refund. The beer is perfectly fine.'

The silence was deafening. Then Big Red's voice blared across the room: 'Get on out of it, Baines, and take your cronies with thee.' His friends, Joe Stone and King Henry, cheered their concurrence and he went on, 'If anyone's for flogging shitty ale, it's your owd man!'

'That's right. Leave the fella and lass be, you young buggers!' said a second customer, getting up from his seat.

'Aye, get gone. Doing a sound job are these new tavern-keepers,' called out yet another.

Eyes steely, the youth glared around. When one or two other men rose to their feet, faces grim with warning, he knew he was beaten. He laughed. 'Sodden bloody fools, the lot of youse. You'll sup owt, it seems. No one brews a better beer than Col Baines.' Then, to Victor, he barked, 'You ain't heard the last of this,' before swinging out of the tavern, his gang close behind.

Phoebe was quite overcome at the support from these rough, solid-gold-hearted strangers who were fast becoming friends. 'Thank you, all of you,' she said thickly. 'You helped to avert God alone knows what, there.'

'Ay, take no notice of that vicious swine,' Big Red told them. 'Takes after his owd man, all right, does he. Jealousy, that's what it is. Got used to the extra custom, Col did, when Fredrick Fennel passed and this place were shut up. He's losing it now you're here – and it ain't just down to the ale, neither. You're decent folk and you run a pleasant premises. Should you have any more bother from that quarter, you just let us know – right, fellas?' he added to the room, receiving a favourable response.

'I saw Col Baines this morning outside his beerhouse,' Phoebe said to Victor when the drama had died down and the customers had returned their attention to their drinking. 'He was just standing there, staring at the tavern and looking none too pleased. You don't think we'll have further trouble from them, do you, Mr Hayes?' she asked, seeking his reassurance – she was proud of his bravery just now in standing up to them. Not so much her: the beer seller's son had frightened her more than she cared to admit.

'No, I shouldn't think so,' he said after a long moment – nonetheless, his face was stiff with suppressed anger. 'Young lads bolshie with drink and sounding off, that's all it was. Don't worry yourself over it.'

Wanting to believe this, she was about to agree with him when the crashing of the door opening sounded, snatching away her response. Whipping around in dread, she fully expected to see Col Baines's son back for another fight. The sight of the figure she was met with instead brought her eyebrows together in dismay and a sigh to her lips. 'Oh, Miss Frost . . .'

Suzannah swayed on the spot, a slack grin on her face. Some of her hair had escaped its pins, was falling over her shoulders like ruby snakes, and her shawl and skirts were dishevelled. Spotting a table of men smiling at her, she staggered across and plonked herself down in the nearest lap. Laughing raucously, she flung her arms around the delighted fellow's neck.

Victor's face was wreathed in disappointment. He crossed the floor and touched her shoulder. 'Miss Frost—'

'Here he is, my Victor!'

'Come, let's get you upstairs.'

'Ooh, hark at him!' she told the men, winking. 'He wants his wicked way with me, I reckon.'

'Miss Frost, please.' A flush of mortification stained Victor's cheeks. 'Come with me and—'

'Come on, Miss Frost.' Phoebe, having arrived at

152

Victor's side, took the woman's elbow and helped her to stand. 'I'll brew some tea.'

Giggling and blowing kisses to the customers, Suzannah allowed Phoebe to lead her out. Victor shot Phoebe a grateful look; nodding, she shepherded her inebriated charge upstairs.

'Sit down here, that's right,' she instructed, easing the woman into a chair. 'Now, you just rest whilst I make that brew.'

'I'd prefer a brandy,' came back the slurred response.

'I think you've had quite enough of that, don't you? What on earth have you been up to?' she added, not unkindly, as she helped Suzannah remove her shawl and boots. 'Anything could have happened to you out there in this state.'

'And you'd have been bothered, would you?'

'Of course I would.' Phoebe meant it. She wouldn't wish harm on anyone, not even Suzannah Frost.

'Oh aye, that's right.' She gave her an exaggerated wink, tongue in cheek. 'We're bosom friends now, ain't we?'

'Well, I wouldn't go as far as that,' said Phoebe with a crooked smile.

Suzannah hooted with laughter. 'You're honest, I'll say that for thee. Aye, Miss bloody Perfect, that's thee, in't it? Well, not for very much longer,' she added on a mumble that seemed meant just for herself.

'What is that supposed to mean?'

'You'll see soon enough, my lass. There's a storm coming your way, aye. Make no mistake about that.'

Figuring it to be but drunken talk, Phoebe went to see to the tea with a roll of her eyes. 'Here, drink up,' she told the woman, helping her to hold the cup. 'Better?' she asked when it was drained.

'Nay, I . . . Oh, Lord!'

Understanding when Suzannah slapped a hand to her mouth, Phoebe rushed to fetch a bowl. Wincing as the woman rid her stomach of the strong spirits she'd consumed, Phoebe held back her hair with her free hand then patted her back.

White as tripe and shivering, Suzannah finally wiped her mouth and flopped back in her chair, closing her eyes. 'God, I feel rotten.'

'Let's get you into bed.'

Through bleary eyes she watched Phoebe plump her pillow and tuck the blankets around her. 'Why you doing this?' she whispered after a while. 'Why you being nice?'

'Common decency is all that I'm providing, Miss Frost.'

'You're . . . you're all right, you know.'

Seeing her bottom lip quivering, Phoebe sighed. A funny thing, was the effect of alcohol. It could leave one on top of the world one minute and in the next drowning in moroseness. 'Get some sleep,' she murmured.

'I mean it, you're all right. I've . . . so *stupid* . . . Lass, I—'

'Sshhh. Rest.'

Hiccupping back sorry sobs, Suzannah fell into a deep sleep. After a last look at her from the doorway, Phoebe made her way back downstairs.

Having called time, Victor was alone and clearing the tables. 'How is she?'

'Sleeping. Look, I think it's best I stay here with her tonight. She was sick just now and I wouldn't like her to be alone should it strike again. The state she's in, she may very well choke.'

Stopping what he was doing to release a long breath,

he turned to face her. His eyes were deep with helpless-
ness. 'Why does she do it to herself? Can't she see people
care, want her to be well? She's so bloody destructive.
It's almost as if . . . as if she feels compelled to harm
herself.'

In this moment, Phoebe now saw Victor's drive
behind his connection with the hapless female upstairs.
He wore a look that could only be described as paternal
worry. He looked on Suzannah as one would a daughter
almost, not a love interest. The realisation was like a
warm hug to her heart, though she couldn't fathom
exactly why.

'I simply want to help her.'

'I know.' Phoebe went to stand in front of him. Putting a hand on his arm, she pressed gently. 'I'm sure
that, deep down, Miss Frost knows that and appreciates
it. But there's only so much one can do, you know? You
can't save the world. No one can. Nor can you force
someone to accept help if they don't want or are not yet
ready to embrace it. You're a kind man, Mr Hayes. Don't
lose sight of that.'

'A fool, more like.'

'No.' Her tone was firm. 'Don't think that. The goodness shines from you like a sunray.' She nodded. 'I
see it.'

'Thank you,' he said thickly. Then, clearing his
throat, 'Well, yes, I think you're right about staying at
the tavern tonight – and I will too.'

She was about to insist he go home and get a proper
rest but, seeing his gaze flick to the window and the beerhouse beyond, she kept her silence. After the scene earlier
with the Baines son, perhaps Victor's suggestion was a
sensible one. Who knew if the lad and his friends wouldn't
plan to return after closing with further mischief in

mind? For tonight at least, it was best they remained on the premises.

Back upstairs, Phoebe went to check on Suzannah. She was slumbering peacefully and Phoebe closed the door quietly. She found Victor settling himself in the chair by the kitchen fire and went to fetch him a blanket. Then she took herself off to the spare bedroom and climbed gratefully into bed.

It had been a long day; she was on the cusp of sleep within minutes.

Who knew what tomorrow held? was her last thought before drifting off completely.

Chapter 10

PHOEBE AWOKE NEXT morning to the smell of warm bread and freshly cooked herring; sitting up in bed, she rubbed her eyes and frowned. The unfamiliar room had her confused for a moment, then memory returned and she nodded. She was at the tavern; they all were, had spent the night. *Suzannah.* A smile tugged at her lips as she wondered how the woman fared. She must have one hell of a thick head this morning.

'Sit thee down, lass.'

'What's all this?' Phoebe asked as she entered the kitchen.

Looking none the worse for her escapades the previous night, Suzannah motioned to the table, where stood a pot of tea and plates of food. 'I rose early and made youse both breakfast. Sit, lass, and get the grub whilst it's hot.'

Phoebe exchanged a look with Victor, already seated and tucking into the meal, and he lifted his shoulders with a pleasantly surprised smile.

'All right, is it?' asked Suzannah as they ate. 'More tea?'

'It's lovely, thank you. You didn't have to go to all this trouble.'

'Aye, I did.' She nodded to Phoebe then lowered her

head. 'Listen, about last night . . . I'm sorry. I don't know what came over me, I . . . I'm grateful to youse for stopping on and looking after me. It'll not happen again.'

She seemed genuinely repentant; Phoebe and Victor were quick to reassure her it was forgotten about. Afterwards, Suzannah brewed a fresh pot and shooed them towards the comfortable chairs by the fireside. As she cleared the table and washed the dishes, Phoebe quietly reminded Victor of their conversation the previous day regarding her taking on the position of cook. It was evident that Suzannah knew her way around a kitchen; now would be the perfect time to put to her their proposition.

'Wha—? Me?' Suzannah murmured, agape with shock, when Victor voiced their idea. 'You'd trust me to do that?'

'Well, of course we would.'

She turned to Phoebe. 'Lass? You agree to this, an' all?'

'I do. I think selling food alongside the drink would be very popular amongst the customers and you seem more than capable – Miss Frost, what is it?' she added, frowning in concern when Suzannah put her face in her hands and burst into quiet sobs. 'You're not agreeable to the idea, is that it?' Phoebe asked, going to put an arm around her shoulders. 'It's all right, you won't be letting us down. We'll find someone else, I'm sure. Don't take on so.'

'It ain't that,' she choked, lifting her gaze wide with anguish to hers. 'I'd *love* to do it.'

'Then what . . . ?'

'I don't deserve this – nor your kindness! 'Specially yours, lass,' she burst out, breaking into tears again. 'I don't!'

'Nonsense.' Aware that Victor was watching the scene,

158

Phoebe tried to portray to the woman with her eyes that the wrong footing they had started off on was a thing of the past. 'Here is a chance to put what has gone before behind you. A fresh start,' she told her with soft encouragement.

'You really mean it, don't you?' Suzannah asked, eyes filled with both wonder and pain.

'Yes. So, what do you say?'

'I say youse are the most generous folk I've ever met in all of my life. I say . . . I'd be honoured to, aye.'

Victor was beaming from ear to ear. 'Right then! Let's get some plans drawn up, shall we?'

Leaving them to it, Phoebe made her way down to the tavern with a smile. Perhaps this would be the making of Suzannah – she certainly hoped so. To put her current way of life to bed, so to speak, and forge a new, safe and respectable direction would clearly be beneficial to her – to all of them. They could really make a success of this place if they all pulled together.

Who would have thought it but a short while ago, she mused to herself with a chuckle as she went about her duties. Working alongside the fiery-haired woman who for a while she'd detested – and actually looking forward to it! She'd got her all wrong, she had. Deep down, Suzannah possessed a decent soul; was likeable even, she was forced to admit. Maybe they *could* grow to become friends – who knew? She, at least, was willing to give it her best try.

At dinnertime later, as the tavern was filling with labouring men in need of a swift beer before their shifts commenced, Phoebe spotted Suzannah enter the drinking room. 'How are you getting on, Miss Frost?'

'Gradely, lass!' She blew at a wayward curl that refused to be confined beneath the scarf wrapped around her

159

head. 'There's pea and ham broth, or sliced ham and pickle with bread for them what prefer summat quick. I'll have had more time to prepare the morrow, am thinking leek pies, an' all. What d'you reckon, lass? Does that sound all right?'

'That sounds excellent, Miss Frost. I knew you could do it,' she added, giving her a soft smile, and received back a delighted grin at the encouragement. 'Now, then.' Phoebe addressed the customers. 'As of today, gentlemen, we shall be selling fresh, affordable food cooked on the premises.' An appreciative murmur went around the room, and she nodded. 'Today's options are pea and ham broth or ham and pickle with bread. Please give your orders to Miss Frost, there.' She pointed across to the woman, who was blushing in proud pleasure. 'She's a wonderful cook, I'm sure you'll all agree. Enjoy!'

Several men, after checking the coins in their pockets, made their way across to Suzannah, and Phoebe and Victor shared a happy look. This venture of theirs was going from strength to strength. Nothing could spoil things for them now.

'Victor. Lass.' It was Big Red. His expression was unusually serious. He drew their attention to the door. 'Look what we've got here . . .'

Catching sight of the two stiff-faced policemen who had entered, Phoebe turned to Victor with a frown. 'Mr Hayes?'

As confused as she, he shook his head.

The law's presence had an immediate effect; a hush went around the room. Customers shuffled on the spot, eyes downcast.

Victor made his way across. 'Yes, officers? Can I help you with something?'

160

'We're here to speak with a Miss Phoebe Parsons.'

All eyes turned to her; the silence was deafening. She glanced from the policemen to Victor, stunned. When she finally found her voice, it was little above a whisper. 'I'm Miss Parsons.'

The officers crossed the room towards her. 'Miss Phoebe Parsons?'

'Yes. But please, what is this ab—'

'Miss Parsons, you are under arrest. Come with us.'

'What? No!' she cried, shrugging off the meaty hands that had clasped her upper arms. 'No, there's been some sort of mistake – Mr Hayes, help me!' she cried, twisting around to look at him.

Victor's face was ashen with shock. 'What on *earth* is the meaning of this? What is she meant to have done?' he demanded.

'We have received a report of a serious theft.'

'You think *me* responsible?' Phoebe was close to tears. 'I have never stolen anything in my life, you must believe me.'

'If you'll come with us, Miss Parsons, all will be explained down at the station.'

'But . . . I'm not guilty of any wrongdoing, I—!'

'The station house, Miss Parsons,' the elder officer snapped, his patience spent.

Phoebe could do nothing but obey. Tears coursing down her cheeks, she gazed at Victor as she was hauled past him to the door. 'Mr Hayes . . .'

'I'll get to the bottom of this, you have my word,' he rasped, reaching out to squeeze her hand. 'Just try to remain calm.'

Out in the street, she craned her neck around towards Victor, who had followed and was standing furious but helpless in the doorway. 'They've made a mistake. They must have, they—' Her speech died suddenly in her throat. For, over his shoulder, she'd caught a glimpse of Suzannah. The woman's face, screaming guilt, told her all she needed to know. 'You?' she gasped. 'This is down to you . . .'

'Miss Parsons?' asked a confused Victor, following her stare. 'Who . . . ?'

'This is Miss Frost's doing. She's done this!'

'What? No, she wouldn't, she—'

'See for yourself! See, ask her!' Phoebe just had time to cry before the officers bundled her into the waiting horse-drawn prisoners' van by the roadside.

Victor called out something after her but, whatever it was, she didn't catch it. His words were swallowed in the scrape of wheels and thump of hooves as the van lurched forward and she was carried off at speed to nearby Oldham Road.

'Wait in there.'

Phoebe was sent with a shove into one of the lock-up's four tiny, ice-cold cells. The heavy door boomed shut behind her, followed by the drag of a key in the lock.

The stark box was empty of fittings, even the most basic wooden boards – with nowhere to either lie or sit, she held on to the damp stone wall for support as dizziness swooped. The strength deserted her legs. She crumpled into a ball on the filthy floor.

Devoid of heating of any kind and badly ventilated, made worse by the terrible stench from the poorly drained building, within seconds the conditions had her shivering uncontrollably and struggling not to vomit. Something scratched in a darkened corner then scuttled away. Biting her lip to stop herself from crying, she pulled her knees to her chin and closed her eyes.

Why? *Why?* The question thumped at her brain, relentless.

She'd been such a fool. She'd put her trust in Suzannah, believed they were becoming friends, and all the time . . . Just what had she concocted? For what reason? Had she planned to have her out of the way all along? Oh, why was she *doing* this?

For what seemed like hours, Phoebe remained imprisoned in the unlit room without sight of or word from anyone. Then footsteps sounded, growing louder as they approached her, and the door moaned open. She squinted through the gloom at the figure who had appeared: 'Hello? Please, I shouldn't be here . . .'

'It's me. Are you all right?'

'Mr Hayes? Oh, Mr Hayes!' She ran to fall into his arms. 'Thank God!'

Victor held her in his thick arms. 'I know an officer of the station here, managed to talk him into letting me see you for a few short minutes. Sshhh, it's all right. I'm here.'

'No one will tell me anything. What am I meant to have done?'

'A Mr Warwick Yewdale has made an accusation against you.'

'Warwick?' She pulled back to look at him. 'What accusation?'

'It's the brooch, Miss Parsons. He's saying you stole it from his stepmother.'

'No . . .'

'He knows you sold it and used the proceeds towards the purchase of the tavern. He's claiming the brooch is a family heirloom, that with Lilian dead the item belongs to his estate. He wants you charged with theft.'

'I would never, never . . . Lilian *did* gift it to me, she

did, she ... my God.' She nodded in terrible remembrance. 'Miss Frost planned this. She planned the whole thing. She told Warwick. They're trying to ruin me; why?'

'I've spoken with Miss Frost, and she insists—'

'Well, of course she would,' Phoebe snapped, swiping at tears that had begun to fall with the back of her hand. 'She's hoodwinking you, Mr Hayes, can't you see? She's *not* who you think she is. Oh, she's believable, all right – she had me fooled up to now, too. She and Warwick are lovers.' Phoebe nodded into his shocked face. 'I've seen them ... together ... with my own two eyes. She asked me only yesterday how I came across the means to go into partnership with you. Naively, I told her, didn't imagine she'd somehow use the information against me. Mr Hayes, you *have* to believe me. She's behind this, she is.'

'I don't understand *why*, Miss Parsons.'

'Nor do I,' she admitted. 'Warwick Yewdale's part in this is clearer: money. It's what drives him, always has been; if there's a sniff of a chance he can claim the brooch as belonging to him, he will. Besides, he's never liked me, for I loved Lilian, whom he despised. The added advantage of hurting me in the process will please him, too. However, as for Miss Frost's motives . . .' She shook her head. 'I just don't know, and that's the truth. I thought we were getting along. I thought she liked me. What will happen to me, Mr Hayes?' she continued, clinging to him once more. 'The law will believe me, surely? They *must*.'

'This is a very serious allegation put against you by a powerful man of the town, Miss Parsons.' Victor's quiet tone was grave. 'But you mustn't give up hope. I'm going to do whatever it takes to clear your name and get you out of here.'

'You harbour no doubts that I didn't steal the brooch?'

'None. None.'

'You'll really help me get free?'

His hold upon her tightened. 'I promise.'

'And Miss Frost? Do you believe me with regard to her also when I say she's to blame for my incarceration?'

'Time's up,' came a gruff voice just then from the cramped corridor, saving Victor from having to respond.

'I must go.' His tone was hoarse as he moved to the door. 'Remain strong, Miss Parsons. I'll be back just as soon as I can.'

'Mr Hayes . . .' The pain of him leaving her was unbearable. 'Make Miss Frost confess. Please, you have to!'

Phoebe was just in time to see him nod before the door slammed shut.

The following hours were a living nightmare – or was it days, weeks even? Phoebe couldn't be sure after a while.

Still, she'd seen no one, least of all the superintendent. Her gaze had remained stuck fast to the door and she'd awaited with petrifying dread a burly officer herding her to the charge office, and her being formally indicted, but no. Not yet, at any rate.

What fate would befall her? She, a nobody, accused of having abused her employer's trust and stealing from one of Manchester's most influential families . . . Dear Lord, she'd be torn to shreds when she was hauled before the magistrate. The verdict was a foregone conclusion. And her punishment?

Imposing New Bailey Prison, situated beside the River Irwell in neighbouring Salford, slammed into her mind, and she baulked. She'd always imagined whenever passing it in her youth the criminals behind its walls,

165

wondered what they must be like, how they coped –
particularly the women incarcerated around the older,
octagonal section with its four-armed buildings branch-
ing off. Was her childhood curiosity about to be salved in
the most horrifying way possible: first-hand experience?

Was that her fate: gaol? A life of back-breaking, physical toil; measly meals; relentless punishment? She'd
sooner die! And maybe she would, she realised, as the
other possibilities pushed through to torment her.

She could get years of hard labour, yes. Then again,
there was also the threat of transportation to some
far-flung land. And worst of all . . . Terror seized her,
making her whimper. *She could even be hanged.* No, no!
She was *innocent*, God damn it!

Please God, Victor was, at this very moment, pleading with Suzannah to confess. His nod upon leaving
earlier was his acceptance that the woman was to blame
for this, must have been. He *would* get her out of here,
as he'd promised, surely? He *had* to.

Hopelessness swooped, threatening to crush her.
Bowing her head, Phoebe gave way to her tears – and in
the same moment, the door opened and an officer
entered the cell.

'Miss Parsons?'

'Yes.' She could barely form the words through her
agonising fear. 'Yes, that's me.'

'You're free to go.'

For half a minute, she could only blink in dumb confusion. 'I'm . . . It's really true?'

He nodded. 'It would seem that fresh evidence has
been brought to our attention proving your innocence.
Come with me, I'll show you out. This way.' Turning on
his heel, he disappeared; scrambling to her feet, she
ran after him, gasping with sobs.

'Please, what evidence?' she asked as they passed through the dim lobby. 'Mr Hayes prevailed, as he vowed? Miss Frost has really admitted her part in this?'

Halting by the main desk, the officer threw her a frown. 'Neither. See for yourself.'

She followed his finger towards the station door. The figure she was met with brought her mouth open in astonishment. 'I don't understand . . .'

'Nor have I time to waste trying to make you; I'm a very busy man,' he said curtly, turning away. 'I'm sure your friend there will explain.'

Alone, Phoebe sucked in a deep breath. Then she was running once more, this time to her saviour and blessed freedom. 'Oh, Mrs Tibbs!'

The Yewdales' housekeeper clasped her to her bosom in a hug. 'Miss Parsons! Oh, you poor girl. Come, let's get you out of here.'

Allowing the older woman to lead her across the road, Phoebe drew in great lungfuls of air. 'I can hardly believe I'm out of that place. How, Mrs Tibbs? How did you know? How did you *do* it?'

'Mr Yewdale's loose piece was at the house last night. I overheard them in the library, lass. She was saying how you'd sold an item of jewellery and pur-chased a tavern, that it was set to be very successful. She planted the seed in his mind to claim ownership of the bauble, to take everything from you, *ruin* you. He sounded more than willing to go along with her scheme.'

Phoebe was trembling with rage. 'I knew it.' *How could she do this to her? Dear God, why?*

'I know you're no common thief, knew it was lies. I wanted to warn you but didn't know where you were, lass. She'd made mention of a tavern, but I had no idea where it was located. That night in bed, I wracked my brains, trying to unravel what on earth was going on.' Coming to a halt, the housekeeper smiled. 'That's when I remembered.'

'Remembered?'

'The brooch Lilian gifted to you on your birthday. It made perfect sense; I was convinced it had to be the piece they were referring to.'

'You're right, it was.'

'And I knew then that it was a definite set-up, had to be, for I bore witness to the fact that the bauble came into your possession through honest means with my own two eyes. Do you recall, I came up to Mrs Yewdale's rooms sometime during that morning to confirm with her the afternoon's lunch menu? As I was leaving, you hurried across to me in your excitement to show me your gift. That dear sweet lady saw. She watched on with a smile, pleased at your happiness.'

'Of course. How could I have forgotten?' Phoebe laughed brokenly. 'Oh, Mrs Tibbs.'

'So you see, you couldn't possibly have stolen it, could you? And I was determined to make sure the police knew it.'

'Thank you, oh, *thank* you. But wait, wasn't Warwick furious when he discovered what you knew, that you planned to clear my name? Didn't he try to stop you?'

The housekeeper shook her head. 'He's none the wiser as yet. The other servants offered to cover for me, make up some excuse or other if he noticed my absence, whilst I slipped out. I figured you'd have been arrested by now – Yewdale isn't one to hang around. It was simply a case of finding out where you'd been taken. The town hall station, as well as Ridgefield Station off John Dalton Street, reaped no reward. Oldham Road was next on my list – thankfully, it proved third time lucky. I said to the lawman in charge that my master had sent me to tell them what I knew, put things right. And here we are.'

Phoebe was overcome with emotion. 'To go to so much trouble . . . for me? I don't know what to say. How can I ever repay you?'

'We're friends, lass, and friends look out for one another,' Mrs Tibbs answered simply. 'Just promise me one thing?'

'Anything.'

'You'll keep in contact. Let's not lose touch again.'

Nodding, she threw her arms around the housekeeper's neck. Then Suzannah's face flashed suddenly in her mind, and her mouth hardened in a thin line. 'In fact, Mrs Tibbs, I can do better than that,' she told her grimly. 'Listen carefully, for I have a proposition to put to you . . .'

Chapter 11

LIGHT FROM THE tavern's windows glowed in the darkening evening, bathing the cobblestones by the entrance in shimmering gold and the promise of a warm welcome. Phoebe stood for a long moment and drank the sight in.

She'd parted company with Warwick's housekeeper at the previous street corner, but afterwards hadn't rushed to return to her place of business. Instead, she took her time, needed desperately to gather her thoughts into some semblance of order before she confronted those inside. She'd show them – all of them – that whatever life deemed fit to throw her way, however much anyone tried to destroy her, Phoebe Parsons wouldn't be beaten. She was made of sterner stuff.

Voices and laughter seeped through to her as she reached the door. She raised her hand to push it open, then, changing her mind, let it fall back to her side and crossed to the window. Out of sight, she peered through the corner of the pane. What she saw had the rage that had been simmering inside her throughout the day bubbling into a fearsome tide.

Victor and Suzannah, standing together by the barrels. And they were laughing. Actually *laughing* whilst she – so far as they were aware – was still imprisoned in some stinking cell for a crime she didn't commit. A crime that had been fabricated by the woman who looked to all intents and purposes to have taken over her role. And the man who had sworn with such heartfelt sincerity to secure her freedom only hours before . . . He appeared completely at odds with the one she was seeing now. Victor cared nothing, *nothing*.

The sear of betrayal in Phoebe's breast was agony. Stalking back to the door, she threw it wide with both hands.

Several heads turned as she stepped inside, then others followed suit and a collective cry of surprise and happy greetings enveloped her. Phoebe barely noticed. Stare locked on the couple now gaping in her direction, she crossed the floor towards them.

'Miss Parsons? My *God*, how—?'

'I'll speak with you later,' she cut Victor off, each word like an ice shard. 'First things first . . .' Swivelling her steely gaze to Suzannah, she murmured, 'You. Upstairs. *Now.*'

By the time the woman's footfalls sounded on the landing, Phoebe had already finished her wild dash of stuffing Suzannah's belongings into the canvas bag. She threw the bundle at her feet. 'I want you gone from here this instant. Go, get out.'

'Lass . . .'

'Out!'

'I, I'm so sorry, I—'

'Oh no you're not!' Phoebe was trembling with barely contained fury. 'I saw you just now – *both* of you – laughing away down there without a care in the world. You're the devil, Miss Frost, do you know that? The very devil himself! I never want to see your face again. Now, please, before I'm forced to do something I may later regret,'

171

she warned, her harsh early days of survival in the slums rising to the fore, 'get *out*.'

Suzannah's pained expression melted into dull acceptance. Crushing a hand to her mouth, she picked up her possessions and fled down the stairs.

The fight left Phoebe in a rapid gust; breathing heavily, she dropped to her knees.

'Miss Parsons. Phoebe . . .'

'Leave me alone, Mr Hayes. Right now, I don't . . . can't . . . Leave me alone.'

It was as though he hadn't heard. He climbed the last few steps and lowered himself to the floor beside her.

'Go away. Please . . .'

'I can't believe you're here. Speak to me. Tell me how – *how* in the world . . . ? What happened?'

Her resolve was crumbling like dry earth on the wind; she shook her head desperately but it was no use. Great shuddering sobs tore from her throat. 'I saw you. Laughing with her. I saw you. How *could* you, how?'

'Oh, Miss Parsons. I see how that must have looked but you must believe me, I wasn't—'

'Wasn't what? Enjoying her company more than mine? Enjoying the fact I wasn't here, that she had taken my place and . . .' She cringed to hear herself, a pink hue of mortification creeping across her face at her petulant ranting and whiny tone. What on earth was the matter with her? 'I'm sorry,' she whispered. 'I sound like a silly child. It's just . . . it's been an emotionally fraught day. I'm wrung out.'

'Well, of course, you would be. Tell me,' he pressed again, gentler now. 'What happened? Why did they let you go?'

In starts and snatches, she explained how Mrs Tibbs had come to her rescue. 'I owe her a great deal. Though what Warwick Yewdale will make of her behaviour, I shudder to think, for her sake. He won't take too kindly to one of his staff members going against him like this. He'll likely evict her from his employ and home without a moment's hesitation – without a character reference, no doubt, in the process. He's only too good at that, as I myself learned to my cost.' Phoebe paused. Then: 'That's why I offered her a job here.'

'Here?'

She nodded. 'The cook and parlourmaid, too, should they want them.'

'But . . . doing what?'

Turning fully to face him, she lifted an eyebrow. 'Well, *Cook* shall have a ready role to fill, for a start.' She waited for him to protest that the tavern already had one – Suzannah – but he didn't. 'The housekeeper confirmed my suspicions about Miss Frost being behind today's nightmare,' she continued, looking him straight in the eye. 'Mrs Tibbs overheard her and Mr Yewdale plotting my downfall. Miss Frost has just moments ago apologised to my face – an admission if ever there was one. So you see, my suspicions were correct all along. I told you it was true. I *warned* you she wasn't all she appears. She's warped, Mr Hayes, wicked to the core.'

'Miss Parsons—'

'I've told her she isn't to show her face here. I will not have that woman anywhere near me ever again. Half of this place is mine, remember; I'm entitled to decide who comes and goes. However, so are you. And, if you insist you can't see that woman on the streets . . .' Phoebe nodded. 'Then she may take my place at your house.'

'What are you saying?'

'I'm saying, Mr Hayes, that from today, I intend dwelling in these rooms here at the tavern,' she blurted, wondering instantly whence the notion had sprung. Then again, perhaps it wasn't such a bad idea. Maybe it was time for a clean break. And yet, to imagine it stabbed more than she'd admit. She'd miss Victor, his company, their safe and cosy evenings in front of the fire, and that was the truth.

'What you saw down there.' His words were careful, measured, as though he was anxious to deliver his explanation concisely now so as not to leave room for mistake or misinterpretation. 'It's true we were laughing. However, it wasn't jollity or happiness at your absence you were witnessing; how could you ever think that of me? I missed you.'

'You did?'

He nodded. Then glancing away, he lowered his gaze. 'You *were* right. I confronted Miss Frost after leaving the station and she finally admitted everything. I insisted she return with me that instant and give a full and frank confession to the police, which she agreed to do. We had at that moment informed the customers we had important business, and to drink up as we were shutting shop, when you walked in. Big Red had guessed to some extent what we were about – at least where we were headed – and had just ordered us to "get a bloody shake on and fetch that bonny lass home". The laughter you saw upon your entrance was mere nervous anticipation, on both our parts. Miss Frost wanted you back as much as I.'

Phoebe narrowed her eyes in consideration. The explanation *was* plausible ... However: 'Please don't insult my intelligence, Mr Hayes, by telling me *she* wanted me returned!'

'Hard as it must be for you to believe it, it's the truth.'

'Mr *Hayes*—'

'Her lover is betrothed, did you know?' Victor announced suddenly.

'Warwick is set to marry?' Phoebe nodded. 'Yes, I knew. And God help the unlucky woman.'

'Miss Frost had foolishly harboured hopes of she herself becoming the future Mrs Yewdale. She discovered the harsh reality last night when she paid him a clandestine visit. He openly announced his plans and, seeing him slipping away from her, she plucked at the first thing to come to mind that she thought would keep her in his favour – the subject of your brooch. It was but a vain attempt to please him, to make him see she'd do anything for him. Her desperation to keep him momentarily skewed her judgement—'

'You sound awfully like you're making excuses for her and what she did,' Phoebe interrupted.

'Well . . . perhaps I am. You see, Miss Parsons—'

'I don't believe this.' She jumped to her feet and paced the small landing. 'Miss Frost was right, wasn't she? You will always choose her over . . . over anyone, any day of the week.' Her hurt was like a physical thing.

'No, no. I'm appalled at her actions! However, she's seen the error of her ways and has repented. She regretted what she'd done almost immediately, hence her state when she returned last night – wracked with guilt, she'd been drowning her sorrows—'

'Stop. Please just stop.' Phoebe felt sick with heartache. 'I cannot listen to any more, I can't. You're utterly blind to her badness. That is an end to it.' And she meant it. Listening to him bleating that demon's praises had switched something in her brain; she felt numb to it all now, to him, and what he meant to her. She would vie for his attention and affection, his friendship, no longer. Let Suzannah have him, if that's what he wanted.

175

She was weary of competing. It was a losing battle she'd never stood a chance of winning.

'I shall have to go and look for her, Miss Parsons, you understand . . . ?'

'Do as you must,' she responded in an empty tone.

'Miss Frost has no one else. I simply can't abandon her to those streets out there.'

'As I said, Mr Hayes, do as you must. Just don't fetch her back here – to my rooms,' she added, her mind made up – this would most definitely be her home now. She could never return to Victor's, go on as though nothing had changed, not after this.

Before descending the stairs, he turned back to look at her. He appeared to want to say more, but he didn't. Instead he dropped his stare, sighed and continued on his way.

Phoebe followed. Reaching downstairs, she was just in time to see him don his hat and disappear through the tavern door into the frost-stroked night. Swallowing down her feelings, she forced her attention on to her work and her customers.

'Yes, sir, what can I get you?' she asked the nearest man waiting to be served – then let out a small gasp. 'You?'

He was as surprised as she. 'Well! And how are thee . . . Phoebe, in't it?'

'It is.' Her tone was clipped. 'I have a bone to pick with you, Mr Lavender.'

Dick leaned in to flash a devastating smile. 'You do, eh? I'm intrigued.'

She tried to ignore the effect his good looks were having on her, but the blush wouldn't be contained; she dragged her eyes from his captivating stare. 'That address you *kindly* took me to the night you came across me in a desperate state in the eating house—'

176

'Betsy's lodging place?'

'Except it wasn't a lodging house, Mr Lavender, was it?'

'I don't understand.'

'I think you do.' Reddening further, she raised an eyebrow.

'You don't mean . . . ? Oh, Phoebe, I am sorry!'

'You're saying you didn't know?'

'Well, of course not! Christ, lass, what do you take me for?'

He looked as embarrassed as she – Phoebe was flummoxed. 'But . . . you seemed to know Betsy?'

'That I do. Least I *thought* I did . . . What's she playing at, at all, running such an establishment? I'm shocked, Phoebe. Yes, shocked and appalled. Oh God, what must you think of me?' he asked, covering his face with a groan.

'Well . . . I *did* find it odd that you would purposely take me to such a place . . .' she told him, biting her lip, beginning to regret her rashness in accusing him of such a deed – his mortification was tangible. 'If you say you weren't aware . . .'

'I weren't, lass. I ain't capable of such foulness, nay I'm not!'

'Then clearly I was mistaken. I'm sorry.'

He inclined his head in gracious acceptance of her apology. 'Let's make no more mention of it. So then, Phoebe, how are you?' His slow grin returned, transforming his face into one of breath-snatching handsomeness. 'You certainly seem to have landed on your feet since the last time we met,' he said, looking around.

'You could say that.'

Watching the smile play about her lips, he tilted his head in playful curiosity. 'Oh?'

'I don't just work here,' she admitted over her shoulder

177

as she busied herself pouring him a drink, 'I own half the place.'

Dick's shock was evident; his mouth opened, his blue eyes following suit. 'Aye?'

She nodded, then when he made to hand coins over for the beer she shook her head. 'Have that on me for my offending you just now. I really am sorry about that.'

'Don't be. We all make mistakes.' His voice was velvet smooth. Taking her hand, he pressed it to his lips, eyes now smouldering, boring into hers. 'Thank God I happened across here the night. I'm happy we've found each other again, Phoebe.'

It was like being struck in the chest by a closed fist – she almost staggered. Her heart beat furiously and all other thoughts but the man standing before her deserted her. Confusion had her in its grasp; lost in his gaze, she could only sigh a response.

During the next few hours, Dick barely left her sight. They talked and laughed, and it wasn't until she felt a tap on her shoulder that she realised Victor had returned. Swallowing down a chuckle at something Dick had been saying, she introduced them, adding to Dick, 'Mr Hayes owns the other half of the tavern.'

Dick touched his cap – 'Nice meeting thee' – then snorted softly in amusement when a stiff-faced Victor failed to return the courtesy.

Phoebe was annoyed at the open rudeness. She shot Dick an apologetic smile then drew Victor to one side. 'That wasn't very polite—' she began, but he stopped her:

'You're making up for that for the both of us.'

'Meaning?'

'I've just been watching you with him from the doorway,' he said, flicking his stony stare across to look Dick up and down. 'A bit of an over-familiar way to treat a customer, wouldn't you say?'

'I was merely being cordial,' she shot back, her cheeks blooming with colour. 'Besides, Mr Lavender isn't just a customer: he's a friend.' That he was the person who had taken her to Betsy's, the episode of which Victor knew about, she failed to divulge. It was no concern of his. 'We met again tonight quite by chance and I . . . well, I enjoy his company.'

'Evidently.'

'Mr Hayes—'

'Look, I'm sorry, I'm just tired,' Victor interjected, rubbing his eyes. 'Ignore me.'

'Any luck locating *your* friend?' Phoebe asked, knowing she was being spiteful but unable to stop herself.

'No.'

'Pity.'

Glancing down at her then away, Victor released a soft sigh. 'It's almost ten. I'd best call time.'

Dick made a great display of saying goodbye, holding on to her hand and murmuring promises of coming back to see her very soon, which embarrassed and pleased Phoebe in equal measures. At the door, he pressed his lips to her hand in a lingering kiss. 'Goodnight, lass.'

'Goodnight, Mr Lavender.'

'Dick, please, remember?'

'Goodnight, Dick,' she concurred, smiling.

When he'd gone, she turned back into the empty tavern to find Victor clearing tables – though she suspected he'd been covertly watching her farewell with Dick, could almost reach out and touch his disapproval. Irritation sparked. He had no right at all to judge her relationships – particularly given the undesirable company he chose to keep! Besides, unlike her own opinions regarding Suzannah, Victor's were unfounded – he knew nothing about Dick, nothing at all.

'I'll see to this lot, Mr Hayes,' she told him, unable to bear another moment of his presence and hypocrisy for one day. 'You get off home.'

'I don't mind—'

'I insist.'

Nodding, he murmured goodnight and was gone.

When she was alone, Victor's unhappy face refused to leave her mind. Her gaze shifted to the door he'd just left through and she was surprised when it appeared to her through a blur of tears. Then another man entered her thoughts and she smiled.

Replaying the hours spent in Dick's company, and imagining those yet to come, Phoebe got on with her duties with a slightly lighter heart.

Over the coming weeks, Dick became a regular patron of the tavern. He was kind and attentive towards Phoebe, made no secret of the fact he was there for her alone. She couldn't recall the last time she'd been as happy. Rediscovering Dick that day had been a tonic, and just what she'd needed after her horrific experience. He'd come at just the right time and their friendship had only strengthened since.

Despite Dick's charm and scrupulous manners, Victor hadn't thawed towards him at all. Phoebe would often find him scrutinising the younger man with undisguised dislike – mistrust, almost – but he didn't voice his opinion again. Not that Phoebe would have been swayed if Victor had. The more she got acquainted with Dick, the more she found to like. She couldn't imagine her evenings without him in them, now.

Then, at the opening of December, there came the day she'd been expecting. It was early afternoon and she and Victor were busy seeing to the needs of their customers when the tavern door opened and two familiar figures entered, small cases in hand.

'Mrs Tibbs! Kitty, hello,' Phoebe called, hurrying to greet them. 'How are you both?'

'Jobless and homeless,' announced the girl Kitty, the Yewdales' parlourmaid.

'He's done it, then?'

Though Mrs Tibbs nodded, she didn't look at all dejected. 'The master discovered what I'd done for you and terminated my employ. Kitty here refused to stop on at the house without me.'

'And Mary?' Phoebe enquired, glancing past them towards the street.

'Cook decided to stay. Well, for a few days, at any rate – she's secured herself a new position in another household, you see. So, it's just us two.' Mrs Tibbs's smile slipped and a flash of worry appeared in her eyes. 'The proposition you put to me when we left the police station that day . . . It does still stand, doesn't it, Phoebe?'

'Of course it does,' she assured her, and the woman released a breath of relief. 'Come on upstairs, I'll show you where to put your things.'

'It's nice here,' said Kitty, looking around and nodding when they were in the kitchen. 'You sure you've the room for us, though, Phoebe?'

'Oh yes. So long as you don't mind sharing a bedroom?' The women expressed that they didn't, and Phoebe went on, 'Then there shouldn't be a problem. In fact . . .' Gazing from one to the other, she smiled. 'I think we are going to get along here together just fine.'

When they were settled in, Phoebe led the way back

to the tavern to discuss their duties. Victor greeted them politely, which she was pleased about; he'd remembered her saying they might be in need of a place to stay and work in the near future, and showed no sign of objection.

'I had thought of Mary for the kitchen but, as Cook's not here ... How would you feel about the role, Mrs Tibbs? I know it's not quite what you're used to ...'

'I'll give it my best shot, lass,' the older woman assured her, chuckling. 'So long as it's simple dishes, I'm sure I'll manage well.'

Phoebe was delighted – Victor, not so much. His face had grown solemn; it was clear that at the mention of the cooking job, he was remembering Suzannah. Though Phoebe felt a pang to see his unhappiness, she ignored it, as she'd trained herself to do.

He hadn't given up his quest to find the red-haired one, despite there having been no sign of her since the day she'd fled the tavern. Daily, he would tramp the streets for hours, but Suzannah seemed to have vanished from the face of the earth. Though she hated to admit it, even Phoebe sometimes found herself wondering what had become of her. Not that she voiced it. In fact, the woman's name was never mentioned between her and Victor, and she preferred to keep it that way.

'What about me, Phoebe?' Kitty was asking now. 'What is there that I can be of help with?'

'Erm ... There's cleaning, if you're in agreement. Dusting and sweeping the tavern, that sort of thing?'

'I'm happy with that. It's what I'm skilled in, after all.'

'You might even enjoy helping us to serve the customers when it's particularly busy.'

Kitty seemed even more pleased with this. 'I'll admit I ain't ever set foot inside an establishment such as this in all my days, but I'm a fast learner. I'd like to give serving a try, aye.'

'That's settled then. Now, we'll start as we mean to go on tomorrow. Rest today, put your feet up.'

'Put our feet up?' Kitty was amazed. 'I ain't never had the time to spare for that afore! Eeh, sounds like heaven.'

'You can say that again,' seconded Mrs Tibbs. 'Thanks, Phoebe.'

'You deserve it, both of you. Things will be different here, I promise you,' she told them earnestly, only too aware of Warwick's total disregard for his workforce and slave-driver ways. 'Go on, make yourselves at home.'

'You possess a kind and generous soul, Miss Parsons,' Victor told her with feeling when the women had disappeared back upstairs. 'I mean it,' he insisted when she attempted to deny she'd done anything worthy of praise.

'I'm indebted to Mrs Tibbs, remember? She risked her position – risked everything – to help clear my name. I'd still be languishing in some godforsaken cell but for her. I'd say I owe her more than what I've provided today. A lot more.'

Victor had reddened; he cleared his throat. 'Of course. I'm sorry, I wasn't thinking. I didn't mean to bring up that terrible episode.'

'But the culprit who wrought that "terrible episode" didn't mean it, apparently, so no harm done,' Phoebe muttered sarcastically, couldn't help herself.

'I'm sorry,' he repeated. Head down, he moved off to busy himself elsewhere.

Throwing him a furtive glance, she swallowed a sigh. She gained no pleasure from hurting him, as she knew she was, quite the reverse. Yet time and again, she couldn't seem to stop from doing it.

She loathed how things had become between them,

yearned for the easy chatter that was now replaced with strained silences. She missed him more than he'd ever begin to know. And she hated Suzannah for that the most. The woman had shattered to dust a special friendship for no other reason than that she could. Her total lack of feeling and decency and own selfish wants had ruined everything. That Victor could excuse this, forgive even, so readily was something Phoebe would never be able to understand. It was a bone of contention that would remain between them always, she knew. The fact was a devastating one but impossible to alter. *Damn you, Suzannah* . . .

The issue was still on her mind later when she donned her shawl and headed out to nearby New Bridge Street and Strangeways Brewery.

Keen to cash in on the beer explosion, common breweries were springing up all the time to supply the barrelage to those who didn't brew their own stock, and ingredients to those who did. Larger premises had even begun buying drinking establishments that came up for sale, ensuring they always had ready outlets for their beer.

Phoebe had placed her order for two sacks of malt to be delivered to the tavern the following day, and had just thanked Mr Boddington and bade him goodbye, when a faint voice she thought she recognised caught her attention. Frowning, she skirted the brewery yard and followed the source.

There it was again – she paused to listen. Up the road ahead, a man was gesticulating angrily. Though too far away to make out what he was saying, Phoebe caught at once his aggression; his tone was thick with threat as he shook a rag-clad woman half his size.

'I ain't swindling thee out of no rotten money. Leave *go*, you swine!'

Phoebe sucked in a breath. She knew the voice had sounded familiar: Suzannah.

She watched as the couple continued to struggle; then the man struck out, catching Suzannah full across the face. Passers-by barely batted an eyelid. Fights and altercations were hardly uncommon in the slums; few were inclined to involve themselves in disputes, especially domestics, seeing it as none of their business. Not so with Phoebe; her feet moved forward of their own accord. She'd opened her mouth and was about to order the brute to leave the woman be when Suzannah managed to twist herself free. She bolted away down the street, her companion's roars of fury snapping at her heels.

Without thought, Phoebe picked up her skirts and set off after her.

She tailed Suzannah for several minutes through the winding roads and side streets brimming with tumble-down abodes, until she reached Ducie Bridge – her childhood stomping ground. Here, she paused for breath. Standing on tiptoe and peering down over the high parapet, Phoebe scanned the banks of the polluted river below.

Sludgy black and choking with rubbish, industrial waste from the surrounding works and mills and domestic sewage, the stench emitted from it turned her stomach inside out even from this height. Unaccustomed to the horror-smell now, owing to her years of absence, she was forced to cover her nose and mouth with her shawl. Flicking her gaze to the sea of foul and festering houses, she squinted harder.

For a moment, she thought she'd lost her; then Suzannah appeared again, darting down a set of ruinous stairs to gain entrance to a knot of dwellings. Knowing she'd be hard-pressed to catch up with her now, Phoebe traced her journey with her eyes, her narrowed stare picking out the flashes of her bright hair.

Seconds later, Suzannah ducked into a broken-down cellar and was gone. Phoebe straightened and retraced her steps back to the tavern.

On the journey, her mind was a tangle of thoughts at odds with one another. There was no marking off a victory this time. She wasn't so vindictive, garnered no pleasure from seeing a body trodden so low. Spying that woman again, her old resentment *had* resurfaced, there was no denying that, and yet she couldn't suppress the niggle of pity that refused to leave her.

That Suzannah had sunk to a new depth was clear; she'd looked terrible. Moreover, if the scene with the brute who had been manhandling her was anything to go by, she was in obvious trouble. But she deserved it, didn't she? Phoebe tried to tell herself. The anguish and terror she'd caused her, her quest to ruin her, and yet . . . Yet worry still tugged insistently at her, much to her chagrin.

The main question, of course, was would she tell Victor?

Phoebe felt herself redden guiltily the minute she saw him. He gave her a tentative smile and it was a struggle to return it. She watched him serving and talking with customers, all the while agonising over what to do, but couldn't bring herself to inform him of what she'd discovered.

Hour followed hour and still she said not a word. Even Dick's company when he turned up later could do nothing to alleviate her troubled mind. Though he did his best to drag from her a smile, she was in no fit mood to comply, and his presence began to irk after a time. She

186

was rather short with him at one point in the evening and, though she regretted it instantly and apologised, the damage was done; Dick made his excuses soon afterwards and left. Still, her conflicted thoughts raged on.

'Are you all right?' Victor asked as the night was drawing to a close. 'Miss Parsons?'

Lost in her own world, she glanced up, frowning. 'Pardon?'

'I asked if everything was all right. You don't seem yourself at all.'

'I'm fine,' she lied, unable to meet his eye.

When the last customers had left and she and Victor had seen to the clearing up, she watched him go to collect his jacket. This was her last chance – *Tell him*, her mind whispered. He returned and she cleared her throat.

'Is something wrong, Miss Parsons?'

Phoebe stared at him mutely; the speech just wouldn't form. Then: 'No,' she said. 'No, nothing is wrong. Goodnight, Mr Hayes.'

When he'd gone, she heaved a ragged sigh and made her way upstairs.

Chapter 12

THE KITCHEN FIRE's comforting crackle and soft glow did nothing to calm Phoebe.

'Here you are, lass,' said Mrs Tibbs, passing a cup across, having made them both a last pot of tea; Kitty had already gone to bed.

'Thank you.'

'It's a nice little place you have here,' the woman was saying, though Phoebe was only half listening. 'And Mr Hayes is a nice man.'

'Yes. Yes, he is.'

'Very fond of you, he is, too.'

She lifted her eyes. 'You think?'

'Definitely. Stands out a mile, it does.'

'We haven't really . . . we're not getting along at present as well as we used to.'

'Oh?'

Phoebe sipped at her hot drink. 'We seem to have drifted apart somewhat, and I hate it. He's a good friend. He . . . means a great deal to me.'

'Do you want the advice of an old wench, lass?'

'Yes, please.' She sat forward to hear it, desperate for a solution.

'Be honest. Whatever it is has come between the two of you can only have the power to do so if you let it. Lay your mind bare to him and all will be resolved, you'll see. For I can bet all I possess that he's feeling as bad about whatever is going on here as you are. Talk to him, lass.'

Long after Mrs Tibbs had retired to her bed, Phoebe sat on, gaze lost in the dying flames. Then she found herself rising to her feet and plucking down her shawl from the peg.

Moments later, she was letting herself out of the tavern and running through the moonlit streets for Victor's house.

He appeared at the door in his nightshirt, his hair tousled and his eyes bleary. However, he sprang fully awake upon seeing it was she standing on the step. 'What on earth . . . ? Phoebe, what is it, what's happened?'

'Might I come inside, please, Mr Hayes?'

'Well, yes, yes of course.'

Following behind him down the dark passage and into the kitchen, her stomach was a bag of knots. He stood with his back to the fireplace and peered at her questioningly.

'I have something to tell you.'

'If this is to do with you and Mr Lavender—'

'Dick?' She shook her head and was puzzled to see Victor visibly sag in relief. 'No, no, my visit here tonight doesn't concern him. Why, what was it you thought I'd have to tell you regarding Dick?'

'Nothing. It's nothing, really. So, what *has* dragged you out at this time of the night? I'm not happy about that, by the way,' he added, frowning. 'You shouldn't be out on those streets alone so late.'

Despite her inner turmoil, his concern touched her. She cast him a soft smile. 'I was all right; I ran all the way. You see, Mr Hayes, the thing is . . . It's Miss Frost.'

'Miss Frost?'

She nodded. Sudden sadness had swooped upon her at giving the admission life. There was no concealing this any longer, no biting back the words now.

'I planned to snatch a few hours' sleep before going searching for her . . . Why, what about her?'

On the way here, she'd pictured Victor out scouring the freezing streets for yet another night, had worried whether she'd even catch him home. 'I thought you might, didn't know if you'd be in, I, I . . .'

'Miss Parsons?'

'I know where she is.'

'But how?'

'I saw her, this afternoon. She was having some trouble with a man . . . She fled. I followed her to a cellar dwelling by the Irk. I can give you the address.'

Phoebe thought he would rush off to rescue Suzannah right away, but she was in for a surprise:

'Sit down.'

'Mr Hayes?'

He guided her to a chair. 'I don't know what to say,' he told her when they were seated side by side. 'You saw Miss Frost this afternoon . . . ?'

'I know what you're about to ask: why have I kept this information to myself all day long? Well, the honest truth is, I . . . I didn't want to tell you.' She hazarded a quick glance at his face then dropped her eyes once more to the tabletop. 'The reason for that isn't just owing to what she put me through, either. I don't want her here . . . with you,' she finished on a whisper. 'I *miss* you, Mr Hayes. Should Miss Frost come back into our lives, her presence will only push us further apart from one another. I don't want her coming between us. Your friendship means a great deal to me—'

'And me.'

'Oh, I'm sorry.' She could hear how she sounded. 'I'm being ridiculous, I know I am, and yet . . .'

'And yet?' he pressed her, leaning closer. 'Tell me.'

'And yet I can't help it, for I need you. More than that, I want you, Mr Hayes, want you in my life.'

'Not Miss Frost nor anyone else could ever come between us or stop me caring for you. No one. Never.'

'You really mean it?'

Victor nodded. Then he bent forward and pressed his lips to the corner of her mouth in the gentlest kiss. 'Always, Phoebe.'

She was quite overcome; laughing softly through her tears, she motioned to the door. 'Go on, Mr Hayes, fetch her home.'

'I'll walk you to the tavern on the way.'

The journey back was for Phoebe over much sooner than she'd have liked – she'd have preferred to have stayed in his company for ever. 'Goodnight, Mr Hayes.'

'Goodnight. And thank you,' he said with feeling. He stooped and once again brushed his lips close to hers, then was gone.

Phoebe let herself into the tavern and, after bolting the door, made her way up to bed.

This night, there was no lying awake for hours staring at the darkness, no troubled sighs and turning over things in her mind. With a whisper of a smile, and touching with the tips of her fingers the spot where the pressure of his kiss still lingered, she was asleep in seconds.

Victor arrived the following morning looking strained but thankful.

'She was at the address that I said she'd be? You found her?' Phoebe asked him.

'Yes.'

'You brought her home?'

'I did.'

'How is she?'

'Exhausted. I've left her sleeping.' He rubbed at his brow with a sigh. 'That's not all. Miss Frost revealed to me she is with child.'

Phoebe blew out air slowly. 'Dear God. Is it Warwick Yewdale's?'

'She'd like it to be, and there is a possibility. However, given her profession . . .' Victor lifted his arms then dropped them back to his sides. 'She can't be sure. She is completely certain of one thing, though: her over-whelming gratitude to you. She is grateful, Miss Parsons, truly.'

Nodding, Phoebe led him to a table, and they sat in silence for a time mulling over what they had learned.

'There's another issue Miss Frost is worried about,' Victor said. 'The man you saw rough-handling her yesterday was her bully.'

'Bully?'

'Yes. It's a term given to those who make their living exploiting streetwalkers. They manage them, shall we say, under the guise of offering protection against trou-blesome customers – and take most of what the women earn in payment. I came across many such specimens during my time in the force; they're void of scruples and can be extremely dangerous. He won't be best pleased about losing her and the money she's been bringing in. She's afraid he may come after her.'

'What's to be done?'

'I don't know,' he admitted. 'I'm thinking about it.'

A series of crashes and cries from the kitchen cut short further discussion; hurrying out, they went to investigate. They found Mrs Tibbs covered in flour on her hands and knees, cleaning a mound of soggy mess off the floor.

'What happened?'

'She dropped the pies for today's fare,' Kitty informed them, struggling not to laugh. Then added under her breath, 'A sign from God, that was, if ever I saw it – I tested one, they were terrible.'

'Don't just stand there gawping,' Mrs Tibbs snapped at the girl. 'Give me a hand!'

Biting her lip, Phoebe escaped back to the drinking room with Victor.

'We can't have her poisoning half the customers. What are we going to do?'

'Perhaps Mrs Tibbs just needs a little more practice . . .' Phoebe suggested, feeling less confident than she sounded. The woman's former role as housekeeper had involved overseeing the staff and the running of the household, which she'd excelled at, not the preparing of meals. It was clear she was struggling to adapt to her new position.

'Let's hope so.'

Their concerns were proven right, later, however, when the drinkers tasted the offerings. Nor were they as discreet in voicing their dissatisfaction as Kitty had been.

'This is bleedin' awful,' growled King Henry, whilst others grumbled their agreement. He spat the mouthful of pie – Mrs Tibbs's second attempt – into his dish. 'Bonny that new cook of yourn might be, but bloody hell, she can't throw a decent bit of grub together for neither love nor brass. Pastry's raw and the tatties are hard as rocks,' he went on, prodding a dirty nail into a piece of potato. 'And I thought my wench at home were useless in t' kitchen!'

'What are we going to do?' Phoebe hissed to Victor

when the food had been cleared away and the disgruntled customers refunded.

'Well . . .'

'Miss Frost,' she said with a sigh, guessing what he was about to suggest. 'Oh, Mr Hayes, I don't know . . .'

'You have to admit she's good at it. Think about it, take your time. I'll leave the decision to you. If you decide you're not yet ready or comfortable being around her after what's passed, I'll fully understand.'

His attentiveness to her feelings warmed Phoebe. That he wasn't automatically acting with Suzannah's needs in mind, was instead considering her as well, left a glow inside her. He'd promised not to let anything – or anyone – come between them again and it looked like he'd meant it. The truth brought to her a sense of security and lent her strength.

'All right. I'll speak to Miss Frost, see how I feel afterwards.' She reckoned it was time they aired their grievances. 'I'm not promising anything, however . . .'

''Course not, 'course not,' Victor agreed, though it was evident he was pleased with the positive move.

'Poor Mrs Tibbs,' Kitty said to them both later when the three of them were serving together. 'She's mortified at how her grub were received.'

Victor pulled a sympathetic face. 'There's really no need for her to beat herself up about it. I'll go up and see she's all right,' he offered, caring of the feelings of others as ever.

Phoebe gave him a grateful smile and had just begun pouring a drink for another customer when Victor's call reclaimed her attention:

'Psst. Miss Parsons.'

'What is it?'

'You've got to hear this.'

Frowning, she joined him at the foot of the stairs. Craning her neck, she listened. 'Mrs Tibbs?' she asked in shock at the astonishing voice floating down.

'Must be!'

'I don't believe it.'

'That's our Mrs Tibbs, all right,' Kitty announced, coming to see what was keeping them. 'A rare talent she's got, ain't she?'

'You knew?' Phoebe asked her.

'Oh aye. Allus singing, she were, in our owd kitchen.'

'How didn't I know about this?' Leaning forward to get a better listen, Phoebe shook her head in wonder.

'Well, the servants' quarters weren't your domain, were they? You were mostly away in the house proper with Mistress Lilian.'

'Of course, you're right. I just can't . . .' Again, Phoebe swung her head. 'She's exceptional.'

'I have an idea.'

The two women turned to Victor questioningly.

'Would Mrs Tibbs agree to put her skills to good use in the tavern, do you think?' he added.

'Entertaining the customers, like? Eeh, that's a gradely idea, aye!'

Phoebe was in full agreement with Kitty. 'Indeed it is. It's a travesty to keep such a beautiful voice to herself!'

As one, the three of them raced upstairs.

By the time Dick entered later, the place was heaving with dancing, happy punters. Mrs Tibbs, delighted to earn her keep without the need to step foot near the kitchen again, had readily accepted their suggestion and had taken to the role of the tavern's new entertainer like a fish to water. A space had been cleared for her by the window, and the traditional Lancashire folk songs delivered in her strong, high strains were an instant hit.

The customers showed their appreciation with applause and feet stamping, and whoops and cries of 'More! More!' – the place had never been so busy.

'Evening, lass.'

'Hello, Dick.' Phoebe was pleased to see him, not to mention relieved that he appeared to have forgotten her shortness with him the previous night. 'The usual?'

'Aye, please.'

Handing his beer across, she inclined her head to Mrs Tibbs. 'Good, isn't she? We've never been so full.'

Dick was quick to agree. 'Hang on, I've got an idea.'

She watched him cross back to the door and prop it open wide. Almost instantly, more people began flocking inside, the bright lights and warm atmosphere, coupled with Mrs Tibbs's velvet tones, drawing them like moths to a flame.

'Well done, how clever of you,' Phoebe trilled, impressed, and laughed when he bowed theatrically. 'Look, Mr Hayes,' she added to the older man. 'See how effective Dick's idea is.'

Victor was frowning. 'It's the depths of winter. The customers will be struck down with pneumonia.'

'Nonsense. The fire's burning brightly,' she pointed out, 'and besides, the natural heat from so many people will keep us all warm.'

A grinning Dick nodded; looking away, Victor let the matter drop.

The night was a roaring success. At one point, Mrs Tibbs had asked for requests, and Dick had shouted out an old favourite. Giving Phoebe one of his dazzling smiles, he'd held out a hand to her and she'd accepted it. Pulled close in his strong arms, she'd swayed with him to the slow rhythm, a hazy sort of pleasure taking her over. She'd never been held that way by a man before and she found that she liked it very much. That it was with someone as attractive as Dick made it all the more enjoyable. More to the point, he seemed to have liked it as much as she; it had been impossible not to be flattered by his attentions.

'Eeh, he's handsome is your Mr Lavender,' Kitty said on a dreamy sigh that night after closing, as the three women partook of a well-earned cup of tea upstairs.

Phoebe felt herself pinken with shy pride. *My Mr Lavender.* Was he? she asked herself, quietly suspecting he was.

'Charming with it,' Mrs Tibbs added. 'You're a lucky lass.'

This time, Phoebe didn't hesitate to agree.

Chapter 13

THE MOROSE MOOD that was becoming a familiar foe crept upon Victor within moments of him waking. Flopping back down and dragging the bedclothes up and over his head, he released a weary sigh. Just what was the point in getting up at all? He may as well stay where he was; it wasn't like Phoebe would miss him, was it? Particularly not later, once *he* showed his face.

His stomach tightened in a misery he could never reveal, not to anyone. He loved her, God damn it. Wanted her with all that he had. Stupid, brainless old fool that he was. Phoebe wouldn't have noticed him in any case – not in the way he'd begun to hope that she could. The likelihood now, with that slippery swine Lavender on the scene, was less than none.

Victor forced himself up and out of bed and crossed to the wardrobe. As he dressed, he ruminated, as he did often of late, over the past few weeks and his shifting feelings. How had he allowed himself to fall for her? He was no young buck with a head full of clouds. He'd been struck senseless with shock when the realisation first occurred to him that what he harboured for Phoebe was changing. The notion was preposterous for a whole host of reasons; he'd wondered for a time whether he was losing his mental faculties altogether.

But no. He wasn't going mad. Every other aspect of his thought process was as structured and sound as ever. His feelings were genuine. Wholly real – and utterly ridiculous.

Even if by some miracle Phoebe was to share for him just a fraction of the fierce love he held for her, what would be the point in it? In fact, the hurt would surely sear far more if she did. Having possession of the knowledge that each wanted the other, yet there being no possibility of there ever being a union between them . . . that would be a torture far greater than the one he was suffering now. Oh, it would.

His mind switched to Kate and he closed his eyes. He was shackled to her for the remainder of his life, that was all there was to it. The marriage vows he'd at one time been happy to have binding them together were now invisible chains he must drag with him for ever. He could never have Phoebe – could never have anyone else. It was a truth he just had to learn to accept.

Dick Lavender. Victor's lips bunched in a scowl of black envy. He had it all. The looks, the silken tongue . . . Phoebe. He had her, all right. He'd hooked her. Worse still, she was making no attempt to wriggle free. How did they even know one another? When had they previously made each other's acquaintance? She'd said the night Dick first made an appearance in the tavern that they were already friends – how?

He could have asked, of course, but hadn't wanted to risk her accusing him of prying and shutting him out still more. Already, back then, she'd been slipping further from him than he could keep up with. Yet even now, when matters between them were back on track, he didn't feel able to probe. When all was said and done, it was none of his business. Who Phoebe chose to forge friendships with was, after all, her concern.

'Morning. Did tha sleep well?' asked Suzannah when Victor entered the kitchen.

He lied to her that he had, then distracted himself with the breakfast she'd prepared for them. Phoebe was calling in here today to speak with her about resuming her position as cook. He just prayed all would go smoothly.

Suzannah needed this for both stability and financial reasons – more so now, with a child on the way. As for Phoebe . . . he couldn't have her upset again. She'd withdraw into herself, would push him away as she'd done before, and he'd be at great risk of losing her for good. No, no. He wouldn't bear her coldness towards him a second time; the first had almost destroyed him.

Working with her day in day out, side by side, with barely a word passing between them had been agony. To have her think for a moment he was putting her feelings second to Suzannah's had never been his intention; he wouldn't hurt Phoebe for the world. Nor was there any basis to it. However, he'd sadly fallen short at expressing his motives clearly enough, as the male species was often wont to do.

The simple truth was, he was a firm believer that people act as they do for a reason. Rarely was it a case of impulsive cruelty – there was almost always another force driving them to commit unpleasantnesses.

Suzannah was damaged, messed up; it often skewed her judgement. He'd been but trying to explain the fact to Phoebe, but she'd interpreted it as him taking the other woman's side over hers. Which was an impossibility, for though he cared a hell of a lot for Suzannah, it was in a mere fatherly fashion. The motivation with Phoebe, on the other hand, was unparalleled; it came from his very soul. His new-found love for her had showed him that. She had his heart. He'd put her first every time.

How ironic, then, that the woman who Phoebe believed had created the gap between them had also been the one to bridge it again without even knowing it. Phoebe spotting Suzannah had got them speaking, healing the rift. And what words she'd uttered . . . !

As he had a hundred times since, Victor replayed in the privacy of his head Phoebe's outpouring. She needed – nay, *wanted* – him. Well, his friendship at least. Even so, the declaration had been a balm to his tortured mind.

For one horrifying moment, he'd thought she was about to announce her betrothal to Lavender, but no, thank God. Putting her own feelings to one side, she'd sought him out to inform him of Suzannah's plight, proving what he already knew: just what a selfless and wonderful being she truly was. And she'd said she missed him, that he was important to her. He could have wept at this, so overwhelming had his relief been that she valued him in any capacity. And that – friendship – he must endeavour to be content with, he knew. Better that than nothing at all, oh yes.

'Did she say what time she'd be here, Victor?'

'Hm?' He blinked up at Suzannah in confusion. 'Did you say something?'

'Aye, I asked . . .' She broke off to frown. 'Are you all right? You don't seem yourself at all.'

'I'm fine,' he assured her – another mistruth. In reality, the knotting in his guts was back worse than ever; he'd been stupidly going over the memory of last night yet again. Phoebe, locked in Lavender's arms as they danced. The way she'd looked up at him, the clear pleasure in her soft brown eyes . . . Stop it, Victor told himself. *Please God, make it stop.*

'Another cup?' asked Suzannah, teapot in hand, slicing through his tumult.

'No, I . . . Sorry, I think I'll go for a walk.'

'Oh. Aye. All right, then.'

It took all the strength he possessed to bring a farewell smile to his lips for her. It melted the second he turned for the door.

Stepping outside, he sucked in freezing air. Then, chin lowered, eyes shrouded in a dark frown, he set off on the aimless trek to clear his head. And the memory of kissing Phoebe – and how much he craved to do so again – went with him.

'Miss Frost.'

'Hello, lass. Will tha come in?'

Phoebe nodded. Doing her best to stem any lingerings of animosity, she followed Suzannah down the hall.

'Please, sit down. Tea?'

'Thank you.'

The minutes dragged by as they sipped at their drinks, the silence growing heavier with each passing second. Finally, Suzannah put down her cup.

'Lass . . . I'm so very sorry.'

'So Mr Hayes informed me.'

'And now I'm telling thee.' Tears glistened on Suzannah's lashes. 'It were a wicked thing I did, *wicked*. I wish I could turn back time and undo it, but I can't. Can you ever forgive me?'

Phoebe met her stare head-on. 'Forgiving is one thing. Forgetting is another matter entirely.'

'I'll settle for forgiveness, lass. Oh, I will.'

'I don't know,' she told her truthfully. 'You've hurt

me a great deal, Miss Frost, and I didn't deserve it. You could have destroyed my whole life, and for what? A few moments in Mr Yewdale's good books?'

'Sounds pathetic, don't it?'

'It does, yes. Callous and extremely dangerous, to boot.'

Suzannah was openly cringing. 'I realised my folly very soon afterwards, I did, honest. But it were too late. I tried convincing myself it didn't matter what came of my telling, that I cared not—'

'Ah yes, your smug drunken warning that a storm was coming my way.'

'But you stayed with me anyroad. You were concerned for my welfare. You looked after me when I were sick to keep an eye on me— Oh, lass,' she cried, covering her face with her hands. 'I felt rotten then, I did.'

'And so you made breakfast . . .'

'I know, I know! It were daft – as if a bit of grub could make up for what I'd done! I couldn't think what else to do. And then you and Victor offered me that job and oh, I could have wept a lake with shame! Tell me, lass, what to do,' she continued, reaching out to grasp her hand. 'Tell me and I'll do it. How do I make it up to thee?'

'Be honest.'

'About what?'

Phoebe folded her arms. 'Warwick Yewdale's attack upon me . . .'

'Aye.' Suzannah's voice was a strangled whisper. 'Aye, I put the idea to him to scare thee. He were raging that you'd found us in that compromising position in his library, were afraid you'd spill what you knew to the town.'

Shaking her head, Phoebe closed her eyes. 'All along I knew it.'

'I'm sorry, I am—'

'Do you love him still?' she cut in.

The woman's gaze pooled with fresh tears. 'Aye.'

'So what of the future? What's to stop you sinking to such wicked lows again, should you deem that the need has arisen? How do I know you won't use me again, and to hell with the consequences, should it suit your purpose with that man?'

'I'll not, lass. I'm done with all that. I'm done with him.'

'Really?'

'Well.' Suzannah spread her arms wide. 'I don't have much choice in t' matter, do I? He's to be wed to another. To a woman of his own breeding. I never even stood a chance, did I? I feel so bloody foolish!' she burst out suddenly, thumping the tabletop. 'How could I have dreamed up such daft notions of us being together proper, like? A man such as him and a slum whore like me . . . ? Ha! Silly, stupid bitch that I am.'

'And the fact that the child you carry may be his?'

'This is my child.' Suzannah's hand swivelled protectively to her midriff. 'Mine alone. No one else's.'

Phoebe eyed her keenly for a sign of dishonesty but could see none. Perhaps impending motherhood had matured her, who knew? But could she really be trusted? Only time could answer that. 'If I was to ask you to come back as cook—'

'Oh, lass!'

'If I did, do I have your promise you'll do nothing to have me regret it?'

'My *solemn* promise, I swear it. Anyroad, Victor's already warned me what would happen if I ever even think to hurt thee again – not that I would, like! – he'll wash his hands of me.'

Victor had said that? Phoebe felt sudden tears prick at this proof of his loyalty, *finally*.

'I'm changed, lass. That I am, for good. Let me prove it to thee.'

'This is purely for business reasons, you understand . . . ?'

'Aye, 'course.'

'Serving food will draw in more trade.'

'Aye, lass.'

She sucked in air. 'Fine. The job is yours again.'

'You mean it?'

Another deep breath, then: 'Yes, I mean it.'

'Eeh, I'm that grateful!'

Whether that was true or not, Phoebe knew, remained to be seen.

'They'll not take kindly to working beside me. I ain't been exactly nice to them in t' past when at Warwick's house.'

'Then you'll apologise.'

They were on their way to the tavern and Phoebe had just informed Suzannah about Mrs Tibbs's and Kitty's employment there.

Suzannah was right – the women were less than pleased when Phoebe announced to them that their former master's lover was to join their workforce. Mrs Tibbs even pulled Phoebe aside to ask was she sure she was doing the right thing – she knew, after all, that Suzannah had created the rumour which resulted in Phoebe being arrested. Phoebe was forced to admit that no, she wasn't completely certain of whether she'd come to regret her decision, but that she was willing to give Suzannah a second chance. Didn't everyone deserve one? Though Mrs Tibbs agreed with this statement, still she didn't seem wholly convinced by the new development.

However, as the day wore on, it was plain to everyone that Suzannah was determined to prove herself. She worked hard, was polite and friendly to customers and staff alike, and by the end of the afternoon even Mrs Tibbs and Kitty appeared more relaxed around her and with the situation in general. Phoebe was mightily relieved. Fingers crossed, things would only improve; she was more than a little hopeful that she hadn't made a mistake after all.

That evening, trade was incredible. With the door flung wide, Mrs Tibbs's singing and the delicious aromas of Suzannah's cooking floated irresistibly down the street – folk seemed drawn to the pleasing atmosphere as though in a trance. Phoebe, Victor and Kitty could barely keep up with the demand for drinks.

'Profits will soar if we can keep this up every night!' Phoebe said to Victor when they found a moment to catch their breath. 'We're really making a success of this venture of ours, aren't we, Mr Hayes?'

However, before he could offer a response, the sound of shattering glass reverberated through the room.

There followed a stunned silence. Then people were gasping and yelling in confusion.

'The window.' Victor pointed to the broken pane and lump of stone on the tavern floor. Then he dashed outside.

Dazed with horror, Phoebe checked that none of the customers were hurt then rushed to join him.

Victor was incensed. 'I'll find out who's responsible for this if it's the last thing I do!' he ground out through gritted teeth.

Scanning the deserted street, Phoebe shook her head. 'Who would do such a terrible thing, and why? I don't understand.'

'I know who did this, all right – *and* why.' Lifting his glare to the beerhouse over the road, his mouth twisted. Moments later, he was stalking his way across.

'Wait, Mr Hayes . . .' Biting her lip, Phoebe ran to catch him up.

Victor thrust open the door and barged inside – Phoebe was right behind. The scene they were met with stopped them in their tracks. 'Dear God,' they murmured in unison.

The cluster of occupants in the stuffy, gloomy little room didn't look up or even seem to notice their entrance. Phoebe and Victor peered around at the haggard faces in grim silence.

Beerhouses were a lower tier of premises and well known to cater for a rougher class of clientele, it was true, but this place was another level of misery altogether. Men of all ages – and some that could hardly be classed as such, so young did they appear – sat hunched around the utterly cheerless space. Worse still was the presence of ale-swigging women, some with grubby babes in arms, who could barely stay upright with drunkenness.

What drew them here was anyone's guess – Phoebe was certainly at a loss to know. Then a man lurched towards the corner, where stood a full and stinking pail, and into which he relieved himself in full view of the room, and she understood.

He'd been a regular of their tavern, she recognised, until last week, when his long-suffering wife had turned up in search of him. Eyes bruised all colours of the rainbow, the woman had wept and pleaded with her husband to come home to his hungry children whilst he still had some money left – witnessing the pitiful scene, Victor had been appalled at his customer's deplorable behaviour. He'd ejected him forthwith, with stern instructions

207

never to return. Clearly, the man had resorted to drinking his family's housekeeping money at the beerhouse instead.

In fact, Phoebe realised, glancing around again, most of the people here wouldn't be permitted entry at any respectable premises. Unwholesome dens such as this, however, had no qualms so long as there was brass to be earned.

That Col Baines had made not the slightest attempt to alter the fact that this was a common dwelling house was evident. On a long table lining the far wall stood tapped wooden barrels from which the beer was directly dispensed – the only clue this was a drinking establishment at all. Yet it was what she spied beneath this that brought the terrible reality home far more.

Victor had spotted it too: a filthy straw mattress, upon which huddled the proprietor's family, beneath some old sacks. Together, he and Phoebe picked their way across.

Snoring loudly, Col's wife lay sprawled along one end, insensible with drink. Beside her, three youngsters turned pale faces up at Phoebe and Victor as they halted.

Victor's tone was gentle. 'Where might I find the keeper?'

'Father ain't here. Nor is our big brother,' offered the eldest in a small voice.

Bar this sorry excuse for a bed, and the orange boxes dotting the floor that the customers were using as seats, not another scrap of furniture existed. That anyone, let alone innocent children, were suffering this wretchedness was heart-breaking.

'They'll be lying low somewhere. They can't be far,' Victor said to Phoebe through the side of his mouth.

'I'll catch up with them at some point. For now, let's get out of here.'

She felt a pang at leaving the beer seller's offspring in such conditions but was powerless to do anything about it. Head down, she followed Victor back to the tavern.

Kitty had swept up the glass in their absence and Suzannah had found a length of board to cover up the window. Mrs Tibbs, though shaken by the disturbance, was refusing to let it spoil the customers' enjoyment and was belting out a local favourite – Phoebe and Victor thanked the three of them earnestly.

'I'm just glad no one was injured,' she told him as they returned to their duties. 'Do you really think it was the Baineses' doing, Mr Hayes?'

'Well, who else? They would have had ample time to bolt back to the beerhouse after launching the missile. Besides, they've clearly got a grudge against us. It was likely seeing us doing so well tonight that prompted them to attack.'

She had to concur it did add up. 'What will we do?'

'Informing the police would be useless: we have no proof and no witnesses – besides, they'll have false alibis as to their whereabouts at the time, you can be sure of that. However, something needs to be done, for this won't end here. Of that, I'm certain.'

'I know word has it that Col Baines has an unsavoury reputation, but I never expected it would be half as bad as that. The state of the place, Mr Hayes . . .' The poor children still on her mind, Phoebe shook her head. 'It shouldn't be allowed. It's just not right.'

He sighed agreement. 'And that is precisely why the likes of him will never prosper in this line of work: because they put profit above the needs of their customers – and sometimes even their families, God help them. Nor does it help when the proprietor – or his wife – develops a taste for the stuff they sell,' Victor added disapprovingly, he himself a staunch teetotaller – rare for a landlord. 'Most of the weekly earnings end up going on drink, ensuring the business is doomed to fail and the family – just like the one back there – spiral into a lifestyle of savagery.'

'Is there anything we can do, Mr Hayes?'

Victor rubbed at his chin. 'I think it's time I had a word in a few ears, for I'm convinced he's breaking more than one law. He's ignoring the hours permitted to trade, not to mention opening when he shouldn't on Sundays, I'm certain of it. Then there's the signboard over the door: it's written in smudged and faded chalk, which is illegal. The wording, which should state his *full* name, which it does not, and that he's licensed to sell beer by retail, must be *painted* in white on a black background or vice versa, *and* in letters of at least three inches in length – the tiny scrawl now is hardly visible. Each of those offences could land him with a hefty fine – possibly up to ten whole pounds.

'As for the fact he should be selling beer only, I'm sure I spied one or two spirit casks in there just now . . .' he went on. '*That* is punishable by having a licence revoked and the premises shut down altogether.'

That Col even failed to keep good order and allowed disorderly conduct at his premises was a crime in itself, Phoebe knew.

She'd seen signs of the beerhouse's nefarious activities over the weeks. Characters of suspicious appearance loitering outside, including women of loose virtue – it was evident that it was a haunt of criminals. The swearing, screaming and fighting from within, which sometimes spilled out on to the street, as did shrieks of bawdy, blush-inducing songs . . . Weekends were especially bad.

Something would have to give, and soon. Matters couldn't continue as they were. It was proving only injurious to the morals of the people who frequented the place, never mind the annoyance caused to decent inhabitants nearby.

There was no denying that alcohol was to many a firm acquaintance. Almost all of life's occasions, from celebrations to devastations, went hand in hand with it. Whether toasting happy moments or drowning one's sorrows when times grew tough, there it was. Moreover, drinking was one of the few leisure activities that could be enjoyed by all. The lower classes in particular saw very little pleasure in life; why shouldn't they get to enjoy themselves in bright and warm surroundings with good company and a glass or two? Moderation was what made all the difference. It was when control ceased and the demon addiction took hold that the problems began.

Given the multitude of low beerhouses mushrooming on every corner, it was little wonder this occurred all too often still. But not on Phoebe and Victor's watch. Both were steadfastly in agreement on this. Knowing your budget and when to call it a night was key – something they kept a keen eye on at their tavern. They were adamant that theirs was and would always remain a civilised and respectable house.

Now, worried there may be further trouble this night, Victor decided it was best that Suzannah, in her delicate condition, went home. They had been gone a few minutes when Dick sauntered into the tavern.

He greeted Phoebe with his ready smile, but it vanished when she pointed out the damaged window and explained what had happened.

'They *what*?' He seemed as livid as if the business had been his. 'You're sure it was these Baineses' doing?'

'Sure as we can be.'

Dick scanned the room. 'Where is the owd man, anyroad?'

'If you mean Mr Hayes,' she said with a small frown, disliking his withering tone when referring to Victor, 'he's walking a friend home. He shan't be long.'

'And what is it he plans to do? Nowt much, I'll bet.'

'Actually, he went over there right away, but neither father nor son was anywhere to be found.' She was growing increasingly annoyed at his attitude. 'What is it that's got you so worked up, Dick? Furthermore, why do you seem to be holding Mr Hayes to blame for all this?'

'I'm fond of thee, Phoebe. I'm fond of thee a lot. That them across the way – that *anyone* – thinks they can show up here and . . .' He breathed deeply. 'As for Victor – well. He might not have it in him to teach them blackguards a lesson they'll not forget, but I do.'

Before Phoebe could respond, Dick swung away from her and strode from the tavern.

Surprised and confused, she was incapable of movement for several moments; then she was shaking her head and hurrying for the door.

When she reached the street and spotted him making his way towards her, her mouth formed a wide O. For he was grasping two wriggling figures by the scruff of their necks – *the Baineses*.

'Dick!'

'These the fellas, are they?' He shook them like a pair of rag dolls, making their teeth rattle.

'Y–yes, but—'

Dick threw them to the ground, sending them rolling

into the gutter. 'Up!' he growled. 'Get the *hell* up and apologise to the lady here.'

Col and his son dragged themselves to their feet. They looked as stunned as she felt.

'Well?' Dick demanded.

'Sorry,' they mumbled in unison.

'So the damage tonight was your doing? But why? What *is* this horrid vendetta you have against us?'

'Whatever it was, it's finished with,' Dick answered for them. 'Ain't that right?' he asked, gripping them once more by their shirt collars.

'Aye,' they were quick to agree.

'And?'

'And . . . we'll pay for the window?'

'That's right. Now, get out of my sight.' Again, Dick flung them with force across the cobbled road, sending them staggering back towards the beerhouse. 'And see to them bloody children in there, an' all!' he ordered before they scuttled away indoors.

For a full minute, Phoebe gazed up at him in dumb silence. Then she was covering her mouth with her hand and laughing hysterically. 'My *God*, Dick. I cannot believe what I've just witnessed!'

Dusting off his hands, he grinned. 'That's them dealt with. You'll have no more bother from that quarter.'

'Come on inside. I owe you a very large drink!'

By the time Victor arrived back, Phoebe was almost beside herself with anticipation. She rushed to greet him: 'Oh, Mr Hayes, you'll never believe what happened . . .' She relayed what had taken place in one long rush. 'Oh, Dick was amazing, he really was,' she continued, reaching across to press the younger man's arm. 'I've never seen anything like it in my life. He put the wind up them, all right! Col Baines and his son have

213

agreed to pay for the damage. Ah, and Dick even insisted they look after those poor children, too. Oh, Mr Hayes . . .' she breathed once more and, turning her eyes back to Dick, sighed happily. 'Oh, it was wonderful.'

Victor hadn't uttered a single word throughout the discourse. Now, when he spoke, his voice was very quiet – likely owing to his shock and gratitude, Phoebe surmised. He held out a hand. 'Well. Thank you, Mr Lavender.'

Dick's smile widened slowly. He looked down for a moment at the proffered hand. Then he grasped it and shook it firmly. 'It were nowt. Any real man would have done the same.'

'That's right. Now, a promise is a promise,' Phoebe laughed, taking Dick's arm again. 'Let's get the hero a drink!'

Chapter 14

'YOU'RE QUIET THIS morning, lass. Nowt wrong, is there?'

Helping Suzannah prepare the pastry for that day's fare for the tavern, Phoebe shook her head. 'No, I . . . No, nothing's wrong.'

'You sure? You're not sickening for owt, I hope? Happen there's summat going around, for Victor were in a similar mood to yours earlier, an' all.'

'Oh?'

Suzannah confirmed her statement with a nod. 'Silent and brooding, he were, aye. Why, mind, I can't tell thee; he'd not say.'

Phoebe frowned, but her curiosity over Victor didn't last long. All too soon, her thoughts clicked back to the other man who had plagued her mind throughout the sleepless night. Or more to the point, what he'd asked her late into the evening.

She cast Suzannah a sideward glance then, unable to keep the news to herself any longer, said, 'Actually, Miss Frost, there is something I'd like to get off my chest if . . . if you wouldn't mind hearing it.'

''Course I'd not, nay.' Wiping her hands on her apron, the woman gave Phoebe her full attention. 'I'd be glad to, in fact, and shall do my best to help if at all I can.'

'Well, it, it's my . . . friend, Mr Lavender.'

'Oh aye? I ain't had the pleasure of meeting him as yet, have I?'

'No, not yet. Well, you see, he . . . he's asked me to marry him.'

'Oh, lass. Eeh, that's wonderful news! It is, in't it?' Suzannah added when Phoebe gave a sigh of uncertainty.

'I suppose so. Yes, I'm sure it is. It's just . . .'

'Just what, lass?'

'Well, it all seems a little sudden.' There. She'd finally put voice to it. 'We haven't known each other for very long. Though I do like him ever so much,' she admitted with a blush and a smile. 'He's incredibly handsome, Miss Frost, and could have any woman he wanted, I'm sure. I suppose I should feel flattered it's me he's chosen to pay attentions to, and I am, but still . . .'

'It's all moving a bit fast for thee, is that what you're trying to say, lass?'

'Yes, I think that's exactly it.'

'Then tell him so. If he's that keen on thee – and it certainly sounds like he is! – then he'll not mind waiting a while 'til you're a little surer in your mind.'

Phoebe nodded, but a small part of her remained unconvinced.

Dick had completely stunned her with his question the previous night, shortly after the scene with the Baineses. She hadn't seen it coming at all, had almost dropped the tankard she was filling for a customer at the time in her astonishment. *Would she be happy for them to get betrothed after Christmas?* She'd gawped at him for an age, his words whizzing inside her brain. Finally, he'd laughed and pulled her to him in a hug, and she'd clung to him with a queer sensation of drowning.

There had been no mention of love or even affection;

216

unnecessary really, she supposed – he wouldn't have asked for her hand if he didn't feel those emotions, would he? When still by the night's end she'd been unable to form an intelligible response, he'd kissed the tip of her nose and told her to mull it over, that he'd have her answer tomorrow. Which was today. And yet she wasn't any closer to knowing what her reply ought to be.

What if he saw her wanting to wait a while longer as a lack of enthusiasm and decided to put a halt on their budding relationship? She didn't want to lose him. She'd grown more than a little fond of him and couldn't dwell on what not having him around any more would be like. However, if Suzannah was right . . . If Dick did care enough for her, then he'd understand and give her more time to come to terms with his life-changing suggestion. Yes. Surely, he would.

'So, lass? Have you figured out what it is you're to do?' the woman asked her when the food was cooking and they were sitting enjoying a cup of tea.

'You were right. I should just tell him how I feel,' said Phoebe decisively. 'I was just being silly; of course he'll be understanding. I shouldn't have doubted it really. I suppose it's that I have little to no experience of men, that is the trouble – as you yourself pointed out not too long ago,' she couldn't help including.

'Eeh, nay, lass. I shouldn't have said that—'

'It's all right, really. It's true. My life as a lady's maid was a solitary one. There wasn't opportunity to meet potential suitors. I haven't ever really been in the company of the opposite sex. Besides Mr Hayes, of course,' she added on reflection, her smile returning. 'He's the first male friend I've had.'

'And now you're on the public scene, the blokes are flocking, lass.' Suzannah chuckled at her bashful laugh, then her eyes grew wistful. 'Eeh, but you are lucky, though. I'd give both arms for a sound fella to look my way.' Glancing down to her stomach and the new life growing within, she shrugged. 'That ain't likely to happen for me now, is it?'

'None of us know what's around the corner, Miss Frost.'

'Aye, mebbe.'

'Well, I'd better be heading downstairs. Mr Hayes will be here any minute and there's the tavern to get ready for opening time,' Phoebe told her, rising.

'All right, lass.'

Phoebe paused by the door. 'And Miss Frost?'

'Aye?'

'Thank you for the listening ear. I . . . well, I appreciate it.'

Who would have imagined not so long ago that she'd be turning to Suzannah for advice? thought Phoebe with a crooked smile and shake of her head as she descended the stairs. My, but it was a queer old world at times.

When Victor arrived soon afterwards, he was in higher spirits than usual, which surprised Phoebe, given how Suzannah had described his mood earlier. 'Good morning, Mr Hayes.'

'It certainly is, Miss Parsons!'

She frowned curiously. 'You're very cheery today.'

'Indeed I am.' He crossed the floor towards her, his face wreathed in smiles. 'Come with me a moment. I have something to show you.'

'Show me what? What are you up to?' She laughed when he tapped the side of his nose and winked. 'I believe you're teasing me, Mr Hayes.'

'Now, would I? No. I have a surprise for you. An early Christmas present, shall we say?'

Phoebe was intrigued. 'Really? Well, where is it?'

'Outside.'

Puzzled as to what on earth it could be but excited to find out, she put her hand in the one he'd held out to her and allowed him to lead her into the street.

'Well, Miss Parsons? What do you think?'

'I don't believe . . . Mr Hayes . . . Oh, I love it!'

Victor put an arm around her shoulders, which were shaking with emotion. 'Hey now, don't cry.'

'These are happy tears, really they are,' she choked, her gaze going back to the fresh new signboard attached to the tavern.

The names of many drinking establishments tended to reflect important topics of bygone days, and theirs had been no different. Now, the old sign from Mr Fennel's years as owner, which harked back to the time of the Napoleonic Wars and displayed the name The Lord Nelson in honour of the bold British naval commander, was gone. In its place hung a new one. And their business's fresh renaming? *The Lilian*. Phoebe was quite overcome.

'I got the idea from what you said about your grandfather naming his tavern The Abbie after his wife. And I know how much your late mistress meant to you. I think a feminine title lends it a nicer touch; it feels warmer, more inviting. Don't you agree, Miss Parsons?'

'Oh, I do. It's a beautiful and fitting tribute to a wonderful woman who made all this possible. Thank you, Mr Hayes, so very much. It's the kindest, most thoughtful thing anyone has ever done for me.'

'You're worth it, and more.'

On impulse, she threw her arms around him and rested her cheek against his broad chest. The comforting feel of his arms went around her in response and she closed her eyes.

'I hope you'll not have notions of holding the lass

219

like that in the near future,' murmured a voice behind them.

Surprised and embarrassed, Phoebe sprang away from Victor with a self-conscious laugh. 'Dick. Hello.'

Though he returned her greeting, his cool stare remained fixed on the other man.

'We were just . . . See the new signboard Mr Hayes has had made? Isn't it just perfect—?'

'You said the near future, Mr Lavender,' Victor said suddenly. He was frowning. 'What were you referring to?'

'You mean to say Phoebe ain't told thee?'

'Told me what?'

'Dick, now isn't the right time,' she tried intervening, but he carried on regardless:

'I've asked the lass for her hand in marriage.' His gaze swivelled to Phoebe – then: 'And she said yes.'

Victor's expression was unreadable. He looked from one to the other. Then he nodded and walked back into the tavern.

'Dick.' Phoebe was less than pleased. 'Why did you say that?'

'Say what?'

'That I had agreed. I haven't given you my answer yet, remember?'

'But you would have said aye, right?'

'I . . . Possibly. *Eventually*—'

'Well, then.'

She blinked, at a loss what to say, hadn't the words to argue it further.

'Now then, soon-to-be Mrs Lavender,' said Dick, looking mightily proud of himself, 'I think this calls for a celebration.'

In a daze, Phoebe followed him inside.

*

'Is it all right if I take myself off home, lass?'

The hour was approaching seven and Phoebe was reaching the end of her tether. Victor was nowhere to be found. Moments after she and Dick had joined him in the tavern following the marriage announcement, he'd left saying he needed to make a few calls and hadn't been back since. She and Kitty had struggled to keep up with the custom on their own, and Suzannah had been forced to step in to help. These added duties, on top of her having been cooking since early morning, were beginning to show. The strain was clearly visible on the woman's face – biting her lip guiltily, Phoebe nodded assent.

'Yes, Miss Frost, you go and put your feet up. Thank you for your assistance. At least *you* can be relied upon,' she told her, unable to keep her annoyance at Victor for leaving them in the lurch like this from her tone. 'Should Mr Hayes be at home, would you kindly inform him we need him here right away?'

'I will, lass.'

Just then, Dick's booming laughter floated from across the room and the women exchanged a weary look.

'See thee the morrow, then, lass,' said Suzannah before making quick her escape; watching her departure, Phoebe half wished she was going with her.

'Another round of ales over here, love!' shouted Dick, pulling Phoebe back to the present, and she dragged herself off to fulfil his request.

She hoped he'd make this his last. He'd been drinking with a group of loud-mouthed men he was acquainted with since the afternoon and was more than a touch merry. Shooting him a glance, she hid a sigh. He was the happiest she'd ever seen him and it didn't take a genius to work out why.

'I've asked the lass for her hand in marriage. And she said yes.'

221

She'd replayed the words over and over in her mind all day. Except she hadn't said yes, had she? Nor, it seemed, would she get to answer either way now. The decision had been made for her and she'd surely left things too late to query it. Neither could she bear to, she knew, taking another look at Dick's beaming face.

'You don't think summat's happened, do you, Phoebe?' asked Kitty a little later, checking the time. 'With Mr Hayes, I mean?'

Her heart gave a few flutters; she was beginning to worry the same. This wasn't like him at all – where could he have got to?

'I hope not, Kitty. Oh dear,' she said in the next breath at the sight of the two newcomers who had entered. 'But he doesn't drink! What on earth . . .'

Victor and his companion, a man around his own age – and in full police uniform – staggered to a table, arms around each other for support. They collapsed, helpless with laughter, into two chairs; Phoebe hurried across.

'Mr Hayes? Oh, just look at the state you've got yourself in. As for you, sir, you shouldn't be in here,' she hissed urgently to his friend. 'Perhaps it would be best that you left now before anyone should discover—'

'I've only just got here. I want a drink.'

'But, sir, you can't.' Lawmen were meant to be active, well behaved and respectable – most importantly, an example to the public at all times. Dishevelled and minus his top hat – he must have mislaid it at some point during the evening – the man before her now presented an image totally at odds with every one of those stipulations! 'You surely know the rules about such things.'

'Poppycock!' he cried, and he and Victor fell about laughing again.

'Sir!'

'Two glasses of your finest whisky for my good friend Bob and me, please, serving wench!' Victor interjected, viewing her through one eye.

'Mr *Hayes* . . .'

'Here.' Having clearly read the situation and surmising it was best to comply with them before they created a scene, Mrs Tibbs placed a small measure before each man. 'And make that your last.'

Phoebe flashed her a grateful look. 'Would you help me upstairs with them, please, when they're done with these drinks?'

'I think it would be best,' said the older woman, eyeing the pair. 'A sozzled landlord doesn't look too good for business. As for him . . .'

'I know what you mean,' Phoebe whispered. 'It won't just be his own job at risk should his superiors find out about this, but ours too.'

Drunkenness amongst the police was commonplace. Strict penalties, therefore, were placed on victuallers who sold alcohol to any constable on duty. Nor could a member of the force lodge in such premises as this – Phoebe just prayed this Bob fellow wouldn't pass out and she'd be pressed into providing him with a bed for the night.

'The punters won't be best pleased neither, knowing there's a policeman in their midst,' Mrs Tibbs added. 'People can be distrusting of the law, lass.'

Nodding, Phoebe glanced around. Fortunately, the crowd were too busy with their own enjoyment to have noticed the pair yet, but it was only a matter of time. Furthermore, would they demand to know why Victor was keeping company with him? Would word getting out that he himself was a former lawman pose a problem?

She hadn't the answers but didn't want to wait around to find out. 'Why don't you and your friend come along upstairs, Mr Hayes?' she said the moment their glasses were empty. 'I'll make you both a nice cup of tea.'

'Beautiful, isn't it?' It was as though Victor hadn't heard her. His bleary gaze was locked on his friend's frock coat and long line of brightly polished buttons. Smiling fondly, he stroked the uniform like a prized thoroughbred, his face full of pride and loss.

Watching him, her gaze softened in pity. 'Mr Hayes . . .'

He turned his stare on her and, to her dismay, she saw he had tears in his eyes. 'But not as beautiful as you, sweet Phoebe.' His speech was suddenly clear and deep with sincerity. 'Not by a merry mile, my love.'

Knowing it was drink talk but touched all the same, she put an arm around his shoulders and murmured, 'Come on, Mr Hayes.'

Mrs Tibbs helped up the constable and the foursome headed for the door leading to the private quarters. They had almost reached it when Dick's voice, high in amusement, carried across to them:

'You're an embarrassment, owd man!'

The insult seemed to jolt Victor wide awake. He juddered to a halt. Freeing himself from Phoebe's hold, he slowly turned to face the other man and his friends.

'Ignore it, Mr Hayes—'

'You smarmy young bastard,' he growled.

Dick merely grinned, and it acted like fuel to a naked flame; Victor's temper erupted. With a roar, he sprang across the tavern.

Phoebe cried out his name in horror, but he was having none of it. Throwing back his arm, he launched a fist at Dick. However, the other man had youth and agility on his side and he dodged it effortlessly. Missing his

224

mark, the force of the swing caused Victor to spin full circle before folding to the floor in a tangled heap.

The group could barely breathe through their guffaws – none more so than Dick. Phoebe was enraged. Rushing forward, she helped Victor to stand then let her glare fall on each man in turn until it came to rest on Dick.

'I want you and your friends gone by the time I return,' she spat in disgust. Without waiting for a reply, she turned Victor around and guided him from the room.

Upstairs, she led him to her bedroom and helped him into bed. Moving towards the window to draw the curtains, she glanced back at him over her shoulder. He was lying flat on his back in the darkness, staring silently at the ceiling. A shaft of moonlight threw its pale glow across his stiff face and she saw that his cheeks were wet with tears.

The stab of deep tenderness for him inside her breast snatched her breath. She climbed beside him and drew him into her arms, and it was the most natural thing in the world.

His warm body moulded against hers and she pressed closer into him and stroked his hair.

'Stay with me, Phoebe. Please . . . stay with me.'

'I won't ever leave you,' she whispered.

Chapter 15

HE'D NEVER BEAR facing them. How could he? The shame would put an end to him.

Eyes closed, head thumping more from crushing remembrance than the after-effects of the alcohol, Victor bit his lip until he tasted blood. Arms that had held her soft body throbbed with emptiness. He dragged a pillow into them and hugged it to his chest, but of course it was no substitute. Nothing could compare to her.

He'd made a complete fool of himself. The man who had begun his day of devastation had ensured he ended it with unequivocal humiliation. Dick Lavender reigned supreme. Victor had never hated another living soul as much in his life.

Pity had drawn Phoebe to his side. Kindness had kept her there. She'd remained with him all night.

He'd awoken in the dawn's cold light and let the previous hours' memories trickle back with nauseating truth. He'd be a laughing stock. He'd ruined it all. And still it had changed not a thing. The reality remained: that man would soon claim Phoebe as his wife.

Victor had disentangled himself gently from her arms. The moment he'd stepped from her bed he'd missed her, but the urge to flee before the house awoke had been too strong. He'd let himself out and scuttled off home like a kicked dog, tail between his legs, to climb heartsore into his own bed. And he'd remain here. He could never return to the tavern, not now. He couldn't look the woman he loved in the eye, for he knew what he'd see: disparagement. And that would surely finish him off.

The better man had won, that's all there was to it. The handsome one, young and strong. The hero who had dealt with the Baineses as he himself had failed to do. That's what she'd called Dick: hero. The pride in that man – *her* man, the man she'd chosen – shone from her. Victor's sense of emasculation, sheer *worth*lessness, in that moment had been unparalleled. And his thought process being what it was, he had conjured up the only thing he could think of to win a small part of her affection back: the sign.

He'd used his heart instead of his brawn; but that would never make enough of an impression, would it? It never did in this world. Strength and bravery were what mattered to man, what won fair maidens. And he couldn't compete with Dick on that score. Even when he'd tried, even when he'd allowed his anger to get the better of him and had battled the younger man head-on, he'd failed – nay, lost spectacularly. The truth was that everything was different now. Phoebe was gone from him for good and he had to accept that.

'Victor?'

He closed his ears to the tapping at his bedroom door. Didn't they know he couldn't face anyone? *Leave me be.*

'Victor, love? There's a sup of tea here for thee.' Suzannah drew back the bedclothes from his head. 'Victor?'

'I'm tired.'

'All right, well, I'll just leave it here for you then.'

227

He heard her put down the cup on his night table. *Go, please.*

'I–I wondered . . . Could I talk to thee about summat?'

'Not now, Miss Frost. As I said, I'm tired.'

''Course, aye. Sorry.'

Her footsteps faded away to the door. 'Wait,' he said, cursing her presence and himself for being unable to ignore her plight. 'What is it that's on your mind?'

She came and sat on the edge of his bed. Her hands were in her lap and her fingers plucked nervously at each other. 'It's that Dick Lavender, Phoebe's fella.'

Victor had to breathe deeply to stem the rush of pain in his chest. 'Go on.'

'I don't think I can carry on working at the tavern with him around.'

'Why?'

'I just, I don't like him.'

He dragged a hand through his hair and nodded. 'No.'

'You don't neither?'

'No, I don't.'

'Phoebe shouldn't wed him. He's not right for her.'

Again, that stab behind his breastbone. 'She's made her decision.'

'She ain't, though, that's the thing. She opened up to me only hours afore they were announcing things in t' tavern – it fair flummoxed me, I can tell you.'

'Opened up about what?'

'She weren't ready to give him an answer. She said them very words to me herself. She planned to ask him for more time to decide. Then the next thing we know, the betrothal's official and she's drinking their news with him like nowt had passed betwixt us. I can't fathom it.'

Victor sat up in bed. 'Miss Parsons . . . she really said all that?'

'Aye, when we were preparing the grub for the day's trade.'

His head was spinning. He cast his mind back to the moment Dick had revealed to him – no, *boasted* would be a more apt description – that he'd asked for Phoebe's hand. She'd tried to stop him, Victor suddenly remembered. *She hadn't wanted him making the issue public knowledge because she hadn't given him her answer.* Yet that arrogant lump of filth had continued anyway, for his own wants came first, above anyone else's.

Or had Dick's main objective been simply to get under his skin? But why would he feel the need to do that? Unless he'd guessed . . . Did he know that Victor's feelings ran deeper for Phoebe than everyone else believed? Then surely Dick saw him as a threat, however small – must do, to go to such lengths to appear triumphant in winning her hand?

The prospect lent Victor a tiny boost of life. Alert now, he sipped at his tea thoughtfully.

'Will you break my decision to Phoebe for me?'

'Decision?' he asked, with only half his attention.

'Aye, that I'm for leaving my position. I couldn't face the lass with it. Please, Victor?'

His behaviour last night slammed back home and he sighed. 'No, I'm afraid I can't. I shan't be going to the tavern today.'

'Why not?'

'I just . . .'

'And last night, an' all,' she pressed on. 'Where did you get to? We could have done with thee there, the place were packed out. It must have been late when you returned; I didn't even hear you come home.'

'I had some, some bad news and . . . I needed time alone to think.'

'Oh, love. Nowt too 'orrible, I hope.'

More terrible than I can even try to put into words. 'I . . . I got drunk.'

'You?' Suzannah was agog. 'But you don't—'

'Yes, I know. Last night, however . . . Well. It seemed a good idea at the time. I bumped into an old friend from the force and we—'

'We? You mean to say you went on a boozy spree with a constable on duty?'

'Yes.'

'And him in full uniform?'

Victor's cheeks were flaming. 'Yes,' he whispered.

'Ha! Oh, good Lord!' Suzannah doubled over with mirth. 'I didn't think you had it in yer! Eeh, I wish I'd have been there to see it.'

'I'm rather glad you weren't.' He glanced at her grinning face then away again quickly. 'I might have . . . well, sort have been involved in a fist-up.'

'Wha—! *You*?'

He nodded. 'With Dick Lavender.'

'Did you thump him one? Oh, Victor, please say you did!'

'Not quite.'

'He didn't . . . ?'

'No, he didn't hit me. He didn't need to – I was on the floor before he could blink. I swung at him and missed,' he explained in a muffled tone, covering his face with his hands. 'I . . . fell. Full force, spread-eagled, on the tavern floor. God, the *shame*.'

'Victor, Victor.' Suzannah had tears of laughter pouring down her cheeks. 'And that's why you'll not show your face there the day?'

230

'Not *any* day ever again!'

'Now, don't be bloody daft! Bloomin' hell, love, I'd never have seen yon sun in t' sky over the years if I'd hid away every time I made a dolt of myself in public! So you took a tumble and went arse over elbow – if you'll excuse the language,' she added with a wicked grin. 'Who ain't at some time or other! You'll live. It's no big deal.'

'But I'm so em*barr*assed, Miss Frost.'

'Aye well. That'll teach thee to pace yourself next time, won't it?' she chuckled.

'Oh no. Never again. Not another drop will pass my lips, I can assure you of that.'

'Well? Are you going to stop feeling sorry for yourself and shift up from that bed, or do I have to drag yer out?'

Victor couldn't help but smile. 'All right.' What he'd learned about Phoebe now seemed worth getting up for. 'On one condition.'

'And what's that?'

'That you come with me.'

The laughter slipped from her face. 'But I told thee, I can't—'

'If I can brave it out with Dick Lavender, then you can, too. You've come so far. You can't give everything up because of your dislike of him, Miss Frost, it's silly. Ignore the man. All right?'

Her voice was small. 'All right.'

'Right then. Wait for me downstairs. It's time I got dressed.'

'Hello.'

'Hello,' Victor murmured. God, the sight of her and the struggle not to wrap her in his arms was immense. 'Miss Parsons, about last night—'

'Water under the bridge, Mr Hayes.'

'I'm sorry. I ran into a friend – the only person from my past, it seems, who still has time for me these days. One drink led to another . . .'

'So I saw. Bob won't find himself in trouble, will he?'

'I shouldn't think so, thanks to yours and Mrs Tibbs's quick thinking getting him out of here. I don't know what on earth I was thinking. It will never happen again. And I, I will of course . . .' He swallowed hard. 'I'll apologise to Mr Lavender.'

'I hope for his sake that he has an apology ready for you, too. He had no right speaking to you as he did.'

A smile tugged at his mouth. 'Thank you for . . . well, you know. Offering your bed up for me last night. And for staying with me,' he added quietly. His eyes were locked to her face and he drank in every inch of her, the yearning to kiss her like a physical pain. 'It's something I will never forget.'

'Nor me. Although . . .'

'What is it, Miss Parsons?'

'I just . . . It doesn't matter.'

He stopped her with a gentle hand on her arm as she made to return to her work. 'Tell me.'

'Well, I . . . I awakened and you'd left.'

'I'm sorry.'

She nodded. 'Me too.'

There followed a quietness that, along with the eye contact, neither seemed willing to break. Then Kitty appeared to help them set up the tavern for the day and the moment was gone. Victor and Phoebe shared a small smile before going their separate ways to begin their duties.

He spotted Dick entering the premises midway through the evening. Gritting his teeth, he busied himself and pretended not to have noticed.

232

When next he looked up, Dick and Phoebe were talking quietly at the other end of the room. Then they were heading his way and he braced himself for the mocking looks and smirks and thinly veiled jibes. Yet they never came. This day, Dick's smile was absent. Expression straight, eyes creased in something akin to regret, he tilted his chin in greeting.

'Dick has something he wishes to say,' Phoebe told Victor.

'That, I do.' Dropping his gaze, Dick sighed. 'I were out of order last night. It were wrong of me to goad thee as I did. It were meant in jest but I took it too far and I'm sorry.'

The speech had seemed sincere, without a trace of dishonesty. Victor looked at the hand the other man had held out and wanted to punch his face in. *Well played, you slimy bastard, well played.* Then he saw that Phoebe was watching with hope in her eyes and his shoulders lost a little of their stiffness.

'I owe you an apology, too.' He took Dick's hand and shook it, doing his utmost not to squeeze too aggressively – for two pins, he'd have happily crushed every bone inside it.

'Bloody drink, eh? It does me no favours neither, and I put away more than my fair share last night. Truce?' Dick added with a disarming smile.

Victor nodded. 'Truce.'

Phoebe's relief was plain. She drew Dick away to pour him a beer, leaving Victor to get on with his work.

Watching them go, seeing the younger man place a dominant arm around her slim waist, she lifting her bright gaze up to Dick in gratitude that he'd made the effort to resolve matters with him, Victor wanted to bellow the injustice to the rafters. He imagined again the soft feel of her in bed last night – and carnal heat smoul-dered in his lower stomach, making his heart hammer. It was a sensation he hadn't known in what felt like an age – the recognition of it surprised him. His marriage, practically devoid of intimacy as it had been almost from the start, had succeeded in stifling those urges years ago – he'd believed *that* was long past for him. Shaking his head, he concentrated his attention on the next customer.

The remainder of the shift passed without incident, though Victor did notice that Suzannah had begun to shadow him whenever possible, which he thought a lit-tle odd. Almost tripping over her as he turned to a barrel and failed to spot she was behind him, he righted himself with a frown.

'What's wrong with you tonight, Miss Frost?'

'Wrong?'

'Yes. You've stuck to my side all evening. What is it?'

She looked as though ready to deny it, then she sighed and motioned across the room. Following her gaze, Victor's frown deepened. 'Mr Lavender?'

'Aye. I just . . . I feel better being nearby to thee when he's around.'

'He hasn't said something to you, has he? Anything inappropriate—?'

'Nay, nay,' she was quick to respond.

'Then what?'

'It's the drinking, I suppose.' She nodded. 'Aye, that's what it is. It makes me uncomfortable being around fel-las what knock it back as much as he does.'

Mystified by this, Victor laughed. 'Miss Frost, look around you. The tavern is full of such men!'

'I know, but he rubs me up the wrong way. Oh, ignore me,' she added, rolling her eyes and smiling. 'I'm being a grumpy cow. Must be the babby, eh, mucking up my emotions.'

'More than likely,' he said; he, too, had suspected the same thing. 'Actually, I'm glad you said that, as I've been thinking: how would you feel about possibly having to endure him for Christmas?'

'What d'you mean?'

'Well, I thought it would be nice for us all to spend the festive day together. You and me, Mrs Tibbs and Kitty if they have no other plans, and of course Miss Parsons. That may mean having to invite Mr Lavender, however, given their union.' The last word stuck in his craw, but he went on. 'What do you say?'

'The lass really means that much to thee that you're willing to suffer that man in your house for the whole day?'

He tried to laugh off her observation but failed. 'Yes,' he admitted.

'Then, aye.' Sighing, Suzannah nodded. 'I suppose I can do the same for your sake.'

Victor could hardly wait for closing time to come around so he could put his idea to Phoebe. Finally, the last customer left and only Dick remained. Victor kept his back to the couple as they bade each other farewell at the door but couldn't hide from the murmurs and soft laughter as they chaffed and teased and said their goodbyes. Then all went quiet and he glanced around to see the night was shut out and Phoebe was alone, clearing tables. He made his way across to her.

'All right?'

Victor nodded. 'You?'

'Tired, perhaps.'

'Yes.' He was silent for a moment, unable to find the words. He'd noticed that with her of late; he found himself tongue-tied like a daft lad whenever they were alone. 'I wanted to ask you something.'

Phoebe paused and put down the glasses she'd been collecting to give him her full attention.

'How would you feel about spending Christmas together this year? You, me, Miss Frost. Mrs Tibbs and Kitty—'

'What?' She looked crestfallen.

'Only if you wanted to, I mean . . .'

'Oh, Mr Hayes, I'd love to. But I'm afraid I can't,' she added, dashing away the smile that had sprung to his face at her initial enthusiasm. 'Dick's just asked me the very same. I said I'd join him this year. He hasn't any family of his own, you see, and I suppose I'm now the nearest thing to that, what with us planning to . . . well, you know,' she finished, dropping her gaze.

He knew all right. Though why, if what Suzannah had told him was true, was she allowing herself to be pulled along with all this? He couldn't stand it any more: 'You know you don't have to go through with the wedding if you're unsure.'

They stared at one another. Victor didn't know who was more surprised by his outburst, himself or Phoebe.

'I'm not getting any younger and Dick is a good catch. I'm flattered he wants me at all. I don't want to spend my life alone. I'd even like children someday. I just . . . I need to be needed. Can you understand that?'

Lost for words at the gentle honesty of her speech, he could only nod. *Oh, my love . . .*

'You will try to be happy for me, won't you, whatever happens?'

I need you, with everything that I am. Be mine. Please, his mind cried out to her, laying bare a tortured truth that his tongue never would. He couldn't give her what she

236

desired – the one thing Dick Lavender could offer her that he couldn't: marriage. And Victor knew she'd never settle for anything less; nor would he want her to. She deserved more than that. More than him. 'So long as you're happy, I'm happy,' he answered.

'What would I do without you, Mr Hayes?'

Savouring her touch on his shoulder as she pressed it softly, he smiled. 'Well, I'd better call Miss Frost down and we'll be on our way, leave you to get some rest.'

'Last night's sleep was the best I've ever had,' she blurted, and glanced away with an embarrassed laugh. 'I mean . . . What I meant was—'

'I know,' he interjected, to save her blushes. Then: 'Me too,' he whispered, winking, and she laughed again, making him smile.

'Miss Parsons can't make it for Christmas,' he said flatly to Suzannah minutes later as they were walking home.

Her innocent enough response had him pondering for the rest of the night:

'I wouldn't bank on that, love. I reckon she just might.'

Chapter 16

THE LILIAN WENT from strength to strength. Providing not only beverages but good, wholesome food and sound entertainment, coupled with the warm atmosphere and fun yet respectable reputation, it was a winning combination. Profit was excellent and still there were yet more new faces every night.

Despite this, just as Dick had promised, they had had no more trouble from Col Baines or his son. The duo gave the tavern and its staff a wide berth, which of course suited all concerned. The last thing they desired was a feud on their hands. That wouldn't have done the business any good at all.

However, the biggest change of all as time went on was in Suzannah. Phoebe had watched the transition with interest and knew Victor had, too. The woman was softer, quieter, her abrasive edges blurred. More unexpected still, she'd developed a deep and unabashed fixation for regular customer Big Red.

No one quite knew what to make of her caprice and so they didn't try, simply let her be. She wasn't harming anyone and she appeared content, so where was the problem? Big Red certainly didn't seem to mind this new attention that the beautiful younger woman showered upon him, that was for sure.

Then one evening, Phoebe witnessed something quite by chance that was to smash their contented coexistence to dust. It left her so shocked and confused that, at first, she questioned herself as to whether she'd imagined it.

The tavern was particularly busy. A large group of pugilists of varying nationalities had stopped in for a good time and, though they were behaving well and causing no bother, they were putting the drink away like it was going out of fashion. None more so than the Italians amongst their number, who turned their noses up at English beer in favour of wine. Victor had expressed worry that they might not have enough of the beverage to last them through the night.

Phoebe left him and Kitty serving to go and check the stock in the cellar. Yet midway down the steps, she realised at once that someone was already down there.

Grunts and heavy breathing – sounds she knew instinctively were carnal, despite her inexperience – reached her first. Then her eyes adjusted to the dim light and, as she peered through the gloom, two figures came into focus.

They had their backs to her, but Phoebe recognised Suzannah right away; there was no mistaking the flame-coloured mane. She was bent over a large barrel, legs parted, skirts up around her hips. Behind her, his top half lost in shadow, stood a man. Gripping her waist with both hands, he was thrusting hard and fast inside her.

Phoebe tore her gaze away and padded back up to the tavern. Mind spinning, she collected empty glasses from the tables absently, her gaze creeping to where sat Big Red, laughing and talking with his companions, completely oblivious to the goings-on beneath his feet. He'd fallen hard for his new love interest – how could Suzannah do this? More to the point, why?

She was earning a decent wage in the kitchen here. Why feel the need to sell herself as she'd done in the past? For that's what this was, Phoebe was convinced of it. She'd seen an opportunity to make some easy money and had sneaked one of the customers downstairs. It was only by sheer chance she hadn't got away with it. For how much longer would she have carried on this activity otherwise? Was this even the first time it had happened? And her with child, too. Dear God, just what was she playing at?

This couldn't continue. Victor must be told; the two of them would have to confront Suzannah, without a doubt.

Then there she was. Eyes wide in her pale face, she slipped undetected into the drinking room and made her way over to Big Red. Sitting beside him, she rested her head on his shoulder, her expression flat, empty of emotion. Frowning deeply, Phoebe resumed her work, her stare flicking continually back to the door.

Several minutes elapsed without a sign of the man. He was waiting a while before following Suzannah up so as not to raise suspicion, she surmised; they had obviously planned this through.

When finally he appeared, Phoebe felt the world tip on its axis – the floor lurched beneath her feet and she staggered.

Dick.

Transfixed, she watched him glance around, then, as though satisfied no one had seen, he plastered in place his stunning smile and headed for a tankard of beer.

Dick had just made love to Suzannah. Dick had . . . with Suzannah. Dick and Suzannah. Dick and Suzannah – the mantra banged at her brain like a hammer.

'There you are, lass.' It was him, fresh drink in hand. Phoebe looked at him mutely.

'Fancy a turn?' he asked as Mrs Tibbs struck up a new song and pulled Phoebe against him with his free arm without waiting for an answer.

Too hazy in mind to either refuse or resist, she swayed with him to the music. Seeking out Suzannah over his shoulder, her eyes remained rooted to her throughout.

When the dance was over, Dick brushed her cheek with the tip of his nose and kissed her forehead. Smiling, he turned and sauntered off back to his friends.

For an age, Phoebe stood, her gaze flitting from him to the woman. Then she nodded to herself and calmly returned to her duties.

Later, after closing, when she and Victor were alone, clearing up, she said, 'About your plans for Christmas. Does the offer still stand, Mr Hayes?'

His surprise was clear. 'Yes, of course.'

'Then Dick and I would love to come.'

'You and . . . Yes, that's fine. What made you change your mind?'

A lump was creeping to her throat – she swallowed it back desperately. 'I realised I'd prefer nothing more than to spend the day amongst friends. You, Mrs Tibbs, Kitty.' She smiled. 'And of course, Miss Frost and Dick.'

'I've asked Big Red along. It seemed only right, given that Miss Frost has taken a shine to him.'

'Excellent.'

Victor scrutinised her for a moment then cocked his head. 'Are you all right, Miss Parsons?'

'Never better.'

'You're sure? Only you seem—'

'I'm sure,' she murmured. 'I'll be off to my bed now, Mr Hayes.'

'Goodnight.'

At the door, something made her pause. She turned and made her way back over to him. Neither spoke as she reached up and drew his head towards her own. She pressed her lips to his in a lingering kiss and he returned it without question.

'Goodnight,' she said, then retraced her steps and headed upstairs.

The moment Phoebe entered her bedroom and closed the door, her legs buckled and she dropped to the floor with a silent scream.

From where she'd found the strength tonight, to smile and chat with the customers, pretend all was as it should be, she'd never begin to know. But she had. She'd done it, and no one suspected a thing. Her idea could go ahead, just like she'd planned.

Forcing herself to regain her composure – it would be good practice during the days to come – she rose and undressed for bed.

Rays from a lacklustre sun were pushing half-heartedly through the thin curtains when Phoebe awoke. Almost instantly, an image of Dick's bare white buttocks pumping back and forth in his ravishing of Suzannah struck behind her eyes and she closed them again quickly.

This morning was a new day and she'd get through it, just like she'd done last night. She would. She had to.

Drawing back the bedclothes, she swung her legs around and got to her feet. Following the same pattern of every other day, she dressed and tidied her hair in the small mirror then made her way to the kitchen.

'Morning, lass.'

'Morning, Mrs Tibbs.' Smiling, Phoebe took a seat at the table and reached for the teapot.

'You're up and about early; Kitty's not yet from her bed.'

'Yes. I got a good night's sleep.'

Placated, Mrs Tibbs returned to her own drink, leaving Phoebe alone with her thoughts.

She'd been on the brink of asking Victor to stay here last night. She'd needed his presence beside her, yearned to have him hold her in bed, soothe her mind and heart as only he could, as she'd done for him. Now, she didn't know whether she was relieved or regretful that she'd stopped herself at the kiss. *The kiss.*

Though her heart tripped several beats, she knew not a shred of shame for her actions. She'd wanted to do that for a good long while, she realised. So why hadn't she? The obvious answer came – loyalty to Dick – and she nearly choked on her tea. The irony was so tragic it was almost funny. Almost.

She'd noticed a shifting recently in her relationship with Victor, sensed his changing feelings towards her – or was that fanciful thinking on her part? He'd sworn once before he'd never act unfaithfully towards his wife. And that's what Kate was, would always be, whether they were parted or not. Phoebe just wished things could be different. For she knew now that if Victor was to walk in here this very moment and declare his love for *her*, she'd go to him like a shot.

Strangely, it was Dick who had showed her what the older man meant to her. Where her heart lay. His treatment of her had proved what, just beneath the surface, she'd always known: he wasn't the one for her. Held up against Victor's moral and correct way of behaving,

243

there was no comparison between the two. She couldn't ever see him doing anything to purposely hurt her, as Dick had.

Victor just didn't have it in him, and that's what she admired and loved the most about him. He was a decent fellow through and through – Kate was a fool. Any woman in her right mind would be lucky indeed to be able to call him hers.

The rest of the day passed much the same as any other. Phoebe did her utmost to avoid Suzannah and when that wasn't possible was as polite as she normally was. The woman suspected nothing of her new-found knowledge and this lent Phoebe strength to see her through to Christmas – when the pretence would be done with and she'd be free to get on with her life. The day couldn't come soon enough.

The same was said concerning Dick – though Phoebe found the act of making out all was as it should be with him infinitely harder. Each small squeeze of her hand and stroke of her hair from him had her flesh scream-ing protest, now. She couldn't bear him even in the same room as her, let alone his touch, and worried she'd explode at any moment and tell him to get away from her. But no. That, she couldn't do. Not here, not yet. The time would come for that soon enough. For just a little while longer, she must endure it. She *would*.

Then, finally, the festive Sunday in question was here, and she knew a mixture of finality and fizzing dread. After today, nothing would be the same, for any of them.

'Morning, Phoebe, and a very merry Christmas to thee!' trilled Kitty, full of yuletide cheer, as Phoebe joined her in the kitchen. 'Sup of tea?'

Phoebe nodded. Then seeing that her hands shook slightly as she took the cup, she set it down on the table in front of her quickly, lest Kitty noticed. The less people knew of her inner tumultuousness – and the events soon to come – the better.

'Mrs Tibbs has left already,' the girl offered as Phoebe suddenly glanced around. 'She said as how she wanted to set off early to make good headway, and that I was to tell thee she hoped we have a reet gradely day.'

Again, Phoebe bobbed her head. The older woman wouldn't be joining them at Victor's, was instead spending the day with her only living relative: a blind cousin named Mrs Price who lived on the other side of Manchester. A kindly customer of the tavern had offered Mrs Tibbs a lift there on his cart. Secretly, Phoebe wished she'd chosen to spend the day with the rest of them, would need her calming presence and all the support she could get later.

'I'd best get a move on. Suzannah's expecting me shortly.'

As Kitty flitted across the room to collect her shawl, Phoebe did her very best to force a smile, saying, 'Yes. I'll follow on just as soon as Dick arrives.'

When the girl had gone, she let her shoulders sag and closed her eyes. She could picture the scene now: Kitty helping Suzannah to prepare the dinner, as she'd promised, whilst Victor and Big Red chatted by the fire. Peaceful, normal. An average, happy little party awaiting the last guests – she and Dick – and expecting an enjoyable Christmas afternoon they would never forget. Except this one was to be anything but. Oh, it would be memorable, that was for sure, but not for the reasons the rest of them anticipated.

The knock came and Phoebe sucked in a ragged breath. Then she was fixing in place that practised smile and, after putting on her bonnet and checking in the mirror that it was straight, she collected her shawl from her room and headed downstairs.

'Merry Christmas, lass,' Dick said as she opened the tavern door to him. 'Are we all set?'

'A very merry Christmas to you, Dick.' She willed herself to reach up and press her lips lightly to his cheek – then turned her face quickly lest he saw the repulsion she just knew would be sparking from her eyes. 'Yes, let's go.'

After locking the door, she led the way towards Victor's house. Dick insisted on putting his arm around her as they walked; the struggle not to squirm at his touch was almost more than she could stand.

'You're certain he wants me there?' Dick asked. 'I'm not exactly his favourite person, am I?'

'Of course – it was Mr Hayes's idea.'

Dick gave a dismissive sniff. 'Aye, well. That were to get thee to agree to go, that's all. He'd not have extended the invitation to me as well if he could have helped it, I'll bet.'

She said nothing to this, simply shook her head in reassurance. Dick hadn't been best pleased when she'd put to him that they take up Victor's offer of dinner at his house with the others instead.

Naturally, he hadn't let it show for too long, had soon checked the tightening of his jaw and plastered in place his dazzling smile. He'd relented, saying if it was what she really wanted and would make her happy then he was only too willing to go along with her wishes. They could always spend the festive day just the two of them next year. To which she'd agreed with a demure nod, all the while knowing there was more chance of icicles forming in hell than there was of that happening. He'd be long gone from her life by then.

'Miss Parsons, welcome. Mr Lavender.' Upon answering their knock, Victor turned his smiling face from her to give the other man a brief nod. 'Please, do come in.'

'Season's greetings, Mr Hayes.' Phoebe touched his hand. 'Thank you for having us today.'

'My thanks to you – both of you,' he added, throwing Dick a half-smile, 'for coming.'

She followed him down the passage towards the kitchen, Dick trailing behind her. Inside, the smell of roasting goose permeated the air and the room was a hub of activity. A laughing and chattering Kitty and Suzannah had the dinner well underway; Phoebe ushered Dick towards the fire, where sat the men, then, taking a breath, she rolled up her sleeves and headed over to the women.

'What can I do to help?' Keeping her eyes averted from Suzannah, her question was directed at Kitty. 'The parsnips, perhaps?'

'Aye, thanks.' Pausing to wipe her hot brow with her wrist, the girl smiled. 'You get them lot peeled and they can be set to roasting with the tatties,' she explained with a nod to the heap of potatoes.

Nodding, Phoebe got to work. Behind her, she could hear Victor and Big Red deep in conversation; Dick, on the other hand, made no effort to join in the discussions. She knew if she'd have turned, she'd have seen him nursing a drink with a haughty air about him, as though he was too good for the company he was in – she shook her head discreetly. He really was an uppity young fool; how hadn't she noticed it before? Or perhaps she had, she realised, and simply told herself she was mistaken? That his false-grandeur ways were a figment of her imagination rather than face the truth of

247

things? Lord, that she'd allowed herself to be so blind . . .

'Nearly done there, lass?'

Suzannah's voice sliced through her ruminations and she brought her head up sharply. To her chagrin, she saw that, despite her question, the other woman's attention was not on her at all but on the men – she was staring intently at one in particular, and Phoebe had no need to look around to discover who it would be. *Shameless, heartless harlot, she was nothing else.* 'Yes, all done,' she muttered, bumping Suzannah out of the way with her hip and crossing to the bowl to rinse the chopped vegetables.

'Ta, thanks,' she gushed to Phoebe, dragging her gaze back and bestowing on her a beautiful smile. 'I'll see to them now then, if you wouldn't mind getting started on that cabbage there . . . ?'

Trying and failing to move her lips in a friendly response, Phoebe could only nod. Lifting the knife, she took her frustration out on the dark-leaved sphere.

Later, as the women took a break before serving up to enjoy a well-earned cup of tea, Phoebe kept Kitty talking about anything and everything that entered her head – rather that than give Suzannah an open window in which to strike up conversation with her. The struggle to act naturally with the woman whom she could now hardly stand to look at was becoming unbearable. *Not long now . . .*

'Right, fellas, if you'd like to take your seats,' Kitty announced finally, much to Phoebe's relief and nerve-jarring anticipation. 'Grub's ready!'

The six of them trooped to the table, which was decorated with sprigs of holly on the bright white cloth, and upon which a fine crockery service and sparkling cutlery had been arranged with care. Victor took his place at the head of the table and Phoebe took the seat facing him. To his left and right were Kitty and Big Red – which left the chairs either side of her open to Dick and Suzannah. Unable to look at them, Phoebe kept her eyes straight ahead.

'This looks magnificent, ladies.' Nodding appreciatively as his gaze travelled the length of the table, which groaned under the weight of the golden bird on its trivet, large gravy boat alongside, and dishes of steaming vegetables, Victor smiled. 'A very merry Christmas,' he told them, holding aloft his glass. 'And may the new year ahead bring happiness and good health to you all.'

'Merry Christmas!' everyone echoed.

As Suzannah rose to begin dishing out the food, Phoebe stopped her with a hand on her arm. '*I'd* like to say a few words, if I may?' she announced calmly, though inside her head was a jumble of pain and bubbling fury.

'Of course, Miss Parsons,' Victor said as Suzannah resumed her seat.

'First of all,' she began, her stare taking in each of the company in turn bar the two beside her, 'I wish to apologise to you good people sitting before me. I've given this careful consideration and, though it saddens me to spoil what should be a harmonious day of celebration and giving thanks, I'm afraid I have no choice. It has to be now, away from the public gaze of the tavern, whilst we're all seated around this table together, as the repercussions shall affect all of you here present.'

In the heavy silence that followed, Phoebe took a deep breath. Then, glancing at the five faces now wreathed in confusion, she began.

'As you're aware, the man seated to my right made me a proposal of marriage—'

'Which tha accepted, lucky fella that I am!' Dick piped up with a grin and a self-satisfied nod.

She ignored him. Then: 'I'm here to say that there shall be no such union between the two of us. For Mr Dick Lavender here is a fraud.' She finally turned her face to his, which was stretched in utter astonishment, his mouth hanging wide open. 'You believed me to be unaware, is that it, *darling*?' she finished in a mocking drawl.

'Phoebe?'

It was Victor speaking. She lifted her gaze to his.

'Phoebe, what . . . ?'

'You want to know what, Mr Hayes? Then I shall tell you – all of you.' Raising both hands, she pointed quivering fingers at the duo either side of her. 'Dick has been having an affair. With none other than this one here – isn't that right, Miss Frost?' she asked, swivelling her glare to the other woman, whose complexion had turned corpse-grey with horror.

For a long moment, the room seemed to hold its breath. Then Dick was on his feet, the speed of the action sending his chair crashing to the floor. 'What in the bloody 'ell is the meaning of this?' he shouted. 'You've gone mad, that's what!'

'Oh no. *Oh* no, Dick. My faculties are running perfectly well, at long last. You, sir, are a low-down liar and I'm exposing you for the viper in the grass that you are.'

'And who's been dripping these lies into yon ears, eh? You tell me that.' He turned on Suzannah. 'This is your doing, in't it? Just what has tha been spouting—?'

'Miss Frost has said nothing – nor would I have expected her to, for she's as sneaky, cowardly and completely void of morals as you are,' Phoebe told him. Ignoring Suzannah's tearful gasp, she went on. 'You see,

Dick, I saw the pair of you with my own two eyes. Together, at the tavern last week. In the beer cellar.' She paused and, leaning forward, whispered harshly, 'Fornicating! Go on, just you try and deny it.'

'Lass?' Big Red rose slowly, his gaze deep with hurt on Suzannah. 'It ain't true . . . Is it?'

Holding out her arms to him in a helpless motion, the woman could only open and shut her mouth – Phoebe answered for her: 'I'm sorry, Big Red, but it is. I witnessed the whole sordid debacle. Admittedly, her lover's upper half was in shadow, but Dick emerged from the cellar after her and—'

'Oh, did I really?' Dick was shaking his head. He was no longer shouting; in fact, his voice held a withering note that threw Phoebe a little – he appeared almost embarrassed for her.

'Yes,' she insisted, her anger at his blatant arrogance mounting. 'You did—!'

'You're wrong.'

'What? That you even have the gall to look me square in the eye and say that? I *know* what I saw.'

'Which was what, exactly? Her carrying on with a fella whose face you didn't even see? And me supposedly coming out of the cellar after her? You witnessed me leaving, aye? Or could it be that you happened to look up as I was passing by the cellar door?'

'Well . . . I think . . .' Slowly, heat trickled to her cheeks. She frowned. 'No, I know. I *know* that you had left, I . . .'

'You're absolutely certain of it, are yer? Think long and hard afore answering, Phoebe. Think and be completely sure.'

She'd expected him to blow and bluster, to outright deny, perhaps even admit his folly and beg from her her

251

forgiveness. What she hadn't anticipated was that he'd turn this around and pin the blame solely on her shoulders. That he'd insist with such vigour that she was unquestioningly mistaken. Yet here he was, doing just that. And more surprisingly still, it was working. Her unwavering conviction of just moments before was rapidly waning. He was right, wasn't he? She *hadn't* seen the identity of the man who had been taking Suzannah over that barrel. And afterwards . . . ?

Desperately, she cast her mind back to what she'd assumed was proof of the mystery person having been Dick. She hadn't actually seen him emerge from the cellar and into the tavern, had she? she thought with sickly realisation. She'd merely caught sight of him walking from the direction of the doorway. *Dear God.*

Had he simply been passing and she'd put two and two together and come up with five? Was it possible she'd got this – got him – horribly wrong?

'Well, Phoebe?' His gaze was clouded in hurt, disappointment and deep offence. 'Can you?'

'I . . .' Swallowing hard, she lowered her head. 'No,' she admitted in a strangled whisper. 'No, I can't be absolutely certain.'

A collective breath went up around the table. Dick fell to his knees in front of her.

'I would never do such a thing, my lass, not to thee. You must believe me.'

Gazing into the bright sapphire pools that were his eyes, shining with unequivocal honesty and desperation to have her see the truth, she felt herself softening towards him with something akin to the old affection she'd known when they first met, and which suspicion had diminished of late. She shook her head. This was the second time she'd besmirched his character by accusing him of something terrible. How did he bear her, at all? 'Oh, Dick. I'm sorry.'

'Eeh, lass.' He enveloped her in his arms and, squeezing her eyes shut, she clung to him. 'Let's not say another word about it, eh? You made a mistake. No matter. You're only human, after all. That's an end to it.'

'But Dick, to accuse you of such a thing . . .' Phoebe craned her neck around to glare at Suzannah. 'This is your doing. You, *again*, have had me suffering untold anguish these past few days with your deplorable and selfish actions. I've been in utter turmoil! So who was he,' she demanded, 'if not Dick here? For there definitely was a man, that much I can be sure of. I saw you, saw it all. A customer, was he? Is that it? You had the audacity to take a punter down into our cellar?'

Silent tears coursed down Suzannah's face. She swung her head in denial. 'You don't understand . . .'

'What is there to? We pay you a decent wage to cook for us, do we not? So what, then?' she pressed at the woman's miserable nod. 'What reason could you possibly have to do what you did?'

Turning away, Big Red reached for his jacket. 'I can't listen to any more of this, I'm going.'

'Nay, wait, please!' Suzannah made to grasp his arm, but he shrugged her off. 'Please, Big Red—'

'Whatever I thought we had . . . It's done, *we're* done.' He swiped the air with his hands. 'Over with, finished. I'll see myself out.' A stiff nod to Victor and he was gone.

'Oh God, nay!' The strength left Suzannah. She broke down and wept. 'This is all your doing, this is!' she screamed suddenly to Dick. 'I hate you!'

Frowning, Phoebe turned to him. 'What does she mean?'

Dick didn't miss a beat: 'I didn't want to say, didn't

want to cause ructions, to hurt thee . . .' He closed his eyes and sighed. 'She's been after me from the off.' Ignoring Suzannah's gasp, he nodded. 'Trying it on any opportunity she can, she is, has been for weeks. I told her I ain't interested, that it's thee I want, but it's like talking to that wall there. She's obsessed. Her snaring Big Red were some daft and pitiful attempt to make me jealous. She told me as much herself. Now it seems – in your eyes at least,' he added harshly to Suzannah, his gaze a mere slit, 'I'm to blame for the fella seeing the light and dropping thee? Nay. It's your whoring what's the cause of that, aye, not me. So you just mind your tongue,' he finished, voice low with warning.

'What?' Phoebe gulped back furious tears. 'How could you?' she whispered to the woman.

Suzannah had turned puce with some unspoken emotion; pent-up outrage, it appeared – likely that Dick had called her to account on her despicable conduct, Phoebe surmised – and she was shaking violently. Then a last look at Dick and now the fight seemed to desert her. She dropped her shoulders, murmuring, 'Oh, what's the point, at all, in any of it any more?'

'What this man says is right?' Victor's voice was low with shock-filled horror. 'Miss Frost? Is it?'

'If you like.'

'What I'd *like* is the truth!'

She didn't look his way, simply nodded. 'Aye. Aye, it is.'

'But *why?*'

Shrugging, she said, 'Well, he's a looker, ain't he? I couldn't help myself. Never could, eh, where men are concerned, and I have the reputation to prove it,' she added bitterly. 'All that bluster I gave thee about me not being able to stand Dick and that he weren't right for Phoebe – well. That were my way of keeping you off my scent, off my real feelings for him. It were nobbut play-acting so as you'd not cotton on.' She nodded to confirm her statement. 'Aye. That were it.'

'Then you leave me with no alternative.' Victor lowered his head. 'Pack your things and leave.'

'But . . . where will I go?'

'That is no concern of mine.'

'But, Victor! The baby—'

'You should have thought of that poor innocent mite before you gave in to your wicked compulsions. I warned you, Miss Frost, warned what would happen if you ever did Miss Parsons wrong again. Well, didn't I?'

'Aye,' she whispered.

'And yet here we are. No, I'm sorry, but all your chances are well and truly spent. You've tried my last thread of patience. I want you gone from this house this minute. Go!'

Phoebe was stunned, had never seen the man before her as angry. Nor could she believe he was seeing through his threat. He was kicking Suzannah out, was actually evicting her from their lives, just as he'd promised he would, should she ever attempt to do anything to hurt her again.

Knowing the man he was, not to mention his fondness for Suzannah, and appreciating how much it must be taking him to do this, Phoebe couldn't have loved him more in this moment if she'd tried. And yet the burning question still remained: why *did* this woman hate her so? Seemingly from day one, she'd done all in her power to try to destroy Phoebe's life. Why? Just what was the motive behind her seemingly sheer hatred?

'Jealousy, that's what it is,' murmured Dick, as though he'd read Phoebe's mind. He stared Suzannah out coldly. 'Go on, then. Do as the man says and get gone.'

After a long hard look at him, Suzannah turned and left.

Stiff silence held them in its grasp whilst, overhead, Suzannah's footfalls filtered through as she flitted around her room collecting and packing her things. Finally, she reappeared at the kitchen door.

'I'm sorry, sorry for everything,' she said simply, before turning and walking from the house.

Kitty rose from the table and without a word hurried down the hall after her, closing the door quietly behind herself. Phoebe did her best to stem the prick of hurt at this – there had been the blossoming of a friendship between the women over the weeks, it was true, but still . . . Suzannah was the one in the wrong in all this; surely Kitty should be siding with Phoebe instead, whom she'd known the longest, after all . . . Oh, how she wished Mrs Tibbs was here.

'I'm sorry.'

Looking to Victor, Phoebe released a sigh. 'You have nothing to berate yourself for, Mr Hayes, nothing at all. It is I who should apologise.' She let her gaze sweep over the table and the much-anticipated fare gone to waste. 'I've ruined the festive day for you, for everyone. I don't know why . . . what I was *thin*king. I should have conducted this matter in private days ago when I first had my suspicions. You've gone to so much trouble here and I . . . Poor Big Red! That was cruel of me, cruel to have him discover what he did in front of an audience. Oh, what a horrid mess!'

Dick put what was meant as a comforting arm around

256

her shoulders, but it didn't have the desired effect – Phoebe found herself shrinking still at his touch. 'Don't beat yourself up about it, lass, what's done is done. Why don't we get out of here, eh? Come on, I'll walk thee back—'

'Actually, Dick,' she cut in quietly, extracting herself from his hold but bestowing upon him a soft smile lest he took offence, 'I'd like a word alone with Mr Hayes, and afterwards I'd rather be by myself, if you don't mind.'

'Oh. Right. I'll call on thee at the tavern, later, shall I?'

'Tomorrow would be best, please. And Dick,' she added, catching his sleeve as he made to turn, 'sorry again for . . . everything.'

He kissed her lightly on the brow, bobbed his head to Victor in farewell and was gone. Moments later, Kitty re-entered the kitchen. Eyes downcast, she made straight for her shawl, hanging by the door.

'Kitty?' Phoebe's voice was gentle. 'Kitty, are you mad at me?'

'Nay, 'course not.'

'Are you sure? Only you seem—'

'I feel heartsore for Suzannah, if you must know. All that she were blathering just now, about her having been chasing your fella and that . . . Well, I don't believe a word of it. She felt forced to spout them lies, she did, I know it. She's frickened witless of him. Aye, she is, she—'

'Miss Frost said all this?'

'Well, no. Not in so many words. I caught up with her in t' street and I asked her if it were all true, and though she said aye, I could tell it weren't—'

'Kitty, Kitty . . .' Phoebe sighed. 'This is what she does. There are things you know nothing about, things she's done to me before you came on the scene. Her

257

spitefulness, this vendetta she's developed towards me from the very beginning . . . She's intent on ruining me for reasons only she knows.'

'Not this time.' Kitty was resolute. 'She's innocent of what Dick's accusing her of, Phoebe. If you'd only hear her out, proper like, without him there shooting warning looks in her direction.'

'No.'

'Just seek her out and listen to her, and you'd see—'

'I said no.' Phoebe's interjection was firm, her patience with the girl before her spent. 'I've wasted enough of my time on giving that woman the benefit of the doubt and second chances. I will not provide her the opportunity to hurt me again. No more. That's an end to it.'

Kitty closed her mouth. Donning her shawl, she said quietly, 'I'll be away home, if you don't mind, only I've a thundering headache on me . . .'

'You go,' murmured Phoebe. 'I'll follow on shortly.'

The instant the front door clicked shut behind the girl, Victor came around the table and enveloped Phoebe in his arms. 'Lass. Lass.'

'Oh, Mr Hayes. What a horrible, horrible day.'

'Sshhh. I'm here.'

'Have I made a mistake of everything? Is Kitty right: am I in the wrong here?'

He shook his head. '*You* have done nothing, nothing.'

This hadn't gone as she'd planned at all. An explosive conclusion was what she'd anticipated and, more predominantly, change. The reality was anti-climactic, to say the least. She felt incredibly deflated. And disappointed. She did, it was true.

'All these days, the agonising . . . It was Miss Frost's betrayal that seared far more acutely, you know,' Phoebe admitted in a whisper against his chest. 'The thought of my letting her back in, that I'd trusted her *again*, given her yet another chance, believed we were after all friends, and she'd trodden it all into the dirt like it meant nothing . . .' She paused, then: 'It overrode any hurt I felt concerning Dick,' she revealed. 'Actually . . . it was like I'd been set loose. That I was free. And now, now I'm back where I started and I . . . I don't know what to do to get out of it and, and . . .'

'Are you saying it's Dick you wish to break away from? Is it? The other night, when you kissed me at the tavern, I'd half dared to hope that, that maybe you . . . Is it?' he repeated.

Lifting her head, she stared up into Victor's face through a wave of shimmering tears. 'Yes, Mr Hayes. Yes. That's exactly what I'm saying.'

'Phoebe . . . My dearest, sweetest girl.'

She closed her eyes and, when his mouth found hers, her lips parted hungrily in response. He crushed her against him and she relaxed, her body melting in his ardent hold.

'You don't love Dick Lavender. Say it,' he rasped. 'I must hear it.'

There was no hesitation – in fact, she knew an overwhelming desperation to instil life into the statement, the *truth*: 'I don't love him. It's you I love. It's you, always.'

The world seemed to hold its breath as Victor gazed on her in dazed silence. Then he was uttering the most euphonious reply – he cried out in rapture:

'And I love you, Phoebe. God, how I love you. Oh, my darling.'

'Victor . . .' She lifted her face once more for his kiss – then drew back with a groan when a sharp knock sounded at the door. 'Who on earth . . . ?'

His breathing was heavy, his voice thick with desire.

'Wait here,' he murmured. 'Don't move. I'll get rid of them.'

They struggled to release one another and when finally they broke apart and he'd gone she yearned for his touch instantly. She heard him open the front door and his shocked gasp – then a familiar voice reached her from across the passageway and the blood iced in her veins. No . . .

'It's Kate.'

Victor's disclosure was unnecessary – she well remembered, all right, the woman who had followed him into the kitchen. Phoebe could do nothing but stare back in painful confusion. *What in the world could she want?*

'I wish to speak with my husband,' Kate announced with definite emphasis on the last word – Phoebe's face instantly blazed with colour. 'Alone.'

Her husband. Mortification locked her in crippling silence as she imagined her lips on his moments before, her famished body aching for him, *all* of him . . . He was a married man. *Kate's* man, in every sense of the word. And she'd . . . she'd thrown herself at him, declared her love for him. Attempted to lay claim to a man she had no right to . . . God above, she was as bad as Suzannah! She must leave. She *had* to get far from here, from it all.

'I'll come and see you just as soon as I can.' Victor had followed her swift exit to the door. That he was as flummoxed as she by his wife's unexpected arrival was clear. 'Kate is likely after me upping her money, I'll bet.'

Phoebe nodded, knew he'd been paying his wife a generous allowance since her desertion, seeing it as his duty; she was, after all, his responsibility, with no disposable income of her own. 'Perhaps.'

'Trust me, that's all this will be about. Wait for me at the tavern. I'll send her away just as soon as I can. And

260

lass?' He caressed her cheek tenderly. 'Remember, I love you.'

But you're not mine to have, never will be, her heart cried out. Nevertheless, biting back tears, she couldn't help but mouth the declaration back to him. Then she turned and hurried through the cold streets for home.

Chapter 17

IT SEEMED SHE was the only soul in Manchester this festive afternoon who hadn't a single special person to call her own. Of course, this she knew to be untrue – for countless folk, this December day would be spent reflecting on those lost rather than in carefree celebration – but it was difficult to acknowledge the fact when despair's cold fingers had you in their grasp.

Loneliness had set in the moment she arrived back and discovered that Kitty had not yet returned. Nor was Mrs Tibbs due for a good few hours; the emptiness was like a physical thing, dark and heavy around her heart, which she found impossible to shake.

One thing she had shed, however, was her earlier shame. She wouldn't berate herself for loving him, married or not – couldn't, no matter how hard she might have tried. He didn't want Kate and she didn't want him. *They* fitted. *They* were meant to be. And yet . . .

Despite Victor's pledge to come to her, Phoebe knew with an almost unearthly certainty that he wouldn't.

Kate's visit was set to change things and, though she couldn't say why, not yet at any rate, she just knew it to be so. The foreboding twisting her guts to ribbons was a sure sign she'd be foolish to try to dismiss it.

Wandering to the kitchen, she put the kettle on the

fire for tea. Then, changing her mind, she removed it and headed for her room, where, after closing the curtains on the world, she burrowed beneath the bedsheets. What seemed like seconds later she was being prodded awake; blinking, she sat up with a frown to find Kitty standing over her.

'Kitty, you're back.'

'I called in on a friend earlier and the hours ran away with me.'

'Hours . . . ? What time is it?'

'Almost seven.'

'Seven?' She was shocked.

'Aye. You've a visitor downstairs, Phoebe.'

She was fully awake instantly. *Victor. He had come after all! Everything was going to be all right!*

Following the girl from the room, she hurried down to the tavern.

'All right, lass?'

'Dick.' The level of crushing disappointment snatched the breath from her; she struggled to keep herself from crying. 'What are you doing here?'

'I couldn't wait 'til the morrow, wanted to check tha were well.'

'I'm . . . yes, fine,' she lied. Then for want of something to say as the silence grew: 'Please, sit down. I'll get you a drink.'

They sat at a table with their glasses – for Dick his usual ale, whilst Phoebe had thrown caution to the wind and opted for a measure of weak beer – and for several minutes, neither spoke as they sipped.

The soft lighting from the fire Kitty must have built cast pale gold shadows along the ceiling and walls and fell across Dick's face, lending his blue eyes shine and his sculptured jaw added definition – he looked the most handsome in this instant that Phoebe had ever seen him. She watched him with only half her mind on the moment, letting the alcohol warm her veins and dull the ache in her soul.

Victor wasn't coming, just as she'd known he wouldn't. He was lost to her before she'd even had a chance to rejoice in finding him. Dick had sought her out instead. He was the wrong man, but he was here. She needed another drink . . .

Mrs Tibbs arrived back at one point, all smiles at the enjoyable hours spent with her family, but one look at Phoebe sitting morose, her glass of beer clutched to her breast, and she quietly retreated upstairs, where Phoebe knew Kitty would be ready and waiting to fill her in on all the disastrous details of the day. The older woman returned sometime later with a tray holding ham and bread, which she placed on the table between Phoebe and Dick without a word, before escaping back to the private quarters. Ever perceptive – of course she'd have been informed by the girl that no one had sampled a morsel of the dinner at Victor's.

Whilst Dick helped himself to the food more than once, Phoebe nibbled on a single slice of ham absently. The pot of tea that had accompanied the plate, however, went untouched in favour of another round of ales.

When winds buffeted the building and rain pecked sharply at the windowpanes, Phoebe's thoughts turned for the first time to Suzannah. She cursed herself for her generosity at wondering, however fleetingly, about the newly destitute woman's welfare. Where would she go this night, and the rest? Just what would become of the child she carried? Why, *why* had she done this to Phoebe, to herself, again? For the life of her, Phoebe just couldn't fathom any of it.

'To think I believed her capable of change.' Phoebe heard the words, caught the alcohol slur within the tone and realised it was she who was speaking, that she'd given her ruminations life. 'A double fool, that's what I am.'

'Nay, you're not. Anyroad, no more dwelling on that one,' Dick insisted, and changed the subject before she could utter anything further on the matter.

Later, their effort at small talk spent, the two of them sat close together mutely, staring into the fading fire. The house and street beyond were still and free from noise, as though the whole world bar them slept. In the deepening twilight Dick's arm went around her shoulders and drew her nearer still. Closing bleary eyes that burned with unshed tears and blotting out Victor's face from her mind – *where in God's name was he?* – she snuggled against the man holding her.

Moments passed, then Dick stood and, without speaking, held out his hand. Phoebe rose unsteadily to her feet and placed her fingers in his palm. With a head full of nothing, she allowed him to lead her towards the stairs.

The sheets were cool on her skin and she gasped a little as he lay her down on the bed, only then realising she was naked. That's right: Dick had undressed her upon them entering the bedroom, she recalled with a half-yawn. Through an unfocused haze, she watched him where he stood at the foot of the bed removing his shirt and trousers.

He climbed on to the mattress and lifted her legs, parting her thighs and moving in to kneel in front of her. A small cry escaped her as he gained some entry with smooth and measured force, which he smothered by putting a hand over her mouth.

'We don't want to waken the others, do we?'

The drink fog inside her head was thickening. 'Dick . . .'

'Shh. Close your eyes, relax.'

Victor's smiling image assaulted her mind once more and she winced on a torrent of despair: 'You really want me, Dick.'

He edged deeper inside her and, now, her body offered no resistance.

'Yes . . . *you* do,' she murmured.

A raising of his eyebrows as to whether she was ready for them to continue, and she nodded.

The face on the pillow beside his was something he'd never anticipated seeing there again. Yet here it was, the truth behind what this meant gut-wrenching. Kate couldn't half pick her moments, he'd say that for her. *God damn it.*

Closing his eyes, Victor shook his head. Just a few short days ago, he'd never believed it possible that he could reach such happy heights until Phoebe kissed him. Willingly, full on the lips, seemingly without an ounce of regret afterwards. It had come as such a bolt from the blue that he'd initially questioned whether he was dreaming; but no. He'd been very much conscious – they both had. She'd chosen to do it, leaving him so delirious with joy that he could have floated from the room, for surely it could mean but one thing: she harboured a level of love for him in return. She must – why else?

Then came the stunning scene in his very kitchen yesterday . . . The memory, lodged in the forefront of his mind for now and always, flowed back. Again, he shook his head. To hear from her own sweet lips that she neither loved nor wanted Dick Lavender, that he himself had captured her heart . . . well. He hadn't adequate words to begin to describe what it had meant to him.

In his fantasy, a future, a new life, had opened up in front of him, for them both. Wives and bonds and sacred vows were forgotten. Nothing else mattered a jot other than that Phoebe wanted him in return, that the one he loved beyond measure could – nay, *did* – share his feelings . . . Then the knock on the door, and everything, *everything*, had withered to rot in the blink of an eye.

Kate had wasted no time in revealing her reason for coming, had announced it the moment they were alone: 'I've decided to give us another try.'

'Why?'

The whispered question, which he'd had to claw from his throat, had visibly thrown her; colouring, she'd glanced away. 'Because, Victor, you are my husband and I am your wife.'

No mention of love, he observed.

'Because,' she went on, 'I believe ours to be a marriage worth saving.'

Rubbish. 'Why now?'

'Why not?' she'd shot back. 'I don't have to have a reason, do I?' Then: 'Look, Victor.' Sighing, she'd crossed the floor towards him. 'I'm not saying it won't be difficult at first, that forgiveness will happen right away. But hopefully, eventually . . . Let's see, hm? What we have is surely worth fighting for. You agree, don't you?'

Did he? In the beginning, maybe. And now? Now, he loved another, but what choice had he? His feelings may have diminished for his wife, but his commitment towards her hadn't. He'd sworn before God to care for her – 'til death did they part. He knew what she spoke was the truth. Devastating, soul-crushing, of course, but no less right. *This couldn't be happening. My own darling Phoebe . . . Forgive me, help me, please . . .*

'The day we wedded, the promises we made . . . You

wouldn't go back on your word, Victor, would you?' Kate had murmured, the flash of victory in her eyes' hazel depths portraying clearly her confidence that he wouldn't.

'If it's what you want . . .'

'It is.'

'Then no,' he'd heard himself pronounce, whilst a part of him perished inside. 'I won't renege on my duty.'

Kate had asked nothing of why he and Phoebe were alone together upon her arrival, nor why there was a spread on the table to sustain a small army and who the guests were that it had been meant for. How he'd fared and what he'd been up to during their separation, she also didn't query. Neither had he offered an explanation. She seemingly wasn't interested enough to wonder, which suited him. In turn, he didn't take the trouble to ask what her sister made of this turn of events. Like his wife, he didn't want or care to find out the answers.

Later, she'd insisted they dine, had warmed up the spoiled food which they ate mostly in silence. He'd watched her from across the table, musing with what concentration he could muster on the ulterior motive for her sudden change of heart. For there had to be one. But what? He'd even offered to raise her allowance, if that was what was behind her decision, but she'd insisted he'd been generous in that regard and that no, it wasn't about money. Then why was she home? Why? Then again, did it matter? There could be no backing out of this now, either way.

He'd craved nothing more throughout that painfully long evening than to flee to the tavern and to Phoebe, to pour out his heart, explain, beg her understanding, but he hadn't felt able to walk out on Kate on her first night back. Instead, he'd stared at his newspaper without

268

reading it, whilst she busied herself with a piece of embroidery she had been working on before her departure and now found in the dresser drawer.

The two of them, facing one another in their usual chairs by the hearth. Little in the way of conversation from either to break the monotony. Back to the same, as though they had never been parted.

This, day following day. Their lives once more. The flat future stretching ahead. Brain-numbingly, spirit-destroyingly normal.

Dead inside.

They had retired to bed at the usual time, resuming the routine of old: Victor upholding the pretence that his task of closing the curtains took longer than it actually did so as to give prudish Kate time aplenty to change into her nightgown and slip into bed unseen. She, with her show of being busy straightening out the already neat bedclothes, eyes firmly averted from him as he undressed and climbed beside her. Giving her cheek to him for the cursory peck before the quick pressing of her lips to his in return. Settling down, him lying on his back to stare unseeing at the ceiling, her turning on to her side away from him.

Hands strictly outside the blankets.

Lights out.

Sleep.

Sleep for Kate, almost immediately, at least. Victor doubted he'd be afforded the same release ever again.

Dawn broke and, as the first white-grey arms of new light played across the pillows and his wife's features, he felt suffocating emotion swell within himself, threatening to consume him whole. How, in the name of God, could he go back to how it had been before? No, he couldn't. Lord, *please*. Gulping down great wave after wave of panic, he shoved aside the blankets and scrambled from the bed.

The tired streets were just beginning to come to life as Victor dragged his feet towards The Lilian. Yearning to see Phoebe and dreading informing her of the shattering change in circumstances in equal measures, he barely noticed the bleary-eyed workers who were equally reluctant to reach their destinations and the start of another gruelling day's toil.

He made straight for the rutted lane that backed on to the tavern, normally sludgy with filth and mud but hardened like jagged rock at this time of year, and paused for a moment to stare up at her bedroom window.

Deciding it would be best not to alert Mrs Tibbs and Kitty to his arrival – what he had to say to Phoebe was private, between the two of them; this would be painful enough without the added burden of an audience – he was scouring the ground for a pebble to throw at the pane when voices halted him in his tracks. Glancing around the premises' wall, he gazed, transfixed, at the two figures that had emerged from the tavern's rear door.

'I'll be on my way, then.'

'Yes.'

Taking Phoebe in his arms, Dick nuzzled her neck. 'I'll see thee later?'

'Yes,' she murmured again. Moving back on to the step and folding her arms around herself tightly, her eyes flitted left to right. 'You should go. If someone should see . . .'

'Let them. What difference would it make? We'll be wed soon enough, remember? It'll matter not then—'

'Yes, but *until* then . . . Please.'

'All right. Fret not, I'm going.' He drew her to him

once more to fondle her buttocks before swinging around and sauntering away.

Having flattened his back against the wall, Victor glowered at the man he'd never imagined he could possibly loathe more but knew in this moment he'd been so very wrong, striding off for home. He watched until he was out of sight then returned his blazing stare to the tavern. Phoebe still stood where Dick had left her. She had her face tilted towards the sky, her eyes closed.

Victor's entire body shook with the struggle not to rush to her, to shake her by the shoulders until her teeth rattled, demand to know what the hell she thought she was playing at. Him and her? They had spent the night together. God damn it, she'd given herself to that slippery, slimy young bastard.

Just like that? What about *him*? What about what they had, what they . . . A moan catching in his throat, he swallowed harshly. Except there was no 'they', was there? Nor could there ever be. He himself had put paid to that when he'd allowed Kate back into his life.

What a difference a day made. He'd lost the two women he felt the most for in the space of a mere few hours, to be left with what? One he neither wanted nor was wanted by, yet who should have been the sole most important person in his existence: his wife. The irony was impossible to miss.

Suzannah. Mother and babe cast out, and for what? *Phoebe*. He'd acted for her. Dick had simply pounced on her not having seen the mystery man's identity when he'd emerged from the cellar, it was obvious. But what could he have done? Suzannah herself had admitted guilt – whilst eliminating Dick from all blame in the process. Why?

Victor had had nothing in the way of proof to

271

support his suspicions that Suzannah was protecting him. Furthermore, he hadn't felt able to speak out, to risk Phoebe thinking he was taking the other woman's side again, for fear of invoking her wrath, of hurting her. *Losing* her, maybe this time for good. Yet he'd done that anyway now, all right.

He'd let them down badly, both of them. May God forgive him – and whilst He was about it, damn and blast Lavender to all the horrors that hell had to give! Just what did the women *see* in that varmint at all?

Victor just hoped Suzannah had been wise enough to seek out a trusted ally to take her in; she'd forged several decent friendships amongst the regulars since working at the tavern. Perhaps she'd taken her chances with large-hearted Big Red, had gone to him to beg his forgiveness?

The alternative, returning to all she knew: the slums – and in her condition, to boot – was a dire one. Her former pimp sniffing her out was a terrible prospect. Yet he could do nothing; his hands were tied. He couldn't even risk attempting to locate her to check on her welfare. Never mind Phoebe's reaction – Kate would kick up one hell of a holy storm if she were to get wind of that. *God damn the female species and the troubles that came with them!*

Turning his gaze back now, he saw Phoebe open her eyes and mutter something silently to the moody clouds. Then she released one almighty sigh and disappeared back inside The Lilian.

Alone, vivid visions of her and Dick together slammed into his brain and lodged there; the torment was like a death. He drew in several ragged breaths. Mouth set in a hard, thin line, he swung about and retraced his steps home.

A waft of fried ham met him as he stepped inside the

272

house. He glanced briefly towards the stairs. Then, eyes narrowing, he stalked across the passageway and into the kitchen.

Kate looked around at his entrance. 'There you are. I wondered where you'd—'

'Leave that.'

'Victor?'

'I said put the breakfast down,' he ordered on a low growl, closing the space between them in two strides and taking from her the pan she held, which he set down on the table with a resounding slam. 'Now, then. I want you upstairs.'

'Upstairs?' Like her figure, her face had stiffened. 'What on earth has got into you? Upstairs for what?'

'What do you think?' He didn't recognise his own voice, was more surprised still to realise it was he who was snapping out these words. 'I am your husband. As my wife, you have certain duties you're expected to perform. One very important duty in particular. *Now*, do you understand?'

'But . . . Well, I—'

'It isn't up for discussion, Kate.' With a flick of his head for her to follow, he made for the door.

In the bedroom, he stood by the wardrobes, arms folded, and watched his wife undress. She got into bed and he made his way towards her. Though she didn't push him away when he pulled her into his arms and planted his mouth over hers in a hard kiss, she remained rigid throughout. Nor did she protest when he pressed her down and manoeuvred himself into position.

He acknowledged he was acting cruelly but couldn't help it, not now. Nothing could contain the raging maelstrom of emotion and pain tearing his mind and heart to ribbons.

He took her without preamble. Not savagely, more primitive – basic instinct in lieu of sentiment in any of its forms. A sharp frown knitting her brows, she lay impassive until he was spent.

Not a word passed between them as he climbed off her. They dressed in further silence then made their way back down to the kitchen.

Sitting facing each other at the table, they ate the meal without looking at each other, the only sound the world beyond the window going about its day.

The cup of tea Phoebe was absently stirring had long since grown cold. A prisoner of her own churning mind and its dark and worrisome thoughts that wouldn't leave her be even for a millisecond, she sat on in the quiet drinking room – her physical self was there, at any rate. Inside her head she was far from the here and now and everything it entailed. Away from reality, from the future. *The future.* What on earth did that have in store for her now?

She'd allowed Dick to make free with her body. Not that she could remember a lot of it due to the drink, however, much to her crippling mortification.

All she'd had was her virtue, and she'd dashed it away in one mad and foolish moment she could never get back. He'd deflowered her. To the outside, she was spoiled goods. No decent and honest man would dream of looking her way after this. Now, she'd have to marry him.

She'd found little pleasure in the copulation. Had Dick? It was difficult to know. He hadn't made mention of the fact either way and, owing to her inexperience, she had nothing to compare it with.

He hadn't exactly been feverish with desire, that much she did recall. No evoking of trembling excitement. No tentative exploration, no caressing. He'd taken her with controlled need. Focused, fully, on the task in hand. Certainly no ardent passion, or even affection. Not really how she'd imagined – how she'd secretly dreamed it would be with Victor.

Victor.

Her breath caught in her throat. She should never have admitted to him her true feelings. She'd frightened him off, that was it. Announcing he felt the same – well. He'd been simply entertaining her for fear of hurting her, for that's the type of person he was. He'd go out of his way to save a body from pain, she knew. *And yet he'd appeared so believable. She couldn't bear this . . .*

Now, he couldn't face her. She'd made an utter fool of herself and probably ruined a perfectly sound friendship into the bargain.

Could she recant, say she'd been mistaken in her declaration? Was there any way at all out of this quagmire she'd created? Oh, what she wouldn't give to relive the last twenty-four hours. *How could she have been so stupid?*

Abandoning her tea, she rose and hastened to busy herself with preparing the tavern for opening, desperate to kill her racing thoughts with work.

She was arranging glasses on the low shelf by the barrels when the door opened behind her – she froze and closed her eyes. *Victor.* Dear God, the *shame . . .*

'Miss Parsons. Good morning.'

'Mr Hayes . . . Mr Hayes, yesterday . . . Oh.' Having turned, she gazed at the duo in numbing shock. 'Good morning,' she managed to stutter after some moments. 'I . . . Tea?'

Victor inclined his head in assent – Kate made no attempt at a response.

Tearing her eyes from the hostile stares of both husband and wife, Phoebe hurried upstairs to her kitchen.

Her hands shook as she busied herself with the teapot and she was on the verge of tears when footsteps on the stairs sounded; she abandoned her task and hurried on to the landing to meet who she assumed would be Victor, desperate now to speak with him, put things right. However, she was bitterly mistaken.

Kate brushed past her into the room then turned to look her up and down.

She knew. She had to. Awash with guilt, Phoebe lowered her head.

'So, Miss Parsons. I hear you and my husband have gone into business together.'

The emphasis that the woman had once again put on her and Victor's connection was painfully evident. Phoebe continued staring at her hands, clasped in front of her, and said nothing.

'It's doing rather well into the bargain, so I hear?'

Finally, Phoebe nodded. 'Yes. Yes, it is.'

'Victor and I have reunited.'

It was as though the flagstones had been whisked away from under her – she took a few wobbly steps sideways and clung to the table's edge for support. *No.*

'As such, I intend to take an active role in the tavern,' Kate continued, nodding, seemingly oblivious to Phoebe's plight. Circling the floor, she peered around through thoughtful eyes. 'Well, the professional side of things, naturally; no woman with an ounce of decency would even think to frequent such a place as a drinking establishment.' Again, she let her stare travel the length of Phoebe, her meaning clear. Then: 'I trust you have no objections?'

Victor and I have reunited . . . Victor and I have reunited . . .

276

The statement refused to leave her ears. She was going to cry. She mustn't cry. *Why, my dearest love, have you done this?*

He could never have been hers, could he? Impossible, for there would always be another woman who would come between them. First Suzannah, now Kate. Though, of course, the one before her was his wife by law – she had from the start held claim to him and forever would. Now Phoebe was to endure her gloating face and acid tongue, her meddling in their special venture, on a daily basis? Week in, week out. Month following intolerable month. Year after year, for good?

She'd sooner walk. She would. Turn her back on the whole damn thing and never look back. Just *how* had things come to this?

'Well, Miss Parsons?'

'Mr Hayes is in agreement with that?' The whispered question hung heavily in the air. 'He supports your decision?'

'In agreement?' Kate laughed. 'And why wouldn't he be? It was his idea.'

Something withered inside Phoebe – she felt it, the finality. Perhaps it was her spirit, or a piece of her heart; she couldn't say. But it was there all the same and she knew she'd never get it back. Irreparable. Gone. And Kate and Victor's reunion was but a part of it, wasn't it? For there was her and Dick, too, what she'd done . . . *All of it was gone.*

'Now that's settled, I'll bid you farewell.' The woman turned on a swish of her skirts. Then, reaching the door, she paused to glance over her shoulder and a hard smile lifted the corner of her mouth. 'But I'll be back soon enough. You'll be seeing more of me from now on, Miss Parsons. Yes, a lot more.'

277

Phoebe had never known pain like it. She staggered around to drop into a chair.

In the solitude of what didn't even feel like her kitchen any more, she gave herself up to her tears and drowned in their despair.

Chapter 18

THE TERRIBLE LOOK of devastation on Phoebe's face upon their arrival had been difficult to bear. Victor closed his eyes on the memory.

So now she knew. He and Kate were back together. Nothing would be the same again.

He hadn't been able to stem his own pain – not to mention anger – on seeing her. Visions of her and that man together had assaulted his brain instantly, coiling his insides until he thought he'd be sick.

Why had she done it? he asked himself for the thousandth time. They had been brought so close, so connected, in that moment in his kitchen when declaring their love for one another. Then Kate had turned up and Phoebe left, taking with her his vow to come to her at the tavern just as soon as he could . . .

'Damn it,' he murmured with sudden understanding. He hadn't gone to her as promised, had he, hadn't felt it right to leave Kate. He'd let her down. Had she been awaiting his arrival throughout the day and into the night, her hope of their future together diminishing with every hour that passed . . . ? Christ, she must have been so bloody *hurt*.

He bowed his head under the weight of his guilt. Phoebe would have surely guessed the reason for his absence, that he was still with Kate, that she'd never left, as he'd assured Phoebe she would once she'd said her piece. Which of course could have meant only one thing, and Phoebe must have known it: his wife had returned home for good. What then? Lavender had called to see her and she'd taken him to her bed out of spite? No. No, that wasn't Phoebe's style.

Comfort, reassurance that she was wanted by at least someone, would be closer to the mark in her decision-making. She'd lain with Dick because he'd been there, and because he himself had abandoned her. Unquestionably, he'd pushed her into that man's arms.

It was all his fault. Never could he forgive himself this. Phoebe really was better off without him, for even if he explained and she somehow managed to find it in her heart to forgive him, wasn't he lost to her? And, more than ever before, she was lost to him. Dick had claimed her completely. He could be in no doubt now that their marriage would go ahead. What had he *done*?

Now, as Kate reappeared in the drinking room, he shook himself back to the present and, hiding his anguish, faked a smile. 'Well?' he asked her. 'What do you think?'

'Very nice. Very nice indeed.'

'I'm pleased you think so.' He ached to ask her if she'd seen Phoebe just now during her tour of the place, which she'd insisted upon and which he couldn't very well have denied her, had to know if she was upset up there, but of course he couldn't. Kate would pick apart his probing, had a knack for that, and the truth was the last thing he desired getting out, for all their sakes. 'We'll be opening up shortly,' he said instead.

'Yes. Well, I'll make myself scarce,' Kate announced, her look of horror at the prospect of still being present when customers started to arrive, plain.

Swallowing down his relief, Victor nodded. 'I'll see you later.'

Following her swift departure, he stood for some moments to compose himself. His feet itched to take the stairs two at a time and seek out Phoebe, but he refrained from doing so. What would be the point? What on earth could he ever say to make things better? It could bring only further pain, for both of them. Everything had changed, immeasurably, and he could do nothing to fix this. Nothing.

'Morning, Mr Hayes.'

He turned at the double greeting and again brought forth the forced smile for the two women who had entered the tavern, woollen shawls wrapped around themselves tightly against the elements and each with a laden wicker basket over an arm. 'Good morning, Mrs Tibbs, Kitty.'

Awkwardness lingered in the air – yesterday's disastrous Christmas lunch was evidently still felt by the girl, and even Mrs Tibbs, who, though she hadn't been present to witness the debacle, had no doubt been informed of what had transpired. He smiled again to lighten the atmosphere and nodded to their purchases.

'You two look to have had a busy morning.'

'Aye, we were out bright and early – buying foodstuff for today's hungry customers,' Kitty told him, holding up the provisions.

Of course. With Suzannah gone, and Mrs Tibbs's shortcomings in the kitchen, the role of cook had naturally fallen to Kitty. 'You're looking forward to your first day at your new job?' he asked her.

She shrugged. 'I ain't mithered what task I'm set to really, Mr Hayes, so long as I'm in honest work.'

He nodded understanding. 'Well, thank you. I'm sure you'll do very well, Kitty.'

'Aye, Mr Hayes. I'll do my best.'

'How's the lass faring this morning?' asked Mrs Tibbs in a hushed tone, swivelling her eyes ceilingwards. 'She was still abed earlier when we left.'

'Miss Parsons . . .' Victor cleared his throat, at a loss how best to respond. 'She's making tea.'

'Dick were here 'til late last night. Mrs Tibbs took them down some grub late on in the evening and he still hadn't gone when we retired to our beds. Him and Phoebe were knocking the ale back summat chronic—'

'That's enough of that!' Mrs Tibbs interrupted Kitty's speech with a click of her tongue. 'You'd do well to mind your own, young lady.'

The girl pinkened with contrition. 'Sorry, I didn't mean to speak out of turn, were only saying what I saw—'

'Yes, well. Idle gossip is unbecoming, and especially in one so young. Mind that you keep your opinions to yourself.'

Lowering her gaze, the girl nodded.

'Now, let's get this lot upstairs,' Mrs Tibbs added, motioning to the baskets. 'And you, Kitty, can pour me a cup of tea.'

Victor was shaking with scorching fury at Kitty's revelations, and the instant the women had disappeared he swore to the emptiness viciously. Phoebe had been inebriated, too? Lavender had taken her innocence, knowing full well she was beyond the realms of lucid thought and common sense? This just got worse and worse. Bastard! And he was the one who had reduced her to this – *him*. In this moment, Victor loathed himself almost as much as he did Dick. *Oh, my precious love! I'm so, so sorry . . .*

Then there she was.

Mutely, he watched her emerge into the drinking room. The sorry sight of her brought a lump to his throat. Face blotchy from weeping, she looked utterly miserable. He took a step towards her, but she sidestepped him and continued towards the door.

'Phoebe, wait.'

She paused. Then slowly, she turned. A world of pain blazed from her eyes. 'How could you?' she whispered.

Before Victor could open his mouth to respond, she was gone.

Shuddering, he dropped his face in his hands. When he felt the touch on his shoulder, he believed for one incredible second she'd returned without him hearing, that she'd forgiven him – his scalding disappointment when he lifted his head and found Kitty standing before him was absolute.

'Sorry if I startled thee, Mr Hayes. Can we talk?'

He bit back a negative response and nodded. 'Talk about what, Kitty?'

'Yesterday, at your house. Phoebe. Suzannah.'

'To be honest with you, I'd rather not have all that dredged back up—'

'Please.'

Releasing a sigh, he led her to the nearest table and motioned that she should sit. 'So?'

'Well, it's like this, Mr Hayes.' The girl flicked her eyes towards the doorway leading to the living quarters beyond and, as though satisfied that Mrs Tibbs wasn't about to appear and overhear her speaking out of turn again, continued. 'I don't reckon it's like that Dick Lavender made out, you know. I don't reckon Suzannah's acted how they all say.'

'Miss Frost her*self* said it, too, remember, Kitty?'

'Aye, I know,' she agreed, shaking her head. 'I know

283

she finished up admitting it were her what was behind it all, that she'd created it, but I don't think it were true.'

'Then why—?'

''Cause she were pushed into it. She said what she did 'cause she felt forced into taking the blame, I think.'

'By Dick.'

'Aye.'

Frowning, Victor rubbed his chin. 'But why would that be?'

The girl shrugged. 'Because she's afraid of him.'

'You believe he has some sort of hold over her? Like what?'

'I don't rightly know.'

'Kitty . . .' Again, he sighed. 'Miss Frost and Dick have no history. They made one another's acquaintance only recently, when she came back to work here. I *do* believe,' he went on in a hushed tone, and now it was his turn to glance to the door in fear of Phoebe reappearing and hearing what he was about to confess, 'that it was he who Miss Frost was with in the cellar. I do. The only explanation I can think of for that is that the two of them were drawn to one another from the off, that they did strike up some sort of affair. Why, I don't pretend to understand. Not love. Lust, perhaps—'

Here, he paused to clear his throat, had forgotten for a moment it was but a slip of a lass with whom he was speaking – this line of conversation was totally inappropriate with someone of her sex and age. 'Forgive me. What I mean is . . . well, unfortunately, it happens. They're both young and attractive – selfish, too, it must be said. They saw something they wanted and they took it, and to hell with whoever else they hurt in the process. Do I think Miss Frost had become infatuated with Dick,

284

as he claimed? I don't know. However, if she did, it most certainly wouldn't have been without encouragement.'

'Do you reckon Dick even loves our Phoebe, Mr Hayes?'

Our Phoebe. He swallowed hard. She was their Phoebe, it was true, was loved by them all. 'I don't know,' he murmured. 'What I am sure of is they're set to marry regardless.'

'I know where Suzannah is.'

He glanced up in surprise at the sudden admission.

'When I followed her from yours and caught up with her in t' street, she told me where she was headed. Do you want to know?'

'Is it somewhere decent? Is she safe?'

'Aye.'

'Then that's all I want to know.'

'But Mr Hayes, don't you want—?'

'No, Kitty. No, I don't. I've done all I can for her. The fact remains that she betrayed Miss Parsons's trust. She took up with Dick knowing full well he was promised to her friend. She hurt her yet again – in the worst possible way. There can be no going back from that. Miss Parsons is the innocent party in all of this; I cannot let Miss Frost back in, not now. This time, she's gone too far.'

'And what of Dick? If what you say is right and he did play more of a part in all this than he's letting on . . . what? He just gets away with it? He ain't to be brought to account, an' all, nay?'

'That has to be Miss Parsons's decision, not ours. She wouldn't thank us for meddling in her business – nor would she believe our suspicions, I'm certain. For whatever reasons, that man seems to draw women like bees to a honeypot, and his smooth tongue ensures they stay there. They can't – or won't – see him for who he is. There is nothing we can do about it.'

Kitty rested her chin in her hand in dejection. 'Aye. I suppose you're right.'

'You'll put the matter from your mind, then?'

'I will.'

'I'm glad to hear it, for no good can come from it, you mark my words.'

'God help us, though, when that fiend gets his mitts on this place. He'll sup us dry in a month, I'll wager.'

Victor had begun to rise from the table; now, he sat back down again slowly. Brows knotted in deep confusion, he asked, 'What was that, Kitty?'

'This place, the tavern.'

'What about it?'

'Well, when Phoebe weds, she'll hand over everything she's got to her husband, won't she? Dick shall be in sole charge of her half of here.'

The colour drained from his face. He nodded. 'My God.'

How had he not made the observation before? Everything this girl said was true: legally, a woman's property became her spouse's upon marriage.

Femes sole – single women and widows – had control over what they owned or inherited. Yet the moment those vows were exchanged, all that changed. Marriage was a patriarchal establishment. Husbandly authority supervened, and wifely subordination was absolute. Therefore, that Phoebe had acquired a share in The Lilian before shackling herself to Dick would make not the slightest difference: once wed, she'd be required to surrender all rights to him. Such was English common law.

Wives had no voice. Their say was virtually nonexistent – less still if they belonged to the lower class. She *would* have to relinquish all she had. And there wouldn't be a single blasted thing they could do about it . . . That was *it*.

Realisation smacked Victor full around the face. He gasped with crushing clarity.

That man held no regard for Phoebe. There was no passionate or romantic attachment in it – and certainly no love. The one desire was money. He hankered to get his sweaty hands on her assets – in particular, her share of the business. *How had they been so blind?*

He had to warn her before it was too late – must.

Whether she chose to heed it was another matter entirely.

With only a general idea of where Dick dwelled, Phoebe was at a loss where to start. Eyeing the row of ancient, decrepit abodes hugging the riverside, she bit her lip then forced herself on.

A painfully thin man, stooped with age and hardship, answered her knock at the first house she tried. He shook his head at her enquiry – no, he didn't know anyone hereabouts by that name – before shutting the door in her face. Directing her murmured thanks to the broken wood, she continued to the next.

She repeated her reason for disturbing them to each occupant who bothered to acknowledge her call, however with varying degrees of politeness they all answered in the same vein. Having yielded no results, her efforts spent, she wandered towards a nearby inn.

Here, Phoebe paused. The place was dank and run-down, the exterior bricks crumbling in parts with decay and neglect. She hazarded a glance through the windows but could see nothing beyond the film of grime coating the panes. She dithered a moment longer. Then, stepping forward, she pushed open the door.

The space, empty of people and eerily silent, was in almost full darkness save for an ugly greyish glow coming from the far corner. Tentatively, she made her way across.

Slipping through what she realised upon drawing nearer was another door, she emerged into a tiny stone passageway. Positioned sporadically the length of the walls, fat stubs of candles in wax-smothered holders threw out the dulled light that had drawn her attention in the main room. Curiosity overriding uncertainty, she carried on towards a narrow staircase.

As she descended through the increasing gloom, yet another dark door came into focus. Now, the nearer she drew, faint noises could be heard from beyond it, increasing in volume with each step she took. Male voices, raised in excitement, and high-pitched squeals that sounded like creatures in pain. Frowning, she turned the knob and nudged the door ajar.

Putrid smells of damp, mildew and general dirt assaulted her nostrils, intermingled with stale beer, tobacco smoke and body odour, and something metallic that she couldn't define. The sight she was met with had her eyes and mouth alike widening in shock.

Blinded by seemingly countless oil lamps blaring brightly, she brought an arm up to shield her gaze and squinted about. A sea of men, of every age and description, had their backs to her and were crowding around something in the centre of the floor.

Though she shifted position to try to gain a better understanding, their bodies were pressed too tightly together to allow even the smallest gap to show; her view of whatever had them engrossed remained completely blocked. Then a shout rang out from somewhere above the melee, demanding silence, and she stopped dead in her tracks.

It was *him*; she'd recognise the voice anywhere. Just what on earth was going on here?

Gathering her courage, she squeezed in between two broad-shouldered spectators to find out.

'By a count of sixteen,' her fiancé announced, holding up in each fist a panting terrier by the scruff of its neck, their white coats splattered with red, 'the winner is . . . Owd Nipper!' He lifted the victorious dog higher and the crowd roared with appreciation. 'Right, then. Who do we have next?'

'Dick?'

His jaw slackened at the sight of her as she stepped forward. 'Phoebe! This is a surprise.'

'I wanted to . . . to see you, speak with you . . .' She shook her head. 'What is going on here?'

'We'll resume after a short break,' he told his audience. Then, cupping her elbow, he led her towards several men by the far wall, who immediately filled two tankards with ale from the line of barrels behind them and thrust one each into Dick and Phoebe's hands.

'No, thank you,' she said, placing the drink on a nearby table; shrugging, Dick took a long draught from his own and, after wiping his mouth on his sleeve, asked, 'How did tha find me?'

'Luck, I suppose.' She had to almost yell to be heard above the fog of noise and, glancing back around, saw that the applauding, whooping crowd were now engaged in showering Owd Nipper with pats and kisses. 'I tried at a few houses first, without success. When I spotted the inn, here . . . Well, I thought there was no harm in enquiring.' Again, she swung her head in increasing puzzlement. 'What *is* this place, Dick? I thought I saw blood on those dogs you were holding . . . was it? Are the poor things all right?'

'They're gradely! Just gradely. The victors especially will be treated like kings tonight, you mark my words.'

Shooting another look towards the pampered terrier, she nodded. 'So I see. But what are they winners *in*? I pushed through the men to find out what was happening, but then you appeared in front of me and escorted me away before I had a chance to get a proper look.'

He drained the remainder of his ale. Then he took her elbow once more. 'Come on, I'll show thee.'

By now, the men were growing restless for the entertainment to recommence, had arranged themselves around the hidden centre again in readiness; spotting Dick's approach, they cheered, parting to let him through. Phoebe joined the circle of spectators and, finally, took in the scene before her.

Dick had taken up position in what looked to be a giant wooden box. On closer inspection, she saw he was standing in a sunken pit bordered by four-feet-high walls. He held up a hand for order and a hush fell around the room.

'Now. Let's get on with the next match.' Turning to a gangly youth standing on the outskirts clutching a bulging, wriggling sack, Dick nodded. 'If you'll do the honours.'

The lad hurried forward. Then, into the square enclosure, he poured from his bundle what appeared to be at least a hundred rats.

After tumbling into a heap on the whitened floor, the rodents darted off in every direction in dumb confusion. One or two, in a bid for escape, attempted to scale the walls but were knocked back into the pit with sticks by members of the crowd.

Then Dick was speaking again: 'Fetch Caesar and Jacko forward.'

Two wiry dogs appeared. They were horribly disfigured. One was missing an eye, the other part of an ear, and the faces of both were criss-crossed with old scars. Catching sight of the rats, they whined excitedly and struggled to be set loose from the firm holds of their owners, who grinned, as though pleased with this.

'Steady on, fellas,' Dick told the terriers. 'Let the timekeeper get everything ready . . .' Satisfied, he continued to the room: 'Right then, you know the rules. They get one minute. The mutt with the most successes wins. Place your bets!'

The crowd readily obeyed, a cloying silence gripped the air, and the dogs were let loose into the pit.

Phoebe could only stare in frozen horror at the grisly contest that unfolded. The animals, evident professionals in their field, dashed to and fro like things possessed, picking off their prey with speed and dexterity. A catch, one swift nip, then they tossed the unfortunate creature into the dank and smoky air. Most of the rats were dead before they returned to the ground.

It was carnage. The screams of agony and terror were unbearable, the nauseating stench of death overpowering; Phoebe gagged. She was the only one. A macabre feverishness had taken over – the rest of the baying crowd were enjoying every second.

Locked in the nightmare, she watched through a film of tears the remaining rats instinctively gather into mounds in the corners of the pit in a vain attempt at concealment, clambering on top of each other in their blind desperation to survive. Their tormentors showed them no mercy. One after another met the same fate – catch, nip, toss – slaughtered in the blink of an eye, until the dogs were almost mad with frenzy and covered in their victims' blood.

One of the last survivors with nothing to lose lunged at Caesar as he advanced, delivering a painful bite to his face. He yelped and backed off – Jacko rushed in to finish the job for him.

Moments later, someone called time and immediately the owners gripped their dogs by the necks and lifted them from the pit. Their thirsty work over, the exhausted terriers were given water and, as they lapped it up gratefully, an officiator entered the enclosure to examine the rats.

Gazing at the mangled corpses lying strewn, Phoebe knew he wouldn't find a survivor. The dogs had completed their task. The whole vicious spectacle had been disgusting beyond description. Never had she experienced anything quite like it.

The Cruelty to Animals Act, passed seven years previously and prohibiting the baiting and fighting of some, mainly large, animals – bears, bulls and badgers, dogs and cocks – had yet to be enforced for rats. After what she'd just witnessed, how anyone couldn't want to prevent their cruel and improper treatment was beyond her. If she had it her way, every last person here involved would be rounded up and prosecuted, would receive the same punishment as those who flouted the law and indulged still in the now-illegal blood sports of those other species: a hefty fine or imprisonment with hard labour. And that included Dick Lavender.

Mouth set in a hard line, she peered around in search of the man in question.

An ugly scene was unfolding nearby; scanning the

angry faces, she spotted Dick in the centre, trying to regain order. The men's grievances reached her ears clearly: Caesar, prized ratter and the odds-on favourite, had missed the win by a single kill. Jacko's mauling of the rat who had attacked his rival had placed the opponents evenly – the contest had been announced a draw. Large wagers were lost and the gamblers were less than pleased – including Caesar's owner, who had been set to receive a healthy purse for the expected victory.

To Phoebe's amazement and horror, the crowd, united in their loss and vexation, turned their blame on to the dog. Caesar had disgraced himself by backing off from his prey and, they were all in agreement, deserved a sound thrashing for his cowardice. *This was too much. She couldn't stand by and allow this, she couldn't!*

'Stop it!' she cried as a twenty-strong mob advanced on the cowering terrier. 'Stop it at once, you brutes!'

The room instantly fell silent. Amongst the rest, Dick gazed at her, open-mouthed.

Phoebe placed herself in front of Caesar and lifted her chin. 'You let this poor innocent beast be,' she told them in a tone now quieter but every bit as firm. 'He isn't in the wrong here. He didn't choose to become a killing machine, he was forced. It is you who are in the wrong – every last one of you. You ought to be ashamed. This barbarity ends now.'

Dick made to step towards her, but she shook her head. Then she turned on her heel and fled from the cellar.

'Lass, wait. Lass—'

'Go back to your friends, Dick.'

'Phoebe, they're not—'

'I said, leave me alone!' Picking up her skirts, she hurried on up the stairs towards the main room. Out in the street, she felt his hand on her shoulder and her anger burst forth – she spun around to face him. 'Who *are* you? I thought I knew you . . . What else aren't I aware of?'

'I don't know what you mean.'

'The hell show back there, of course! Good God, Dick . . . it was terrible, terrible! How can you involve yourself in something so brutal? I never would have believed it. I really don't know you at all.'

'Aye, you do,' he coaxed. ''Course you do.' Smiling, he made to take her in his hold, but she thrust away from him and folded her arms. 'Phoebe—'

'I want the truth, Dick. Or I walk away from here, from you – us – for good.'

He visibly blanched at the threat. 'All right.' Nodding, he released a huge sigh. 'All right, the truth. The first thing you should know is that that shower back there, they ain't no friends of mine. Aye, I do work at that there inn when I'm needed. And aye, I am involved in blood sports – there's allus a ready supply of rats from the river nearby, after all. But it's just a job, lass. A man's got to eat.'

'No. No, I'm sorry, I can't accept that as adequate reason. There are plenty of other means to make a living—'

'What? How?' His face had turned angry. 'Look around you. Folk ain't exactly falling over themselves to offer the people of this town regular employ.'

'But . . .' Casting her mind back to a conversation she'd had with him months ago, she frowned. 'I thought you said you were employed at a brickworks?'

'Nay, I said I work there when I can grab a day's toil, and that ain't often. The same can be said for a number of other premises I can manage to get to take me on forra few days – weeks if I'm lucky – whenever they're a pair of hands short. But it ain't guaranteed brass, you know? What am I meant to do in t' meantime: go hungry? Work's work, and in times of desperation we'll do owt to earn a crust. We do what we must.'

'Do you agree with that . . . that horr*ific* violent game back there, Dick?' Phoebe asked him, close to tears. A trickle of guilt that she'd judged him so harshly had set in – she should have heard his reasons for being involved there through fully before berating him as she had. He was correct in what he'd said: the whole country was in a crisis. What else was a body with no reliable income to do in these climes of austerity? But she must know, she must, couldn't associate herself with a man who lacked such a basic quality as compassion: 'You aren't someone who condones such a thing as that, are you?'

'Nay, lass! I'd ban the whole soddin' show, were it in my power. But it ain't, is it, and the bare fact remains: animal sports are big business and even bigger money. Me, I referee through need, not greed. I hates it, lass.'

He looked thoroughly ashamed. His sincerity cut her to the quick. 'Oh, Dick, I'm sorry.'

'Eeh, no need for that,' he told her, taking her hand. 'We'll not dwell on it a second more, aye?'

'Yes. Thank you.' She shook her head. 'I don't know how you put up with me. All I seem to do is cast aspersions on your character, am forever accusing you of wrongdoing.' *Never more so than with regards to Suzannah Frost. How mistaken she'd been there.* A flush of affection for him, her only true constant of late, washed through her. Whatever else may be lost to her, Dick was here to stay. She smiled softly. 'Things will be different when we're married, I promise you. No longer will you have to subject yourself to such things in order to earn a living, for you'll always have a position at the tavern.'

His face spread in a heart-winning smile. 'Aye.'

'Life is set to get a whole lot better, Dick.'

'Oh, you're right, there.'

They embraced and, when they drew apart, a frowning Dick asked, the matter reoccurring to him, 'What *did* you come here to see me about the day? You said you needed to speak to me about summat . . . ?'

Victor slammed into her thoughts, making her wince with further remembrance of all that had passed and was over with. He was quickly replaced by the image of Kate's vindictive face and the fresh problems her return was set to create; Phoebe closed her eyes. But before she could spill all to him about that woman's unwanted intentions, a shout from close by pierced the misty air – blinking in confusion, she followed Dick's gaze towards the open inn door.

'And don't come bleedin' back, you swine, else I'll do for thee well and proper next time!' came the voice again from beyond the main drinking room – and this was swiftly followed by a flash of white careering past them into the street.

'Caesar . . . ? Oh, Dick!' Phoebe cried, taking stock of the sorry animal, who had limped to a halt by the roadside, looking bereft and confused. 'Oh, they've beaten him, look!'

'Easy, fella.' Crouching to the terrier's level, Dick shifted towards it, speaking softly. 'It's all right, we'll not harm thee.'

His gentleness with the unfortunate creature brought tears to Phoebe's eyes. 'That's it, Dick. Careful, now. He's terrified.'

Head down, tail lost between his shaking hind legs, Caesar watched his approach warily, his one eye wide with apprehension. He allowed Dick to stroke his head then lift him with care into his arms.

'His owner has abandoned him?' she asked, and Dick nodded.

'After today's loss, he'll have reckoned that Caesar's ratting days are over.'

She clicked her tongue in disgust. 'So he's simply cast his dog out on to the street?'

'Oh aye, common as night follows day, that is. If an animal ain't fit to earn brass no more, he's gone quick smart. Caesar's master's a successful breeder – he'll have a replacement trained up in no time.'

'Discarded, just like that? That's all the thanks they get for countless years of faithful service and keeping their owners' purses plump?' Phoebe was incensed. 'Black-hearted devils, the lot of them! Well, we can't just leave him here. He's coming with me.'

'Aye?' Dick appeared extremely pleased with this.

'Absolutely. And I'll tell you something else,' she vowed, holding out her hands for the dog, who went to her readily and snuggled close to her chest, 'Caesar will never have to suffer the rat pit ever again. For him at least, those days are over.'

Dick looked as though he was about to say something at this, then he nodded and smiled. ''Course, aye.'

'Have you to get back to your work?' She had to force herself not to grimace on the last word.

'They'll do without me, I reckon, for one day.'

'Good. Then let's get this poor thing home.'

Chapter 19

THE TAVERN WAS steadily filling with revellers when they arrived. With Caesar tucked safely under her arm, Phoebe led the way inside. Immediately, she spotted Big Red, at his usual table, looking decidedly down in the mouth despite the best efforts of his friends, the brothers Seth and Elias Dodd, Joe Stone and King Henry, to cheer him up.

Her heart went out to the gentle giant. She wondered, not for the first time, whether she should have exposed Suzannah in private and left it to the woman herself to break the news of her infidelity to Big Red, away from the others' gazes. His hurt and mortification had been hard to witness – and all of that for what? Phoebe asked herself now. So she could ensure that Dick and Suzannah were as humiliated as she could have them be when she broke the news of her findings?

She'd chosen Christmas Day, when they were all together, to cause maximum embarrassment and damage to the pair. The frame of mind she was in, she'd hardly given a thought to how it would affect the others. She'd been wrong – in more ways than one, she admitted, glancing to Dick – and she felt ashamed. She must try to make this right. Motioning to her fiancé to follow, she braced herself and headed across to the men.

'Big Red? May I talk with you?'

'Aye.'

Phoebe perched on a stool facing them and lowered her eyes. 'Yesterday . . .'

'What's done is done, lass' said Big Red dully.

'No. No, I was thoughtless,' she told him, shaking her head. 'I went about things in completely the wrong way. The pain of betrayal, what I'd convinced myself was true – it clouded my judgement. I shouldn't have involved you and the others in the confrontation. I know you had become fond of Miss Frost . . . I'm sorry.'

'Ay now, we'll have none of that.' Big Red fumbled for her hand and pressed it. 'I were fond of her, lass, aye. I'll not deny it. But as I said: what's done is done. You're not to berate yourself for nowt, all right? I hold no grudge against thee. Or thee,' he added after some moments, his gaze swivelling to Dick. He held out a mammoth calloused hand. 'Bygones be bygones?'

'Bygones be bygones,' Dick agreed, shaking it warmly.

Phoebe smiled through her tears of relief. 'Thank you. Let me get you all another drink – on the house, of course.'

'Well, we'll not say no, lass!' Big Red chuckled. ''Ere, who's that you've got there?' he asked suddenly as the terrier popped his head out from beneath her arm to glance around. 'Poor divil don't look too clever.'

'This is Caesar, and you're right, he isn't too good. He was beaten, Big Red.'

A disapproving murmur went around the table.

'Who did that to him, then?'

'His owner. He thrashed him and abandoned him on the street for losing a match. Caesar is – *was* – a ratting dog. I couldn't very well leave him out there.'

The men shook their heads then nodded agreement,

with Big Red adding, 'You pass him to me, Phoebe, whilst you see to the drinks. I'll look after the young scrap.'

She did as he bid, smiling when Caesar went to him without fuss, then made her way to the barrels. 'You sit down,' she told Dick, who had followed her. 'I'll bring them across.'

'Sit with them lot?' He threw a look over his shoulder at the men whose company they had just left.

'Yes, why not?'

A look of superiority twisted his features. 'Huh.'

'What's wrong with them?' she demanded, frowning. 'You didn't seem to mind shaking Big Red's hand just now—'

'And why d'you think?' he cut in witheringly. 'He's fists on him like sledgehammers – I ain't daft enough to get on t' wrong end of his temper, am I?'

'They're good men, Dick.'

'Gutter maggots, the lot.'

'Dick! They are not. They're honest and decent—'

'All right, all right. Just don't be too long with them ales, eh?'

Watching him swing away and drag himself back to the group, Phoebe's brows knitted further. She really did dislike that side he had to him. Though for the most part he did his best to conceal it, it slipped into the open at times and she'd find herself wondering just which one the true Dick Lavender was. He had more faces than a clockmaker's shop, and it unnerved her. *Which would she get behind closed doors once they were married . . . ?*

'Perhaps it's exactly those qualities you mentioned – honesty and decency – that he's repelled by, for he doesn't possess an ounce of either.'

She jumped at the voice close to her ear and whipped around. 'What?'

300

'You heard me well enough.' Victor's tone was low but the fire in his eyes spoke volumes.

'You were eavesdropping on our conversation? You had no right—'

'We need to talk. Urgently.'

His intensity killed her budding anger, and dread shivered through her. She leaned in closer. 'Mr Hayes? What is it, what's wrong?'

'Not here,' Victor murmured, glancing along the room at Dick. 'Later, when it's quiet.'

For the remainder of the day, Phoebe couldn't keep her mind to anything. Boxing Day trade proved brisk and, a pair of hands short owing to Kitty now being employed in the kitchen, she and Victor barely had time to blink, never mind talk.

Dick had left not long after expressing his scathing opinion of Big Red and the others – Phoebe had been secretly relieved. She'd been drawn to seek him out in her upset but his attitude towards those she'd come to regard as friends still smarted and she felt she'd had enough of him for one day. Before making his departure, he'd suggested he take Caesar home with him, but she'd insisted the dog stay with her at The Lilian. Though she'd thanked him nonetheless for his kind offer, he hadn't looked best pleased with the decision, which flummoxed her somewhat, but all too soon Victor's earlier remark had returned to consume her thoughts and she'd quickly forgotten all about it.

Throughout the remaining hours, guesswork had stalked her mind, her imagination inventing numerous possibilities as to what Victor could have been referring to, each more worrisome than the last, and she was reaching breaking point. Hadn't she herself discovered something new about Dick this very day: his connection

301

with the seedier side of life and shocking involvement with blood sports? Had Victor learned of something else equally as disturbing that she wasn't aware of? Finally, as they were nearing closing time, she managed to pull him to one side.

'Please . . . Mr Hayes, I must know.'

He nodded. Mrs Tibbs and Kitty had retired to their beds shortly before, and he indicated that he and Phoebe see the remaining customers off and then they would talk.

Big Red was amongst the last drinkers' number and, spying how his rugged face fell when she held out her arms to relieve him of Caesar – the dog hadn't moved far from his lap since arriving here – she smiled softly. 'He's taken a real shine to you,' she told him, 'and it's evident you feel the same for him.'

'You're right there, lass, I do. A sound hound, he is, sound.'

She nodded, satisfied. 'In that case, how would you feel about taking him off my hands?'

'Aye?' Big Red's pleasure was plain.

'I probably wouldn't have the time to care for him anyway, what with most of my hours taken up with this place . . . Besides, I don't think we could tear him away from you now, even if we tried!'

Beaming from ear to ear, Big Red went on his way, whistling a merry tune, Caesar trotting happily by his side. Then Victor bolted the tavern door, shutting out the world and leaving only them and his dark findings soon to be disclosed, and the mood instantly changed – all trace of Phoebe's smile vanished. He inclined his head to a table and she obeyed in silence. Face grim, he took a seat facing her.

'Dick Lavender loves you not.'

The unexpected statement completely threw her; she blinked, thinking she'd misheard.

'It's true,' Victor went on. 'I'm sure of it. He has his sights set on this place once you're married. That's his reasoning behind him snaring you. The Lilian. Money. Nothing more.'

'This is what you've been waiting to tell me?' The subject of the revelation, and in particular the brutally blunt fashion in which he delivered it, cut her to the quick. 'I don't believe this . . . What is *wrong* with you? Why are you saying these things?'

'Because they are true. Dick—'

'Loves me! Do you hear?' Tears spilled over to splash to her cheeks. 'He does.'

'Phoebe . . .'

'Why are you so intent on hurting me? Haven't you done that enough already?'

His face fell. He made to reach for her hand on the tabletop and sighed when she snatched it away. 'I never meant . . . The last thing in this world I wanted to do was hurt you. But Kate *is* my wife, Phoebe, and I—'

'I don't want to hear it!'

'I had no choice, God damn it!' His breathing was ragged and he looked close to tears himself. 'It's my duty, as her husband . . . I had to take her back. Don't you see? I had to.'

'I'll tell you, shall I, just *exactly* what I see?' Phoebe could barely get the words past her choking sobs. She'd been holding all this emotion at bay since he failed to show up yesterday, she realised, and now it was impossible to suppress. 'I see a man I no longer recognise. I see a man who lied about his true feelings, who expressed to a woman a love he didn't really hold, who *pretended*, and crushed her heart to pieces in the process. I see a man who then left her waiting, without a word of explanation. Left her believing herself to be unwanted, worthless, *nothing*.

'You discarded me. You tossed me aside then had the gall when you finally had the nerve to show your face to do so with your wife in tow. Have you any idea how that felt? The agony, humiliation? *Have* you? And now, now you sit there and tell me that the only person I had to turn to, who was steadfast, is a fraud? You believe just because you could never love me, no one else possibly could either? Well, you're wrong, Victor Hayes. You're wrong, and I'll prove it!'

He was openly weeping now; silent tears coursed down his cheeks. Half rising from his seat, he shook his head slowly. 'Not a single syllable of what I said to you was pretence. Please believe me, Phoebe, I swear it. I have loved you from afar for months, yearned for you with everything that I am, and to discover you felt something for me too . . . I almost had you, and I lost you. I know now it can never be with us. That is something I shall have to suffer – my penance for trying to do what I believe to be right – for the rest of my days.'

Phoebe couldn't help herself – holding back now was an impossibility: she ran to him. He clasped her to him with a cry and she clung on like a victim at sea hanging on to driftwood – indeed, her very survival in this moment depended on it. *He loved her back, but it couldn't be. It could never be* . . . 'I'll die if I can't be with you!'

'My love. Oh, my dearest love . . .'

'It's so *unfair*. Why is she back? Why now?'

'I just don't know. My world ended when she announced her decision to return home, but there wasn't a thing I could do – still can't.' His inner torture coated his next words: 'You . . . you have to put me from your mind.'

'I cannot!'

'You must. I have a responsibility to Kate, but you . . . you owe Dick Lavender nothing. Be free. Find happiness with someone who can give themselves to you wholly and truly, who will love you for you and not what you can bring to the table. He's not who you think he is, he's not. I'm certain.'

'But I do feel I owe him in some ways. He has been dependable whenever I've needed him, has helped me – the business, even: you remember the trouble we had with the beerhouse over the road and Col Baines and his son, how Dick put a stop to it? He needs me and I suppose I am fond of him,' admitted Phoebe. *And last night . . . last night I took him to my bed. Should a child result from the sin . . . Oh, may God – and you – forgive me.* It was hopeless, hopeless. 'I'm promised to him,' she finished on a dull murmur.

'Please. Please. Don't do it.'

'But if I can't have you, what does it matter? What does *any* of it matter?'

'Those vows are for life, Phoebe, as I've found out to my cost. Don't make the same mistake I have. And the worst of it is,' he continued, heaving a sad sigh, 'you're a woman. Upon marriage, Dick would hold full control. You'd no longer have the right to do anything with your property. This property. You'd no longer manage it if he chooses not to allow it—'

'Well, that wouldn't make much of a difference to me, would it?' she shot back.

'What do you mean?'

'You've given Kate free rein over The Lilian, have you not? You *suggested* she involve herself in the running of it. She told me so herself earlier.'

'She's a stinking liar! I don't believe . . .' He gave a

brittle laugh. 'Well, that woman is in for one short, sharp shock if that is her intention, I promise you that! The threat that Dick would pose, however, *is* a very real one, Phoebe,' he went on ominously. 'You could do nothing without his approval, would require his consent in everything. Inasmuch as he'd be at liberty to do whatever he wished with your half of this place – as well as all profits that result from it. You wouldn't be permitted to have an income of any kind separate from your husband's, nor be the legal owner of any money you earned. All we've built up, all the hard work . . . Please, don't throw everything away.'

'No.' She shook her head in growing horror. 'Dick wouldn't . . . wouldn't do that . . .'

'You're without a shred of doubt on that? How well do you actually know him? The *real* him?'

The one behind the mask.

Visions of the rats from earlier, poured like potatoes from that sack, and the horror that followed, popped behind her eyes. Whispers swirled amongst them: Dick's disparaging remarks for anyone he deemed beneath him. How cruelly he'd goaded Victor into shaming himself that night in front of the whole tavern. His drinking. His pomp and arrogance and ability to talk his way out of anything. *The image of his smirking face by the cellar door following his tryst with Suzannah . . .*

It *had* been him. She wasn't mistaken, as he'd vehemently claimed.

Or was she?

Her mind picked at her, prodding forth specks of uncertainty, until everything coiled into one grey mass and she could no longer process anything clearly.

'Phoebe?'

'I can't . . . I need time to think.'

'Has marriage been mentioned again lately between the two of you?'

She nodded. 'Yes, only today.'

Victor swore under his breath. 'Then he's still intent on seeing this through . . . Listen to me.' Drawing back, he held her by the shoulders and stared deep into her eyes. 'You must hold him off for a while. Promise me you'll try, that you won't agree to anything rash just yet.'

'What do you intend to do?'

'Find out as much as I can about that man. He's hiding something, I'd stake my life on it. There has to be some clue, something we've missed . . . Let me prove to you my suspicions aren't unfounded. Will you trust me on this, Phoebe? Do I have your support?'

After a long hesitation, she gave him her word. And a part of her hoped beyond hope he'd succeed.

Chapter 20

'YOU DID *WHAT*?'

Barely listening, her mind too consumed with perfecting the plan she would shortly put into practice, Phoebe shook her head. 'Sorry, Dick . . . what did you say?'

'I *said*, what the bloody hell did you go and do that for?'

She blinked in surprise at his anger. Then her thoughts cleared, bringing her back to the moment, and she frowned. 'I gave Caesar to Big Red last night because they had taken a shine to one another. What does it matter?'

'Well, you can just go and get the mutt back, can't you?' he responded through gritted teeth. 'Tell that gormless sod you've changed your mind, that the dog belongs with us.'

'I will not. What has got into you?'

Evidently doing his level best to quell his annoyance, Dick released a long breath. 'Nothing. Sorry. Sorry, lass. I just . . . well, after what little Caesar's been through, I'd like to be sure he's going to be looked after proper from hereon in, as he deserves.'

'Big Red will more than provide a good home for him, there's no fear of that.'

'Even so . . .'

'Dick, I can't ask for the dog back now, can I?' she insisted. 'How would that look? He'd think I didn't trust him after all and, besides, they're fond of each other. It would break both their hearts.'

Seeing a muscle in his jaw throb furiously at this – her refusal to comply – her frown grew. 'What's the real reason for your outburst, Dick? Why do you really want Caesar back? Surely not . . .' she added as a terrible thought occurred. And then Dick glanced away, confirming her suspicions: 'I don't believe you. How *could* you? You thought to use that poor animal to make money, didn't you? That's why you were pleased for me to take him in – you planned to exploit him, return him to the rat pit. I'm right, aren't I? Aren't I?' she pressed when he didn't answer, grasping his arm.

The sound of splintering glass as he snatched from her the tumbler she'd been polishing and launched it at the wall behind her was deafening – Phoebe cried out in shock.

'Dick! What on earth—'

'Don't you ever speak to me like that again, my girl. I won't be interrogated, not by no one, d'you understand?'

'Dick, please . . .' He'd taken her by the wrist and hauled her towards him. His face, taut with fury, was so close she could see the veins in the whites of his eyes. 'Let me go.'

'My business is mine alone. You'd do well to remember that.'

It was a full minute after he'd stalked from the tavern, slamming the door behind him, before her senses returned; gasping, she dropped into a chair and pressed a fist to her mouth to stem the rising emotion.

She'd believed he was about to strike her for a

moment there, she really had. His temper had seemingly erupted from nowhere and she hadn't been prepared for it. Finally, the true Dick had made himself known, just as Victor had predicted he would. Phoebe felt sick with the hideous confirmation of it.

Heart still hammering, she rose and went to drag the bolt across on the door. The last thing she wanted was him reappearing and a repeat performance of what had just transpired. However, she was steadfast on one thing: if and whenever he did show his face again, she wouldn't submit to his demands, no way. Caesar was staying exactly where he was, where he was safe. Though whether she could keep up the pretence of their sham relationship after this – for that's what it was, she saw it clearly now; gain was his sole motive here, probably always had been – remained to be seen. However, she must. Well, just for as long as it took for her scheme to bear fruit, at any rate.

Victor had left shortly after their discussion the previous night, but not before they had shared a sweet and lingering kiss. Each knew it must be their last, and the parting had been unbearable for them both. He'd dragged himself off – gone, back to his wife – leaving Phoebe all alone once more. The pain, indescribable, persisted still; she doubted it would ever go away.

She'd lain awake in bed in the pale moonlight, eyes that refused to grant her release in sleep raw from crying, her tired brain regurgitating all she'd learned. Her feelings were reciprocated. Victor did love her. *And what did that matter now?* her mind would always scream, taunting her with the fact, until she thought she would go mad. Then Dick's face would slip into her thoughts and she'd wonder afresh about all he might be hiding from them, what life as his wife could be like, leaving her numb all over.

Held up against Victor, she didn't love him, no, not in that pure and unadulterated sense. She was fond of him; in the most part he treated her acceptably, and wasn't someone better than no one at all? She wasn't getting any younger and the prospect of spinsterhood left her cold with dread. And should she find herself with child – *his* child . . . ? Well. *Then*, the decision would be out of her hands entirely. She'd have to wed him for certain, there were no two ways about that. A fallen woman with an illegitimate to raise alone was a fate far, far worse than a lifetime of singledom, that was for sure.

Was it the tavern Dick desired, and not her? Would he change – or rather revert to his true form – once the vows were uttered? And what irony in those words of the service! *With all my worldly goods I thee endow.* That was what the man was made to promise to his betrothed before God, wasn't it? An absurd line, then, when it was the other way around.

Everything Victor had reminded her of was true: upon marriage, husband and wife became one entity. She'd no longer be a separate person in her own right. Phoebe Parsons would be absorbed into Dick Lavender and her basic identity would cease to exist. So far as the law was concerned, she'd hold the same legal status as convicted criminals or those certified insane – little to none – for no other reason than becoming someone's wife. The injustice was monstrous.

Matrimony, therefore, had to be done right, or you would spend the rest of your days in regret. Marry in haste and repent at leisure, so went the age-old adage – never in her life had a thing been more fitting. All she could do was simply pray until she ran out of words that Dick wasn't who they feared him to be. And, if he was, that a baby didn't result from that single night of down-right stupidity and so force her to shackle herself to him regardless.

And on, and on . . .

Eventually, sheer exhaustion won through and her agonising had, blessedly, abated, allowing her to fall into a fitful slumber. But not before a crucial factor in this whole debacle had rooted itself in her mind and her idea had been formed. Victor had vowed to sniff out whatever he could find regarding her fiancé. She intended to do the same concerning his wife.

Kate Hayes was back for a reason – one that wasn't born from a desire to save her marriage due to any natural objective such as love, Phoebe was sure of that – and she was determined to find out what.

Now, as she swept up the broken glass from Dick's outburst, she glanced once more towards the door; only now she found herself wishing he wouldn't stay away for too long after all. He'd be back once his mood had cooled, surely? For her quest of outing Kate to have any chance of succeeding, she needed his cooperation.

She'd been prepared when he turned up shortly before, but his unexpected rant concerning Caesar's new living arrangements and subsequent sharp exit had put a halt on proceedings for now. And temporary it was – she'd set the wheels in motion at the next opportunity. Whenever that might be.

In the meantime, there was something else she could do – something to assist Victor's hunt for clues on Dick – this very moment. For one other thing had occurred to her before she'd fallen asleep last night: her unpleasant encounter at the lodging house Dick had taken her to months before on their first meeting.

Had he been honest with her about his connection

with the place and the woman, Betsy, who managed it? Or was she foolish to have pushed the memory of it to the back of her mind? Well, she intended to find out. It was time she did a little digging of her own.

'Another cup of tea, mister?'

Dragging his eyes from the window, Victor gave the serving girl an absent shake of his head. She flitted off to another table and he trained his stare back on the street.

There! *Finally*.

Releasing a sigh at the sight of the uniformed man heading in his direction, then taking a few deep breaths to curb his nervous anticipation, he rose in readiness to welcome his friend. Yet his relief turned out to be short-lived:

'What, *nothing*?' Victor rasped.

'Nothing.'

'But surely . . . surely there must be something?'

'He's clean as a whistle. Sorry, old chap.'

Victor dropped back in his chair in crushing disappointment. He'd been so certain they would have some record of him. That viper Lavender was cleverer than he'd given him credit for. No recent or even historical misdemeanours, no brushes with the law, no trace. *Bastard*.

The constable left soon afterwards to return to his beat, but Victor sat on, his mind in turmoil.

What would he do now? He'd pinned all his hopes on Bob uncovering something of worth on Dick. What the hell was left? Worse still, how would he break the news of this development – or lack thereof – to Phoebe?

As though thought of her had conjured her up, the eating-house door opened and he watched in surprise as she entered. Head down, as though in a world of her own, she crossed to an empty table in the corner. She looked as dejected as he felt. Frowning, he made his way across.

He had to say her name twice before she noticed his presence. 'Are you all right? What's happened?' he asked, taking a seat facing her.

'Yes, I'm fine, I . . .' She shook her head. 'I went to see someone who might have had some information to impart on Dick.'

'Oh? Who?'

'Someone he introduced me to on our first encounter . . .' Her face reddened and she lowered her gaze. 'I told you about the incident at that lodging house, that a man I met took me there under the pretence of it being respectable, however it was anything but? Well, what I failed to reveal was that the man in question was Dick.'

'*What?*'

She nodded miserably. 'He denied all knowledge of its true nature, of course. Like a fool, I believed him.'

'The filthy, low-bellied . . .' Victor had to force out the words through gritted teeth – he'd kill the swine for this!

'And now,' Phoebe went on, 'the woman, Betsy, who ran the place, the only person who might have been able to shed light on him, is gone.'

'Gone, you say? You're sure?'

'Well, of course I'm sure; I've just this moment come from there. The lodging house is boarded up, empty. Betsy and her girls must have moved on.'

'I have some news of my own,' Victor admitted. 'You remember my constable friend, Bob? I paid him a visit after leaving you last night to ask him to check the records for any information on Dick.'

'And?'

Seeing the glimmer of hope that had appeared in her eyes, he swallowed in bitter regret. 'Nothing.'

'Oh.'

'I'm sorry.'

She shrugged. 'Don't be. You tried.'

They sat in silence for a few minutes, each lost in their own dispiritedness. Was there no bringing Lavender down?

When a lone tear hugged her lower lashes for a moment then splashed to her cheek, Victor reached beneath the table for her hands, which were resting in her lap. Shielded from the other diners' view, they clung to each other.

She believed herself shackled to Dick for certain now; he saw it in her gaze. All hope of finding good reason to break off their engagement had left her – Victor's own eyes misted at the sight. He wanted to sweep her up in his arms, assure her that it mattered not that she'd lain with Dick, that she needn't dash her freedom to the wind because of it. But he couldn't, for her shame should she discover he knew would crucify her, he was sure. Besides, should new life ensue from their night together . . . No. There would be no child. He wouldn't – couldn't – consider that.

His own folly – the recent copulation with Kate – trickled into his mind and he frowned. Thoughts of what he'd done filled him with lucid regret. Why had he acted so? To prove himself a man? Well, it hadn't worked. It had served only to make matters worse – his wife could barely look at him, seemed on edge when they were alone at home, as though expecting him to pounce on her at any given opportunity. However, she need have no worries on that score.

315

Never again would he behave in such a way. He'd been angry, upset, blinded by desperation for a release from what he'd witnessed at the tavern's back door – Dick stealing away, having spent the night with the woman he loved. He'd taken his pain out on Kate and for that he was sorry. For all her faults, despite him being fully entitled to his conjugal rights by law, she hadn't deserved that.

Husbands aplenty wouldn't have given the matter a second's thought, this he knew, but he wasn't of the same mind. Lovemaking was special, so far as he was concerned, a precious joining of two people who held one another's hearts. It shouldn't be undertaken when only one half of the pairing desired it – or had manipulated the other when in drink into thinking they did, as Dick had done with Phoebe.

That he could be clubbed together with a specimen like Lavender in anything, let alone something of this nature, made him sick to his stomach. Men, in effect, really were the worst.

'I'd better be getting back,' said Phoebe. 'Mrs Tibbs and Kitty will wonder where I've got to.'

He released her hands reluctantly and watched her drag herself to her feet. She drew her shawl up and around herself tightly, as though in need of its comforting embrace – the pinched face peeking out at him from the woollen folds tore at him and heightened his sense of hopelessness still further.

'I'll see you later?'

Victor nodded. She turned and disappeared into the frosty morning, and he dropped his head in his hands in despair.

There was nothing else for it. There was but one person left who could possibly help them now.

The question was, given all that had passed, would Suzannah be willing to oblige?

'Mr Lavender's up yonder.'

Phoebe paused on the tavern's threshold to lift an eyebrow at Kitty in surprise. 'He is?'

'Aye. He said as how he needs to speak with thee, that you'd not mind him waiting upstairs.'

Which, Phoebe observed, the girl clearly did. Dick encroaching on their private quarters wasn't something she was pleased about, it was plain to see. And Phoebe was wont to agree. Yet at the same time, she was curious to find out what he had to say for himself – and, glory be to God, have the opportunity to put her main plan into action. *Pray she'd have more luck with this one than she'd had in seeking out Betsy* . . . After thanking Kitty, she took a deep breath and made her way to the kitchen.

'Lass . . .' Dick rose from the table at her entrance. He wore an expression of deep contrition and she swallowed a sigh of relief. His anger towards her was spent – it was he who sought forgiveness. Her scheme would go ahead.

'Hello, Dick.'

'Lass, I'm sorry.' He crossed the space to wrap her in his arms. 'My conduct earlier . . . I'll never treat thee like that again, I give thee my word on it—'

'It's all right, Dick. Let us forget it.'

'Aye?' He was visibly delighted. 'You mean it matters not? We'll put it behind us?'

'Of course.' She brought a sweet smile to her lips. 'You were upset at my letting Caesar go – and not for any undesirable reason, I'm sure, as I initially suspected,' she lied. 'I understand that now.'

'Eeh, Phoebe . . . I'm glad you've seen sense.'

She nodded, smiled again. *Oh, I've done that, all right.* 'Sit,' she told him, motioning to the table. 'I'll make some tea.'

Cups in hand, they chatted lightly for a few minutes until Phoebe, deeming the time right, said as innocently as she could muster, 'Did you know that Mr Hayes's wife is back on the scene?'

'Nay.'

'Yes, Kate's returned home. The thing is . . .' Here, she dropped her gaze and shook her head. 'No, I can't, shouldn't really . . . It may cause ructions, should she discover I've discussed this with anyone.'

'What is it?' Sitting forward with a frown, his interest piqued now, he pressed, 'Tell me, lass.'

'Well, it's just . . . Mrs Hayes intends on taking over the running of this place. She informed me of the fact herself.' It was true: Kate had. However, the woman hadn't been near the tavern since – clearly, Victor had put her straight, nipping her desires in the bud before they had the opportunity to bear fruit. But of course Phoebe omitted this small detail. Dick certainly couldn't know it if she wished him to comply.

'What?'

'Yes, Kate's adamant.'

'Well, she can just go to hell!' Dick was furious. 'Laying down the law like that – and her a wench, to boot? What could she know about business? We'll just see about that, won't we, for when we're wed, she'll have to get through me. I'll put the uppity bitch in her place, all right!'

And there she had it. Clear evidence that, all along, Victor had been totally correct in his assumption: Dick had no intention of allowing his wife a mind of her own. His scathing reaction just now concerning Kate – the very prospect of a member of the fairer sex even daring to consider something so bold as to run an enterprise – was proof enough. Even so, Phoebe knew she had to hear it definitively, out loud from his own two lips.

'Will that go for me, too, Dick, once we're married?' she put to him, her tone even, aware that he was more likely to speak freely and not feel pressured into glossing over the truth than if she tackled him on this with affront.

'When tha becomes Mrs Lavender, working *will* be a thing of the past for thee, aye. You'll not need your own income, will you, for I'll look after thee.'

Annoyance was brewing inside her, but she managed to swallow it down. 'Whether I need to or not aside . . . what if I *wanted* to continue on here?' she asked carefully.

'Look, Phoebe.' He smiled blandly. His voice had taken on a condescending edge, as though he was trying to explain something very simple to a complete idiot, which had her hackles rising further. 'Independence ain't decent in a wife. No wedded women trade in their own right – what would folk think of me, were I to allow that? Nay, lass. Your main responsibility will be in t' running of the household and taking care of my needs, as is a woman's place. Like any right-minded fella, I'd expect full cooperation from thee once we're married.'

'I understand.' Where she found the strength to resist slapping him in the mouth, she didn't know. 'Husbands are in charge, after all; it's just the natural way of things, isn't it?' she added demurely, whilst inside she raged.

'Exactly!' He seemed relieved and not a little pleased that she'd grasped she would be in no way his equal and was fully accepting of the fact. 'Fret not, mind, for I

319

shan't be a tyrannical ruler,' he went on, puffing out his chest as though proud of this generosity. 'You'll find I'm a fair husband – within reason – aye.'

'Well. Thank goodness we've straightened all that out.' Smiling brightly, she reached for the pot. 'More tea?'

'Aye, why not.'

'So,' she continued a little later when her anger had abated enough for her to do so, 'the subject of Mrs Hayes.'

'Worry not on that one,' he growled, his temper instantly resurfacing at the mention of Kate. 'As I said afore, I'll put her in her place, all right, once we're wed—'

'Yes, but until that time . . .' Phoebe gave a long sigh then bit her lip. 'There's nothing stopping her just now, is there, Dick? However, that's not the worst of it,' she added gravely, and was gratified to see his eyes narrow in concern – she had his full attention, all right. *Now for her plan.* 'I believe Kate is up to something.'

'Up to something? Up to what?'

'I cannot be certain . . .'

'Tell me.'

'Well, I think she may be deceiving Mr Hayes as to her true reason for returning. She loves him not, I'm sure of it, which can mean but one thing . . .'

'It ain't him she's back for,' Dick finished for her, stroking his chin.

'Precisely. So, what else?'

'Brass. This place.'

Phoebe nodded. 'I think she means to be rid of me somehow. Make my time here so unbearable that I'll be forced to quit the tavern, sell my share perhaps, just to be shot of her—'

'But that's what I—' He clamped shut his mouth, a red hue spreading across his face. 'I mean . . .'

'*But that's what I had in mind.*' Was that what he'd been about to blurt? she asked herself with sickening realisation as she watched him attempt to claw back his composure. He'd hoped to marry her then drive Victor from The Lilian, have the business for himself? Of course it was. How hadn't she seen it? She'd been so blind, so stupid. *God damn you, Dick Lavender!*

'What I meant is,' he blustered on, and Phoebe hid a grim smile, savouring his discomfort, 'I reckon you're right. That must be this Kate's intentions. Aye, well, not on my watch! Victor might not have the backbone nor the balls to put her straight, but I do. I'll show the pair of them what I'm made of when I'm running your half of here.'

'Oh?'

'I've some big ideas. I intend on exploiting all opportunities. Stopping open later shall be the first thing – to hell with the fools what want to drink themselves to death. Foresight, not to mention a bit of devilment, is what's needed to succeed. It's the road to ruin else, aye.'

'You know best, I'm sure,' she forced herself to say, before bringing the conversation back on track: 'In the meantime, I think it would be wise to find proof of what Mrs Hayes is up to. Who knows what problems she could create if left much longer to her own devices. It's better that we gain the upper hand, don't you think?'

'Aye, but how? She ain't likely to admit to owt should we tackle her, is she?'

'No. However . . . her sister might. And that's where you come in.'

'Me?'

'Yes, Dick. It's more than likely that Kate spoke of me to the woman after our first encounter, described me even – I can't risk her guessing who I am. You, however, she knows nothing about. I have an idea . . .'

A short while later, the plan was secured. Phoebe could have danced, so immense was her relief. Dick had agreed to it all. *Pray God it was going to work.*

She walked with him to the door when he rose to take his leave and even allowed him to kiss her on the lips in farewell – anything to keep him on side. 'Thank you for this, Dick. Good luck.'

'I'll think of summat to get the sister talking, fear not,' he assured her. Then: 'Mind, it's more than wishes of good luck *I* expect from *thee*, lass.'

Her smile slipped. His tone had been low but firm and there was a definite sly glint in his gaze – searching his face for a clue as to his meaning and finding none, she whispered, 'Such as?'

'Oh, I think tha knows. I do this on one condition.'

Seeing the prospect of exposing Kate and having her rid from Victor's life for good slipping away, Phoebe nodded. 'Name it.'

'We set a date for the wedding. Done?'

'You have been,' she uttered under her breath when, at her nod, he turned and walked away.

Chapter 21

'CAN YOU MANAGE without me for an hour or so?'

'Yes, of course. Kitty's here, should I require help.'

At the mention of the girl, Victor cleared his throat with increasing guilt. He'd secured from her Suzannah's new address, meant to call on her right now and see what she had to say concerning Dick, but he hadn't revealed his intentions to Phoebe. Unsure what her reaction would be, he didn't want to take the chance of her knowing, not just yet, at any rate. Should Suzannah have anything important to tell him, then he'd make Phoebe aware of what he'd done. For now, he must keep her in the dark about him seeking out the woman who had caused her so much unhappiness; it was the best thing all round.

'There's nothing wrong, is there?' Phoebe asked now, pulling him back to the present, and he smiled reassuringly.

'No, no. I just need to pay someone a visit. I'll be back before the rush begins.'

On his way to the door he passed an unfamiliar man, who had just entered. As Victor made to exit the tavern, he overheard the stranger query Phoebe's name – something made Victor pause to watch the exchange. Moments later, he was glad he had.

'I'm Miss Parsons, sir,' she answered him politely. 'Now, what can I get you—?'

'Miss Phoebe Parsons?' the young man cut in.

'Well, yes, but . . . May I ask who *you* are and what your business is?'

'Apparently, I'm just an errand boy,' he replied, and Victor caught the disgruntlement behind the self-description. 'My business is to deliver something to these premises, to a woman bearing your name. So, here you go, this is for you.'

Victor had crossed back to Phoebe and she glanced up at him with a frown before tearing open the small paper-wrapped package that the man had thrust into her hand.

'Oh my . . . !' Phoebe almost choked on a gasp. 'What in the *world* . . . ?'

Victor was just as stunned as she at what had been revealed. He turned to ask the man what on earth was going on, but he'd vanished.

'Mr Hayes, why . . . what can this mean?'

'I don't know,' he admitted. He held out his hand. 'Let me see.'

Phoebe placed the ornament in his palm and, gazing down at it, he shook his head in perplexity. *Lilian's brooch*. This was it. It had to be, was identical in every way. But *how*?

'You're sure you don't recognise that fellow just now?'

'No, not at all.' Phoebe was adamant. 'I've never seen him before in my life.'

'Well, then. That leaves only one other who can shed light on this mystery.'

'Yes.'

'Mr Rakowski,' they said in unison.

Victor hurried for the door, saying over his shoulder, 'I'll go, you watch the tavern.'

Twenty minutes later, he was back. The heavy frown that had accompanied him from the jeweller's shop remained rooted still to his brow.

'Well?' Phoebe asked the second she spotted him. 'What did Mr Rakowski say?'

'Nothing.'

'But I don't understand.'

'Nor me.' Victor scratched the hair at his chin. 'I'm completely flummoxed.'

'But what did Mr Rakowski say, Mr Hayes? Surely he must have been able to offer you some explanation – the brooch was in his possession last, after all.'

'He said he sold it for a very good price just this morning.'

'To whom?'

'A young man – who matched the description of the errand boy who deposited it here with you.'

'What?'

His frown growing, Victor nodded. 'I'm afraid Mr Rakowski could tell me nothing more. Just what the devil is going on?'

Fingering the brooch, which she'd affixed to her bodice in his absence almost without realising she'd done it, Phoebe chewed her lip, eyes thoughtful. 'It was taken off the jeweller's hands for a very good price, you say?'

'According to Mr Rakowski, yes. Why?'

'That man who delivered it here didn't appear wealthy, did he?'

Recalling his serviceable footwear and plain fustian suit, Victor shook his head. 'No.'

'Which means he must have been instructed to make

the purchase for someone else. Someone whom, it seems, has money to throw around in abundance. But who? I know no one who fits the bill – least of all someone who would desire to then gift such an expensive piece to me.'

Victor could offer no response. It made not the slightest bit of sense to him either.

'Oh. I almost forgot.' Reaching into her apron pocket, Phoebe brought out an envelope. 'This came for you whilst you were out.'

Taking it from her, Victor broke the wax seal and unfolded the sheet of paper. As he scanned the words printed there, his lips bunched together. 'Eh? What in the world could *he* want?'

'Who? What is it?'

He passed the note to Phoebe and watched her brows meet in shared confusion. 'Chief Constable Summers?'

'My former boss from the force.'

'He wishes to see you as a matter of urgency. Mr Hayes . . . ?'

'I have no idea. Wait,' he added. 'Who delivered this?'

'A street urchin. He said a man paid him a penny to fetch it to you . . .'

'Your errand boy, do you think . . . ? For the love of Christ, just what is going on!' he burst out, suspicion and worry of the unknown darkening his mood. Well, he was going to solve this enigma once and for all!

Mumbling to Phoebe that he'd be back soon, the summons clutched tightly in his fist, Victor set out with grim purpose for the chief constable's office.

'You're back.'

'Looks like it.'

Phoebe hurried to pour Dick a drink, saying through

326

the side of her mouth as she placed the full tankard before him, 'Well? Did you . . . ?'

'Oh aye.'

'What happened?'

He took a long draught of his ale before turning his dazzling grin on to her with a wink. 'I told thee to trust me. Didn't I say I'd get answers, that I can spin *any* female around my little finger when I choose?'

Yes, he had, and this she could well believe. He'd hooked her just as surely, after all, hadn't he, not to mention Suzannah Frost – likely countless other women in the past besides.

'I told her I were a travelling tea salesman.'

'And Kate's sister swallowed it?'

Dick laughed. ''Course. I reeled her in with a bit of convincing blather and one of my smiles, and she invited me in to discuss business willingly.'

A bogus tea company? That's what he'd come up with? True, they had failed earlier when discussing the plan to decide upon how he'd strike up conversation, but Phoebe had been willing to trust his suggestion of him playing it by ear when he reached the house. It could have so easily gone wrong. She couldn't help but admire his steely confidence and sheer audacity. Either Kate's sister was spectacularly gullible or Dick's skills at flattery surpassed anything Phoebe had imagined. Was no woman immune to his charm?

'The old modus operandi never fails,' he went on, with a definite air of smugness. 'They're asked to put in an order to be delivered at the week's end – payment upfront, naturally – with the deal clincher being that for every pound of tea they buy, they get two ounces free. Simple. Folk, whether they be stinking rich or starving poor, allus love a bargain. Add to that a stroking of their ego – surely a body as intelligent as themselves wouldn't be fool enough to miss out on such an opportunity? – and you've got them hook, line and sinker. You think how many houses that will work at. Aye, it's a lucrative little scam.'

'You sound awfully skilled in these nefarious activities. This wasn't something you concocted for Kate's sister's benefit only today, was it? You've committed such frauds before. How in the world have you got this far in life without accruing a criminal record?' she added too late, blushing furiously when Dick cocked his head in curiosity at the statement – curse her slack tongue!

'And what makes thee so sure I ain't known to the law?' he asked her quietly after some moments.

'Well, I'm not, I, I simply assumed . . .'

'Needs must at times, I've told thee that. I ain't proud of my past, nay, but I survived it – survived it my way – and am here still to tell the tale.'

Past, my eye. You never stopped. 'Of course. Forgive me,' she hastened to murmur, sensing his rising anger at her judgement and afraid he'd storm out before she learned what he'd uncovered about Victor's wife. Inside, however, her mind was spinning.

It was one unpleasant revelation after another. He had his finger in every possible pie. He – all this – ran deeper than she'd anticipated. Dick Lavender was an out-and-out rogue. Just what else didn't she know?

'You finished criticising now?' he muttered eventually.

'I . . . Yes. Sorry.'

'So, d'you want to hear what occurred the day, then, or what?'

'Yes, please.'

'Well, I knocks on the door and spin her my line, as I said, and she invites me in. We chatted for a short while, and then I asked, all casual like, whether I were keeping her from her household duties. She laughed and said I was, actually, but she'd forgive me – took a reet shine to me, she had. Anyroad, she says how her sister used to see to the chores but that she'd recently moved out. Apparently . . .' Here, Dick paused for effect, a smile stretching across his mouth, and Phoebe had to fight the urge to shake the rest from him.

'Go on,' she encouraged.

'Apparently, she's newly betrothed and it seems Kate became surplus to requirements. With a new beau on t' scene, she wanted shot of Kate and encouraged her to go on home.'

'Kate's sister told you all this?' Phoebe was stunned.

'Oh aye. Right forthcoming, she were.'

'So she hasn't returned to Mr Hayes for love but because her sister outgrew her companionship. She's here through naught but necessity. I *knew* it.'

'That's the top and bottom of it. Victor's wife has bamboozled him good and proper, and he's fell for it, daft owd bastard.'

The slur brought angry colour to Phoebe's face, but she quashed it, saying, 'Well, at least now we have ammunition to fire back at her, should she try to throw her weight about here. We could threaten to tell Mr Hayes her true motive for coming back.'

'Aye.'

'Thanks, Dick. I couldn't have done it without you.'

'So?'

She shook her head. 'So . . . what?'

'Our wedding.'

Oh God. Not this again.

'Remember? We agreed we'd set a date?'

'Well, I . . . of course, it's just—'

329

'Just what?'

Licking her lips, she scrambled around inside her head for something – anything – to hold him off. But nothing came. She had *nothing*.

'How's about I see to the arrangements?'

She swallowed hard. 'You?'

'Aye, sort out getting the banns read and what not. In fact, I can call in at the church right now, what d'you say?'

'Now? But Dick—'

'There's no time like the present, eh?' he insisted, as though he hadn't heard her. A big smile stole over his features. He nodded. 'Aye, I'll do that. See thee later, lass.'

'I, I just think we should . . . should discuss this further, Dick, I . . .' But her words floated away on the air, her hope of holding at bay this whole messy situation along with them, at the closing of the tavern door behind him.

Phoebe was standing lost, staring into space, when Victor entered. He looked as dumbstruck as she felt – concern for him snapped her from her reverie. 'Well?'

'You're not going to believe this.'

'What is it? What did Chief Constable Summers have to say?'

'He's offered me back my position,' Victor murmured, tone soft with incredulity.

A quiver of horror ran through her; she couldn't help it, despite knowing she was being selfish. Victor, with the chance to be a police officer again within his grasp? That he missed the role was no secret; he'd snatch the opportunity in a heartbeat for certain. But good God, if he should, what of the tavern? She'd never manage the place alone! 'What will you do?' she forced herself to ask.

'I don't know . . . Why now? What on earth changed his mind?'

'Did you ask?'

'Yes, of course. He said that, after reviewing my case, he's decided to give me another chance. He said that though they had to take the course of action at the time that they did, the force had lost a damn good lawman when they terminated my employ. And that was that.'

'So this . . . it carries no connection with the return of the brooch?'

'Seems not.'

'A coincidence?'

'Looks that way.'

Folding her arms, Phoebe frowned deeply. 'So we're still no nearer to understanding why Lilian's gift was returned to me.'

'No,' Victor agreed, but it was clear he had his mind on different matters – it didn't take a genius to work out what.

'Mr Hayes.' She took a deep breath. Who was she, after all, to stand in his way? 'I'll understand if you decide to accept the chief constable's offer. Really, I will,' she added, when Victor lifted his eyes to search her face. 'I know how very much you miss it. If it's what your heart truly desires . . . I shan't stand in your way.'

'The Lilian is my priority now. Besides, I couldn't leave you in the lurch,' he told her, alleviating her dread – only to have it slam back again when he uttered, 'And yet I . . .'

'You what?' she whispered.

'I need time to think. I'm sorry.'

Nodding, she turned away to busy herself with serving a customer, but her thoughts were all awhirl. He was going to leave here, leave *her*, she just knew it. And that's exactly what reclaiming his former role would mean, had to.

Even if it were possible for him to manage both positions – which of course it wasn't; there were not enough hours in the day – he wouldn't be permitted to do so. After all, lawmen couldn't be associated with drinking establishments. He'd have no alternative but to let the tavern go.

What then? She certainly hadn't the means to buy him out, so to whom would he sell his share? She'd be forced into partnership with a stranger. What if they didn't see eye to eye? Her working life would be intolerable.

However, all of that paled in significance when she allowed herself to delve deeper into what the change would really mean. For oh, worse still, so much worse, would be the loss of this great man she couldn't live without. He was more than just her rock; he was the whole mountain. What would she *do*? The prospect of being parted from him was unfathomable. No, impossible – her heart wouldn't take the pain. *Lord, she couldn't bear it, she couldn't!*

When a short while later Dick breezed in, the wolfish grin he wore said it all – Phoebe's last vestige of strength snapped. Her mind had been so consumed with Victor she'd forgotten about this more pressing problem; just how much more of this day could she endure?

She could do nothing but stand numbly by as Dick regaled the drinking room with how well his meeting with the rector had gone, how in no time he'd be making an honest woman of Phoebe Parsons, that the wedding could very shortly go ahead.

Throughout, Victor sat mutely, his face impassive, but Phoebe noticed the clenching of his fists and the hollow pain behind his eyes and berated herself for not warning him of Dick's intention. For him to have to sit here and listen to the man spouting such talk must be hell. This, she knew, for wasn't she feeling it just as acutely? Just what had she got herself into? Was there to be no end to this nightmare she'd created?

Victor rose abruptly and, separating himself from the cluster of customers raining congratulations on Dick, crossed to Phoebe. 'What I mentioned earlier,' he said to her stiffly, 'that I had a call to make—'

'Oh, yes,' she cut in, her wretchedness absolute. She wanted desperately to throw her arms around him and reassure him that this, Dick's display, wasn't what it appeared, that she'd had no *choice*, damn it. But of course, she couldn't. 'You go ahead. I'll manage here.'

Victor threw a final glance in Dick's direction. Then he nodded once and was gone.

That turgid swine wasn't for giving up. Well, neither was he. Dick Lavender would strong-arm Phoebe into marriage over his dead body!

Turning left, Victor stomped on towards his destination, but there was no escaping his own mind.

She'd sworn to do her utmost to hold Dick off; what had changed? he asked himself again. From what he'd just heard that man spewing back at the tavern, it seemed Phoebe had actively encouraged him to put the wheels into motion . . . But surely not. It was a distortion of the truth, had to be. This was yet another of Dick's warped antics. Christ, what he wouldn't do to have her rid of that vermin! Pray be to God this visit would prove successful and that Suzannah would possess the means to help him do just that.

He arrived at the address Kitty had given him in no

time, but it took him a good deal longer to pluck up the courage to knock.

What would be Suzannah's reaction upon seeing him? he fretted, glancing up and down the street as he contemplated whether he'd done the right thing in coming. Would she rant and rail, slam the door in his face? *But she was their last hope. Please let her show understanding.*

'You won't get to find out one way or the other by standing here like an idiot, doing nothing, will you?' he muttered finally, pulling himself together.

Taking a deep breath, he rapped on the wood.

'Victor. It's thee.'

'Hello, Miss Frost.'

Suzannah stared at him for a moment then held open the door. 'Will tha come in?'

Thank God.

'It's all right, there's no one else present.'

He nodded and followed her inside.

The dwelling was clean and well kept, and the modest fire lent the room a cosy feel. At Suzannah's instruction, he took a seat at the scrubbed table and looked at the woman before him properly for the first time. The flames' glow picked out the warm hues of her luscious hair, giving it the appearance of polished copper, and her creamy skin shone with health. He smiled.

'You look well.'

'Ta, thanks. Mrs Reed is looking after me gradely. Mrs Reed, the wench what agreed to me lodging here,' she explained, at Victor's frown. 'Her husband, Jim – you know who I mean: owd fella what sups in t' tavern, allus sits in the nook by the fire?'

'Oh yes, I know him.'

'Well,' Suzannah went on, 'he asked me a bit back whether I knew of anyone seeking a room, that their last child had recently married and left home, and with less brass coming in they were finding it a task making ends meet. I called in after leaving your house that day and they let me move in on t' spot. I ain't earning a living to pay my way here by doing what's gone afore,' she added, as though reading his mind – he had wondered. 'Nay. That Suzannah Frost is in the past, where she belongs, and that's where she's stopping. I saved a few shillings from my wages cooking at the tavern, you see. And when those are exhausted . . . well. I'll find myself a little scrubbing job somewhere, aye.

''Ere, Mrs Reed's reet good to me,' the woman went on, smiling now. 'Feeds me on porridge and fresh buttermilk of a morning, she does, to aid the babby's growth . . .' She broke off and lowered her gaze. 'Kitty tell thee where I were headed, did she?'

'That's right.'

'She's well? Mrs Tibbs, an' all?'

'Both are fine.'

'And Phoebe?' Suzannah added in a whisper, flicking eyes now deep with sorrow back up to meet his.

'To be honest with you, no, she isn't all right. That's why I'm here. I – we – need your help.'

'With what, Victor? What's happened?'

'Dick Lavender happened. He's intent on destroying Miss Parsons's life. I need you to tell me everything you can concerning him. Don't you see, you're the only one who may have it in their power to put a stop to him.'

Pale-faced, Suzannah rose shakily and crossed to the window. Her back to him, she folded her arms. 'I have nowt to tell thee.'

'Please—'

'I'm sorry.'

'Look, Miss Frost.' Victor went to stand behind her.

'What occurred on Christmas Day . . . I was wrong to evict you from my house as I did without giving you a proper chance to explain. I'm ready to listen – really listen. Tell me, please. Just who is that man, and what hold has he over you?'

'The truth's so terrible you'd not believe me even if I were to speak it.'

The statement, and the chilling tone in which she'd delivered it, made the hairs on the back of his neck stand up. He swallowed hard. 'I shan't doubt a single word, Miss Frost, not for a second.'

'I can't. What he'll do to me . . . I'll be done for!'

Taking her by the arms, he turned her around gently to face him. 'Listen to me. You have nothing to fear, not any more. Stop protecting that man and I'll be with you every step of the way, that I promise you.'

'Nay, I can't, I *can't* . . .'

'Do it for Phoebe. You owe her that much at least. Please.'

To Victor's sheer relief, she heaved a sigh and dropped her shoulders in defeat.

What she revealed was far, far worse than anything his speculating could have conjured up.

'You're willing to repeat all you've just told me to Phoebe?' he eventually rasped. And at Suzannah's small nod: 'We've got him, lass. We've *got* him.'

Chapter 22

'DON'T BE AFRAID. I shan't leave your side.'

Suzannah was trembling violently as they reached the tavern; Victor placed a reassuring hand on her elbow. To his dismay, the first person they encountered when they entered was Big Red – at the sight of him, Suzannah faltered.

'I can't, Victor, can't do this, I . . . I shouldn't have come—'

'Sshhh. All will be fine, you'll see,' he soothed, urging her on.

Wearing a heavy frown, Big Red watched their approach. Though his eyes strayed to Suzannah and stayed there, he didn't speak.

'Something has come to light, and I think you have a right to know what,' Victor told him. 'Will you hear it?'

After a long hesitation, the man mumbled an acceptance. He passed Caesar to his drinking partner, King Henry, and folded his arms to await further instruction.

Victor shot him a grateful look then scanned the drinking room. Of Dick Lavender, there was no sign. Neither could he see Phoebe. He went to speak to Kitty, who was serving customers with Mrs Tibbs, to be told that Phoebe was taking a short break upstairs.

'Ready?' he asked, having returned to Suzannah.

'Aye.'

With a decisive nod, Victor motioned for her and Big Red to follow then led the way to the private quarters.

Phoebe was pouring tea at the table when they entered the kitchen – the sight of them all together seemed to freeze her to the spot. She put down the pot and rose to her feet slowly.

Victor hurried to her side, saying quietly, 'Please don't be alarmed. Miss Frost has something of great import-ance to tell you.' He eased her back into her chair and, too stunned to argue, she offered no resistance. He then indicated with a tilt of his chin that the others should sit before taking a seat himself.

'Is it to do with Dick?' Phoebe managed to ask him after some seconds.

'Yes.'

All eyes swivelled to Suzannah. They waited in charged silence for her to begin.

'I knew him only as Dick. On the odd occasion that folk referred to him following my return here as cook, it were as Mr Lavender, so you see, never did I dream . . . Then I "met" him for myself. It were the day him and Phoebe announced their betrothal, and that night Vic-tor was nowhere to be found. I stepped in to help with the customers, and there he was. I couldn't believe what my two eyes were seeing . . .'

Suzannah paused to press her fingers to her quiver-ing lips. 'Horrified is what I was – aye, and so was Dick, for that matter. He pulled me aside the first opportunity he got and threatened me into keeping silent. Eeh, I were that frickened. He said as how I weren't to utter a word to anyone, least of all to Phoebe, that I knew him, and how. Knowing what he's capable of, I had to go along.'

338

'I remember now,' Phoebe murmured. 'Dick was drinking heavily with a group of his friends. You cried a headache and went home early.'

'That's right, lass. My mind was all of a jumble, the guilt at holding my tongue eating away at me; I couldn't bear his presence another second. But it were useless, there were no getting away from him, for he was here the next day and the next and the one after that, I . . . I feared I'd never be free of him, not *ever*. I told Victor I no longer wished to work at the tavern but couldn't tell him the truth as to why, just said I didn't much care for Dick. And not imagining the real reason behind my decision, he persuaded me to stop on, to just ignore the man.'

'I'm sorry,' Victor whispered in the silence that followed, lowering his head. 'I had no clue.'

''Course tha didn't, don't blame yourself, nay,' Suzannah was quick to tell him. Then, turning back to Phoebe, she continued, 'So you see, I stuck to Victor's side at work for safety whenever Dick were around – it were all I could do. 'Course that weren't allus possible, and Dick . . . well. He seemed to somehow allus find a way to get me on my own.'

'Get you on your own? For what purpose?' Phoebe asked – then instantly blushed scarlet with realisation. 'The cellar . . .'

'Aye. But you see, one night, I got chatting to Big Red.' Flicking her gaze to the man in question, Suzannah smiled softly. 'And d'you know, Dick bothered me less after that. I knew it were Big Red's size, that Dick wouldn't take the chance with him by my side, and so I . . . I . . .'

'Tha pretended to like me to keep Lavender at bay,' said Big Red. Eyes on his clasped hands, he shook his head. 'It were nowt but play-acting. Tha used me.'

339

'In t' beginning, aye, for I were desperate,' she admitted, visibly cringing. 'But lad, my feelings grew into real affection, they did, honest. And later . . . later, love.' She nodded, and a single tear rolled down her cheek. 'Surprised me, that did. Scared me a bit, too. I ain't never really known owt like that afore, not for any bloke. Oh, I believed I had.' Her hand travelled south to stroke her rounded stomach, undoubtedly with thoughts of Warwick Yewdale. 'But with thee, lad . . . That were real,' she whispered, whilst her eyes added: *It still is.*

'Tell me, please. I must know.' Phoebe's face was as white as the tablecloth. 'How was it you already knew Dick? Just who the hell is he, Miss Frost?'

'He's my bully.'

'What?'

'That's right. The fella tha witnessed getting rough with me near the brewery that day is one of Dick's cronies. Why d'you think he never came looking for me after I escaped his clutches, as we feared he would? It were because, by sheer foul fortune, Dick was here to keep an eye to me instead. There's a band of them, with Dick at the helm. They work Manchester's slums together, exploiting unfortunates – women who ply a trade using what's betwixt their legs – have for years.'

Phoebe slapped a hand to her mouth as though she'd be sick. 'My God.'

'That's not all,' Victor put in grimly. He nodded encouragingly to Suzannah to reveal the rest. 'Go on, Miss Frost.'

'Dick, he . . . he were master of the bogus servants' agency whence I first found myself sucked into the life of debauchery.'

'No . . .'

'I told you, lass, of how I came to make Miss Frost's

acquaintance,' said Victor gently, taking Phoebe's hand. 'Turns out that the one behind that deplorable operation was none other than Dick Lavender himself.'

'I believed myself free of him after going to the police, but it weren't to be,' Suzannah added in a voice thick with tears. 'He caught up with me weeks later and forced me into working the streets for him instead.'

Big Red scraped back his chair and leapt to his feet to pace the room. 'I'll kill him. I'll tear his head from his *neck* for him. I'll—'

'Nay, lad, you mustn't, for he'll find a way to wreak vengeance, he will. He's rotten right through to the marrow and dangerous beyond belief! Lord only knows what he'll do.'

'So what, we do nowt? Is that what you're saying?'

'I don't like it any more than thee, but there's no other way, lad. Least now Phoebe knows the way of things, can be shot of him afore it's too late. I prayed everything would come to light sooner. Though I were too coward to loosen my tongue, I hoped *someone* would notice . . . *something*. You remember, Victor, I said to you when yer told me that Phoebe wouldn't be spending Christmas at your house, I said not to bank on it? I truly believed it would have all come out by then, for surely it had to. But nay.'

Victor closed his eyes on a sigh. He *had* thought her words queer at the time – why, oh why, hadn't he pressed her for an explanation? 'Yes.'

'Dick, he reckoned he owned me, treated me as he liked. He took me when his lust needed sating, hit me and degraded me at will. I thought, when I learned you'd seen him taking me in the cellar . . .' Suzannah turned eyes swimming with unshed tears to Phoebe. 'I thought it were all over, finally. That it would bring an end to it and I'd know peace. That you, lass, would banish him from your life – aye, and mine, into the bargain.'

'But I didn't, did I? I'm sorry. So sorry . . .'

'Nay, I blame thee not. Really, I don't, for that were on me. I'd wronged you so often it were no surprise you didn't want to hear me.'

Phoebe's response was deep with sincerity: 'I'm hearing you now, Miss Frost.'

'Eeh, lass.'

'Thank you for your courage in telling me the truth.'

'It's the very least I . . . Oh, how I've treated thee!' Giving way to her emotion, Suzannah burst into miserable sobs. 'I never wanted to hurt thee again, I didn't! Say tha forgives me, lass, please.'

Gulping back tears of her own, Phoebe patted the woman's shoulder. 'It isn't forgiveness you're owed, Miss Frost, but gratitude. You've saved me from God alone knows what fate. For that, I'll be for ever in your debt.'

'I know it ain't much after all I've caused, but I hope that goes some way to making it up to you,' Suzannah gulped, nodding to Phoebe's bodice.

Frowning, she glanced down – and at the sight of the brooch winking back at her, her brow cleared. 'It was you? You're behind its return?'

Suzannah nodded. Then, turning to Victor: 'You heard word from the chief constable yet?' she asked.

He and Phoebe gazed at each other. But how could this be?

'Warwick,' Suzannah confessed. 'He made it happen.'

'Why on earth—?'

'I went to see him, yesterday. I were desperate, needed to do summat to try to make it up to youse both the only way I knew how. Warwick's the only soul I know of with money and influence aplenty that I knew could help. I threatened him, told him to make it happen else I'd tell the town about our child and destroy his reputation in the process. Eeh, he were that mad, but he agreed. I remembered you mentioning, lass, that you'd sold the brooch to a Mr Rakowski – Warwick had his new footman buy it back for him and return it to thee. Warwick said he'd speak to the chief constable and persuade him to reinstate you, Victor, hisself.'

'The errand boy was his footman ... Fresh in his employ, you say? Well, of course, that explains why I failed to recognise him. I, I don't know what to say,' Phoebe murmured, reaching up to stroke her precious bauble.

'Warwick banished me from his land. He said I'm never to show my face again, and I vowed I never would.'

'You mean you found yourself with a solitary opportunity, could have asked him for anything and he'd have granted it, and you chose to utilise it to benefit us?' asked Victor in wonderment.

'Aye, for I love youse both,' Suzannah answered simply.

'I don't know what to say,' he told her, echoing Phoebe. He was quite overcome.

'All you've done for me, the pair of youse ... Nowt felt more important than giving summat back, however much you might have detested me. And ay, I know what you're thinking: I could have demanded Warwick set us up for life, me and the babby. Brass, a home of our own ... But nay.' Suzannah shook her head. 'This child shall want for nowt, but it's me what'll provide. He or she – me, an' all, for that matter – neither want nor need owt from that man, not never. I have my friends again, least I hope, and that's more than enough, aye.'

Victor and Phoebe shared a soft smile. It was the

latter who said: 'You'll come back, won't you, Miss Frost? The tavern hasn't been the same without you.'

'Oh, lass. Eeh, you really mean it? I'd be delighted to, that I would!'

'And I'm sure Mrs Tibbs wouldn't mind coming in with me if you'd like to share Kitty's room—?'

'Nay,' Suzannah cut in, though her eyes shone with thankfulness at the offer. 'I'll be much obliged to return here to work, but I prefer to stop on at Mr and Mrs Reed's, if tha don't mind? I'd not want to disrupt things, am settled there, you see.'

Smiling, Phoebe opened her mouth to utter assurance that she understood, but the words never reached her lips – Big Red got in before her:

'Aye, you stop on where you are,' he told Suzannah. Then, taking the room by surprise, he added, 'Well, just until we're wed, that is.'

'Wed?' she stuttered.

A hand the size of a dinner plate caressed first Suzannah's cheek then dropped to encompass her neat bump in a tender touch. 'Aye, lass. If youse'll both still have me?'

'Lad! Eeh, come here, you big daft bugger, 'course we will!'

Motioning to Phoebe that they should give the emotional couple some privacy, Victor shepherded her from the room, closing the door behind him. Alone on the landing, they gazed at one another in stunned stupor at all that had transpired.

'You're not too disappointed, are you?' Phoebe asked eventually. 'About the police, I mean?'

'No, not really,' he lied – truth was, it smarted that he'd been offered back the job not because they truly rated him an asset to the force but because of coercion. However, there was little point in dwelling on it. What was done was done, and Suzannah had meant well. That part of his life was dead and buried; he'd known it, deep down. As he'd stated to Phoebe only that morning, The Lilian was where his priorities lay now.

'You shan't accept the position, then?' she asked.

'No, lass.'

'Oh, thank God!'

'Steady, steady,' he murmured on a chuckle as she threw herself into his arms. 'You didn't honestly believe I could leave you, did you?'

'I . . . don't know.'

'Never.'

'Mr Hayes, what am I going to do?'

By the tone of her voice, now suddenly flat and thoroughly beaten down, he guessed she was referring to Dick. Victor held her closer. He knew precisely what she meant and it both pained and frustrated him equally.

What if I'm to bear his child? What then?

That was what was tearing her up inside, and he felt it too. Evicting Lavender from her life went without saying in light of all they had learned, they knew that. It didn't lessen Phoebe's troubles or fears, however – how could it? A pregnancy would make everything infinitely more difficult. Until she knew for certain either way as to what fate decided, she could never know peace.

'Whatever happens . . . no matter the outcome . . . I'm here for you,' he whispered fiercely into her hair. Feeling her stiffen against him, he knew she understood his meaning. 'It's all right. Everything's going to be all right.'

'You . . . know?'

'I do.'

'Please don't hate me.'

His arms tightened ever more around her. 'As if I could.'

'I'm so very ashamed. Why did I *do* it?'

Because of me and my treatment of you, his tortured mind yelled out. And he knew all this was far from finished.

The real battle had only just begun.

Chapter 23

AN ODD SENSE of calm had greeted Phoebe upon awakening and remained with her still. Grateful of the fact, she didn't question it.

Keeping at bay the chill of the winter afternoon, a merry fire danced in the grate. The teapot sat ready in the centre of the table, two cups alongside. Downstairs, the tavern was filling with thirsty customers, Mrs Tibbs and Kitty tending to their wants. Ordinary, normal.

Taking a last glance around, Phoebe nodded. Everything was as it should be in preparation for Dick's arrival.

Everything, that is, besides the two men secreted in her bedroom across the small landing.

Dick's footsteps sounded on the stairs and he swaggered into the kitchen. He greeted her and she returned it, a feeling of all-encompassing relief washing through her to keep company her composure. *Soon, it would be over. So very soon.* The knowledge was like a balm to her soul and the moment his buttocks touched his chair, she began:

'Dick, I have something to tell you.'

'Does tha, now?'

Noting the arrogant curl of his lip at her announcement, she was reminded of his changed attitude towards her of late. Whereas before, he'd appeared attentive to her every word and action, now he could barely hold in check his disparagement of everything she said and did. That he no longer felt the need to be as mindful of his behaviour was evident.

His quest to hoodwink her was complete. The chase was over; he'd secured his prey. Or so he believed.

'Have you summat to impart or haven't yer?'

She inclined her head in affirmation.

'Well, go on then, spit it out.'

'There's no easy way of saying this and so I'll come straight out with it. I don't wish to marry you.'

'Eh?'

'You heard.'

'I *know* what I heard, girl. Only it seems you're talking in tongues, for I could have sworn you said you're not for wedding me.'

'That's because it's true, Dick. I've changed my mind. That's how it is, and you'll have to accept it.'

He breathed deeply, eyes turning thoughtful. 'What's afoot? Come on, out with it. Summat's brought this fool-ishness on, and I want to know what. I want to know *now*, damn it,' he growled when she didn't answer, thumping the tabletop hard. 'Well?'

Doing her best to stop her gaze from straying to the door – and Victor and Big Red beyond – she kept her stare fixed on Dick. 'I don't believe we're compatible.' *That, and the fact you're a deplorable, revolting specimen and you make my flesh crawl,* her mind added.

For two pins, she'd have told him exactly how she felt and what he was, but a promise was a promise. Short of going down on her knees, Suzannah had begged her, Victor and Big Red not to make mention of her revela-tion, that it had been for their ears only, to spare Phoebe a life as Mrs Lavender and all that would have come

348

with it. Suzannah had been adamant she'd never hope to live in peace if Dick knew she'd blabbed about their past. Seeing how terrified the woman was, Phoebe and the men had reluctantly agreed.

'So let me get this right,' Dick said slowly now. 'You're wanting to toss away all we have 'cause you reckon we don't "fit". Is that it?'

'Yes.'

'Well, tough, for I ain't soddin' having it!' he exploded. Puce with fury, the veins in his neck looked as though they would pop. 'You're marrying me, and that's an end to it.'

'An end . . . ? Just who the devil do you think you are?' Her building temper becoming increasingly impossible to suppress, she glared at him. 'I don't have to marry you, Dick Lavender, if I choose not to do so. You don't own me, you know. Nor do you get to make my decisions. I intended to do my best to let you down gently, but if you're intent on refusing to accept this, then I'm afraid I must be blunt: I carry no love for you. In fact, if I'm perfectly honest, I oftentimes struggle to find you so much as likeable. Nor do you hold any sort of love for me. This I know,' she continued quickly before he could bluster a rebuttal. 'Please, don't insult my intelligence any further than you already have by denying the fact to my face.'

If a wisp of ash had at that moment floated from the grate, it would have had the power to knock him down flat, so absolute was his shock. His head performed a queer sort of jig, jerking left and right in an attempt at contradiction. 'You're lying,' he finally managed to squeak. 'You do love me! And I, I love thee, 'course I do—'

'You're the liar, on both counts, and you know it. I've slowly come to realise that it was only ever this place you wanted, Dick, not me.' There, she'd said it. She watched the range of emotions pass across his face and inwardly revelled. *Deny that one, you swine, you!*

'Oh, I see.' Recovering suddenly, his brow cleared as though in understanding. 'It's my past, in't it? That's what bothers thee.' Definite relief that he'd apparently solved the reason behind her decision – and confidence that a dollop of his infallible charm and persuasion would bring her round – had him sighing with a disarming smile. 'You think I'm with thee for your assets? Eeh, lass. Them ain't my intentions, nay.'

'You reek of deception.'

'Them ain't, I tell you—'

'Stop! Just stop, for God's sake.' She couldn't take much more of this. Of course, she hadn't expected him to accept all this lying down, but how much longer would he put up a fight? She just wanted him *gone*. 'Your numerous petty and fraudulent operations mean naught to me. The same goes for your involvement in blood sports and our Lord alone knows what else you have a hand in. Not any more. I convinced myself you were merely unfortunate, a victim of circumstance who had been dealt by life a harsh hand. But no. This goes beyond that. You were after the bigger prize all along, a permanent meal ticket, if you will. Well, you shan't get it from me. Your plan to bleed me dry and take the tavern has failed. Now, please, will you just leave.'

'Phoebe, nay. You're wrong, you are.'

'Get your *filthy* hands off me,' she spat, lurching from his reach as he made to embrace her. She'd lain awake for half the night, going over in her mind all she'd learned of him, had shed bitter tears for the poor women and girls he'd ruined and was doing so still. Now, to have him touch her . . . 'You make me sick, what you are . . .'

Recalling before her tongue ran away with itself her vow to Suzannah, she bit back the rest of her sentence. *But oh, how she longed to speak it, tell him exactly what she felt.* 'There is something dark, the blackest of black, about you. You see people as mere commodities, don't you? Simply objects to use as you see fit. You'd take the eyes out of one's head if you could – and still come back for the eye-lashes. Have you no scruples, no shame at all?'

'You're a fine one to preachify about having no shame.' As though he'd realised sweet talk was pointless now, his attitude shifted tack and his expression turned altogether more sinister. 'You spread your thighs for me willingly not a handful of days past. I claimed thee, aye.'

I claimed thee. My God, how had she been so stupid? He planned it, of course. Bedding her had simply been part of his scheme, a way in which to bind her to him, to trap her.

'Well? What says thee to that?'

'It means nothing,' she said as firmly as she could muster. But tears were not far away, much to her chagrin.

'Nay? And others would hold the same belief, would they, were it to become known?'

He was threatening to besmirch her character publicly. Why was she even surprised? Though the prospect made her want to wilt with the horror of it, she drew together all her strength and held firm. 'You can't blackmail me. You shan't. I. Do. Not. Want. To. Marry. You.' She threw every word at him like daggers. 'Do you understand? It's over with, finished. Now leave my home and don't ever return – or you'll regret it.'

'Oh, will I now?'

Cursing letting slip the warning, seeing how it had stoked his rage to worrying proportions, she swallowed down her own anger and attempted desperately to claw

351

back her self-control. Meanwhile, Dick had circled the table to stand in front of her. Fists bunched by his sides, he dragged in air through flared nostrils.

'Just what are you going to do, eh? Nowt, that's what, so don't come the threats with me. Now, I'll say it again one last time, so you'd do well to listen good: I've toiled too hard and for too long at this to give it all up. We're marrying, and that's all there is to it.'

The tension had thickened ominously and, now, her eyes travelled in the direction of her bedroom of their own accord. She'd insisted she speak with him by herself, but the men had been adamant she wasn't to face him entirely alone. Unbeknown to Dick, they were hiding out mere feet away, ready to offer her assistance should the need arise. A need which, she feared, was rapidly approaching. She'd never seen the real Dick this clearly before and it was safe to say she was scared. Now she understood Suzannah's terror. He cut an intimidating figure when at his worst.

'D'you hear me?' Dick pressed on a bark, looming closer.

From where Phoebe found the strength, she didn't know: 'No. I won't do it.'

'Bitch, I'll show you!'

Before she had time to blink, let alone dodge his advance, his hands were around her throat. Then the door burst inwards, and Victor and Big Red were hauling Dick off her. Sobbing and gasping for air, she sent up a thank you to God for the men's quick actions. 'Please . . . just get him out of here!'

Pinned against the wall, both arms twisted painfully up his back, Dick craned his neck to leer at her. His eyes were those of a being possessed and spittle bubbled at the corners of his mouth – he looked like a rabid dog.

'Bitch, you've no idea what you've done. By God, you'll pay for this, every last one of youse!'

'Shut that rancid trap of yours, Lavender, before I do it for you,' Victor hissed close to his ear.

His response was wild laughter – Phoebe baulked to hear it. It put her in mind of the shrieking banshees in the stories her brother had scared her with as a child. The female spirits of Irish folklore were predictors of doom, well known for heralding deaths . . . her blood ran cold. Was this an omen of things to come?

She squeezed shut her eyes as Dick was dragged past her from the room, yet his parting promise remained with her long after he'd gone:

'You'll know suffering afore I'm through! The reaper's got you marked – *marked*! I'll finish you all!'

Chapter 24

DAY FOLLOWED DAY. To their initial unease then relief, nothing happened.

After a fortnight, they were all learning to breathe a little easier. Though Victor and Big Red hadn't mentioned it, and nor had she asked, Phoebe suspected they had sent Dick on his way that day with more than mere words to stay away. She didn't go in for rough justice, however justified; however, she was willing to make an exception with this. Mercifully, it seemed to have done the trick and Dick had got the message after all.

At The Lilian, normal service resumed. Suzannah had taken up her former post as tavern cook and was settling back in well. Released from Dick's control, her mind free now to be consumed only with impending motherhood and a wedding on the horizon, she went about her duties with a song and a smile. Kitty was pleased to have her friend back, and the ever-benign Mrs Tibbs was simply happy that the rest of them were happy. They dared to hope that things were finally on the up.

Then dawned the fifteenth day of January, and with it brought revelations that would set in motion irreversible changes to all their lives.

Phoebe had been woken in the early morning by a

familiar dragging ache in her lower back and stomach. Throughout the agonisingly long hours that followed, she'd checked and rechecked herself at the privy, prayers falling relentlessly from her lips – finally, her doggedness paid off. The crimson staining made its appearance; her monthly bleed had come!

In blind joy, she dashed inside to find Victor. She located him in the kitchen enjoying a quick break with a cup of tea – laughing through ecstatic tears, she told him how there would be no child.

'You're certain?'

'Absolutely so. Oh, Mr Hayes, I cannot tell you . . . the *relief*.'

'Come, it's all over,' he soothed, holding her close, and she rested her cheek against his chest. 'A fresh start. Your life begins here. Promise me you'll make the most of it.'

'I . . .' But the words refused to come, and she wept bitterly. 'Life is meaningless, though, Mr Hayes, don't you see? It offers nothing . . . without you.'

'My own sweet love . . . please, you mustn't think that way . . .'

'I cannot help it,' she confessed. 'Kate doesn't deserve you. She—'

'She what?'

Now was the time. Phoebe had put off revealing what Dick had discovered about Victor's wife – so much had transpired afterwards, there just hadn't been the right moment. Victor deserved the truth. What he chose to do with the knowledge of it was up to him, but at least she could say she'd done the right thing in making him aware.

'Kate's sister is soon to remarry. Inasmuch, she no longer required Kate as a companion.' Lifting her face,

Phoebe met his eye. 'That's why your wife is back. The *only* reason. I'm sorry, but she doesn't love you, Mr Hayes. She doesn't, but I do. I do, and I can't have you, and it's so unfair. *Why* must life be this cruel?'

Victor shook his head. 'I don't know.'

'I haven't upset you, have I?'

'No, no. I suspected as much, knew in my heart of hearts that Kate hadn't returned through choice.'

'It's merely a home she required.'

'Yes.'

'Then ...' Phoebe's heart had begun to drum. 'Couldn't you give it to her? The house, I mean. Perhaps she'd let you go, then, and we—'

'She wouldn't. It wouldn't be enough. She wants to punish me, I'm sure of it. She's miserable, and so I must be, too. She'll cling on to this wreck of a marriage of ours until her dying breath just to spite me. It's useless.'

Nevertheless, Phoebe saw the spark of hope that had appeared in his eyes. When he kissed her brow and murmured could she spare him for half an hour, she could barely squeeze her voice past the lump in her throat: 'Yes, of course . . .'

He hurried from the room and she felt her way to the table to drop into a chair. *Dear God, could their wish really come true?*

Several hours later, Phoebe was still no closer to knowing.

Victor had failed to return.

She wandered about the drinking room listlessly, completing her duties with only half her mind on the task, her hungry gaze riveted to the door. By closing time, she was teetering on the cusp of breaking point. After seeing the last of the customers on their way, she bade Kitty and Mrs Tibbs goodnight and went to sit on the wooden form by the open fire. Locked in utter misery, she wrapped her arms around herself and watched the dying flames through a blur of tears.

This was just like last time. He'd promised to come to her at the tavern and hadn't. It didn't bode well. Again, it could mean but one thing: bad news. She was thoroughly fed up with disappointment.

Kate had refused him his freedom as he'd predicted she would. It wasn't enough she didn't want him – she wouldn't abide the notion of anyone else having him either. He could never be Phoebe's, it was true.

A tapping at the door finally came and, despite herself, Phoebe couldn't contain a hopeful cry. She raced across to admit him.

Avoiding her eye, Victor skirted past her into the room. He removed his hat, which he wrung in his hands as though his mind was in great turmoil, but still he didn't look at her.

'Mr Hayes?'

'I told her. I told Kate I love you.'

'And?' she whispered.

'She . . . She . . . Christ, I cannot speak it. For if I do, you'll hate me, and that I shan't bear!'

Dread was filling her. Frowning, she shook her head. 'Never could I harbour for you anything but love. Please. Tell me.'

'Kate, she . . .' Victor took a great shuddering breath. 'She's with child.'

'But she can't be.'

'Phoebe, lass . . .'

'But how? I don't understand *how*, I . . . You said it was me you loved—'

'Yes, and you said the same about me, only that didn't stop you lying with Dick, did it?' he shot back harshly, then, when she winced, dropped his head in his hands. 'I'm sorry. I shouldn't have . . . I didn't guess about you and him, as I think you assume. I saw you both together, saw him leaving here the morning after . . . I wanted to get my own back. My male pride had taken a battering, I was in turmoil, I . . . I went home and I bedded Kate. I regret it, did so the moment it was over. Now, she's to bear my child. And I, I can't . . .'

'Oh, Mr Hayes.' Phoebe drew him into her arms. 'Oh, Mr Hayes,' she repeated, having nothing else at her disposal. She felt numb with loss, the finality of it all. What a titanic mess they had made of everything.

'Tell me what I should do.'

His agony tore at her, but she couldn't make this right. No one – nothing – could. 'You don't need me to do that. You know what must be done.'

He could never leave Kate now.

'Sing us another, Mrs Tibbs!'

'Aye, go on, wench! One of them slow, romantic numbers tha does so well. Fair bring a tear to my eye, them do,' called another customer, then blushed scarlet when his friends pointed at him teasingly, guffawing like donkeys. 'Scoff all youse want, I likes 'em!' he roared, making them laugh harder still.

Any other time, Phoebe would have watched the harmless scene with a chuckle. Right now, however, she wanted to run as far away as possible. She hadn't the strength for pretence, doubted she'd ever even smile again, let alone anything more. Alive her physical form may be, but her soul had withered and died last night, and she knew she'd never be the same. Nothing would. Nothing.

One glance across the room at Victor's haunted expression and her heart tore in two all over again.

Desperate for distraction, she escaped towards Big Red's table, where sat the man enjoying a drink with Suzannah. As she drew nearer, she saw he wore an expression as downcast as her own – frowning, she asked, 'Big Red? Is something wrong?'

'Aye, lass, you might say that. It's Caesar.'

'The dog? What about him?'

'Gone missing, he has. I let him out this morning to do his business, like, and he never returned. Queer, it is. He ain't never strayed afore.'

'I am sorry,' Phoebe told him, adding, to try to lift his worry, 'but fear not, for I'm sure he'll be back. He's likely wandered off somewhere, that's all.'

'That's what I said,' Suzannah put in, shooting her a grateful look. She stroked her beloved's arm in reassurance. 'The little fella will be home when he grows hungry, you mark my words.'

'Aye, happen you're both right,' Big Red began, but he never got to finish his sentence. An almighty crash rent the air, swallowing the conversation – with a collective gasp, they gazed at the object that had been launched through the tavern window and landed on their table. Dark and twisted, it was difficult to make out just what the mass was. Then Big Red nudged it with his tankard, turning it over, and they staggered back in horror.

'Nay. Oh, Christ!'

'Mother of God . . .' Spinning around, Phoebe heaved up a stream of bile.

Big Red was openly crying. Lifting the blood-soaked lump that was Caesar's headless body, he held it to his chest and released a beast-like roar to the ceiling. Then he was charging across the floor, sending flying with his beefy arms anyone in his path, on his race to the door.

The road was empty.

'Come, my love, sit thee down,' Suzannah pleaded with him, and, seeing her distress, he allowed her to usher him back inside. 'A dram of brandy for his nerves, please, lass, and quick,' she told Phoebe.

'Follow me,' Victor told them, leading the way upstairs to lend them privacy.

Easing the dazed-looking man into a kitchen chair, Suzannah sat facing him and chafed his hands as though to instil life back into him. 'Talk to me, lad. Say summat.'

'Lavender.'

'Nay, it can't be, he's gone. It's likely just wicked kids and their games—'

'Lavender,' he insisted on a low growl. 'This is a message, this is. I should have throttled the swine when I had the chance, should have guessed he'd not slink away quietly.'

Phoebe shared with Victor and Suzannah a look of dread. Could it be?

'Big Red! Oh Gawd, where are thee?' came a sudden cry. Heavy footsteps on the landing beyond accompanied it, then King Henry burst into the room. 'Eeh, lad.'

'What is it? Speak up, man!'

Struggling to catch his breath, Big Red's friend pointed towards the street. 'Your . . . your dwelling,' he panted. 'I ran as fast as I could . . . It's up in flames!'

'*What?*'

'Quick, lad, come on!'

'Drink this,' Phoebe told Suzannah, placing a cup of tea in front of her. 'I know you're worried, but you must think of the baby.'

With a reluctant nod, the woman wiped her wet face on her sleeve and sipped at the hot brew.

It was just the two of them. Victor had accompanied Big Red and King Henry to the house, and Phoebe had done her best since to reassure Suzannah and help keep her calm.

'I didn't want to believe it, but Big Red's right. This is just about that bastard Dick's style, aye. He's been lying low is all, licking his wounds, waiting for the right time to strike.'

'Miss Frost, you don't know that for cert—'

'He's found out I'm back here,' Suzannah went on dully, as though she hadn't heard her. 'He knows I've spilled the truth and made you wise to him, that it's me what's ruined everything. I've destroyed his life, ripped from him all he had. Now he means to do the same to me. This . . . this is just the start. He'll not rest 'til he's made every last one of us pay.'

Suspecting deep down she was right, Phoebe hugged herself. Just what were they going to do? What else would they have to face before they woke from this living nightmare they had found themselves trapped in?

Catching sounds of movement on the stairs, they rose as one as the men entered. Faces black with smoke and grime, they dropped into chairs at the table and Phoebe hurried to pour them tea.

'It's gone, I've lost everything.'

'Eeh, lad!' Suzannah ran to throw her arms around Big Red.

'Completely gutted out, it is,' King Henry agreed. 'Fret not, mind, for as I've said already: you've a home at mine for as long as needs be.'

'Ta, thanks,' he murmured. Then, turning to Suzannah: 'You look fit to drop. Come on, lass, let's get you back to Mr and Mrs Reed's.'

'You'll not do owt daft the night, will you, lad?' she

beseeched him as he walked her to the door. 'You'll not go in search of Dick? Promise me.'

'I promise.'

Placated, Suzannah gave a sigh of relief.

Only Phoebe saw the look of pure murder he shot to the other men before he slipped from the room.

Chapter 25

DAYBREAK BROUGHT A cutting downpour and sharp winds which, by mid-morning, still showed no sign of letting up. When Suzannah arrived at the tavern to prepare the food for the day's customers, she was soaked to the skin. Tut-tutting, Phoebe shed her of her sopping shawl and ushered her to the fire before pouring her a steaming cup of tea.

'Eeh, ta, lass.' The woman drank it gratefully. 'By, it's foul out there.'

'How are you feeling this morning?' Mrs Tibbs asked her gently, Phoebe having filled her and Kitty in on developments so as to prepare them for possible further onslaught.

Tears instantly filled Suzannah's eyes, but she blinked them away determinedly. 'As well as I can be, you know?' she said quietly.

'A crying shame, it is, about Big Red's place. And oh, poor Caesar, the little love!' chipped in Kitty. 'Reet fond of him, I were. Place shan't be the same without him.'

The women lapsed into sombre silence and the only sounds in the small kitchen were the pitter of rain against the windowpanes and the crackle of the fire. Eventually, Mrs Tibbs and Kitty drifted off to give the drinking room the once-over, ready for opening. Soon afterwards, satisfied that Suzannah had regained the colour in her cheeks and was sufficiently recovered, Phoebe left her to get on with her own duties and went to give the others a hand downstairs.

At some point during her work, Phoebe noted the sound of Suzannah descending the stairs and the rear door opening as she visited the privy. When minutes passed, followed by several more, and realising she hadn't heard the woman return, she went off in search of her.

'Miss Frost?' she called, tapping at the privy door. Receiving no response, she knocked louder. 'Miss Frost, are you quite well in there?'

Still no answer was forthcoming. Worry now building inside her, Phoebe pushed open the door. The privy was empty.

She stood for a moment, frowning in confusion, before making her way to the back lane behind the tavern. What she saw had her crying out in horror: 'Oh, Miss Frost!'

'Lass . . .'

'What on *earth*?'

'St—st—stabbed. Phoebe . . .'

'Sshhh, don't try to speak,' she choked through her terror. Dropping to her knees beside the pool of blood spreading beneath Suzannah, she cradled the woman's head in her lap. 'Everything's going to be all right.' In the next breath, she yelled over her shoulder: 'Mrs Tibbs, Kitty! We need your help. Oh please, come quickly!'

'Dear God above . . . !' Mrs Tibbs was first on the scene. Taking in the situation, she turned to the girl who had followed on her heels. 'Kitty, fetch Mr Hayes from his home whilst I dash for the doctor. Run like the devil, lass, go on!'

'Big Red,' Suzannah breathed, struggling to keep open her eyes.

'Mr Hayes shall bring him to you just as soon as he arrives. In the meantime, you must try to remain calm. It's all right, it's all right, I'm here.'

Dick. This was his doing, had to be. That she'd actually considered marrying someone who could commit an act this monstrous made her sick to her core. Well, this couldn't continue. He *had* to be stopped.

Sudden thoughts of the child robbed her concentration – damping down her panic, Phoebe cast a discreet eye over Suzannah in search of the source of the injury. Locating it, the colour drained from her face. The crimson flow looked to be coming from the woman's lower stomach. *Good God, no.*

'Is she . . . ? Is she . . . ?'

Victor! Thank the Lord. 'She's breathing,' Phoebe reassured him as he skidded to a halt beside her, Kitty close behind. 'Mrs Tibbs is collecting the medical man, he should be here any minute.'

'This cold and rain . . . we must get her inside before she perishes from pneumonia.'

Nodding, Phoebe stepped aside and watched as Victor murmured soothingly to Suzannah. He lifted her gently and carried her towards the tavern, and Phoebe ran on in front to open wide the doors.

'Put her down in my bed, Mr Hayes,' she told him when they reached the landing. 'Then I think you ought to fetch Big Red.'

In case Suzannah doesn't make it. The unspoken observation hung in the air between them, devastating in its probability. *Her betrothed must have a chance to say his goodbyes.*

When Victor had gone, Phoebe instructed Kitty to

make tea and turned her attention to her patient. She'd just finished making her comfortable when the doctor arrived.

Assessing the situation, he nodded grimly. With instructions that he'd need clean rags and hot water fetching immediately, he ushered Phoebe from the room.

His request fulfilled, the three women sat at the table in heavy silence. All they could do now was wait and pray.

The doctor was still working on Suzannah when Victor returned with Big Red. The latter man's expression of sheer terror was painful to witness – Phoebe went to him and squeezed his hands.

'You must hold faith,' she told him, but her words sounded hollow to her own ears. 'Miss Frost is in good hands.'

Twenty agonising minutes later, the doctor finally emerged.

Locked in dread and fear, no one moved. Then he spoke and the room resonated with their collective breaths:

'She'll live.'

'Thank God!' Big Red fell to his knees at the doctor's feet. 'Thank *you*, sir. Thank you.'

'And the child?' asked Victor quietly.

'By some miracle, that too shall live. The knife penetrated the mother's hip, causing minimal damage. An inch or two to the left and it would have been a wholly different outcome. Both she and the child have been extremely fortunate indeed. She informs me she didn't see her assailant, that they struck from behind. She has no known adversaries?' he added with a frown, glancing at them in turn.

366

'Nay, none,' Big Red answered him quickly.

'Then it would seem it was a random attack.'

'Aye, likely so. The desperate and devilish alike are plentiful round these here parts.'

'Yes, quite.'

'The lass, can we see her?'

'One of you only, for a minute or two. The patient mustn't be taxed, needs plenty of rest.'

Big Red hurried to the sickroom whilst Victor saw the doctor out. The moment they were alone, Kitty threw her hands in the air in perplexity.

'We know very well who's to blame for this – why didn't Big Red name that swine Lavender?'

Phoebe and Mrs Tibbs exchanged a look. They knew the answer to that, all right. The last thing he wanted was the law involved in this; it had gone too far for that. Besides, what proof had they? No, the courts wouldn't mete out punishment on Dick. Not they, for he intended to dole that out himself.

Their suspicions proved founded when the man himself re-entered the kitchen. His face, normally florid with health and good humour, was now bone white with unspeakable fury – he looked as though he might explode at any moment.

'Miss Frost is comfortable?' Phoebe asked him gently.

He gave a stiff nod. Then: 'This savage attack was wrought by that black-hearted spawn of Lucifer,' he growled. 'Worse still is who was Lavender's main target: he went deliberately for the child. How much *lower* can a body get than that? My lass in there, she's distraught, reckons this is all her fault. Caesar, my house going up in smoke: she blames herself for them, an' all. She says she should never have got involved with me, that she's harming me, hates herself for dragging me into her troubles. She wants to call off the wedding for my sake, to set me free from this feud, thinks it would be doing me a kindness.'

'Oh, Big Red, I am sorry—'

'Don't be. *Don't* be, for it shan't happen. Nay! I'll *not* allow Lavender power to smash to ruins our love! Now, more than ever, I shall teach him a lesson he'll not forget. Walked the length and breadth of this district last night, I did, in search of him, but without result. Well, I'll not fail this time. I'll sniff him out, you mark my words. By God, I will!'

'He means to do Dick great harm, and I can't see that happen,' Phoebe whispered to Victor soon afterwards, pulling him aside on the landing. 'Big Red will kill him – he can't hang for that despicable man, he shan't. I need to try to sort this out.'

'What? But how?'

'Just leave it to me,' she insisted grimly. 'I have an idea. Knowing Dick as I do, he'll find it impossible to resist.'

Before Victor could press her further, she hurried downstairs and out of the tavern.

Scanning the street and spotting a group of barefoot urchins playing nearby, Phoebe called the eldest of the boys across.

'Would you like to earn yourself sixpence, child?'

'Eeh, would I, missis!' he cried, rubbing his grubby hands in glee.

'I need a message delivering.' She relayed the address of the inn in which she'd recently witnessed the rat massacre. 'Do you think you can find it?'

'Aye, no bother.'

'You must ask for a man named Dick Lavender.'

'Aye, missis. And the message?'

'Tell him Miss Parsons wishes to see him at The Lilian. Seven o'clock tonight. Tell him . . .' She paused to think, knew it was important to get the words just right for maximum effect. 'Tell him that his pocket will much benefit from the meeting. You'll remember all that?'

The boy nodded. Snatching the coin she held out to him, he skittered off to fulfil her request.

Her heart beginning to drum in anxious anticipation, Phoebe made her way back to the tavern to inform Victor of what she needed him to do.

Everything was in place.

Upstairs, Suzannah slept, and Mrs Tibbs and Kitty were at her bedside, keeping an eye to her. Assuring Big Red that she was in good hands, Victor had persuaded him to go home to King Henry's and rest. Lastly, having decided not to open today in light of events, the tavern was empty of customers. All had gone to plan. Phoebe was confident they wouldn't be disturbed.

Sitting side by side at a small table, she and Victor kept their eyes rooted to the door.

By eight o'clock, Dick still hadn't shown.

'He isn't coming,' said Victor.

'But he *has* to. Money is what feeds his very blood – the temptation will be too much for him.' Rising, she wandered to the window and glanced outside.

'Any sign of him?'

She shook her head. 'I don't understand it.'

Dick would have been watching the place, would be well aware it was only them here, Phoebe was certain of that.

She'd come to the realisation this morning: he'd been keeping tabs on them ever since she'd broken off their betrothal. How else had he discovered Suzannah was back on the scene and had revealed all concerning his despicable behaviour? How else could he have taken Caesar and destroyed Big Red's home without knowing where Big Red lived? The *only* way was by tracking their movements. There was no other explanation.

So why, tonight, hadn't he shown? He'd have surely seen Big Red leave earlier, would be conscious of the fact there were no customers. That should have lent him confidence to deem this meeting safe enough. The fewer the people here to confront him, the lesser the threat. It just didn't add up.

'Perhaps the lad you paid simply fled without upholding his end of the bargain,' Victor offered now. 'Lavender might never have received your message – that would certainly account for his absence.'

'Yes, maybe you're right . . .' Phoebe began, but her words trailed away as movement across the road caught her eye.

'What is it?'

'Col Baines's place. I could have sworn . . .' Peering harder, she let out a small gasp. 'It *is* him.'

Victor came to stand beside her and she motioned across. 'Dick's inside the beerhouse; I've just spotted him passing by the window. That's it, of course,' she added, nodding. 'I should have guessed. It's the Baineses' beerhouse whence he's been spying on us all along.'

'The perfect vantage point.'

'Indeed.'

'In that case, he's certain to put in an appearance soon,' Victor told her. 'He's likely just biding his time, wanted to make absolutely certain that no one would turn up at the tavern as our back-up and ambush him when he was meant to be here.'

Sure enough, moments later, the beerhouse door

370

opened and Dick poked his head outside. After looking left and right, he slipped out and headed across to The Lilian.

'Quickly,' Phoebe hissed, drawing Victor back to the table.

They just had time to resume their seats before the tavern door creaked open and Dick stepped inside.

Having lost none of his arrogance, he sauntered over, pulled out a chair and sat down. With a cocksure tilt of his chin, he smirked at them in turn. 'Missed me, have youse?'

Phoebe felt Victor stiffen with anger beside her but, to her relief, he didn't rise to the jibe. She'd made him promise not to lose his temper and to let her do the talking – thankfully, he was keeping his word.

'So, lass?' Dick said, smiling amiably, as though the past few weeks had never occurred and he was conversing with a friend. 'To what do I owe the pleasure?'

'Enough is enough.'

'I don't understand.'

'Yes, you do, Dick.' She spoke calmly but firmly. 'You know precisely what I'm talking about. I want an end to it. Right now. What will it take to get rid of you for good?'

Leaning back in his seat, Dick rested his boots on the table and folded his arms. He smiled. 'I see.'

'Well?' she asked as the silence grew.

'What are you offering?'

Phoebe reached up and unpinned the brooch from her bodice. She placed it on the table and pushed it across.

'What's that?'

'That, Dick, is a very expensive item of jewellery. One hundred pounds' worth, to be precise.'

Sitting up slowly, he glanced from her to the ornament. 'Is that right?'

'It's yours. Take it and never bother us – *any* of us – again.'

Dick picked it up. Turning it between his thumb and forefinger, he scrutinised it through narrowed eyes, and Phoebe held her breath. Finally, and much to her confusion and great dismay, he tossed it back on to the table.

'No, ta.'

'No? But . . . I thought—'

'Aye, well, tha thought wrong. You reckon a measly hundred quid is compensation enough for all you took away from me? Nay, lass.'

'Then what the hell *do* you want?'

'Your half of this place forra start. Only now,' he added over her snort of derision, 'that alone ain't enough no more. The price has risen, I'm afraid.' Turning to Victor, his eyes were hard as flint. 'I want *your* share, an' all, now, too.'

'You're mad,' Phoebe whispered.

'Oh, I'm that, all right. Raging, in fact, you might say.' Each word was like an ice shard in its sharpness. 'You did me over good and proper, played me like a soddin' fiddle! Well, now it's me what wields the bow. You owe me. You'll do as I've asked and sign this place, lock, stock and barrel, over to me. Otherwise . . .' A grin spread across his face. 'You reckon you've seen the worst of me, what I'm capable of? Ending the life of that whore Suzannah's brat ain't nowt to what else I'm prepared to do.'

'Bastard!' Victor roared. In a lightning-fast move that surprised them all, he threw back his arm and smashed his fist into Dick's face. The force of the blow

372

lifted him from his seat, and he and the chair were sent careering backwards, landing with a crash on the hard flagstones.

Phoebe gazed at him then covered her face with her hands. 'Oh, Mr Hayes. You promised you'd hold on to your temper . . .'

'I won't apologise.' Victor was breathing heavily. 'He had it coming to him, by God he did.'

'He isn't moving. You've rendered him unconscious. He'll be furious when he wakens; now he'll never agree to my suggestion—'

'He had no intention of doing so at any rate. You heard him: he wants this place, nothing less.'

Phoebe heaved a heavy sigh. She'd had a task on her hands earlier when she'd put her notion to Victor of buying Dick off with the brooch; he'd been aghast and dead set against it. However, she'd insisted it was her decision, that she planned to do it with his help or without. There was no other option; Dick's reign of terror would never end otherwise, and who next would suffer his wrath? She'd worked hard to talk Victor around – now, it had all been for nothing. The disappointment was crushing.

Minutes passed as they waited in quiet dread for Dick to stir.

Yet he never did.

Eventually, Phoebe and Victor glanced at each other to share a frown. Then they walked slowly towards the prone man.

'Dick?'

Nothing.

'Dick, can you hear me?'

'No.' Victor spoke in a whisper. 'Don't you do this, Lavender. Don't you *do* this.' Folding to his knees, he reached out tentatively and pressed two fingers to Dick's neck. 'No . . . *No!*'

'He's dead.' Phoebe's voice sounded oddly calm to her own ears. 'Dick's dead.'

'Mother of God.'

'The impact of the fall . . . He must have banged his head.'

'I've killed a man.' Scrambling to his feet, Victor backed away. 'I'm a murderer.'

'No.' Again, that evenness of tone – Phoebe shook her head firmly. 'No, you are not. You didn't kill him. The fall did.'

'But it was me who caused it! It was me, *me* I tell you, I . . . !'

'Listen to me.' Taking his shoulders, she shook him hard. 'You must pull yourself together. Victor! You must. Dick has finally stumbled upon the sword he lived by. His actions alone have determined the outcome. You meant this not.'

'How can you speak so, Phoebe? The man's dead!'

'Yes, he is. However, I can't pretend to be sorry.'

'But—'

'You are a good man; he was not. You deserve a life; he did not. All he's done, the pain he's wrought – not just to us but to countless others . . . I'm glad Dick Lavender is no more. I'll tell you something else: I refuse to see you punished for this. They shan't hang you. I won't lose you, I *won't.*'

'But justice . . . justice must be *served*—'

'And so it has,' she said fiercely.

They lapsed into silence. After an age, Victor raised his head to look at her and asked quietly, as though dreading the answer, 'So what *do* you suggest we do?'

'Get him as far from here as possible.'

374

'Dump his body? Are you mad?'

'No, not mad – sensible. It's the only way.'

'But how? Where? We'd never get away with it. Questions are bound to be asked regarding his disappearance. The Baineses – they'll attest to him having been there tonight.'

'The beerhouse may have been Dick's last known sighting, but that means not a thing. Him leaving there for The Lilian doesn't necessarily mean he reached it. No one actually saw him enter here, I'm sure of it. Besides, I highly doubt the Baineses will trouble themselves to wonder or go out of their way to probe. No doubt Dick will have been throwing his weight about with them these past weeks – remember how he was the last time when warning them off the tavern? Col and his son shall just be glad they've seen the back of him.'

'But . . . someone else . . .'

'Who? Who is there to wonder? He has no kin; he'll be missed by very few people. If anything, his demise will be to many a blessing. He must have made his fair share of enemies over the years. Another thing: he isn't known to the police, you said so yourself, so can't be identified from that quarter if he's discovered. Nor shall they break their backs to find out who he is, not for a man of his class, and you know it. He'll simply be another dead slum dweller amongst the many who have gone before him.'

'Surely it's impossible . . .'

'Nothing is impossible if one puts one's mind to it.'

For a long moment, Victor gazed at her in awe. 'Why are you doing this?'

'For you, I'd do anything,' she responded simply.

This went against everything Victor had been taught, trained in, *believed* to the very core of him. He'd spent a

375

lifetime battling for righteousness and the good, the truth. Would he agree to this? Could he shift, however briefly, on to the side of lawlessness? Did he really have it in him?

'Please,' Phoebe whispered when his eyes filled with agonised tears. '*Please.*'

'The river. We'll dispose of him there.'

On a sob of sheer relief, she ran to him and held him tightly. 'The river,' she echoed.

The scrape of wood on cobblestone sounded preposterously loud in the gathering twilight. Nerves strung beyond endurance, they winced with every step of the way.

Wracking their brains for a way in which to transport Dick to his watery destination, they were initially stumped. Until, that was, the perfect solution had crept upon Phoebe.

Rushing down to the cellar, she and Victor had scrutinised the empty barrels, selecting a thirty-six gallon – the largest they had at their disposal. Deftly, quietly, so not to alert those blissfully unaware upstairs – no one would know about this: it was the best way, for all their sakes; Phoebe and Victor would carry the truth of tonight's events to their own graves – they had worked together to squeeze Dick inside before fastening in place the lid. Feeling strangely detached from the situation, they had given one another a determined nod and set off for Ducie Bridge.

Now, as they rolled the barrel towards Long Millgate through the stubborn drizzle, they were mindful to keep their heads down and avoid meeting anyone's eye. The last thing they wanted was for a customer of The Lilian to recognise them and enquire as to what they were about. The sooner this necessary evil was done with, the better.

They continued along dingy streets riddled with the dwellings of the toiling masses – mere glorified lumps of sooty masonry, reeking of poverty – past towering mills and foundries, onwards towards the bridge.

They were just about to descend into the web of narrow passages and filthy nooks leading down to the river when a voice called out to them, piercing every corner of their brains and turning their knees to wax:

'Victor? Victor Hayes?'

'Bob?'

'Dear God,' Phoebe murmured beneath her breath.

The constable closed the space in several long strides. He slapped Victor friendlily on the back. 'Good to see you, man!'

'And you,' he croaked.

'Where the devil are you going with that?' Smiling, Bob nodded to their cargo.

'A fellow tavernkeeper,' Phoebe blurted, seeing Victor break out in perspiration as he floundered for an answer. 'He's run out of best ale, yes, and . . . and we offered to loan him a barrel until he can get to the brewery in the morning.'

'That was kind of you,' the lawman said, then a frown creased his brow and he shook his head. 'However, I can't stand by and see a fair maiden straining herself; you'll do yourself a mischief, lugging that thing. Here, allow me.'

'No!' she said, a little too sharply, as he made to reach for the barrel, then hastily lightened her response with laughter. 'I'm stronger than I look. Besides, rolling it along the ground, it isn't too taxing, really.'

'If you insist.'

'I do, but thank you kindly for your offer, Constable.'

Bob touched his top hat to her then shook Victor by the hand. 'Well, I'd better return to my beat.'

'Yes.' With what was more a grimace than a smile, Victor waved his friend on his way. 'Goodnight.'

When Bob had disappeared around the bend, they both emitted a ragged sigh.

'Let's get this over with,' said Phoebe grimly.

Thick fog rose from the hungry river. Allowing the mist to encompass them in its moist curtain, binding them for ever in their secret, they knelt side by side on the sludgy bank. A final glance around, then they removed the lid and tilted the barrel's mouth towards the Irk. Dick slithered noiselessly into the black waters.

'Thank you.'

Standing close together at the foot of the tavern stairs, Phoebe and Victor gazed at one another with an altogether different and deeper understanding than either could have imagined possible. This was more than another layer to have fused their connection this night. They were as one, now. Just a single being which nothing could sunder.

'I love you,' Phoebe responded.

'And I love you, now and always.'

A brief touching of lips and they went their separate ways.

Chapter 26

'I WISH I knew what ailed that girl,' Mrs Tibbs said to Phoebe as she poured them their first cup of tea of the day.

'Who, Kitty?'

'The one and only. Look, see the shoddiness of her work on this floor? If she's shown it a brush this morning, then I'm the Queen of England. I don't know where her mind's at, really I don't, but it certainly isn't here.'

Reaching for a piece of bread from the plate in the centre of the table, Phoebe's brow creased. 'She's not herself, then? Could she be sickening for something?'

'I don't know, lass.'

'Have you spoken to her, Mrs Tibbs?'

'I have, but she wouldn't say. She insists all is well, but I know that girl, and untroubled she is not.'

Phoebe's frown grew. The last thing she wanted was for Kitty – any of her friends, for that matter – to be unhappy. 'Perhaps I could have a word with her?' she suggested.

'Would you?'

'Yes, of course.'

The woman nodded, relieved. Then, glancing once more to the floor, she clicked her tongue. 'Well, good luck to you, lass, for she's testing my patience and that's the truth!'

Hiding a smile, Phoebe went in search of the girl. She found her sitting on the edge of the bed and gazing out of the window as though in a world of her own. 'May I speak with you, Kitty?'

'Phoebe.' At the sight of her, colour instantly rose to her cheeks. 'I . . . suppose so.'

'Kitty, what's wrong? Mrs Tibbs is right: you don't seem yourself at all. You can talk to me,' she assured her gently. 'What is it?'

'I, I can't. You'll think me daft, Phoebe, you will . . .'

'I shan't, I promise. Oh, please tell me,' she coaxed, beginning to worry as the girl's eyes pooled with tears. 'What's upset you so?'

'I just, I fret at times whether . . . well, whether *I'll* ever meet a nice bloke to call my own.'

'Oh, lass.' Though Phoebe was smiling inside with relief, she made sure to conceal it. Deem the issue un-serious she might – and glad she was too, had been fearing all sorts just now – but Kitty, in the complicated throes of blossoming womanhood, certainly did not. Sensitivity was what was needed here. 'Kitty, of course you will, in time. There's a young fellow out there some-where just waiting to meet you – and fortunate he'll be, too. Has Miss Frost and Big Red's betrothal brought this on?' she added as the thought occurred. 'Is that it?'

'Partly, aye, but it's not only that. It's also . . . well . . .' Glancing up bashfully, Kitty blushed harder. 'It's thee, an' all,' she finished on a rush.

Her eyebrows rose in surprise. 'Me?' Then quieter, reluctant to even mention his name: 'But Kitty, Dick and I are no more, you know that—'

'Nay, not him. I mean Mr Hayes.'

'What?' Her shock was intense. 'Kitty, what do you mean?'

'I'm sorry, really I am. I weren't eavesdropping on purpose, Phoebe, honest I weren't . . . I heard youse. Last night on yonder stairs. I'd got up forra drink and I caught what youse said to each other. You said you loved him. And Mr Hayes – well, he said it right back!'

'I see.' It was all Phoebe had; there couldn't very well be any denying that, could there? How could they have been so foolish . . .

'You're not angry with me, are you, Phoebe?'

She let out a sigh. 'No, Kitty. No, I'm not angry.'

'I'll not breathe a word to nobody, really I'll not.'

'Thank you. It would create only problems and upset if the truth were known, for Mr Hayes and I . . .' A lump had risen to her throat. She swallowed hard. 'It can never be.'

'But why, Phoebe? He don't love his wife, does he, so why can't—'

'It's not that simple,' she interjected. 'Marriage is complicated; love doesn't always come into it. And besides . . .' She paused for a moment then shrugged. What was the point in hiding it? Kitty and the rest of the tavern would know soon enough, at any rate. 'There is also the matter of the child. That's right: Mrs Hayes is to have a baby.'

'But . . . No, she ain't.'

'I tell you, Kitty, it's true.'

'It's really not, Phoebe, I tells thee!'

The girl's insistence threw her. 'Kitty, why do you appear so convinced of this?'

''Cause I've seen the proof of it with my own eyes.'

'What proof?'

'Yesterday, when Miss Frost were attacked, and Mrs Tibbs sent me to collect Mr Hayes from home.'

'Yes, what of it, Kitty?' Phoebe pressed, beginning to lose patience. 'Speak out.'

'Well, I went the back-entrance way, as I'm used

to – force of habit, you see, from working at the Yewdales'. Anyroad, I bangs on t' door and Mrs Hayes answered.'

'Yes, and?'

'It were clear she'd been doing laundry when I arrived – I saw the pail holding garments in soak.'

'So?'

'Well, when I say garments, I mean . . . well, *you* know. Her unmentionables, like.'

'Her underwear?'

'Aye. Them and her monthly rags.'

'You're correct about this?' Phoebe's breaths came in short bursts. 'Kitty, you must be absolutely certain—'

'Oh, I am. I saw them just as sure as I'm seeing thee now. Honest, Phoebe.'

'Thank you, Kitty. If you'll excuse me, I . . . I must get on.' She rose unsteadily from the bed and fled from the room.

On the landing, she paused to gulp some air. Then she was snatching up her shawl and running as fast as her legs would carry her down the stairs.

'May I come in?'

To say Kate was displeased to see Phoebe on her doorstep was putting it mildly. Eyes turning hard, she drew her lips together in a thin line. 'What do *you* want?'

'To speak with you.'

'Speak with me? And what, pray, could you possibly have to say that I'd be interested in hearing?'

'Please,' Phoebe pressed quietly.

Silence, thick with hostility, hung between them.

'Very well,' Kate ground out. Turning on her heel, she made off abruptly down the hall. 'I can spare a minute or two only. I have far more important things to be getting on with, you know.'

When Phoebe entered the room, Victor rose slowly from the table, his breakfast forgotten. 'Miss Parsons? What is it? Has something happened?'

'You could say that,' she murmured. Then, seeing him blanche, and realising he believed this to be about their actions at the river the previous night, she gave him a discreet shake of her head. 'I wondered if I may speak with your wife. In private.'

'Speak . . . ?' Victor looked to Kate, who raised an eyebrow, as flummoxed as he. 'Yes, I . . . Of course.' He glanced at them in turn once more. Then, face wreathed in confusion, he left the room.

'Well?' shot the woman when she and Phoebe were seated.

'Mrs Hayes, I know you're not with child.'

Kate's mouth dropped open. 'You what?'

'I said I know you're not—'

'How *dare* you! That you have the gall to walk into my home and spout such wicked untruths—'

'I don't blame you, not really. I don't,' she insisted when Kate gazed at her. 'Your husband had just told you he was in love with another woman. You were angry, hurt, afraid you were about to lose everything. In desperation, you blurted the first thing that came into your mind. I understand. Oh, Mrs Hayes . . .' Phoebe's tone was soft. 'How did you think to get away with it? Surely you knew that at some point your husband would start to wonder when your stomach didn't grow . . . ?'

Kate's words were barely audible. 'How did you find out?'

'That matters not. But Mrs Hayes, this has to end. You know that, don't you?'

'Yes.' As the admission was uttered, the burden of guilt seemed to rise from her; she seemed almost relieved

383

her deceit was out in the open. Her frame loosened and she closed her eyes. 'Yes,' she repeated. 'I meant not for this to happen, whatever you may think . . .'

'I know. I believe you. And Mrs Hayes?' Sudden tears filled her voice. 'I'm so very sorry. Though *you* may not believe *me*, Victor and I falling in love . . . We meant not for that to happen, either.'

Though Kate didn't say it, her eyes spoke for her: she knew Phoebe told the truth.

'Please be frank, I have to know for certain. Do you hold any love for your husband at all?'

'Would it make a difference to the two of you if I did?'

'Yes,' Phoebe answered honestly.

For a full minute, Kate stared at her and Phoebe held her breath. Finally, she murmured, 'Perhaps at some point early on I thought I did . . . No. I don't love him.'

'Then will you set him free?'

'You would spend an existence in sin?'

'A lifetime with Victor could never be that.'

The woman glanced to the table.

'This, your life at present . . . it can't be what you want,' Phoebe added.

Kate shook her head.

'Then will you agree? Can you find it in you to grant us all contentment? Please?'

'The house?'

'Ownership shall pass to you, naturally. I'd also see to it personally that you receive a generous allowance for life. You needn't fear of ever going without.'

'Really?'

'Of course. You'd be entitled to nothing less. Whatever else may happen, there's one thing we cannot change: you'll always be Victor's wife.'

When the women eventually rose from the table, their futures secured, Phoebe had tears of joy running down her face. Before turning to leave, she reached for Kate's hand tentatively and squeezed, and Kate acknowledged their shared assuagement with a nod.

Meeting Victor in the hall, Phoebe saw that he knew. And as she walked into his outstretched arms, a familiar voice, clear and refined, whispered its plea for a final time, and Phoebe smiled.

'Always, Lilian. Always.'

A SHILLING FOR A WIFE

Emma Hornby

Sally Swann thought life couldn't get much worse. Then a single coin changed hands.

A dismal cottage in the heart of Bolton, Lancashire, has been Sally's prison since Joseph Goden 'bought' her from the workhouse as his wife. A drunkard and bully, Joseph rules her with a rod of iron, using fists and threats to keep her in check.

When Sally gives birth, however, she knows she must do anything to save her child from her husband's clutches. She manages to escape and, taking her baby, flees for the belching chimneys of Manchester, in search of her only relative.

But with the threat of discovery by Joseph, who will stop at nothing to find her, Sally must fight with every ounce of strength she has to protect herself and her son, and finally be with the man who truly loves her. For a fresh start comes with a price . . .

Available in paperback and ebook now . . .

MANCHESTER MOLL

Emma Hornby

Moll thought she could keep her family safe . . .

Eighteen-year-old Moll Chambers works her fingers to the bone doing all she can to support her family. With an ailing father and a wayward mother, Moll is the only one who can look after her siblings, Bo and Sissy.

But Manchester is an increasingly dangerous place to live, overrun with a ferocious rivalry between gangs of so-called 'scuttlers': young men and women bent on a life of violence and crime. And they have her brother in their sights. Soon even Moll can't protect Bo from the lure of the criminal underworld.

Then the scuttlers looked her way.

When she herself falls for the leader of a rival gang, Moll's choices place her and Bo firmly on opposite sides of the city's turf war.

With her loyalties now torn in two and tragedy lurking round every corner, will Moll be able to rise above the conflict and protect those she loves the most? Or will stepping out with a scuttler spell ruin for them all . . .?

Available in paperback and ebook now . . .

THE ORPHANS OF ARDWICK

Emma Hornby

After a cold, hard winter on the streets, three orphans are about to give up hope when an unexpected turn of events brings them to the doorstep of Bracken House.

Taken in by the firm but kind-hearted cook, the young friends can hardly believe their luck. But behind Bracken House's impressive façade lies a household steeped in troubles and mystery, with residents above and below stairs battling their own demons and dark secrets.

Not everyone is happy with the new arrivals, and soon the orphans' safety is in danger. If they want to stay in the first home any of them have known for years, they must unravel the past and bring hope to the future. Will they succeed? Or will they come to regret ever leaving the mean slum streets they once called home?

Available in paperback and ebook now . . .

A MOTHER'S DILEMMA

Emma Hornby

Minnie Maddox cares deeply for mothers and their babies – she makes a living by taking in unwanted babies and finding them good adoptive homes – and is delighted for her neighbour when she finally becomes a mother after decades of trying. But when the baby dies of natural causes while under her roof, and knowing her neighbour will be devastated, Minnie swaps it with one of the infants in her care.

Now seventeen, Jewel Nightingale knows nothing of her true origins. But, assaulted by her hateful cousin and making the dreadful discovery that she is pregnant, she faces a desperate dilemma. Fleeing her job as a domestic maid, she follows an advertisement to a house in Bolton's dark slums, where a woman promises to help her when the child is born. Little does Jewel know that there's a terrible price to pay . . .

Can she keep herself – and her baby – safe? And what will happen when Jewel discovers the truth about where she came from?

Available in paperback and ebook now . . .

A DAUGHTER'S PRICE

Emma Hornby

Laura Cannock is on the run. Suspected of killing her bullying husband, his family are on a merciless prowl for revenge. Fleeing from her beloved home of Bolton to Manchester, Laura seeks refuge with her coal merchant uncle. But her relief is short-lived as it soon becomes clear that a roof over her head comes with a price – of the type so unbearable she must escape once more.

Destitute and penniless, a stench-ridden housing court in the back streets of the factories is Laura's only hope of a dwelling – a place where both the filth and the kindness of neighbours overwhelm. Here people stick together through the odds, leading Laura to true friendship, and possibly love. But with the threat of her past still hanging over her, there's still one battle she must fight – and win – alone . . .

Emma Hornby's page-turning sagas are perfect for fans of Dilly Court and Rosie Goodwin.